The Young Accomplice

'Wood is a seriously talented writer, able to enter the
minds of his characters with eerie precision' *FT*

'A British novelist who deserves more attention than he
has had . . . Wood blends storytelling punch with
literary sensibility' *The Times*

'Tense and full of menace' Johanna Thomas-Corr,
New Statesman, Books of the Year

'A treat . . . What, it asks, are the opportunities available to
someone who wants to leap clear of their wrong beginnings,
when everything that hurts has already been cut?'
John Self, *Critic*, Fiction Books of the Year

'His most original [novel] yet . . . *The Young Accomplice* has
already been compared to Thomas Hardy novels and
there are echoes of *Tess of the d'Urbervilles* in the story of a
vulnerable young woman whose past catches up with her.
Wood is also wonderful on the intricacies of love
and architecture as a means of enriching people's lives.
It's a novel that feels as if it has been imagined with slow
and tender care – and I suspect it will be cherished
by readers for a long time' *Sunday Times*

'*The Young Accomplice* is finely constructed, with themes of
wrongdoing and innocence woven naturally into the action.
Benjamin Wood's attention to detail, his smooth writing style
and his strong beliefs give the novel an unusual dignity'
Times Literary Supplement

By the same author

A Station on the Path to Somewhere Better
The Ecliptic
The Bellwether Revivals

The Young Accomplice

BENJAMIN WOOD

PENGUIN BOOKS

PENGUIN BOOKS

UK | USA | Canada | Ireland | Australia
India | New Zealand | South Africa

Penguin Books is part of the Penguin Random House group of companies
whose addresses can be found at global.penguinrandomhouse.com.

First published by Viking 2022
Published in Penguin Books 2023
002

Copyright © Benjamin Wood, 2022

The moral right of the author has been asserted

Epigraph from *Frank Lloyd Wright: An Autobiography* used courtesy of the
Frank Lloyd Wright Foundation, Scottsdale, AZ, USA

Typeset by Jouve (UK), Milton Keynes
Printed and bound in Great Britain by Clays Ltd, Elcograf S.p.A.

The authorized representative in the EEA is Penguin Random House Ireland,
Morrison Chambers, 32 Nassau Street, Dublin D02 YH68

A CIP catalogue record for this book is available from the British Library

ISBN: 978-0-241-98885-5

www.greenpenguin.co.uk

MIX
Paper from
responsible sources
FSC® C018179

Penguin Random House is committed to a
sustainable future for our business, our readers
and our planet. This book is made from Forest
Stewardship Council® certified paper.

For Isaac and Oren

'We do not learn much by our successes:
we learn more by failures – our own and others',
especially if we see the failures properly corrected.
To see a failure changed to a success – there is what
I call Education.'

Frank Lloyd Wright

PART ONE

The Mayhoods

June 1952

The old man had been treading couch grass in the field since dawn, halting now and then to hack a nettle stalk with his dull scythe. Sometimes, he'd inspect the heads of flowering weeds and peer back, agonized, towards the house, as though he'd sighted a pernicious species long presumed extinct. Arthur Mayhood watched him from the steps of his back porch. It was the sort of clear, bright morning that made him recognize how close he was to happiness – a wholesome sunlight over Ockham that seemed as thick as tallow, and the verdancy of every acre in his view like something rendered for a postcard. If he looked far enough into the distance, he could forget the dire state of his farm and feel good about himself again, remember what it was that brought him out here in the first place. There was so much to do at Leventree that he'd not anticipated. It had been less than a year, all told, and the house was in good order, but trying to restore the land had broken him, one fruitless day after another. A stubborn part of him used to believe he was invulnerable to the drudge of manual labour: for as long as he still had the use of one good arm, he could manage twice the work of anyone. Well, that streak in him was gone now, too. Lately, he'd resolved to take whatever crumb of help or wisdom anyone could throw at him. The old man was a case in point.

His name was Hollis and he'd shown up in the yard at six a.m., as promised, wearing a large straw sunhat on a string across his back. A glower had set upon his face as he'd considered the condition of the fields a moment, but his feelings had remained unspoken. In the dawn light, he'd seemed thinner than he had the day before, his complexion rough as grout. He'd said he wouldn't mind a cup of tea himself before they made a start on things – 'Seeing as you've got one on the go already' – so they'd stepped into the kitchen, eyeing one another, for as long as it had taken to drink up. There'd been some discussion of the lovely weather they'd been having, but the topic had run dry.

Hollis had glanced up towards the ceiling. 'Mrs Mayhood a late riser, is she?'

'Not usually,' Arthur had replied.

'Thought I'd say hello while I was here.'

'She's gone to town to fetch a part. How loud's your voice?'

The old man had snickered. 'Saw your tractor out there in the garage. If it were a horse, I'd shoot it.'

'Wish I had the luxury.'

'What's the part she's after?'

'Damned if I know.'

'Just to Leatherhead, she's gone?'

'Yes.'

'Could've put it in the post for you.'

'I think she wants to barter down the price.'

'Well, good for her.'

This had been as much of an exchange as could be wrung from the old man. There was a dourness to him that seemed reflexive, born of wretched luck in days gone by. Civility and candour were the best assurances for men like Hollis – it had been the same with lads in borstal and a fair few of the sergeants in his company – while others favoured toadying and politicking. In Arthur's view, a bit of gruffness in a fella was a sign he wanted to be taken seriously. As they'd gone out to the yard together, he'd suggested that the windbreak was the place to start: 'I think it might be causing us more problems than it's helping.'

The old man had nodded. 'If you say so.' They'd moved off together, heading for the bank of ash trees at the far side of the meadow, but then Hollis had stopped walking. 'There are two ways we can go about this. Either I can tell you what you want to hear or I can tell you what I really think – which one suits you best?'

'The truth is all I need for now.'

'Then stay put here. I'll have a wander on my own.'

There was a time, barely a week ago, when Arthur might've been embarrassed to expose the dearth of progress he had made at Leventree. He didn't like to advertise his limitations, even if he could admit to them. But replenishing the grounds of this old place – just making the land functional again – was going to take more than his reserves of industry and patience. It required native wisdom. Men like Hollis had a vast resource of local knowledge and experience to draw from, inherited from their fathers and grandfathers. It was in their bones and blood. They could gauge the character of a soil by sight and feel. But Arthur had no instinct for this type of work. He'd learned the rudiments from books and tried to put the complicated business into practice. He'd scrutinized the survey map a hundred times, inserted augers to determine depth, variety, but ask him the condition of his soil today – the very thing upon which Leventree relied – and he couldn't give an answer. Florence always said he ought to be more tolerant of his failings and celebrate his talents: 'You're not a farmer, you're an architect. There's not a man round here who knows the right end of a T-square, let alone could run a farm and keep a practice going all at once – you're too hard on yourself.' Still, he couldn't help suspecting there were people back in London who were taking a dim view of him already. Another city exile with delusions he could work the land: the countryside was teeming with them.

Florence had been first to notice he was struggling. Was there anything she couldn't glean from the small shifts in his behaviour, or had he just become transparent? Two, three months ago, he'd been out scything nettles in the north field, more or less where Hollis was hunched over now, and she'd whistled in that way she always did when summoning him in for supper: a spike of noise that sent birds bolting from the hedges. He'd traipsed in and washed the dirt from his fingers, then sat down at the kitchen table, where she'd laid out a spread of Sunday's leftovers and a fresh-baked loaf for him to tear the crust off. Bringing the water jug, she'd said, 'You want to get a proper tool for it, or borrow one. Won't be hard to find if you'd just ask around. It's not the sort of work that you can do without the right equipment.'

The mere mention of the dismal job that he was doing out there in the weeds was injuring, and he'd not taken kindly to her suggestions for improvement. He'd found the old scythe in the hay barn with a box of other ancient implements, none of which he knew the purpose of, or even how to hold correctly. 'It'd go a damn sight quicker if I understood what I was doing,' he'd said. 'Perhaps I'm letting them all seed by cutting them. They'll likely reach our doorstep by next year, you watch.'

'I wish you'd let me help you.'

'You've enough to do. We need that tractor working.'

'I've still got the extras notice for the Proctors to type up.'

'Leave it. I can get to that tonight.'

'As well as their corrections? You're exhausted.'

'One big pot of coffee, I'll be fine. See if you can't get that engine going while I'm at it.'

She'd gone quiet then, busying herself at the range, wiping down the surfaces.

'What is it, Flo?'

'I'm just wondering when I agreed to being the resident

6

mechanic. We were supposed to share the work. I thought that was the point.'

He'd set his fork down a little abruptly. 'The tractor's a priority and you're the only one who's got the nous to fix it.'

'Yes, but I can still do other things. The letter to the subcontractor – let me do that, surely?'

'Suit yourself.'

She'd gone quiet again. 'I was thinking we could sell the Austin.'

'Don't be daft. We can't be driving to meet clients in the wagon.'

'Why not? We'd get something a bit more modest, spend the difference on the tractor.'

'Your father wouldn't like that very much, God rest him.'

'No, I know, but –' She'd slung the dishcloth into the sink. 'Maybe you could wait until the Savigears arrive? Attack those weeds together?'

'I'm not going to give them that impression.'

'What impression?'

'That I let a pile of weeds defeat me.'

'Well, I don't wish to sound unkind, but they'll be in their sixties by the time you've cleared that field. Sometimes the best thing is to admit you're beaten and seek help. I'm going to put the word out in the village.'

'You bloody well are *not*.'

But his wife knew better than to listen when he got indignant. She'd never been too proud to ask for help, because she rarely needed it – Florence was the most proficient person in his life and also the least interested in other people's judgements. Her face was known to everyone from Ockham to West Horsley, and that was all the currency she needed. One afternoon, while he was hacking at the weeds again, she'd taken it upon herself to go into the village and announce their problems to the landlord at the Barley Mow. Arthur had begun receiving visitors soon afterwards.

At first there'd been a few well-meaning strangers, asking for a daily rate: strawberry pickers, orchard workers, planters with chapped faces and bruised fingernails – he'd turned them all away. Then his neighbour to the east had rolled into the front yard in a flatbed wagon, honking the horn. He'd had a team of farmhands sitting in the back with a variety of tools, and an expression like a tank commander sizing up a bridge. 'We heard you had a weed problem,' he'd said, scanning the north field. 'That where you want us to begin?'

But Arthur's self-defensiveness had overtaken him; a cold-ness had spread slowly through his body. 'I think I've got to grips with it now, thank you.'

'Doesn't look that way from where I'm standing. Let us pitch in with you.'

The men had all been staring down at him from the back of the wagon, half-amused, about to jump.

'No,' he'd said. 'Thanks very much, but no.'

His neighbour had climbed out, ensnaring both his thumbs inside his belt loops. 'Seems to me as though you've got a lot of couch grass there that needs uprooting. Thistles, brambles, nettles, all sorts on the verges. That'd take me near enough a fortnight to sort out by myself, and I'm not half as –' He'd paused to find the right articulation. 'As *encumbered* as you are, so . . . Look, the offer stands. Between the six of us, we'll have it weeded out by supper.'

'It's all right, I'll manage.'

'Are you sure? Don't let your pride get in the way.'

But grand gestures of charity, when made like this, were only meant to glorify the giver – that was something Arthur had learned in his youth. 'Sorry to waste your time,' he'd said.

His neighbour had sucked in the air and spat a disc of phlegm

8

towards the ground. 'Is your wife home? I've known Flo since she was –'

'Florence knows my feelings on the subject.'

'All right, then, we'll leave you to it. But tell Flo we dropped in.'

'Will do.'

He'd guessed that she was somewhere in the house, observing from a window. The four men in the back had turned away, laughing, and his neighbour had thrown up his hands and climbed into the driver's seat. They'd semicircled in the yard and rolled off in a spray of dust.

Later, when he'd tried to justify his actions to his wife, he'd found her strangely muted on the subject. All she'd said was, 'Better get an early start on it tomorrow, then. We've other jobs that you're neglecting.' And so he had. In the cool of dawn, he'd gone out with a scythe and spade to pulverize the beanstalk nettles on the fringes of the fields, some of which had grown above six feet, and he'd razed them all by sunset, dug them out, come in with his cheeks and ears stinging, bubbled with an orange-peel texture, his palm raw with blisters underneath the glove, the whole of his good arm pulsing. It had been a satisfying day, but the worst of it was still ahead. Couch grass was a dogged weed to shift. According to his books, the only certain means of purging it (without the use of chemicals, which he and Florence were opposed to) was to tease it out with a hand fork, one devious white root at a time. The north field was almost three acres.

He'd tried not to wake up in a defeated frame of mind. He'd tried to ignore the aches and pains and rashes. He'd tried to pull his boots on and stride out every morning, steeled, envisioning the north field bare and primed for cultivation by week's end. But the couch grass had conquered him slowly, drained his energy and self-esteem. There were certain tasks that didn't lend themselves to single-handed men: he'd struggled to get purchase on the fork to prise the roots out, and when he'd finally managed it, they'd broken into fragments, leaving him to forage in the dirt on bended knee. His prosthetic had been useless, slipping, hanging by its straps; a more secure appliance for the job was needed. The muscles all along his back had locked up. His knuckles had begun to seize: they'd swollen to the size of chestnuts. After three days, he'd carved out a channel, running east to west, about the width of a cinema aisle – and he couldn't bear to look in its direction, let alone pick up his fork and carry on again tomorrow.

So, that evening, he'd driven to West Horsley, walked into the Barley Mow, and heard the conversations fade as he came through the doorway. He'd ordered a pint of mild and the landlord had prepared it for him wordlessly, taking his payment and returning his change. Then: 'How're things going at your place? I heard you had some trouble.'

'Nothing that some petrol and a lighter couldn't fix,' he'd answered.

The landlord had winced. 'That bad, eh?'

'At the moment.'

'Well, perhaps you shouldn't be so stubborn. Let folk help you out a bit.'

'You're right, I know. And I appreciate them taking pity on me.' He'd sipped his mild, which tasted watered-down. 'But there's a trick to learning, isn't there? I mean, you can't depend on other people all the time. You've got to put the graft in, work it out alone, even if you get it wrong.' He'd paused then, getting the impression he was being listened to for listening's sake. 'What I'm saying is, if I'm going to fail at something, I like to know exactly why. And now I do.'

'How's that?'

He'd lifted up the baggy sleeve on his right side, patting at the space where his arm used to be. 'I need to wait till this grows back, you see.'

The landlord's grin had been uncertain. 'Best keep watering it, then.'

'Exactly. One pint at a time.'

He'd seen a lot of dingy public houses, growing up, and never understood the fuss that people made about them; but sitting there at the bright counter with his glass of Truman's, speaking his mind amid the rumbling conversations, he'd felt somewhat consoled. The landlord had returned to the back pages of his *Advertiser*, browsing the classifieds with one lens of his spectacles held up to the print; he'd had a pencil viced inside the hinges of his jaw and, now and then, Arthur could hear the shucking noise of him inhaling his own drool. At some point, years ago, this man had been a patient of Flo's father. It was strange to think that every filling in that mouth – and likely everybody else's in the building – had a faint connection to his wife. As a child, she used to help her mother mix the mercury amalgam. There were people in these parts who still canted their heads when they addressed her, lightening their voices, as though she was that kindly little girl with plaits who'd sat at the reception desk in summer holidays. But Arthur had no such associations. Everyone he knew when he was young was either dead or far away or out of touch.

He'd been counting out his pennies for another pint when a voice had carried to him from along the bar: 'You must be that architect I've heard so much about. Doing up that place of Mr Greaves's.' And he'd turned to find a weary-looking fella on a stool, hunched over an ashtray with a mound of fag ends large enough to fill an urn. This old man had smoked his rollie with a pleasing eccentricity, clamping it between his thumb and middle finger like a dart.

'I am. Who's asking?'

'Hollis. Geoffrey Hollis.' The old man had stared back at him, but softly. 'Used to know your in-laws a long time ago.'

'Is that right?'

'Oh yes, he'd a lovely way did Mr Greaves. Always made you comfortable. Until you heard the drill go on.'

Arthur had smiled and signalled to the landlord for another. 'You must know my wife, then, too.'

'Not seen much of her since . . . it would've been a good few years back now. I always liked her. Everybody did.' The old man had stamped out his rollie. 'Are you still looking for a bit of help there on the farm?'

'I am. You offering?'

'Depends on what needs doing.'

'Killing weeds, for starters, but it's good advice I'm after really. Someone who can show me the best way of doing things. There must be tried and tested ways I haven't tried or tested yet.'

'Ah, you're looking for short cuts.'

'No, I promise you, I'm not afraid of the hard work. Most jobs I can manage on my own. But if you read a thousand books on farming, all of them assume you're doing it two-handed. So I'm having a few difficulties.'

'Right, I get you. That's a shame.'

Arthur had fished out a shilling from his pocket, planted it beside the pennies on the counter. This had been the cheeriest he'd felt in weeks. He'd slid his pint along the bar to stand with the old man. 'Thing is, if you're able to help out, I can't afford to pay you. All that I can offer is a trade. Building work, carpentry, plumbing – I'm your man for that. Planning applications, surveys, drawings. Say the word.'

'Sounds fair,' Hollis had answered, 'but I don't have need for anything like that.'

'Then maybe you know someone else who does? Family, friends, it's all the same to me.'

'I've got a brother down in Devon, but he hates my guts.'

'Oh, I'm sorry.'

'Don't be. I deserve it.'

And he'd been about to turn away when Hollis had come back at him: 'You haven't even asked if I'm a farmer. I suppose you must be desperate.'

He'd admired the old man's leaning gait, his calloused hands, the worked-in quality of his shirt, whose whiteness had become a shade of buttercream. 'I just presumed. From the way you were talking.'

'As it happens, I've been working farms round here since I was in short trousers. Never managed to save up enough to get a piece of land to call my own – liked the horses and the fights too much, and probably a bit too much of *this* –' Hollis had lowered his eyes down to his drink, muttering his words into his chest as if he were incanting the Lord's Prayer. 'But give me a fair patch of earth and I can get the best out of it.'

'That's exactly what I'm looking for. I'll wash your windows, clean your gutters, anything you like.'

'No need. I'm only in a caravan. But, tell you what – d'you have running water?'

'We do.'

'Is it hot?'

'If you're patient.'

'All right. Let me have a bath round your place every Sunday, we'll be even.'

'That's it?'

'That's it.'

Arthur had leaned over for a handshake, but there'd been an awkward meeting of their fingers – the rules of modern civilization were unfavourable to lefties.

13

'Can't promise you that I'll work miracles, but I'm not short of good ideas.' With this, the old man had gathered his cardigan, his tobacco pouch, his keys. 'Tomorrow morning do?'

'Yes. Perfect.'

They'd shaken hands again with more assurance.

'I'll be over nice and early. Sun's up around six-ish.'

If a measure of good people is how true they are to what they promise, Geoffrey Hollis didn't disappoint. His arrival in the yard had been so spiriting that Arthur found himself revisiting the numbers in his head: was there not some way that he could budget for the old man's expertise? What position could they offer him? Caretaker? Agrarian consultant? *Farm supervisor*. Perhaps a day a week on basic wages to begin with? Once the next cheque from the Proctors cleared, he could section off a portion of the funds – it'd be worth it in the long run.

The sun was slanting down now on the old man's giant straw hat. He was out there in the north field with the scythe across one shoulder, going about his quiet survey of the land, unhurried. As he approached the fringe of grass that spilled into the yard, he crouched to dig his hands into the soil again, holding the dry earth up to his nose as if to breathe in its bouquet, then tossing it aside. The more that Arthur watched him, the more relieved he felt. Not just because he'd found someone who knew what he was doing with his land, at last, but because its problems were no longer his to bear alone. There was even an uplifting tune the old man hummed as he strolled back towards the house – a repetitious melody like something from a hurdy-gurdy – and it reminded Arthur of those perfect afternoons he'd spent with Flo on Southport pier when they'd been courting.

He didn't get up from his seat on the back porch, but let Hollis approach him, humming, until he came to rest at the foot of the steps, leaning on the pilaster. He couldn't see the old man's eyes beneath the brim of his enormous hat, and couldn't gauge much from the straightness of his mouth as he went on with his hurdy-gurdy tune.

'Well, come on, what's the verdict?' Arthur asked. 'Do I have to torch the place, or what?'

Hollis lifted a tobacco pouch from his back pocket. 'It's not half as bad as I expected. Not the best, but we can save it.'

'Are you sure?'

The old man pursed his lips. 'Yup, we can bring this back to life in no time.' He was curling a cigarette paper now in his dry-looking fingers, stuffing it with pinches of Old Holborn. 'Your soil's in fairly decent nick, considering. You've got a clay loam, but it's not too heavy – we can spread some sand to lighten it, plough in some manure if need be. Main thing is, it's nice and black – you've got no drainage problems I can see.' He licked the paper's edge and sealed it with his thumb. 'Wouldn't mind a glass of water, if you'd be so kind.'

Arthur stepped inside to fetch it. When he came back out, the old man was smoking peacefully, sitting on the top step with his hat off. 'Here.'

'Thank you.' Hollis gulped down the entire glass in one. 'Dry mouth all the time, these days. I think there's something wrong with me.'

'Maybe you should knock those on the head.' Arthur gestured at his rollie. 'I gave them up a while ago. Wasn't easy, but I got my breath back.'

'No chance. Got me through a lot, these things.'

'You must've seen a bit of action in your time.'

'I have indeed.' The old man picked a fleck of loose tobacco off his tongue. 'Langemark, for all the good it did me. Where'd they ship *you* off to?'

'North Africa, at first. Then France and Belgium. And a bit of Holland.'

'Quite a picnic, that.'

'For all the good it did me.'

The old man nodded gravely. 'Holland's where you lost the arm, is it?'

'I got off lightly, too.'

'I know the feeling. Where'd it happen?'

'In a town called Ravenstein.' He could see that Hollis wanted more, so he surrendered the whole story, thinking it might help his cause. 'I was in the Sappers. Our platoon was taking down a bridge. Thick snow and ice for miles. None of us had any feeling in our fingers and our coats were worse than useless. We were shifting iron transoms, unloading them in six-man teams. Suddenly, I think, *My God, we're taking fire*, because the fella up ahead drops to the ground as though a sniper's had him. Micky Davis was his name. We called him Plank. He'd only been with us a month or two, since we came back through Normandy. Well, Plank had gone and lost his footing in the snow. And once he let go of the transom, so did everyone. Except for me. They reckoned I was lucky it was just my arm got trapped.'

'Still, it must've hurt like billy-o.'

'You can't imagine. Anyway, I try not to relive it, if I can. It catches up with me sometimes and I get moody. But not often. I prefer to keep my eyes on the horizon.'

'That's the way. No looking back. You can't dwell or it kills you.'

He hadn't known the old man long enough to start inquiring, but he got the sense – from nothing really, just the downcast tone in which he spoke sometimes – that Hollis's regrets outweighed his satisfactions. Here was a man who'd given up most of his days on earth to tending it, making it pay dividends for someone else, and Arthur didn't want to be the next one to exploit him.

'All right, then. My soil is fine – that's welcome news,' he said, sitting in the shade beside him. 'What about the weeds?'

'They're about the worst I've seen, but we'll get rid of them. I'm afraid the old ways are the only ways I know: a bit of mowing and a lot of pulling. We could try smothering them for a while with tar paper, see if it softens the roots. It all depends how fast you need the money.'

'From the crops, you mean?'

The old man looked at him. 'Didn't notice any livestock. Just your hens.'

'Oh, we're not trying to make a profit here. It's all a matter of subsistence.'

'Let me check I've got this right,' said Hollis. 'You're not *selling* what you grow?'

'Not unless we have a surplus. Even then, we'll donate what we can to folk who need it.'

'Well, what kind of farm is this supposed to be?' The old man clutched the rail and pulled himself up to his feet. 'I'm not going to put my back out for a hobby. There's folk who'd give their – well, they'd *kill* to have a bit of land like this to make a living from.' He handed back his empty glass. 'I'll have to think about it.'

'It's not a hobby, I assure you. It's going to be our livelihood. Mine and Flo's. It's just a little different from the ways you might be used to.' Arthur had to follow him into the yard. 'Let me walk you to the gate. If I can't convince you by the time we reach the road, then I won't bother you again. And you can still have your hot bath here every Sunday, no matter what's decided.'

At the pace the old man was walking off, his hat was dragging on its string, biting his throat. It was only when his lighter and tobacco pouch slipped out of his back pocket that he stopped at all, noticing the clatter on the gravel. He picked up his belongings with a flash of his long arm, then stood up, saying, 'Let me tell you something, Mr Mayhood. You had best consider what you plan to do with all this space. Because there's too much here for you to manage on your own and not enough for you to take for granted.' He dusted off the pouch, blew on his lighter and inspected it for scratches. 'You seem a decent bloke to me – and I mean that – but you can't go about the job of farming like you go about the job of being an architect. The ground will eat you up.'

'I understand that.'

'No, see, I don't think you *do*. Not yet.'

Arthur grinned at him. 'Farm supervisor.'

'Excuse me?'

'That's what your title's going to be. And we're going to discuss a proper wage for you. As soon as I get payment from a few things I've been doing.'

Hollis crossed his arms. 'You've a peculiar way of going about things, you know that?'

'So I've heard.' He didn't know what sort of explanation would be satisfactory – there was a sudden coolness to the old man's attitude that was approaching disapproval. A bit of forthrightness was called for now. 'You've got to understand, we've risked an awful lot to move our practice here, and that's what this place is: a practice, not a farm. We're trying to make a little Taliesin here in Ockham, which I don't expect will mean that much to you. But it's everything to us. This farm, sustaining it – that's central to our cause. We need our land to function just as well as what goes on inside the draughting room. And there isn't much that I don't know about designing buildings, but when it comes to farming, well – you've seen, you *know*. I'm struggling to cope.' An early heat was settling around them. He felt the perspiration at his temples. It was going to be another glorious June day.

'You're not as hopeless as a few I've seen,' the old man said. 'You've got the guts for it, I'll give you that.' He heaved out a sigh, slipped the Old Holborn into his back pocket, tucked the lighter in his front. 'Farm supervisor, eh?'

'Job's yours, if you want it.'

It was then, as Hollis was deliberating on his offer in the shadows of the elms, that he caught sight of someone coming up the track from the direction of the road and said, 'You know this fella?'

'Who?'

Hollis jabbed a thumb into the distance. 'He's left your gate wide open.'

The figure coming up the track was heavyset and bearded. One side of his shirt was hanging free, leaving a swatch of pale flab exposed above the belt-line. There was a composure to the way he walked, with both hands tucked behind his back, but his shoulders had a forward lean that gave him a mean air, a look of shiftlessness – qualities that Arthur didn't want around him or his farm. 'He's probably just asking after work. There's been a load of people coming by of late. I'll tell him to move on. Won't take a minute.'

'If he's short of money,' Hollis said, 'his belly's yet to hear of it.'

'Well, let's give him a chance.' Arthur shielded his eyes and called along the track, 'Hello there, fella. Can I help you?'

The man didn't respond until he'd taken ten or twelve more strides towards them. There was a sweaty shine about his forehead, a blotchy dampness to his shirt around the armpits. 'I was passing by,' the stranger said, 'and got to wondering about your place, that's all.' His accent wasn't local and his tone was slightly hostile. 'What is it that you do here? I can't tell.'

'Farming,' Arthur told him. 'We're not hiring at the moment, if that's what you're after.'

Hollis cleared his throat.

The stranger stood there, scratching at the little continent of hair remaining at the centre of his scalp. 'Well, I suppose that's that, then,' he said. 'Pardon the intrusion.'

'It's no trouble. Close the gate on your way out, please.'

The man's face tensed with something like antipathy. 'It was open when I got here,' he said, 'but I'll shut it. You can watch me and make sure.' He slung a heavy look at them and turned on his heels.

They let him traipse away along the gravel.

'You meet all sorts in this game,' Hollis said. 'A lot of them are kind and decent, and the rest are more like him.'

The stranger reached the gate and, with a sham dispassion, pulled it closed. He was gone at last, but Arthur could still see his mammoth bootprints in the dirt. There was a chill about the air now in the shaded driveway and he was thirsting for another cup of tea. He couldn't keep from staring down the track, recalling how the stranger's shape had passed along it like a tram he'd missed. If it hadn't been for Hollis slapping a big hand upon his shoulder, saying, 'I'd better take you up on it, your offer, seeing as beggars can't be choosers,' he might've stayed there until dusk. 'First things first, I recommend we plough that field as soon as we've dug out those weeds,' the old man barrelled on, 'then sow it with a cover crop. Rye'd be the best bet. Plough that when it comes through, harrow it. Sow rapeseed next and turn that under, too. And after . . .' They began to walk back to the house again instinctively: no pledges made, no contract, just a mutual direction.

A shot to test the camera, out of focus. The shadow of a hand moves to the lens. The picture tightens. All the grey tones in the foreground deepen. And there's Florence on the doorstep, hands on hips. In overalls. A scarf tied in her hair. She's mouthing to the camera. 'No, no. Arthur. No.' A playful cut-throat gesture. 'Stop it! Stop!' She hides her face behind the crossbones of her arms. The camera lingers on her till she turns away. It pans up slowly, to the transom window. The picture lurches with a sudden zoom. Brickwork now and mossy pointing. A little downward shift. And there's the fancy plaque. Its painted letters judder in the frame and settle. LEVENTREE. *Another awkard zoom out. Camera shake. A momentary sky. A flash of knee. A pair of bootcaps. Gravel. Blurry darkness. Keep it.*

August 1952

The Savigears had already alighted and were waiting for her at the bright end of the platform. Their supervising officer had followed her instructions to the letter, dispatching them on the mid-morning train from Waterloo and providing a few pennies for the phone at Horsley station. Around eleven, the call had come – a deep and cheerless voice said, 'Morning, Mrs Mayhood. It's Joyce Savigear. I was told to ring when we arrived?' – and this first conversation, brief and stilted as it was, had felt momentous. They weren't just faces in a file any longer, or names she raised in speculation. It was as though, with everything she uttered on the phone that morning, she was going over pencil lines of them in ink.

She'd changed out of her overalls and climbed into the car without a word to Arthur, who was so deep in the field with Mr Hollis, spreading bucketloads of sand, that all her whistling went unheard. In any case, it was her husband who'd forewarned her not to make a special fuss of their arrival. He'd decided they should walk to Leventree or take the bus – 'It'll be a decent test of their initiative' – and it was only after several days of needling him with counter-arguments that he'd relented: 'Pick them up, if that's what you think's best, but go without me. Come and find me when they're ready to start work.'

The drive from Ockham was a short one, but she hurried all the way, because she didn't want them to mistake her lateness for indifference – no one liked to be an afterthought. She remembered getting fidgety at Horsley station as a girl, watching all the strangers disembarking and diffusing while her mother held her hand, moaning every time a car came up the hill without her father in it. A momentary anxiety like this could turn into a lifetime of resentment if you let it and she didn't want that for the Savigears. Besides, there was a certain thrill in breaching the speed limit in the Austin, bringing it to that sweet point above forty where it seemed to hover in mid-air. The car park was quite empty so she rolled up right outside the station house.

As soon as she saw them looming on the sunny platform, she realized how much she'd misjudged them. The Savigears were not the scrawny pair she was expecting. Standing half a yard from one another in the fug of their own cigarettes, they had the restful attitude of two navvies on a lunch break. The eldest, Joyce, had shoulders broad enough for work unloading cargo at the docks, a frame so tall she could've looked a draught horse in the eyes. The youngest, Charles, was shorter by at least a foot, but he was hard-faced, compact, and he seemed to wear his shirt a size too small. He was not exactly handsome in the sense that he could grace the cover of a magazine – there was just a certain sangfroid to him, a ruminating quality about his eyes that she felt uncomfortable observing. He had the same determined look she'd noticed in her husband at that age: eighteen and ready to tear down the world.

In January, she and Arthur had received a set of photo-graphs from the borstal records showing two glum adolescents with a spread of pimples; they'd spent hours gazing at these images, tacked them to the pinboard in the draughting room where they couldn't fail to stop and look each time they passed into the hall. It was hard to reconcile those young deliquents with the pair she saw before her now.

She assumed their supervising officer had dressed them up to look like architects. Joyce had on a long grey skirt and stockings, a white blouse with a button collar, which seemed to bother her especially – she kept circling the inner edge of it with one hooked finger. Charles was in a dark blue poplin suit, the jacket slung over his shoulder now, the heat being so cloying; he was clean-shaven and a fair bit pink around the neck, with short hair combed and brilliantined; even his shoes were shined.

As she came along the platform, neither one took notice. Charles just peered into the distance, toeing the flank of his suitcase; he was chuntering about something that he must've viewed out of the window on the train, while his sister stood by, listening. 'Yeah, but these were more like speakers from a record player,' he was saying, 'and they were strapped on to the roof somehow with rope about this thick, going down to the front bumper. Don't know how they stayed on, mind you, but it worked. And that was just the start of it, because –'

She let him trail off, striding up to introduce herself. 'Hello there, you two. I'm Florence Mayhood. Wonderful to meet you both at last. I'm sorry to've kept you waiting.'

'Hello, Mrs Mayhood,' Joyce said, dropping her cigarette, trampling it.

'Hello, Mrs Mayhood,' Charles said, doing the same. 'Good to meet you too.'

'Please – Florence will do fine. I'm not your landlady. Well, not officially.'

'All right.' Joyce simpered at her brother, huffing smoke out of her nostrils. 'You're in charge.'

'I am for now.'

'In that case, you can call me Joy. He goes by Charlie.'

'I'll make a note of it,' she said, tapping the plate of her forehead. 'Welcome to our little patch of nowhere. You must've brought the sunshine with you – absolutely chucked it down last night.' It was only when she offered them her hand that she spotted its condition: engine oil encrusted so deep underneath the fingernails she'd have to take a scrubbing brush and Epsom

25

salts to them when she got back. 'Excuse the state of me. I was working on the tractor when you rang, but – well, let's just say it won't be moving for a while.'

'What's up with it?' Joyce said, gripping her hand indelicately.

'Transmission.'

'Oh. That's going to cost you.'

'Maybe so.' She smiled back at the pair of them. 'I haven't given up yet.'

Charlie straightened out his posture, shook her hand. 'They had me doing motor mechanics all last year at Huntercombe. If you want, I'll take a look at it. Tractors can't be that much different.'

'Better take him up on that,' Joyce said, amused at something. 'He's always had a knack for getting engines running, even when he's not supposed to.'

'Leave it out,' said Charlie, and for a short time afterwards, his confidence appeared to drain. He went back to kicking his suitcase, eyeing the tracks.

'Well, I'd appreciate you pitching in,' she told them. 'Mr Mayhood has a lot of talents, but he's no use in a garage.'

Joyce sniffed. 'Must be hard in his condition.'

'Oh, he's never let that set him back. It's just he's never had much interest in machines.' She gestured to their meagre luggage: two brown cases, shabby at the edges, no doubt issued to them on their discharge. 'Are these your only bags?'

They nodded.

'Good. The car's just at the front. Let's go.'

She turned and led the way. Above the iron footbridge, the sun was giving off its white and formless shimmer, permeating like a headache; she could feel one brewing. Their footsteps clomped and scraped behind her.

'What about you, miss?' Charlie's voice rang out, but she didn't stop or turn; and even though the honorific made her feel like a schoolteacher, she let it go unchecked. It would do no good to keep instructing them to use her given name. They would need to think her worthy of that trust. Give it time and it would happen. 'Where'd you learn to fix an engine?'

'I took classes when the war was on,' she answered, pushing through the station door and holding it ajar. 'But they might've been a waste of time.'

'Ha ha.' Joyce had a chugging, low-pitched laugh that was quite endearing.

'We had a fella teaching us who'd let us take his motorbike apart, and –'

'Give it a rest, will you, mouse?' Joyce said. 'Let the lady have some peace.' And, taking the weight of the door, she added, 'Sorry about him. He's not always such a moaner.'

'I'm not moaning. I'm just making conversation.'

'He doesn't realize when he's doing it.'

'Because I'm not doing it.'

'You see? *Moaning*.'

Florence waited for the two of them to settle down. Perhaps they were a little less mature than she'd considered. 'No need to apologize,' she said. 'I don't like to talk about myself too much, that's all – and you'll find Mr Mayhood is the same. In fact, he's worse.'

They passed through the cool of the station. Behind the kiosk window, the attendant – whom she didn't know but dimly recognized – leered when she wished him a good morning. 'You too, Mrs Mayhood, you *too*,' he called back. The mill of rumours in these parts required no grist to thrive. There were too many people round here with too many small-minded preoccupations and she was long past caring about any of them. Still, she couldn't help but think it must've been the ripest gossip of his working week, to see a married woman

27

strolling through his station with two handsome youngsters off the London train.

When they reached the car, the Savigears were noticeably quiet and she couldn't tell if they were looking at the Austin with approval or contempt. They stowed their luggage in the back and Charlie sat beside the pile, deferring to his sister's greater size without a second thought. Once the key was turned in the ignition and the engine stirred, Joyce said, 'Lovely motor, this.'

'Well, it's reliable enough.'

'They're built to last, these,' Charlie chimed in from behind. 'Heavy, mind you, but I bet they go a fair old whack.'

She cleared her throat. 'I'm sure you're right.'

'We're not used to being driven round like royalty,' Joyce said. 'We could've walked it, easy.'

Florence jounced the gearstick into reverse. 'I'm not used to having passengers. But it's only so that you can get acquainted with the route. Next time, you can hoof it.'

'Suits us.'

On the way back home, she kept to the speed limit, while the Savigears fell into another silence, taking in the scenery. It seemed that they were quite content to orient themselves without her saying anything, so she spared them the guided tour that she normally conferred on guests – they didn't get too many visitors, apart from her old friends from architecture school in Liverpool, dear Fred Cort and his array of sweet-hearts, and the more capricious clients who came to check they hadn't lost their minds by setting up a practice so far from the city. She found it a refreshing change to drive without the burden of small talk and local history.

They dipped under the railway arch and skirted by the fields along the narrow Ockham Road, with sunshine flickering behind the trees and a pleasing, intermittent shade from every house they passed, until they came to the thin strip of junction, islanded by grass, that she would often tell people (as part of her tour patter) was the turning that her father used to miss at least three times a week, even after twenty years of living here. This road – Alms Heath – was the one she always liked to walk down after school, in the days when she still knew her neighbours and they crossed their driveways just to ask how she was doing. They'd be banging mud and cowpats from the heels of their boots as she went by, or hosing down their weekend boats and horseboxes, or sitting out in their front gardens with enormous pitchers of gin fizz and home-made cider. And it struck her now, as she coasted on towards the house, that no part of what she saw out there today was visible to the Savigears. When they peered through the windscreen, they must've seen a place entirely untouched by their own footprints, as yet meaningless, unspoiled. The Ockham of her parents' time was gone and she could only think of it as necessary ground – a site on which to build something important and long-lasting.

'You see,' she said, turning the wheel towards the crooked entry gates. The timber struts were desiccated, grey as chicken bones. 'It isn't such a cinch to find us, is it?'

'Where's the house?' Joyce asked, scrunching up her eyes to get a view beyond the treeline.

'We've a little bit to go yet. The track curves up to it. Would one of you mind jumping out and opening the gate?'

They'd thought of putting up a sign when they'd moved in. But as nice as it had looked when Arthur painted LEVENTREE on to the plaque and varnished it, they couldn't find the right position for it at the entrance. In the end, they'd both decided it was best to fix it to the body of the house, above the transom window. But they'd always known, no matter how much ground they could prepare ahead of time, the spirit of the place would be established when their first apprentices arrived.

Looking at them now – ungainly Joyce with both knees kissing the glovebox, sombre Charlie opening the gate beyond the windscreen – she wondered if the right selection had been made. She could still recall that day in late October when a batch of drawings had come in from Redditch, Lowdham Grange and Huntercombe – a set of envelopes so thick and heavy that the postman had complained of a sore shoulder – and the sanguine exercise of laying each one out on Arthur's trestle table to scrutinize their worth.

How many of those sheets of work were mediocre, showing no basic glimmer of potential (lazy marks impressed by too-blunt pencils, inconsistencies of scale, indifference to perspective). How many evinced a certain competence that they found spiriting yet somehow ordinary (nicely put-together sketches of exteriors that looked traced from an old print; faithful replications of original details by Wren or Lutyens without much nuance or precision, as though made at the behest of an over-eager tutor lacking knowledge of his own). And then one exceptional piece had surfaced in the pile, bearing the stamp of Huntercombe and the number 27: a line drawing of a bridge between two buildings that had clearly been imagined, one being Gothic, crumbling, the other being a futuristic block of intersecting oblong beams. They were as confused by it as they were exhilarated. Not only did it show technique – an early draughtsman's accuracy – it displayed an eye for composition and peculiar inventiveness. They knew, right then, they'd found what they were looking for. When Arthur followed up with Huntercombe to ask the name of number 27, he was told about a boy called Charlie Savigear, generally well behaved, a bit intense, a decent athlete.

Then, a few weeks later, in a packet from the girls' facility at Aylesbury, they'd discovered something almost as exceptional – a study of a church's flying buttress with a wonderful exactness of detail; the mossy growth between the bricks appeared to stand up on the paper. It demonstrated talent that was perhaps more painterly than architectural, but it was striking and persuasive. Again, Arthur had phoned up the housemaster at Aylesbury who'd been in charge of organizing their submissions and at a certain point he'd covered the receiver to collect his thoughts. His brow had furrowed. 'Spell that for me, please,' he'd asked, scribbling it on to a notepad. 'Do you know if this girl has a brother . . .? Well, do you think you could find out for me?' Then he'd slumped into his chair and lobbed the notepad over his desk so she could read it. 'Two needles in a haystack,' he'd explained, 'and they're related.'

Even when she was a child, Florence used to marvel at the way the farmhouse would appear behind the avenue of elms. Her parents used to lease the fields for grazing – throughout the year, the sheep and goats would nuzzle up against the fence and she would pet them, only to be chided for it later: 'Those animals are other people's property,' her father would complain. 'Walking meat is all they are to us. Don't touch.' This time, driving with the Savigears, she could only wish the land was in a healthier condition. 'All of this has to be ploughed through and harrowed soon,' she said to them, 'and Mr Mayhood wants to cut back some of these old trees – they give a lot of shade, but they're diseased. We'll have to grade this road and do something about the driveway, which gets to be a nightmare when there's a good amount of rain. And most of this is down to us, unless we can enlist some local volunteers.'

'What are the chances of that?' Joyce asked.

'Low to none, I'd say. A lot of bridges have been burned already.'

'Blimey.'

Charlie leaned into the space between their seats. 'It's a lot more normal than I thought it'd be – the house, I mean. I was expecting something, I don't know, more modern.'

'It's nothing special from the outside, I'll admit,' she said. 'We've got ideas for improvements, naturally, but we've been holding off on all those plans until you got here.' This seemed to cheer them, the promise of participation in a grander scheme. Charlie leaned back, folding his arms, and Joyce gazed forward, saying, 'It's better than a boarding house in Hoxton, anyway. That's where they put a girl I knew – and she was bleedin' miserable.'

Charlie said, 'There's nothing like a bit of country air.'

'I'm glad you see it that way.'

Passing by the north field, she took pleasure in its baldness – the dreaded weeds all plucked out by the roots and cleared away, leaving one vast patch of rain-struck soil, part-doused in sand. Mr Hollis was still out there, towing a handcart through the mud, but she couldn't see her husband anywhere. She parked up before the garage, where the rusty tractor sat unmended in the gloom like something rescued from a ditch.

'How long has that old thing been out of order?' Charlie said.

'About a decade, but I love a challenge. And we were given it for nothing.'

'You were robbed.'

'We'll see about that, won't we?' After she turned off the engine, all that she could hear was the hens' bickering. 'Come on. Get your things. I'll show you round.'

They went in through the front door, which was usually reserved for clients and visitors, but she thought the Savigears' arrival should be lent a proper note of ceremony. If she could've smashed a champagne bottle on the wall to bless the house and all who lived in it, she would've done so. 'Welcome home,' she said instead. 'It might not feel like it yet, but it will soon, I promise you.'

The Savigears offered no response. It was Joyce, stopping a moment on the patchy gravel with her case at heel, who saw the plaque above the transom. She said nothing to begin with, seeming almost fearful, eyes shifting downward, downward, till they landed on the threshold. 'There's nothing to wipe my feet on.'

'Are they muddy?' Florence asked.

'Not sure.'

'Don't worry. We've a sturdy mop, if need be. Leave your cases by the table there.'

Joyce came inside, dipping her head, and muttered to her brother, 'Why've they always got to give their houses fancy names?'

'*Shh*. Give it a chance,' he said. 'Don't wreck it.'

Later, Florence would deliberate on those words, *their houses*, with regret and trepidation, but, for now, the only thing to do was act as though she'd not been listening. If she asked them to explain what they'd been whispering about, she'd seem no different from a borstal officer. In the first place, what had made her so excited by the thought of Leventree was the prospect of some youthful company – she'd spent too much of her life in service of the old and the infirm – and although that motivation hadn't waned exactly, it was now more complicated. Nobody had ever tried what she and Arthur were attempting to achieve with these two youngsters. There were no accepted guidelines for how everybody should behave. In only half an hour with them, she'd observed enough about the Savigears to know what they could tolerate. For one thing, it was senseless to presume that she could be their mentor, or their mother, or their matron – these were certain routes to failure. No, she thought, let Arthur be the one they couldn't bear to disappoint. Her aim would be much simpler from the outset: friendship.

Charlie slid his case under the console table and looked up at her expectantly. His jacket was now draped over his forearm.

Somewhere between the platform and the hallway, he'd unbuttoned his shirt several rungs and she could see a wheatish covering of hair beneath. His features seemed to vary with the viewing angle – sometimes square and unremarkable, sometimes deft and curvilinear. She found her eyes were drawn to looking at him in the same way they would linger on an Aalto building when she flicked through *Architectural Review*.

'Now, I assume that Mr Mayhood will be upstairs, getting changed,' she said, leading them along the hall. 'Most days, he likes to spend the first few hours in the fields, and seeing to his duties round the house. We've a strict rota for chores, as you're about to learn. You might've seen that old man slogging in the mud as we passed by – that's Mr Hollis. He's helping us around the farm until we're self-sufficient, but we've no one else on staff. So, if you're hoping maids and butlers will be picking up your laundry, you'll have to think again. Everything we do here will be done through our own labour and cooperation.'

She paused before the dining room, discovering the inlays of the panelled doors were dark with dust. 'Look at that – my fault for spending all week in the garage.' She ran her finger through it, showed them. 'You'll be used to honest graft, I know, except there's no one here who's going to try and keep you on the straight and narrow – you'll see your supervising officer every month, that's all. You're free to come and go whenever you see fit, to learn your trade with us or not, to work the land with us or not, to join in with the spirit of this place or not. And what we hope is – just by living here, by seeing what you can achieve with us – you'll want to stay, you'll think of this as home. Not just for now, but, well –' She hadn't planned to deliver any sort of speech, yet here she was, at the tail end of one. The occasion had compelled her and the words had gathered a momentum of their own. 'For as long as you both wish to,' she concluded.

The Savigears just smiled politely. It saddened her to notice how the two of them were standing: single file against the wall, straight-backed, waiting to be let inside the doors. One little burst of oratory had rendered them submissive. They were so like Arthur it unnerved her. There were certain habits, she supposed, that were ingrained in borstal leavers, such as being quiet and listening when adults spoke at length. From now on, she would have to keep from sermonizing. It had taken years for her to learn which subjects to avoid with Arthur, what sort of language she could use with him, which reactions fuelled his anger or upset his mood. 'Anyway, you've heard enough.' She gave the big oak doors a push and they swung back with a satisfying heft, meeting the magnetic stoppers on the other side. 'Let's start here in the dining room.'

She showed them the long table Arthur had designed and built from cherry wood, with its chevron patterning around the rim and the slatted underframe that brought to mind the pipes of a church organ. Joyce expressed a liking for it: 'Makes me feel dainty,' she said, smoothing her palms over the surface. Charlie seemed unsure. 'I suppose you save all this for best, miss. Entertaining and the like?' he said, and didn't look entirely convinced by her assurance that their mealtimes would be spent together in this room. 'Who wants to live in a museum?' she said. 'Everything we have, we use. Beauty shouldn't be distinct from function – that's the way we see things.'

'Wait until you've seen my sister eat, though. You might change your mind.' When Charlie smirked, it came across as self-rebuking; his voice became a little softer at the edges.

'Oi,' Joyce said. 'Remember I've got plenty on you, mouse.'

In the kitchen, they seemed more at peace, more comfortable. Charlie spent a good few minutes at the window by the sink, gazing out into the yard, across the fields. 'It's really pretty here,' he said. 'I won't mind washing up if there's a decent view.' She directed them towards the household rota Arthur had prepared – they didn't flinch at the requirement to cook and clean and launder, studying the grid with blank expressions, receiving all her information on the whereabouts of things (her book of failsafe recipes, the scullery, the washing powder, clothes horse, ironing board, and so on) without questions or resistance. 'Have you cooked on a range like this before?' she asked them. 'It takes a bit of getting used to.' Joyce told her there had been one similar at Aylesbury, and she'd seen enough of it over the past two years that sometimes it intruded on her dreams. 'I'll get the hang of it, I'm sure,' was Charlie's answer. 'I can make a mutton stew and dumplings – that's all we learned to cook while I was in the kitchen party, though we had to use enormous vats for that. It always needed more salt in it than they said.'

She decided it was best to take them straight upstairs and show them to their rooms. The parlour could be saved for later. It was the only space within the house that she and Arthur hadn't finished to their satisfaction. All her parents' furniture remained, in more or less the same arrangement it had been in since she was eight, playing by her father's slippered feet as he read periodicals. They'd stripped the walls and painted them – a rich autumnal shade called Middle Buff that Arthur had got cheaply from a wholesaler in Peckham. She'd patched the ceiling cracks, torn out the phoney cornices, sanded down the beams to show the grain of all the oak and given them a shine of beeswax. But until they could afford to shift the furniture and make more of their own, the room was an embarrassment of styles: the lace and gilt-frame gaudiness of the Victorians (her mother's taste) and the tweedy blandness of a country hotel lobby (her father's). Arthur liked to keep the parlour door closed so their clients wouldn't see it and preferred to rest beside the fire in the draughting room: his soundest sleeps, it seemed to her, were always in the armchair with his feet up on the coal bucket.

For now, the Savigears were boarding on the first floor, in the east wing of the house. She and Arthur had discussed the allocation of their rooms for weeks, trying to see the arguments from both sides, but now it all seemed moot: just like the Savigears, one space was much larger than the other. Still, as she escorted them up to the landing, she felt obliged to give the rationale. 'I'm sorry, Charlie, but your sister has the bigger room.' She heard a crack of Joyce's laughter from behind. 'But if and when we take on more apprentices, she'll have to share it and we'll put up a partition wall or two. So things will even out eventually.' At this, Charlie turned and gave his sister bug eyes; then he said, 'I don't mind, miss. It's good enough for me. A comfy bed and a good reading lamp, that's all I need.'

Florence almost wished that she could put her arm around him. 'Those things we can promise you,' she said. 'And if you get a hankering for any other furniture, well, you let us know. Mr Mayhood thinks it would be nice if you'd consider how you want these rooms of yours to look – right down to the finest detail. They're extremely bare, but you should see them as blank canvases.'

She showed Joyce to her bedroom first: a broad, white space with a bay window overlooking the north field. It had an iron bedstead, an ottoman, a desk, a wardrobe and a simple rag rug she had woven out of fabric scraps. What a thrill it was to watch Joyce sitting sidelong on the bed, giving out a short sigh as she bounced the mattress with her backside, taking in the softness of the counterpane and pillow with her palms. 'Mr Mayhood wants you to submit designs for his approval,' Florence went on. 'We've a budget for materials, and we can help you with the carpentry, the decorating. But that's all for later on.'

The bathroom, she explained in passing, was all theirs, as

she and Arthur had their own en suite; and there was an out-side privy in the back yard they should use when working on the farm. 'It's more practical and stops you traipsing mud and God knows what in from the fields.'

'I thought you had a sturdy mop,' Joyce said.

'Well, not *that* sturdy.'

The view from Charlie's room was of the front yard and the chicken sheds, and he went straight up to the window to absorb it. 'Does the sash stay up?' he asked, sliding it and seeing how it held. He turned to his sister – 'Found my smoking spot' – and then began reviewing the dimensions of the space. 'I'm getting some ideas for what to do with it already,' he said. 'Won't take much to make this perfect.'

'Glad to hear it,' Florence said. From her position, she could see the wretched tractor jutting from the doorless garage down below. Her stomach ached a little. 'Do you need to wash up or get changed before I take you down to Mr Mayhood?'

'Not me,' Joyce said.

'Nah, I'm fine,' said Charlie.

'Come with me, then. He's expecting you to start work right away.'

Their procession down the stairs and back along the hallway was more solemn. She sensed some apprehension in their whispers (they were mouthing things she couldn't quite discern). 'You needn't look so worried: even at his prickliest, my husband has the softest heart of anyone you'll ever meet. All you have to do is show him that you have a strong work ethic and an appetite for learning. Try to listen to instructions and consider his suggestions. Suffer his bad singing when he's in a cheery mood and drink the awful tea he makes.' They reached the draughting room. She knocked lightly on the door and waited to hear Arthur's voice. 'Most of all, remember: everything that landed you in borstal – the mistakes you've made – he made them, too, when he was your age. I don't think you'll ever have a bigger ally in your life than Mr Mayhood.' She could hear his footsteps on the parquet, so knocked louder.

'Yes, come in, come in!' he called.

She found him in the nook behind the door, riffling in the guts of their old filing cabinet. He had his reading glasses on and both the lenses were smeared thickly with his fingerprints. 'Have you seen that bill of quantities?' he said, not looking up at them. 'I thought I filed it.'

'Which one?'

'The amended version. I've a nagging feeling I miscalculated something.'

'Really? What?'

'It doesn't matter,' he said, bringing out a sheet of paper. 'Got it.' And he took sight of their two apprentices at last, lifting his chin faintly. 'Wait there, please. Won't be a minute.' He turned and marched towards his little bureau, where he liked to do his paperwork.

Without a word, the Savigears stepped inside. She wanted to apologize for Arthur's lack of courtesy – or was it plain dismissiveness? He was presenting such a cold front, as though he hadn't spent the past two years preparing for this moment. But if the Savigears felt disregarded, it didn't register in their expressions. In fact, they seemed more animated than they'd been since she'd first seen them on the platform: they were studying the room, admiring it, gesturing towards the things that took their interest – the shining draughtsman's tables organized in a four-square pattern and the clean new instruments set out for them to use. They were pointing at the drawings for the Proctor house that Arthur had pinned up on the noticeboard behind them, the Lawson sofa where he sometimes lay in the hope of finding a solution in his work, the wing chair by the dull brass hearth where he took brandy in the evening. They were a little wonder-eyed. And she understood at once that this had been her husband's plan from the beginning: let them find the inspiration in the room all by themselves, give them a short moment to project their dreams into the space.

Arthur stayed there at his bureau for at least another minute, circling things in pencil. When he was done, he pulled the glasses from his face and dropped them to the table with the bill of quantities. Underneath, his cheeks were flushed and blotchy, as they often were when he had shaved right after bathing. As he came towards the Savigears, he held the open fist for his prosthetic arm in his left hand; a shiny silver disc remained exposed inside his blazer cuff until he made a show of fitting the appliance – it gave a loud metallic snap. She knew that he'd arranged this for the Savigears' benefit, too.

There were people – some of whom she used to view as friends – who were repulsed by Arthur's stump, who baulked at noticing the hollow drape of his shirtsleeve; but it was the artificial limb and its attachments people had the damnedest time accepting. She guessed that they equated it with a deception of some kind, like dummy legs in a magician's box. Well, it had never troubled her the least bit. She'd always found the engineering of it beautiful – the deftness of the mechanism, its ingenuity and practicality – and, except for when he hung it on their towel rail at night, she never paused to think about it.

'Did you make that for yourself?' asked Charlie, awkwardly.

Her husband thinned his eyes. 'I'm sorry?'

'The arm. Did you design it?'

Arthur gave a heavy exhalation. The question had surprised him, but he didn't seem insulted. 'You know, it never once occurred to me. Beyond my expertise, I think.'

'If you can build a house, an arm can't be that difficult.'

'Yes, I suppose you're right. I hadn't thought of it.'

Joyce spoke up then: 'Sorry, Mr Mayhood. He can't keep his gob shut sometimes. Please don't pay him any mind.'

'No harm done at all.' Arthur nodded back at her. 'My skin is thicker than it looks.'

'I could say the same about my brother.'

Florence had to bite her lip to keep from laughing. She didn't want poor Charlie to feel rounded on – he was looking so deflated, scraping his shoe-tip over the parquet, hands thrust deep inside his pockets. 'I'm sure he was just curious,' she said. His head had dropped so low that short strands of his hair had worked loose from the grip of brilliantine; and when he straightened up again, casting his eyes in her direction, she caught a hint of his affection in the sharpness of his face.

'Have they seen their rooms yet?' Arthur asked her now.

'Of course.'

'Good, then. Good.' He headed to the noticeboard, motioning for them to follow. 'I want you to submit your renovation plans within a week. Does that sound feasible? Something a bit like this –' He knuckled the dead centre of a drawing tacked up on the cork: it was an early sketch for the interior of the Proctors' living room. 'Cross section or two-point perspective, up to you. I just want to see some logic in relation to the space itself.'

'Absolutely, Mr Mayhood,' Charlie said. 'There's plenty I could do with my room. Plenty.' The boy was putting in the extra effort now: she really felt for him.

'Shouldn't be a problem for me either,' Joyce said. And she dropped a hand upon her brother's shoulder, peering down at him. 'We're both extremely grateful to you, Mr Mayhood, for this opportunity. We don't intend to let you down. Do we, Charlie?' They might not have been sentiments that she'd been coached to say, but they were delivered with the flatness and the fluency of wedding vows, rehearsed so many times inside her head that all the music had gone out of them.

'No,' said Charlie. 'We're extremely grateful.'

'Thanks aren't necessary,' Arthur said. 'Without you two, we'd only have an empty house and too much land to cope with. You're the reason for this place, not the excuse.' He waved them forward, into the spread of sunshine that the shutters couldn't block: a white trapezium of daylight that burned in from the picture window every summer afternoon, vanishing the pattern on the rug, fading the lampshades and the spines of all their books. It was a blessing and a curse. 'Let me show you to your places. Then you'll really feel at home.'

They each had a draughting table of their own: Joyce's faced the window at the north end of the room; Charlie's faced the stone partition to the south. They took their seats with reverence, as though they'd found positions at the bridge of some great ocean-going vessel. At first, they didn't seem prepared to touch a thing that lay before them. Then Arthur told them, 'Please, it's fine. You needn't wait for my permission. We've given you the basics – have a look there, in the drawers. Some of it is second-hand equipment, but it's all top quality. Florence has made sure of it.'

Months ago, she'd gone to Guildford to procure supplies: a few mahogany T-squares with ebony edges; celluloid set squares ($45°$, $60°$, plus a couple of adjustables); some folding two-foot rules; two boxwood scales with divisions; pencils (regular, mechanical); pots of waterproof ink; India rubber and erasers; watercolours, sable brushes, draughting tape. And she'd gone slightly over budget for two cases of used instruments in pristine condition: bow compass sets with good sharp needles. Returning home that day, seeing the bench seat of the Austin stacked with what she'd bought, she'd glowed with a sensation other women must've felt when nesting for a newborn. Those women had their Moses baskets, woollen hats and booties, little muslin squares in pretty tissue parcels; and there

42

she'd been with all her draughtman's implements, wrapped in the supply store's thick brown paper. That was just the way things had to be for now.

'What's this, Mr Mayhood?' Joyce asked. She was skimming through the home-made pamphlet Arthur had prepared and planted in their drawers. Fifty-something pages, typed and carbon-copied from the published volume, held together with brass fasteners. The title, *An Organic Architecture*, was hand-lettered in red. He'd made these pamphlets a few nights ago, while she was stripping down the tractor motor in the garage.

'That's your bedtime reading,' he said. 'Lectures from the great man.'

'I usually prefer the cowboy books. You know, Zane Grey, that kind of stuff.'

'Well, my aim is to enlighten, not to entertain.'

Charlie was already reading through his copy. 'It's Frank Lloyd Wright,' he said.

His sister called, 'Who's that when he's at home?'

'A famous architect. He built this fancy house beside a waterfall – somewhere in America, I can't remember where. I heard a programme all about it on the radio.'

'Oh,' Joyce said. 'I must've slept through that one.'

'Well, you'd best start reading,' Charlie said. 'There's bound to be a test . . .'

Florence watched her husband as he leaned upon the plan chest. There it was: that gladness he'd been hiding all day long. No man ever looked as handsome when he smiled as Arthur Mayhood. His lopsided mouth regained its symmetry and the creases of his face became more interesting, coherent, like the patterns of a leaf pressed in a book. 'No test, no test,' he said, 'it's just for inspiration,' but they didn't seem persuaded.

May 1939

His ovation went on just a fraction longer than it had the previous two evenings. If Mr Wright was pleased by this, he didn't let it show. He waited at the lectern, blinking slowly at the crowd, as if to say, *I'll tell you when I've had enough*, until the hall was poised and hushed. Latecomers jostled in the doorway for an inch of standing room. Four hundred sets of eyes were pointed at him. Still, he took a beat to organize his cuffs, arrange his necktie, clear his throat. He looked much older underneath the slanting lights: white hair, turkey neck, a cane, a suppleness about his features. When he finally spoke, his voice was deep in tenor but genteel, and Arthur felt as though it was addressing only him.

'Good evening, everyone. In light of our discussion last time, we shall start proceedings with a short film of our work at Taliesin. My apprentice Jimmy Thompson is the man to thank for putting this together. What you're going to see is just the first of many reels of footage he's compiled . . .' With a sudden gesture to the wings, the hall went dark and up came the long beam of a projector. The film was grainy but in glorious full colour, and the images washed over one side of Wright's head and shoulders, causing him to squint.

Rocky desert land, blue sky, no clouds. A caravan of loaded trucks and motorcars winds down a sun-baked highway, spuming dust. The jointed wooden frame of a large building stands in silhouette. A shirtless man atop a ladder drives nails into a joist. He looks down at the camera, gestures with his mallet, grins.

Arthur had a view between the heads of strangers packed into the aisles. He was among the rest of the associates and students who could barely stand still or keep quiet, while the more esteemed guests took the padded seats. At first, he found it hard to focus on the speech. Not only was he bothered and uncomfortable, the amplifiers echoed in the hall. But once his ears adjusted to the interference, he could hear the great man's words for what they were: a campaign for a better way of life.

Lank-haired children in worn overalls play hopscotch at the base of a long gangway. High above their heads, a team of shirtless men push wheelbarrows.

Here, says Wright, the Taliesin Fellows are at work, erecting buildings for their camp in Arizona. They live and practise there, five months a year, to spare them the harsh winters in Wisconsin, where it gets as low as thirty below zero. Taliesin West, they call it. Home from home.

Other men in shorts and boots are chipping at stone beams with rockhammers. A lanky redhead in dark glasses leans against a doorjamb, laughing. Wright himself, wearing a beret and white cape, draws in cramped, unfinished quarters. He's erasing pencil lines and sweeping rubber leavings with quick backhand strokes.

Here, says Wright, they've made the walls from desert stones with concrete reinforcements. Redwood frames and canvas roofs, as soft as bedding. He keeps a modest study of his own, of course he does. But there are thirty cubicles for his apprentices. They like to work in close proximity.

An angular brick building on the brow of a vast hill planted with
apple trees and elderberry bushes. A field of shaking grass. Three
men are lifting bales of hay on to a wagon.

And here, says Wright, are pictures of their real home: Taliesin in Wisconsin. The original and best. In summer, there is nowhere else he'd rather be.

Tables, lamps and draughting boards inside a large, still room.
A kitchen table stacked with provender. A line of Mason jars
with spices and preserves. A horse-drawn plough. A tractor
scaling a vast mudheap. Women washing turnips in a long
ceramic basin.

Here, says Wright, their principles of fairness and cooperation are in evidence. The boys and girls together. They've got many hundred acres to maintain, so nobody is ever shy of duties. On a Monday, boys might get involved with all the cooking and the cleaning while the girls are at the market; on a Tuesday, they'll be mixing mortar, laying bricks or bringing in the crops together, and so on and so forth throughout the week. A spirit of collaboration is important. When it comes to the division of the labour, girls and boys aren't treated any differently – as much as such a thing is possible. Knowing the land is knowing life, he likes to say. The most important thing to learn in architecture is appreciation for materials: the weight of stone, the roughness of a brick, how wood can be pared down and shaped. The hand will discipline the mind this way.

A smiling lady in a gingham shirt carries a pail of apples through
a field. Wright lugs a watermelon on his shoulder through the
festooned gateposts of a county fair. Next, he's drawing at a table

46

under lamplight, flanked by two apprentices. Across the room,
a woman in a trailing headscarf and white trousers draws a crisp
arc with a set of compasses.

Here, says Wright, is the most vital organ of their operation: the draughting room. The boys and girls spend hours drawing, drawing and more drawing. Everybody learns by doing, but it's not a school they're running. There is no tuition. Taliesin is their home, their practice, and they value their apprentices as colleagues. Comrades.

A gathering, as if for a class picture, at the entrance of the Taliesin
building. Wright, in a tremendous wide-brimmed hat, stares up at
something he has spied off-camera.

Here, says Wright, is what's surprised and pleased him most. With only some direction on his part, these bright young men and women have developed skills to last a lifetime. His aim is to encourage their resourcefulness, instil a good work ethic, so later he might watch them thrive and practise an organic architecture of their own. It is, he says, a model for a better nation. For the place he calls Usonia.

Wright ambles through the tall grass with his cane, towards a
single, wind-stirred tree.

The film went on, so bright and strange and fluid, and the great man continued his narration, swaying at the lectern. It had stirred Arthur's blood already, sent a tremble through his legs, up to his neck. Those young apprentices on-screen, attending to their work with such a unity of purpose – he knew exactly how they felt. He saw their jokey solidarity and happiness. He recognized their inhibitions, too – the woodenness to their expressions, smiling under scrutiny. They weren't quite being themselves. They were acting for the camera. On their best behaviour. Maybe that was all the feeling was – affinity with strangers – but he had the strongest sense that he was one of them.

*

Later that night, he lingered on the entrance steps at Portland Place and smoked a Woodbine in the rain. The day had been so pleasant only a rank pessimist would've thought to carry an umbrella, and the RIBA building had no portico, no awning – but, for Arthur, getting drenched was a small price to pay for privacy. He'd come upstairs after the lecture to discover half the audience still pressed inside the foyer, waiting for the shower to pass. He'd shunted through the crowd to reach the doors and rushed out with his hat sloped down. There was a hum inside his body that nothing but tobacco and fresh air could pacify. It was making his toes twitch inside his shoes. He didn't know if it was possible to be in love with a philosophy, but that was how it seemed. And it was only as he struck a match to light up that he realized he'd abandoned both his colleagues in the lecture hall.

He'd been trying not to think about them: Miles Ibbot and Fred Cort. The three of them had walked to Portland Place together after work, chatting about office matters. 'As far as I'm concerned, unless a bomb can bounce right off it, I don't see the point in building with it now,' Ibbot had been bleating on the way, 'but Mr Stack is still insisting on that riven slate. It's so short-sighted.' When Cort had answered, 'I should think a *bouncing* bomb would do a lot more damage,' it had only prompted Ibbot to begin a rant about it being men their age, not Mr Stack's, who'd have to shoulder the responsibility for fixing Europe's mess, just wait and see. It hadn't taken Arthur long to understand that when his colleagues got into a rhythm it was best to nod along and keep his mouth shut. Once they'd shown their tickets to get into Jarvis Hall, he'd gone to use the lavatory and made sure they'd remained apart all evening.

'So this is where you're hiding, Mayhood, you sly devil.' Now the big bronze doors were opening and Fred Cort stood upon the entrance steps, shielding his head with a newspaper. 'Ibbot had a bet with me that you'd gone straight back to the office. Easy money, it turns out.'

Arthur stared across the street, into the spray of traffic. 'How'd you know I hadn't?'

'Because you've got a lovely girl to spend your nights with, haven't you? Unlike our dear Ibbot, who's afraid to speak to one in daylight.' Cort shut the doors, came closer. 'I'll tell you this much: if he's serious about the navy when it all gets started, then I'm trying for the air force.'

'I've known plenty worse than him, believe me.'

'You don't have to share a table with him every day. The man's a perfect bloody misery.' The rain was battering the *Telegraph* above Cort's head – it was saturated, limp. 'Is there a reason you can't smoke inside?'

'Quieter out here,' he said. 'A bit of rain won't hurt me.'

'Well, I'm getting drenched.'

He eyed the ground. 'I didn't ask you to come out, Fred.'

His colleague seemed to take offence at this. He stood there with his mouth ajar, his tongue working the ridges of his teeth. 'I was hoping you'd stayed on, that's all. I wanted your opinion on the talk, but it can wait till Monday.'

'*My* opinion?'

'Yes. Is that so strange? I can't decide if he's a genius or a raving loony. Possibly a bit of both. You see? I'm terribly conflicted, and I hate to be conflicted. But you always seem so sure of everything, I thought you'd have a view on it.'

'Sorry, Fred. I've come out here for peace and quiet. I'm not really in the mood for a debriefing.' In truth, he'd tuned out several times during the lecture. His mind had kept on skipping backwards to Wright's colour film instead. He couldn't stop his thoughts returning to it. He was thinking of it now.

'Perhaps on Monday, then.' Cort ditched the newspaper and let the rain attack his scalp. Again, he seemed a little stung. 'Look, Mayhood, I'm not sure we've really got to know each other since you joined the firm. I'd hate to think you see me as a rival.'

'Why should I think that?'

'No reason. I'm just trying to say, we're not in competition.'

'Something tells me Ibbot doesn't feel the same.'

'God, no. He'd trample on your grave to fetch a paperclip for Mr Furnish.'

'Oh, I'd bet he would.' At least Cort had a sense of humour – that was one mark in his favour. Water was now beading at the fella's earlobes, too, but there he was, still trying to engage him in a conversation. Either it was hardiness or plain stupidity. 'You ought to go back in before you catch pneumonia.'

Cort just sniffed. 'So *are* you waiting for your girl out here – is that why you're so keen to brush me off?'

He threw his Woodbine to the kerb. The fact was, he and Florence had their normal weekend planned but, for the past few days, he'd been auditioning his reasons not to travel out to Ockham at the final hour – variants of sickness, tiredness, poverty, emergency, all of which were hollow and pathetic. There was an eight fifteen from Waterloo tomorrow morning she expected him to board, and then he'd have to walk two miles from the station to her family's farm in what the wireless forecast said would be a gale. And he knew, deep down, that he would do it, just to see that smile blooming on her face when she pulled back the door. She'd draw him forward, as she always did, by the loose knot of his tie and kiss him softly on the mouth, and say, 'Dear Lord, I've missed you, Arthur.' But, as soon as they were past the threshold, everything would start to feel uncomfortable again. She'd be agitated by his company, her mind still on her father in the room upstairs.

Every time he was in Ockham now, he loathed himself, because their circumstances caused him to behave contemptibly. He'd started to resent the diligence with which she cared for Mr Greaves. She bathed the man, spoon-fed him every meal, escorted him to the commode and back, wheeled him up and down the road, exercised his idle limbs, put him to bed; it was an infinite routine, and there was something marvellous about it all in the beginning. But lately Arthur had been huffing when she got up from the sofa to attend to duties on her list. Clumsily, he'd once attempted – after three too many brandies, bored – to persuade her into bed, half-grasping at her hips, when she was clearly too depleted to stand upright in the doorway and still had to prepare her father's supper. 'Leave it, eh?' he'd said. 'Who's going to notice if it's late?' As these words had slipped out of his mouth, he'd felt revolted with himself, and so had she. 'Go and sleep it off, Arthur – this isn't like you,' was how she'd put it, 'and I'm hiding that decanter from now on.' But she'd barely spoken to him the next morning and he could tell that he'd sunk fathoms in her estimation.

If things carried on this way, he feared that she would see his selfishness emerge so often that she'd stop forgiving him. What if this ugly side of him was really all there was? It seemed he was incapable of courtship from a distance – it made him shameless and irrational. But he simply didn't know how he could spend so little time with Florence and remain content. He couldn't manage London life without her – all the loneliness he had to bear just to maintain a stable distance from his colleagues – not unless he could reset himself with Florence at the end of every day. Seeing her in Ockham on the weekends wasn't going to be enough. It was torment, having her beside him but not really *there*. 'In actual fact,' he told Cort now, 'I'm seeing her tomorrow. Early train and all that, so –' He made a drama out of looking at his watch. 'I'd best be going.'

'You're a lucky man,' Cort said. 'I never seem to reach the going-steady part.'

'Don't worry, Fred, I'm bound to ruin it eventually.' He rummaged in the sodden lining of his coat to check he had his keys.

'Do you have a picture?'

'Pardon me?'

'Of her – your girl. I'm sorry, I don't know her name.'

'It's Florence,' he said. 'And yes, I've got one, thank you.'

As soon as it was obvious he wasn't going to share the photograph, Cort laughed and shook his head. 'My goodness, you're not easy to make friends with, are you, Mayhood? I mean, a fellow really has to earn it.'

'We're colleagues,' he replied. 'We needn't be blood brothers.'

'That's a shame.' Cort smoothed the rain out of his hair. 'I've always found it easier to work with people I get on with.' There was a note of approbation in Cort's voice and then a slight contraction of his eyes after he spoke. 'You and I should get a drink. That's what we ought to do.'

'It's nearly past my bedtime.'

'Come on. Just a half? Have mercy on me.'

Thunder rumbled overhead. The rain was growing heavier. It seemed that Cort was only going to pester him until he ran out of excuses. 'All right. Where?'

They went just round the corner to the Masons Arms. The snug was busy, full of drinking men's unvarnished chatter, but compared to Portland Place it felt subdued. They hung their coats beside the fireplace and Cort dried off his hair with an enormous hankie; then he bought two halves of mild and carried them to a free table.

'Cheers,' Cort said, raising his beer as they sat down. 'Here's to Mr Wright and – what was it? Snowdonia?'

He had to laugh. '*Usonia.*'

'Ah yes, that's the one. Usonia!'

They clinked their glasses. He was lighting up again when Cort said, 'I'll never understand how you can smoke those gaspers. You might as well chew on a lump of coal.'

'They're cheap, that's all.'

'So's tripe, but I don't eat it.'

'Good for you, Fred. Some folk have to eat whatever they can get.'

He didn't mean to be so blunt. Most of his hours in the office at Stack Furnish were spent avoiding frank exchanges such as this: exposures of his background that could make him vulnerable to judgement. He'd been shaped by his mistakes, his hardships, and would not deny them. But somewhere down the line (in fact, he knew exactly when it was: the morning of his interview for the assistant's job, when Mr Stack and Mr Furnish had asked him to describe his time in borstal, as though it were a stint in Gandey's Circus) he'd realized it was better to deflect attention from his past. It was bad enough he had to speak with Bootle in his voice, buffed out and made presentable, but still apparent, still remarked on. He'd become the office curiosity, a lightning rod for condescension from the Harrow boys like Ibbot. Sly comments were already being passed in whispers – he was sure of it. He'd seen their faces simpering when he came back from lunch or went into the storeroom. *Oh dear, there goes Mayhood in that cheap hat from the market.*

'You're right,' Cort said, surprising him, 'I shouldn't be so glib. I'm sorry.'

They sat there for a moment, saying nothing else. There was a crack of raucous laughter from the bar. He'd never known his colleague to be so contrite or tongue-tied. He wondered if the things that he'd disliked about Cort all this time – his bluster and immodesty – were symptoms of another type. Perhaps Fred Cort was no more certain of himself than he was. Perhaps he wasn't like the rest of them at all. 'I'll tell you what, though, Fred,' he offered as a consolation, 'even if they're cheap, I never share them.' Then he put his nearly empty packet on the table. 'Go on. Seeing as we're not in competition. Have one.'

Cort scratched his chin, amused. 'All right. Might as well.'

He watched him take a Woodbine, light it, have a puff. All the while, he weighed the prospect in his mind: that he could let somebody get to know him for a change. That he could sacrifice a measure of control to ease some of his loneliness. Why not take a reading of Cort's goodness here and now, as it was just the two of them? Survey the ground a bit before he trusted it to build on. Why not try? He couldn't keep on shrugging people off in case they disappointed him.

'You know,' he said, as plainly as he could, 'I started smoking these in borstal. Actually, it would've been before we got there. We were held for a few days at Wandsworth nick, just in the sorting station, and a lad there offered one to me while we were lining up. I thought the same as you did now: *Go on, might as well*. I'd never smoked before, but I've been faithful to them ever since. Old habits and all that.'

'Bloody hell,' Cort said, exhaling. His eyes had gone quite rheumy with the smoke. 'I never knew you were in borstal.'

'Yes, two years at Feltham.' He was going to have to hold the reins of conversation tightly now and stop them veering off into the gloom. 'Please don't spread it round the office, mind.'

'Of course I won't. What did you *do*?'

'Held up a cargo train,' he said.

'Good heavens. Really?'

'No. What do you take me for?' He saw Cort's face relax again. 'They caught me with some stolen goods, that's all – about ten crates of pipe tobacco.'

'Why? What made you do it?'

'Circumstances. I was hungry and I had to. There's a story, but I'd rather keep it to myself.'

'This happened up in Liverpool?'

'Yes, but a long time ago. You'll want to knock the ash off that. They burn up quicker than you think.'

'Oh, blast.' Cort rubbed a big grey streak into his trousers. He was not a seasoned smoker. 'Well, it can't have been *that* long ago. We must be the same age – at least, I thought we were. I'm twenty-four. How old are you?'

'The same.'

'And how old at the time?'

'Fifteen.' He found that Cort was looking back at him with something like esteem – his lower lip thrust out, his nostrils flared.

'*Nine years?* Blimey, that's a turnaround. It took me five to get through *Ulysses*.' And then he leaned in, blinking. 'You're a bit of an enigma, Mayhood. Do the partners know about all this?'

'Well, it was in my covering letter. I could hardly keep it secret.'

'No, of course, I didn't mean to –'

'It's all right. The truth is, half the firms in London wouldn't even interview me. But Stack Furnish wrote straight back.'

'Fair play to them. I wouldn't have expected it of Mr Furnish.'

'I suppose it helped that two of his old pals were my instructors and they recommended me.'

'He trained at Liverpool as well?'

'Yes, under Reilly.'

'That explains a lot about his style. Am I the only fool who didn't go there?'

'You and Ibbot.'

'Damn.' Cort arched his back to vent the fumes over his shoulder, laughing. 'I think I'm getting used to these. They're not so awful.'

'Everyone surrenders in the end. You'll be on ten a day before you know it.'

His colleague drained the last few inches of his mild and put his glass down. 'Well –' He burped into his fist. 'The partners didn't bother showing up again, I noticed. That's three lectures in a row they've missed.'

'It's odd, to say the least.' There was a dampness still to Arthur's clothes, but he was warmer now and more at ease. His spirits had been lifted, seeing the honesty of Cort's reaction. There'd been some surprise when he'd first mentioned borstal, as expected, and a bit of idle curiosity. But not much pressure to explain himself. No pity. And then – *done*. As though what he'd revealed was no more consequential than the landlord's prattle at the bar, the conversation had moved on to other matters.

'I know for sure that Mr Furnish was invited,' Cort went on. 'I asked his secretary. But I can't imagine they're on board with Wright's ideas. Organic this, organic that. A million miles from their approach now, isn't it?'

'I find them so frustrating,' he replied. 'They're clearly in a rut, but it's so comfortable for them they haven't noticed.'

'Absolutely, I agree. And it's a great relief to hear you say it. I've been going slowly mad.'

In fact, a general dissatisfaction with the projects at Stack Furnish had been festering in Arthur for a while now. But he couldn't tell if this was caused by apathy towards the low-risk style the partners were inured to, or if it was because he was still cleaving to his happy memories of architecture school – those dream-drunk days he used to share with Florence. It was just over a year ago that they were living a short tram-ride from each other, existing in a heedless syncopation, going from his lodgings to her halls of residence and back again, making plans out loud. Liverpool was much too small for their ambitions; London was the next place on the list. The world seemed braced for them to conquer. He missed those years with her so deeply he relived them every night inside his head on a despairing loop.

Not long after he'd arrived and taken up his rented room in Dulwich, reality had shouldered him into submission. Working at Stack Furnish was sobering and monotonous. He'd found that being an architect in practice required little vision or imagination; if he took the partners as his standard-bearers, architecture seemed to be about the mindless service of rich clients who couldn't tell the difference between lateral and perpendicular, but who could still be invoiced for a spate of meetings to discuss the smallest of adjustments to designs – nothing ever got completed, just continued. The longer he was at Stack Furnish, the more he felt he was releasing the balloon strings of his principles, forgoing every instinct and good habit he'd acquired since his first draughtsman's class at borstal. Now the world was definitely braced for something, but it wasn't him and Florence or their big ideas.

'I get the feeling you approve of Mr Wright and what he preaches,' Cort went on. 'Please tell me that you do, because I can't keep up the act. I'm not *at all* conflicted. Not one bit. I think the man's a visionary – and now it looks as though I'm only saying it because you are, but ever since those first few articles of his in *Wendingen*, I –'

'Stop, Fred. I believe you. And you're right, I think the same.'

For the first time, he could look at Cort and see through the veneer of him: those three-piece suits he wore on a rotation, the rule-straight parting in his hair, the news broadcaster's accent. It was just another way of blending into the drab scenery at Stack Furnish, giving the partners what they wanted. 'Let me get us the next round, eh? Unless you'd rather go back to the office.'

Two more halves of mild apiece and then they switched to brandy. After this, the wall lights started shimmering like campfires far away. The pub got so loud he was shouting things to Cort across the table that ought to have been whispered. 'I've not given any thought to what I'll do when it kicks off, have you? I'm sure we'll get dragged into it before too long. Perhaps I'll just present myself wherever I'm supposed to go and they can put me where I'll be most useful.'

'Sounds all right to me. I have an uncle who was in the Sappers, so I might as well look into that. As long as they don't put me in a tank, I'll do just fine.'

'I wouldn't mind. It's ships that bother me – the water, anyway. Every time I go to Birkenhead, I chuck up on the ferry.'

'Skip the navy, then.'

'I don't trust aeroplanes much neither.'

Cort made wide, reproachful eyes at him. 'Sounds like something I heard Ibbot say once.'

'Oh, God. Sorry. Change the subject.'

'Fine by me.' Cort snapped his fingers twice. 'Let's have another of those gaspers.'

'We finished them already.'

'Then let's find a cigarette machine.'

'It's out of order.'

There was a blurry half an hour or so in which they scrambled on the pavements of Great Portland Street, looking for a corner shop, before they gave up altogether. The rain had long abated. Hotel canopies were dripping on the heads of passers-by, the gutter pipes were sluicing by their feet and all of London's fairground dazzle seemed undignified. After this, a quietness began to settle, prompting him to think about tomorrow.

'I should turn in for the night, I think.'

Cort came and shook his hand. 'I'm really glad we did this, Mayhood.'

'Take care, Fred.'

'I'll see you in Usonia. Or maybe just the office.'

'Monday morning. Bright and early.'

'Cheerio.'

He watched Cort shamble round the corner, clattering the railings with his fingers like a kid. His own legs felt unsteady as he wandered down to Oxford Street to catch the last bus home to Dulwich. When he got back to his lodgings, it was some time after midnight and his landlord's reading lamp was still aglow in the front window, shutting off as soon as his key met the lock.

The starkness of his room was dismal. There'd hardly been a spare hour since his move from Liverpool to hang a picture, let alone bring in an aspidistra or replace the furniture. Florence had stayed over with him only twice, and there didn't seem to be much sense in dressing up his digs for his own benefit. The brandy and the beer were churning in his stomach now. He made himself a plum jam sandwich and ate it in the partial darkness, feeling suddenly alone. No matter how much he denied it, there was goodness to be found in the companionship of other men. A different sort of happiness, less bewildering or engulfing. But he'd had to leave too many of these friendships at the gates of Feltham and, since then, he'd been afraid to lose another.

All this time, the judge's voice was still clear in his memory:

'Arthur Patrick Mayhood, you shall go to borstal for a period of training. Three years, with a minimum of one year to be served.' *Training*, he'd thought, and imagined long days hiking up a mountainside in shorts and vest, performing shuttle runs on muddy football fields. Whatever *training* meant, it had to be a vast improvement on the cells at Walton Prison. He'd seen enough of them while he was on remand there, counting down the weeks until his court date, separated mostly from the con men, muggers and wife beaters, but thrown in with a pack of them for Sunday services, hearing things that chilled him, murder tales that wouldn't leave his head. For a while, his name had been replaced by a cell number on a uniform: K-186. He'd had a six-foot room with a barred window and an iron frame to sleep on. Mornings were for exercising on the ring, the afternoons for sewing mailbags – no talking was allowed, just stitch, stitch, stitch for hours. By nine o'clock, his door was bolted shut and lights went out. His dreams had frightened him so much he'd rarely slept.

He'd found another kind of life at Feltham. In with boys his age from up and down the country, most of them the same as him – no family to speak of, and no money to their names, persuaded into thieving by necessity. An older lad he knew, John Parker, had been serving time for pilfering a case of baking powder, which he'd tried to flog back to the bakery he'd pinched it from in Colchester. John had been a mouthy sort, but harmless. There were rougher lads you had to steer a path around: the thugs who came to shove you down while you were minding your own business in the dining hall, who bloodied up your nose for pointing your eyes at them in the plunge bath. But trouble had been easier to avoid in borstal than it had been on the streets of Bootle.

He'd gone in like the rest of them: resentful, clueless, cursing his bad luck. Dispatched into a house with eighty others, then a group of twenty with a prefect leading them. In grade one, days were regimented and mundane (parade drills in the yard at six a.m., then cleaning duty), supervised by warders in civilian clothes. No speaking with the other boys at mealtimes and no games allowed or common recreation. For a few months, all he'd done was sweep the floors and scrub the lavatories. But at least he'd slept on a thick mattress, under blankets, in a cubicle with MAYHOOD on the door, and not a bolt-lock to be seen. In fact, the Feltham gates were always left unmanned, with only seven feet of concrete wall at the perimeter – anybody could've scaled it with a bit of application. (The two lads he'd seen try it had been apprehended in a nearby village that same evening, and they'd done six months on stoneyard duty, smashing rocks to powder. No one else had bothered after that.)

In time, he'd earned a stripe and was allowed to join a working party. Every lad from grade two onwards had to learn a trade before he got discharged. Some had chosen tailoring or bootmaking; others had gone down the engineering route, or blacksmithing, or carpentry; the rest had found they liked it better in the kitchen or the laundry. He'd considered signing up for farming party to begin with. Just outside the boundary wall, there was a tract of land for them to cultivate, with guidance from a local resident – it wasn't quite the many hundred acres Frank Lloyd Wright had bragged of owning in Wisconsin, but it kept them occupied throughout the year. Half the veg they ate at Feltham were produced on that small farm, and this made their meals good and wholesome; not the pigswill they doled out at the men's prison. He'd seen lads planting, mowing, raking in the fields with sunshine on their backs, and thought it looked appealing: honourable work that wouldn't tie him down to one place on the map. But then his pal John Parker had decided on the building party, so he'd followed him and joined the navvy gang.

By then, he'd lost his sense of bitterness about his situation. There were certain privileges he'd won from his first stripe: more recreation time, no limits on his conversation in the dining hall, a later call to bed. And there'd been hobby-hour classes, taught by volunteers from the outside. He'd taken woodworking, then draughtsmanship: a simple ten-week course that had awoken him to architecture. While it wasn't true to say that he was ever satisfied with being a prisoner, borstal had allowed him to discover things he hadn't known existed, skills he'd never thought that he possessed.

The strangest part about tonight was seeing those Taliesin boys engaged in work no different from the navvy gang's routine. Heaving wet cement around in barrows, laying bricks, affixing joists and roof beams. In the navvy gang, they'd had no famous architect to guide them, just Ken Siddle, a retired engineer who'd given up his weekdays to inspire their love of building, showing up each morning in the same blue overalls and a cloth cap. They'd put up a machine shed, starting with shovels to dig out foundation trenches, ending with door locks and hinges – it wasn't much to look at, but it had a pitched slate roof and windows edged with stone, and it was still the only finished building he could put his name to.

Now that he was brooding on it in the glumness of his room, he couldn't stop the film from flashing in his mind again, the *tick-tick-tick* of it. There was nobody he could explain it to who would've understood. But there was Florence, who would listen.

It was much too late to call her. Even so, he went out to the hall to use the telephone, adding his name quickly to the logbook – he'd accrued a small debt to his landlord in the past few months, entirely with calls to Ockham. She picked up after half a dozen rings. 'Yes? Hello? Who *is* this? Do you realize the time?'

'Sorry, Flo. It's me.'

A long breath of forbearance. 'Goodness, Arthur. What's so urgent?'

'Only just got home . . .'

'Have you been drinking?'

'Might've had a few after the lecture. With a colleague.'

'Well, you ought to get some sleep if you still plan to catch the eight fifteen.'

'I'm not so sure I can.'

'Oh, please don't cry off now. It's been a dreadful week. I need you.'

'I'm still coming. I just meant that I can't sleep.'

'Why not?'

A blade of light appeared beneath his neighbour's door. He had to lower his voice. 'I wish you could've seen this film I saw tonight, Flo.'

'You were at the flicks without me?'

'Sort of.' None of it could wait until tomorrow. By the morning, all the surfacing ideas that buoyed him now would surely sink again, or he would have to drown them. But if Florence heard the wonder in his voice, she would remember and remind him.

August 1952

A hole in the air-inlet pipe had caused most of the damage. She'd already had to scrap the cylinder, the camshaft bearings and the pistons. Finding the replacement parts had been a feat of correspondence, but she'd done it, sending letters, making calls, driving the wagon halfway round the country to acquire what she needed, arriving in the yards of working men who advertised their spares in *Farmers Weekly*. They'd all asked her the same question when negotiations started: 'Did your husband not come with you?' But she'd been steadfast to her valuations. Sellers always buckled when she showed her readiness to leave without a deal. The kindliest of all the men she'd bartered with, a snub-nosed fellow who had teeth like sweetcorn, claimed that it was dirt that wrecked most tractor engines: if there was the slightest hole in the air-inlet system, so he'd told her, muck got drawn into the cylinder. Arriving home, she'd re-examined the old Fordson and discovered a small fissure in the pipe. Well, that explained it. She'd been hopeful for a while that she could get the damned thing operational before the end of summer. But although she'd patched the hole, replaced the parts and got the motor running with the crank – rumbling sweetly, with a force that rattled through her bones when she climbed up and took the wheel – the gears would not engage, no matter what she tried.

A transmission problem: that had been her educated guess. To check, she'd siphoned off the gear oil, mixing up a sample with some paraffin, dunking in a horseshoe magnet. When she'd pulled it out, there'd been a layer of metal shavings at the poles, thick enough to spread on toast, and she'd concluded that the bearing was abraded; probably, the worm gear had been sheared down, too.

Every day since then, she'd thanked the Lord for Charlie Savigear's arrival, because having one more pair of hands and someone to confer with made the problems easier to solve. Dropping by the garage late on his first afternoon, he'd said, 'Did you get the housing off it yet, miss? I can do it, if you like.' She'd given him a set of overalls – they were Arthur's size, so rather swamped him – and, working in the shade of the garage together, hunched beside the rusty chassis, they'd found an easy synchronicity. He'd proved that he could handle a rachet set as well as he could use a pencil. And he seemed to have a knack for following the terse articulations of the owner's manual, whose vagueness often mystified her. Once the gearbox was dismantled, they'd surveyed the ruins inside: every bit as bad as they'd anticipated. 'What now?' he'd said. 'Where d'you even find stuff for these old machines?' She'd shown him the back section of the latest *Farmers Weekly* and they'd composed their own 'Parts Wanted' ad to run in the next issue, walking to the Alms Heath post office together to dispatch it.

For a while after this, she'd seen much less of Charlie. They'd had their routine hours in the draughting room, of course, with Arthur overseeing matters from his station by the window, going to and from the Savigears' tables to scrutinize their work or offer his advice. Sometimes, she would demonstrate a technical concern to Charlie or his sister – how to vary line weights to suggest a difference of material, say – and they'd be effusively apologetic, as though it wasn't every trainee architect's experience to fail a little less with each attempt.

Charlie had submitted a design for renovations to his bedroom after only a few days and she couldn't help but think he'd rushed it. The drawing showed a raised bed with a ladder and a small desk in the hollow underneath, plus a built-in wardrobe unit: it was a clever use of space, rather like a sailing boat's interior. Functional, discreet, overtly boyish, and drawn with a nice looseness of expression. Her husband had been most impressed when they'd reviewed it: 'See the rungs there, on the ladder, how he's thought to make them thicker at the base and thinner at the top – I like that sense of detail. But it should be ash, not oak . . . I've got to say, I'm glad to see so much restraint, aren't you? It bodes well for the future.' Compared to the extravaganza Joyce had put together, it was practically monastic: Arthur had instructed her to scale down her ideas. 'That big four-poster bed is an indulgence,' he'd said. 'And how exactly do you plan to make that stained-glass window? I don't know a glazier who could do it to those specs – at least, not for the amount of peanuts we could pay him.' Since then, Charlie's doorway had been covered with a tarp – the carpentry was under way inside and he'd been making furtive progress every day with Arthur's help, while Joyce was left amending her initial plans. 'A good lesson to learn early,' Florence had maintained to both of them. 'Compose within your means.' But, quite honestly, she felt that Joyce's rather clumsy drawing showed the most imaginative range. And though she'd grown accustomed to the din of hammering and sawing inside Charlie's room each afternoon, she missed his company in the garage.

Eventually, there came a phone call from a dairy farmer near Worcester, claiming that he had the tractor parts she needed. The only problem was the price: a whole pound steeper than her husband was prepared to entertain. She enlisted Mr Hollis to her cause, suggesting, 'Please could you remind him how expensive it'll be to keep a horse in food and shelter through the year instead. We've no room for a working animal. It's looking like we'll have to drag that plough on someone's shoulders – are you going to volunteer for that?' Her husband listened better to the old man's supplications, it transpired.

This morning, she agreed a deal with the dairy farmer on the phone. After breakfast, she got straight into the wagon and drove there without stopping – three hours on the outbound leg, the loose boards of the flatbed clanking all the way. She took a flask of sweet tea with her and some home-made bis-cuits in a napkin, nothing else. The farmer let her give the parts a long inspection and then made her count the money on the still-warm bonnet of the wagon. 'Sorry, love,' he said, 'I've had the wool pulled over me before. Don't take it personal.' On the way back, near Burford, she parked up on the verge of a through road to relieve herself behind a tree. Her stomach started whining for a feed. She wanted fish and chips with reams of bread and butter, but no shop was open on a Sunday.

Arriving home, she stepped out of the wagon at the front gate, leaving the engine running, as she always did. The latch was slightly rusted and there was a certain knack to lifting it. She was pushing back the gate, facing all the hedges and the bracken on the neighbour's side, when she saw movement in the copse. It wasn't rare to spot a fox stalking the woods this time of day, and roe deer had been known to spring on to the track, so she didn't find it too perturbing. But then she noticed how the bracken quivered, splayed, and she was sure, when she glanced into the copse again, that a man was squatting there amid the tangle of the ferns and bushes. A rather large man, was her sense of it. The bald cap of his head was poking out above the greenery.

'Who's there?' she said. 'Come out, please, or I'm phoning the police.'

She paced backwards to the wagon. A spike of trepidation scratched along her spine. As she got behind the wheel, the man skulked from the bushes with both hands in the air. He was thick around the middle, hunched and bearded. And the buckle of his belt hung down.

'Don't bother the police,' he called. There was no panic to him, which she thought surprising. Not a blink or twitch. 'I was only – look, you've caught me short, that's all.' He steered his eyes down to his trousers. 'Could I make myself present-able again?' Lowering his hands, he tightened up his belt and clasped it shut. 'I was about to wet myself. I'm dreadful sorry. There was nowhere else with any sort of coverage – I thought it'd be private. More fool me.' The face he gave her then was childlike, fraught with shame. 'If it's all the same with you, I'll just be on my way, dear. That all right?'

Well, she could hardly punish him for doing exactly what she'd done herself ten minutes out of Burford. 'Go on,' she said, 'be off with you. Don't ever let me see you on my land again, you hear? Or the police will know about it.'

'Thank you,' he said. 'Much obliged.'

She slammed her door closed, trying to make a point, to shoo him off.

He grabbed his belt and started walking, stepping round the wagon's flank. She eyed the mirror till he passed behind her and then drove on a few yards. Getting out to shut the gate, she was disappointed with herself for being so uncharitable, so protective of her property – it undermined the spirit they were trying to foster round the place. She hadn't meant to sound so scathing, but that scratch along her spine had caused it: she'd felt vulnerable before the stranger in a way she hadn't with the farmers she bought parts from. Why? The man had seemed no more suspicious than the rest of them, just *larger*. She decided it was best to leave these details out when she reported the encounter to her husband later on; he'd only rant and rave about her lack of caution.

Coming down the drive, she spotted Charlie at his bedroom window, and he waved back when she tapped the horn. By the time she'd slow-reversed the wagon into the garage and climbed out, he was standing in his overalls by the workbench, ready to begin.

'I was thinking you were lost somewhere,' he said. 'Did everything turn out all right?'

'I think so. Had to pay a few more bob than I was hoping. Plus a tank of diesel.' She retrieved the box from the front seat. 'Mr Mayhood won't be pleased.'

'Ah, he'll make it back in time saved, won't he?' Charlie lifted up the clump of straw the farmer had put in the box for cushioning. Underneath: a new thrust bearing and a worm gear, used. 'These are in good nick.'

'We'll see. The proof is in the pudding.'

He looked up with a face of mock alarm. 'Don't remind me – Joy's in charge of supper.'

'What time do you make it now?'

'It's nearly five.'

'We have at least an hour, then. Good.' Her overalls were hanging on a peg in the dim recess by the doorway. She buttoned herself into them and pinned her fringe back with the kirby grips she kept inside the pockets. 'What's your sister cooking?'

'I dunno. But don't expect a feast.'

'If it's warm, I'll eat it. All I've had today is toast and biscuits – gave the last fried egg to Mr Hollis when he came this morning.'

'That old man can look after himself, if you ask me.'

'I owed him one this time.'

'Is that why he's been coming round to use our bath and all?'

'That's not my doing. But yes.' The procedure to attach the parts was fiddly and she wanted to review the manufacturer's

69

diagrams before they started. 'Where's the manual got to? It was here on the seat.'

'Sorry, miss, I moved it,' Charlie said. He went over to the bench where all her tools were spread out in a neat arrangement and then ambled back, the grease-stained Fordson booklet scrolled up in his fist.

'Does it say what grade of oil the gearbox needs? We'll have to top it up again.'

'Yeah, hold on a sec.' He turned the pages. 'Ninety viscosity.'

'All right. We've got a can of that, I think.'

'What does "SAE" mean?'

In the past few weeks, she'd learned that Charlie was the sort of boy who never asked a question twice. As soon as he received the information he required, it filled a little vacancy inside his brain for ever. 'Society of Auto something,' she said. 'Engineering, maybe. Not important.' She rubbed her hands, examining the disconnected parts that sat upon a sheet beside the two back wheels. Every last component had been cleaned and polished to the best of her ability. Between them, they'd plotted out the disassembly in her notebook, accounting for each tiny step and measure. All they had to do was trace back through the sequence and swap in the new parts; but no machine was ever so amenable to her intentions. 'I suppose it shouldn't take us long, in theory.'

'A few parts and a bit of grease – ta-da – it's up and running.'

'Simple as that.' She smiled.

'Simple as that,' he said.

It was curious how young she felt sometimes in Charlie's presence. There were moments when she caught herself adopting the complaining attitude she used to have when she was seventeen: 'This old pile of rubbish better be worth it . . .

Makes no difference, anyway: something else is bound to break before too long . . .' At other times, she felt so elevated by her sense of duty that she began intoning like a reverend at the pulpit, stressing the importance of old tractors like the Fordson ('the majestic Model N', she called it) and even veering into stories about girls she knew who'd served in the Land Army. She couldn't understand why she was stumbling so much in pursuit of his respect. Had she always been this eager to be liked?

That hour seemed to stretch and slide away. They stood together at the workbench reassembling the entire transmission, talking only in relation to the job at hand. Charlie passed her tools when she requested them, applied his brute strength to the worm gear with a mallet when she asked him to, but mostly he stayed next to her, recounting the procedure from her notebook, squinting when he couldn't read her cursive. 'What does that say – *level* or *bevel*?' At a certain point, he put the book down on the bench, and she could feel the sudden press of his attention. 'Miss,' he said, 'there's something I've been wanting to bring up with you.'

She kept her eyes on the components. 'Oh?'

'It's just that . . . look, d'you remember when you picked us up that morning from the train? My sister had a dig at me for – well, she said that I could get an engine running even if I wasn't meant to.'

'I remember.'

He was playing with the lever on the vice, making it clink up and down. 'I didn't want you wondering about her meaning on that front. It only happened once.'

'All right.' She wiped her brow upon her sleeve. 'Which part goes next? This little one?'

'Miss, do you understand what I've been trying to –'

'I just said it was all right.' She always seemed to sweat more at the peak of concentration than she ever did when scrubbing floors, or chasing hens around the yard, or scraping paint off walls. It was peculiar. The hair beneath her kirby grips was wet and frazzled, and she felt the need to reposition them, but her hands were black with oil. Charlie went on clattering the vice, until she reached to grab the lever and he stepped away. 'You needn't fret,' she said. 'We know what you did wrong and, frankly, it's of no concern to us.' She couldn't tell from his long exhalation whether he was troubled or relieved.

'How? I mean, who told you?'

'Well, for a start, we asked for copies of your borstal records and they sent us what they could. Then Mr Mayhood spoke with all the officers who knew you, and both your old housemasters – even had the top brass calling him. The governors. So, if you're looking to feel guilty about something, you should see our phone bills.' This almost brought a flicker of a smile to Charlie's face. She went on: 'Honestly, we've never worried about what happened in the past. The only thing we care about is what's ahead of you.'

For a moment, he was quiet. His Adam's apple climbed and dived inside his throat. Then he said, 'The coppers reckoned we were on a joyride when they pulled us over. That's not true. I never even knew that car was stolen. It was all a big mistake, and Joy, she wasn't really –' He trailed off, in search of the vocabulary. 'All I really mean to say is that we've put those days behind us, miss. I swear to God we have. We've never been more grateful in our lives for where we are.'

'I know that, too,' she said. 'And so does Mr Mayhood. There's no need to second-guess the rest of it.'

She didn't want to prise open the subject of his past and stir it. No one had a right to wallow in another person's pain. What she knew of Charlie Savigear's life had been condensed into summations on thin sheets of paper, refracted through the phone calls

Arthur had held with borstal personnel and then recapped for her. But certain details were immutable. And how could they not shape her attitude to Charlie and his sister? Surely she could recognize their hardships without lapsing into pity.

The fact was they were children when they lost their parents, and that was tragedy enough. She thought about this often, knowing how she'd mourned her mother's passing, how that grief had spread throughout the fabric of the everyday. It must've left them feeling anchorless. The records said a single German plane had emptied out its payload over their home town of Gillingham one night – this was summer 1940 – and a bomb had struck the back end of the Savigears' house. Their father (a sign painter whose deaf ear kept him from enlisting) and their mother (whose occupation was not cited, so a housewife) were sheltering beneath the stairs, and that was that. Either it was good luck or misfortune, depending on which angle she regarded it from, that Joyce and Charlie had been sent away to live with distant relatives six months before – maybe they were spared the bombs, she thought, but not the damage. It explained the troubles they got into later, even if it didn't excuse them. Skirmishes with other kids, at first. Some petty thefts (apples from the greengrocer's, cigarettes from a machine, a teacher's bike). Receiving stolen goods (a petrol mower lifted from a garden shed). And then that joyride through the streets of Maidstone in a stolen car, which landed them in borstal. When she compared their history to hers, she felt something like vertigo.

Now Charlie pushed his hands into his pockets and leaned hard against the bench. 'I can't tell if Mr Mayhood likes us yet.'

'Whatever gave you that idea? He thinks the world of you. He told me.'

'Well,' said Charlie, 'we get on all right. But I'm not sure about it.'

'About what?'

'I don't know how to put it. Our chances, I suppose.'

She noticed he'd been speaking in the plural. 'Is it *your* relationship with him that you're concerned about or Joyce's?'

He went quiet again. Then he admitted, 'It's just hard to know how well she's doing. In Mr Mayhood's eyes.'

'Well, I'm afraid my husband's very hard to read sometimes,' she said, by way of reassurance, though it didn't quite come out as she intended. 'But if he isn't happy with the job you're doing, trust me, he won't spare your feelings. Anyway –' she smeared more grease into the housing – 'at this point, you're just here to watch and learn. We want you both to listen and get used to how we work. And, while you're doing that, you'll need to muck in on the farm as much as possible. Did you read the lectures Mr Mayhood gave you – in the pamphlet?'

'Yeah. A few times, actually.'

'There you are, then. Our ideas are the same as Wright's. We're trying to give you both a real grounding. Not just in our practice. Life in general.'

Charlie angled his head until she was compelled to look at him. 'Do you believe in all that stuff?' he asked. 'Organic architecture?'

'You make it sound like a religion. It's just a way of thinking.'

'That's a shifty answer, miss, if you don't mind me saying.'

'Is it?' She was forced into a shrug. 'All right. Ask me that again in a few years.'

Charlie nodded, grinned. He diverted his attention to the notebook. 'Three-inch seal's the one you're looking for,' he said. 'I'm guessing that small squiggle is a three.'

She checked. It was. 'Smart alec.'

In an hour, they had the new parts fitted and the housing back together. There were four bolts left to tighten when she heard Joyce calling, 'Supper's on!' and clattering a saucepan with what sounded like a ladle. 'Supper's on!'

Charlie wiped his hands on his lapels. 'I think supper might be on, don't you?'

She laughed. 'I'll just tighten these last few.'

They hung up their overalls and went inside to wash: Charlie to his bathroom halfway down the hall and Florence to her en suite in the bedroom. She fetched the Epsom salts from her side of the cabinet and filled the basin to a froth, scrubbing the dark oil from her fingernails until the water turned a sooty shade. In the mirror was a tired version of herself she hardly recognized, with soft grey crescents underneath her eyes that looked like bruises and a gungy sheen about her nose and fore-head. There never seemed to be enough time to attend to her appearance. It was a quick spritz here, a dash of make-up there – repairs she fitted in between her main priorities. It had been years since she'd put on a dress and gone out dancing, though she'd never much enjoyed it when she had.

The clamour had begun downstairs already – Joyce's thump-ing strides along the hallway as she carried in the serving dishes, the water jug's dull chink against the glasses, murmured voices. They'd started to acquire the rhythms of a family. Comfort was beginning to breed habit. It was all that she could ask for. She scrubbed her arms up to the elbows till the skin was ruddy, rinsed them under the cold tap. She cleaned her face and brushed her hair. She changed into a skirt and blouse, even though she knew another hour in the garage would be needed after supper.

Coming out on to the landing, she noticed that the blue tar-paulin outside Charlie's room was gone. He'd painted his door white – a high-gloss finish – and now the purpling daylight took to it so readily it almost seemed like a French window. She'd been smelling paint fumes for the past few days and suddenly she had the explanation. The far end of the corridor was brighter, but its symmetry was lost. She had a foot on the top stair when she heard a handle turning. Charlie backed out of his door and shut it. Clean blue T-shirt. Hair slicked back. His face freshened with soap.

She cleared her throat and it startled him slightly. 'I thought you were already down there.'

He spun round, amused. 'No, miss. I just needed a quick smoke.'

'The tarp is gone, I see.'

'It is.'

'So when's the grand unveiling?'

He waved her over. 'Right now, if you like.'

Behind him, in the window, afternoon was waning into evening. What was it about him that was different from the boy in baggy overalls who'd left her in the garage? Perhaps a new-found peace within himself, an inner confidence restored. She didn't know. But as he stood there by his doorway, thick-browed, restful, waiting for an answer to his invitation, he looked so much like Arthur in his youth that she could feel the strangest dislocation from herself. He had the same involuntary pout, the same relentless motion to his eyes, as though observant of particulars that only he could see. And his carriage: borstal-trained into uprightness, yet so languid and serene.

From down below, the clank of cutlery, the smell of stewing apples. 'Your sister's gone to so much trouble,' she said, remembering where she was again. 'We don't want it to get cold.'

*

It was only Joyce's second try at making supper since she'd been with them; the first had been a small catastrophe of burnt Welsh rarebit and split custard. Tonight, there'd been tinned-salmon rissoles with mashed potatoes, swede and carrots, followed by stewed apples drowning in Carnation. It was clear that certain aspects of the recipes had been ignored, and the whole week's butter ration had been squandered in the mash alone; but Florence knew that to complain about a person's efforts in the kitchen was the most ungrateful sort of whinging. Her husband was uninterested in the artistry of food. It was fuel to him and nothing more. He'd shovelled in great forkfuls, making noises of encouragement, saying how well Joyce had done 'to give us such a spread', and Charlie had seemed pleased to find him so expansive in his praise. 'Yeah, well done,' he'd chimed in, 'not half bad.'

Joyce had gazed at her across the table. 'Was it up to snuff then, miss, or what?' It was clear that her opinion was the only one she cared to hear. There was such a hopeful tone about her voice, a brittleness.

Arthur had said, 'Let's not leave the poor girl in suspense, Flo. Tell her.'

She'd tried to find a way to moderate her answer. 'The rissoles were a touch too sloppy and a little bland,' was how she'd phrased it. 'But, besides all that, you did extremely well. The pudding was especially nice, I thought.'

'Oh well, there you are, then.' Joyce had rocked back in her chair. 'I can still make it as a housewife, after all. I knew it.'

Charlie had said, 'Now you've got to find a bloke who'll marry you. Good luck.'

She'd been quite dismayed to hear him talk that way to his own sister. But, then again, she'd never had a brother. Maybe this was how it was supposed to be.

'Stranger things have happened, mouse.'

'Yeah? Like what?'

'Well, take a look around you,' Joyce had said. 'Who'd have thought we'd end up here?'

'True.' Charlie had gulped down the water in his glass. 'But there are miracles and there are *miracles*.'

'Will you shut up now, please?' his sister had replied, with so much fury bottled up inside her that it gave her a red tint from nose to neck. 'Perhaps I'll have a wander into town and see who takes my fancy. Bound to be someone whose eye I'd catch.'

At this, Arthur had stood up. 'I should think we've all got better things to do this evening, no?' He'd started gathering their plates. 'Thank you very much for supper.'

When he'd left the room, Florence had regarded both the Savigears and sighed. She'd made the widest, most beseeching eyes that she could make. 'You two need to settle down, and quickly.'

'Sorry, Florence.'

'Sorry, miss.'

While washing up the dishes – it was Arthur's turn to scrub, her turn to dry – she told him that the tractor would be up and running by tomorrow. He didn't seem too cheered at first, picking at the crusted bottom of a saucepan with his thumb-nail, saying nothing. Then: 'Running, as in *moving*?'

'Yes, with a bit of luck.'

'Well, that's terrific.' He rinsed the pan under the tap until the suds ran clear. 'I'll let Hollis know, first thing. How certain are you?'

'I've only got to reconnect the gearbox, fill the oil again. If I manage that tonight, you might be ploughing by Tuesday. How soon can they deliver the manure?'

'I'll find out.' Arthur leaned to kiss her cheek. 'You cracked it, Flo. Well done, my love.'

'Oh, don't get too excited till you're doing circuits in the fields.'

'Straight lines up and down – that's all we need.'

That night, she worked alone in the garage, because the Savigears were needed in the draughting room: Charlie had been given elevations from old projects to redraw and his sister had to finish off her bedroom sketches. Crouching underneath the tractor with the floodlight shining harshly into all its cavities, she refitted the gear housing, bolted it in place. She fetched the oil from the cupboard, checked the grade and funnelled in a fraction more than strictly recommended in the manual. It seemed to take no time at all, but when she looked up at the clock, an hour had passed already and she was much too tired – and much too wary of another failure – to crank the engine. In the morning, she would have more strength and more resolve. She pulled a sheet over the Fordson, shut the lights off and went inside to take a long soak in the tub.

When she emerged from the bathroom in her nightie, hair all clean and coiled in a towel, she felt revived. Arthur came in as she sat applying her cream before the mirror at her dressing table. He unbuttoned his shirt and drew its tails from his trousers. 'You smell fresh,' he said. 'It's nice to catch you for a change, before you've made it into bed.' He smelled of brandy and stale perspiration, but she didn't tell him so. She watched his quiet reflection as he loosened all the straps of his prosthetic arm. It was in his hand as he came over to her, stooping down to kiss her neck. 'Did you manage it?' he asked. 'Dear God, you smell nice.'

She hummed. 'It's done.'

'So that's the glint I'm seeing in your eyes, is it? You're demob happy.'

'You could say that, yes. The next time it breaks down, *you're* fixing it.'

'Come on, have some faith in your own handiwork, my love. That tractor will outlast us all.' He stroked her shoulder.

On his way into the bathroom, he stopped to drape his limp prostethic on the towel rail.

'I meant to tell you,' she called in to him. 'There was a funny thing that happened when I got home earlier, with the parts.' The taps went on and she could hear the gentle thunder of the basin being filled.

'Oh really?' he called back.

'Somebody was walking in the copse. A man. Only a few feet or so inside the gate. I saw the bushes moving. Anyway, it turned out he was trying to spend a penny, but I don't know – I didn't like the look of him.'

After a moment, he appeared back in the doorway, rubbing a white flannel on his face. 'I hope you told him to clear off,' he said. 'But nicely.'

'Of course.' She began to towel the damp out of her hair. 'And he did. But I just got a funny feeling from him.'

'Did he threaten you?'

'No. Nothing like that. He seemed quite embarrassed by it all.'

Arthur's skin was shining wetly now and mottled underneath the eyes. 'What did he look like?'

'He was, well, quite fat. And tall. With a beard.'

'Hang on.' Arthur threw the flannel and she heard it splash into the basin. 'I think I know him. Well, I've *met* him. He just came along the drive, about a month or two ago. Hollis saw him, too. Baldy fella with a clump of hair here in the middle. Patchy sort of beard up to his eyes, like this.'

'Yes. *Yes*. That's him. Who is he?'

'I don't know. He's odd, though.'

'Well, I mentioned the police and he came out of the bushes in a hurry.'

'Did he now?'

'I thought I was a bit abrupt with him. But now I think I handled it quite well.'

'Sounds as if you did.' And Arthur came across to grip her fingers lightly. 'Has this been on your mind all day?'

'A little bit.'

'You should've said.'

'Other things got in the way. I'm sorry.'

'Did you see this fella go?'

'Yes. At least, I think I did.'

'I'd better take a look.'

'Right now?'

'Absolutely.'

'But it's dark.'

'I'll just drive down there and shine the headlights. Bring my torch along.'

'No. It's late now. What if he's still there?'

'I'll chase him off again.'

'No, Arthur, please don't bother. Wait until the morning.'

'I won't sleep unless I check.'

'He's gone now. And, besides, he wasn't dangerous.'

'You can't be sure of that.'

'He wasn't, just a little strange. I watched him walk away. Don't bother going out there now. Take Hollis in the morning.'

But he was readying the straps of his prosthetic. 'No, this fella's come back once already. Who's to say he won't again? Believe me, I've seen plenty of his type before. You've got to drive them off with sticks or they'll keep showing up.' With that, he put his shirt and pullover back on, and hastened down the stairs.

From a gap between the curtains at the landing window, she watched the wagon's headlamps brightening the yard and arcing round the driveway. Soon, all that she could see were brake lights jerking in the distance, and then nothing whatsoever. She thought about the times she'd stood in this position as a girl, dreading the arrival of her parents' dinner guests on Saturdays, listening to their drunken conversations as they came out to their cars long after dark. And she remembered all those nights she'd waited quietly outside her father's door, a numbness in her legs, while Dr Pask had run his checks. Most of all, she thought about the final afternoon, when Dr Pask had stepped out with his leather bag and pulled the door shut with great care – out of habit, she supposed – to say, 'I'm sorry, but it won't be long for him now, dear. All there's left to do is hold his hand on the way out.' So that's what she had done – and, afterwards, the purity of the relief she'd felt had horrified her. That week, she'd scrubbed the walls with soapy water. She'd dusted down and polished every stick of furniture. She'd hung all of their rugs up on the washing line and cricket-batted them. She'd scoured every fireplace in the house with Vim and a stiff brush. Until, eventually, she'd given up on punishing herself with mindless chores and let herself feel glad to have her life back.

Now, at last, the wagon was returning to the yard. Arthur left it parked across the face of the garage and climbed out. She went and tucked herself under the bedcovers, if only so that he would come upstairs and find her lying there, unworried by the situation she had caused. He walked in, turned off the bed-side lamp and whispered, 'Nothing out there I could see. I'll check again tomorrow.'

So she opened her eyes and gave her best impression of a yawn. 'That's good,' she said. 'I really wish I hadn't brought it up. A silly thing to land on you so late at night.'

But when she turned the covers back, he said, 'I'll be up soon. I'm wide awake now, so I might as well do something useful,' and she knew that she would find him passed out in the wing chair come the morning with a book still open on his chest.

The north field. Barren in the light of dawn. Crows skip in the mud. Suddenly, the tractor rolls into the frame. The driver slumps. It's Mr Hollis in his sunhat. Coming back round with the plough. A second row. The blades carve up the earth and darken it. A seam of soil and manure expands into the distance. Soon, the tractor turns to start another furrow. It's coming back, towards the camera. Mr Hollis twists his body, one hand on the wheel, to check the straightness of his work. Meaty chunks of dirt spit up behind him. He gets closer, closer, closer, till the white roll of his cigarette is visible, clamped in the flat pocket of his mouth, the lit end bobbing. A slow pan left, towards the copse, the boundary fence, the driveway and the yard. There's Joyce, blowing on a mug of tea. How young she looks. She gives a thumbs up to the lens and grins. Pan to the right. The tractor stands at rest, its engine throbbing. Mr Hollis climbs down from the driver's seat and trudges over to assess the plough. He beckons to the camera. Cut this.

September 1952

It was a fine and honourable thing that they were doing to help these borstal kids, no doubt, and Hollis knew they had the best intentions. But he couldn't stand to watch the Mayhoods have their hearts wrung out by folk who didn't recognize a good thing when they had it, which is where all this was headed in the long run, wasn't it? He had a sense for other people's disappointments, a way of reading changes in their temperament. Not that it had done him any favours down the years. There'd been steady jobs he'd had to walk away from in the past because of it, and ones that paid him a good wage to boot; he'd cut ties with his family because of it, and even his own childhood sweetheart, Maureen Bull, who'd had it in her mind to marry him.

He'd hated ducking out of his responsibilities like that, without folk hearing the particulars of why. But how could he describe it to them without sounding like some batty palmist at the fairground? There was a *knowing* in him for these things, that's all it was, and people never liked to hear about it. Who wanted to be told bad news was coming down the road? Who cared to hear about another person's intuitions? Still, he didn't take much pleasure in being proved right neither, when the troubles finally reached their doors. His brother and that prissy lady book-keeper who'd fleeced him of his savings – what a sorry situation. The lovely grain farm that went under like he knew it would, because of foolishness and greed – another sad affair. And Maureen Bull – he never did find out who she was seeing on the side, but if the pair of them weren't happy, that was their bad luck.

Before long, he was going to have to leave this place behind as well. Leventree was five and a bit acres of good land to work, and he'd enjoyed being in charge of it. He'd liked it best of all when it was only him and Mr Mayhood in the fields, taking their short tea breaks on the back porch, jotting down their plans for what to grow and how they should rotate the crops. Nobody had ever trusted him with managing their farm before, but Mr Mayhood had consulted him on every last decision, asking what provisions he required to make it run the way he wanted (to begin with, he'd mistaken 'resources' for 'race horses', which had caused a laugh or two between them – he'd put it down to Mr Mayhood's northern way of speaking).

But since the borstal kids had moved in, nothing was the same. He'd decided that a year would have to be his limit. He'd stay to gather in the winter crops and for the harvest in the spring. He'd get the ground just right for seeding in the sum-mer. After that, he'd give his notice to the Mayhoods and find something else to do. He had a lot of fondness and affection for them both and it'd pain him to move on. But he couldn't stop the knowing part of him from ringing in his head like funeral bells whenever those two youngsters were around. They weren't ever going to have the stuff it took to work this land. And, at his age, he didn't have the wherewithal to cover for them.

Take the sister, Joyce, for instance. She had a lot of power in her shoulders – probably enough to haul the corn drill all the way to Leatherhead and back – which only made her lack of effort harder to forgive. There was slyness to her ways: she was the sort who'd pay you compliments across a bar as long as you were paying for her drinks, then leave with someone else at closing time. A proper schemer. Last week, when they'd all been spreading the manure in the north field, she'd lifted six or seven forkfuls from the trailer before asking for a fag break. 'Isn't there some sort of a machine for this? God knows there ought to be,' she'd had the gall to say. All right, so it wasn't pleasant to be standing on a pile of horse shit with that rotten fruity stink inside your nostrils, getting underneath your nails, into your skin – but she had no right to gripe. 'Just bloody well get on with it,' he'd warned her. 'Stop your bellyaching.' Well, her eyes had turned to slits. He could've sworn she'd balled her fists up tight. 'If I wanted to be bossed around all day,' she'd said, 'I would've stayed in borstal.' He'd been thinking, *Don't you worry. Keep this up and they'll be sending you straight back.* But he'd just taken up his fork again and told her, 'We're not doing this for me, it's for the Mayhoods.' That'd cowed the girl, and he'd been proud of the achievement.

Meanwhile, her kid brother was all industry and no results. For every dozen fork-loads of manure the boy had spread, there must've been eleven that were left an inch too thick and Hollis had to go back over them himself to get them evened out. It wasn't that the boy had an aversion to instructions – Charlie listened well, you had to give him that. No, it was more that he was simply useless with a rake.

When he'd mentioned all of this to Mr Mayhood afterwards, he'd got the normal level-headed answer: 'Surely you remember how it was when you were discharged from the army? All those orders you'd been taking every minute, all that *yes sir no sir*. Once the war ends, your routine ends too. It's back to civvy life again and it feels strange. Well, it's the same for them. It takes some getting used to. *As do you*, it must be said. They're still adjusting.' Hollis hadn't cared much for that verdict, so he'd tried again with Florence, just to get a measure of her own mood on the subject. This was Monday morning, right before they'd gone to buy the rye seed. He'd popped his head into the kitchen about six o'clock and, bless her heart, she'd fried him up an egg and let him eat it at the kitchen table while she swept the floor and wiped the range. He did enjoy the sight of her, he couldn't lie.

'Exactly how much of this seed will be enough?' she'd asked.

'I'd say we need about a bushel and a half per acre,' he'd replied. 'Shouldn't be too dear. We'll have to clean it, mind.'

'Does that take long?'

'Depends how fast it can be winnowed. The old-fashioned ways are best.'

'Just show us what to do . . .'

'It won't be easy teaching those two.'

'Oh. Why's that?'

'Well, it's a job that takes a bit of grace and patience. So there's no point asking Tweedledum and Tweedledee. You'll end up picking seeds out of your yard for months.'

'Don't call them that,' she'd said, her tone not far from scolding. 'Please. It isn't kind or fair, and Mr Mayhood wouldn't like it either.'

'Just a joke,' he'd answered.

Later, as they'd walked the long way round towards their neighbour's farmhouse with the drizzle in their faces, he'd said, 'Look, I know I can be hard to please. But that girl's bugging me. She's not the type you can rely on in the fields. Her brother's not too bad, might get there in the end, but her? No chance.'

'It's early days,' she'd said. 'They're learning as they go.'

'I'm speaking of her attitude. Her mind's not on the job.'

'Not everyone is suited to the outdoor life, at first. Including me. She'll come around eventually, I know she will.'

'Let's hope you're right.' He could admit they hadn't been there very long and there might still be duties they could handle better: basic yardwork, for example. Mucking out the chicken sheds, that sort of thing. 'But up till now, the signs aren't good. I reckon you could give the village idiot a pitch-fork and he'd do a decent job of spreading your manure. At least he'd put a proper shift in.'

'Hold on, Mr Hollis. Either she's not working *hard* enough or *well* enough – which is it?'

'One's no different to the other, in my book. Result's the same.'

'You have to set the standards for her, then she'll follow.'

'Mr Mayhood doesn't pay me to be nursing them through simple bits of work. They're your apprentices, not mine.'

'All right, I can see your point on that one.' They'd approached the neighbour's door. A soppy-looking dog came running up to meet them and she'd crouched to give its fur a ruffle. 'I'll raise it with my husband, see what he advises.'

'Did that yesterday. It got me nowhere.'

She'd almost smirked. 'Well, Arthur is a fair man, as you know, and sometimes it's about how sensibly you make your argument. I'll mention it again.'

If anybody cared for his opinion on the subject, Mr May-hood was a very lucky man to have a wife as capable and handsome as she was. Even as a young girl, playing in the wait-ing room of Mr Greaves's place, she'd been a cheerful little thing; he'd seen her bring a smile from men in blinding agony, who'd come in to get wisdom teeth yanked out and cavities filled in. In her teens, she'd sat at the reception desk in summer, reading books and drawing pictures, opening the post and fix-ing the appointments. There were lads her age he'd known to fake a toothache just so they could go and talk to her a moment. So he couldn't understand why Mr Mayhood wasn't doing everything he could to keep her safe. Letting her go round the country buying tractor parts. Who knows what sort of crooked fella she might come across?

For months now, he'd been pestering them both to get a farm dog – not a mawkish thing like next-door were content with, but a proper German shepherd or Jack Russell terrier; a smarter breed that you could train. But they didn't even have a cat at Leventree for catching rodents, because Mr Mayhood was allergic. With no dog to bark or any shotguns in the house, they were making themselves vulnerable. He must've said as much to Mr Mayhood fifty times, but the answer always came back no: 'I gave up firing guns in Holland, thank you, and I won't go back to it. Besides, we can't keep weapons in the house – it's a condition of their borstal licence.' Only a few weeks ago, they'd gone out on a recce of the driveway because Florence had found someone pissing in the bracken on her way back home. He couldn't quite recall the bloke himself, but Mr Mayhood thought it might've been some scrounger who'd come by the place in June. They'd done a full sweep of the drive, the verges, the entire copse, and found no sign of anybody tresspassing. There'd been a few big footprints in the dirt, that's all, but they'd been right where Florence said she'd seen the bloke the first time, near the gate. Mr Mayhood's final judgement had been: 'We should keep an eye out, but I don't think we've any grounds to be concerned about the fella now.' Hollis had stayed watchful, and the only oddity he'd noticed since was Tweedledum.

Around that time, he'd seen her going off to post the May-hoods' letters. It would've been a Friday morning, as he liked to save the niggliest of jobs till then and he'd been sawing off an overhanging branch along the driveway that had scraped their last delivery lorry. That's how come he'd spied her from his perch up in the tree as she'd come out, not realizing he was there. A short while after, she'd trudged back again, while he'd been gathering the cuttings from the ground. There'd been a parcel in her hands. Brown paper and a lot of packing tape. No sooner had she spotted him, she'd shoved it in her coat. It looked peculiar. 'Been ordering from the catalogue?' he'd said, and might've simpered at her just a bit. She'd stopped right next to him, stared back without a twitch. 'It's a present for a friend of mine. I didn't have enough on me to post it, did I?' she'd explained. 'It'll have to wait for payday now.' With that, she'd wafted at the air as if it reeked. 'Phew, Geoffrey, that won't do. A stink of booze like that before it's even noon – you'll get a reputation.' All right, so perhaps he might've had a drink the night before. No more than usual. 'I've not had a drop for days,' he'd answered, flummoxed. 'Calm down, I won't tell,' she'd said, and carried on towards the house. 'You'd better not go spreading lies about me,' he'd called after. She'd given him the shrug-off. But, since then, he'd taken care to suck a peppermint each morning on his walk to Leventree. No further wisecracks had been uttered.

Two weeks extra. That was how much longer it'd taken for the tractor to be mended than he'd planned for, but it hadn't set them back too much. Ploughing had gone well this Tuesday. There'd been one rough moment when he'd felt the blades hit something solid early on – he'd feared it was a rock, so when he'd found a chunk of rotten fencepost jammed in there, he'd almost cheered; the thing had come out with a bit of pushing and the blades weren't even damaged. Crack of dawn this morning, they'd been winnowing the seeds, with Florence high up on the ladder, dropping handfuls, watching all the chaff float westwards on the breeze, while Joyce and Charlie held the sheet out underneath to catch what fell (a task even a simpleton could do). And Mr Mayhood – well, he'd stood there in the yard and filmed it all for reasons that escaped him. Not a day went by at Leventree without that little wind-up camera being pointed in somebody's face and Mr Mayhood telling them to act as though he wasn't there. Which wasn't easy, given that he had to clamp the thing between the pincers of his dummy arm to operate the focus with the left, and he kept cursing the contraption every time it didn't do what he was asking. Hollis had begun to wish that he could drop it in a ditch.

This afternoon, the forecast was for perfect sowing weather. He escorted everybody out to show them what to do (apart from Mr Mayhood, who was stuck indoors with paperwork for a surveying job, or so he claimed). They heaved the corn drill through the yard and hitched it to the tractor. They attached an old chain harrow behind that, and Florence had to smear a bit of axle grease into the drawbar where the hooks were nearly rusted through to get it dragging straight. Then he told her to get up and take the wheel so he could ride the corn drill. 'Someone's got to make sure that the seeds are broadcast nice and even, and the harrow's got to cover them – about *this much* of earth is what we're looking for.' After a few passes, he intended to jump off and let the youngsters have a turn. That way, she could get a close-up view of how they worked, and then she'd understand what he'd been telling her.

But wouldn't you just know it? The Lord had other plans.

With the fine job she'd done fixing up the tractor, well, it should've come as no surprise to him that Florence was a skilful driver, too. She handled that machine far better than he ever could, going at an ideal pace, no jolts or swerving. But what happened next was unexpected. Her manner with the youngsters changed all of a sudden: she dropped the friendly stable-girl approach and started talking like the stable owner. She didn't ask for Hollis's opinion or permission either, she just beckoned Charlie over as they came back to the south end of the field. 'Come and take the wheel from me,' she said, 'and keep it steady – we're not at the Monte Carlo rally. Straight lines up and down, that's it. You hear?' The boy, a little startled, nodded and climbed on. But didn't he just prove himself to be a natural? Making smooth, tight turns before the drainage ditch and barely taking a glance down to line up the back tyres with the furrow edges. He made Hollis look a fool for doubting him. So, on the seventh pass, he shouted to the boy, 'Oi, Charlie – wait a mo! Let's get your sister.'

Hopping off the corn drill, he trudged across the apron of the field to speak to Joyce. 'Take my place up there, will you? It's time you rolled your sleeves up and got mucky.'

'All right. If I have to.'

'Follow me.' When she was up there on the little platform with her boot heels on the edge, he passed on his instructions. 'Keep your eyes down on those chutes and watch for anything that gets clogged up,' he said. 'And if it does, you take this stick right here and give it a stiff prod until it falls away. Another thing to watch for is those coulters – see them? Make sure they stay fixed right where they are. If any of them break, you let me know. You get all that?'

'I did,' she said. 'Sounds easy.'

'Then what are you both waiting for?'

He gave Charlie the go signal and the tractor lumbered forward. Treading his way back towards the porch steps for a smoke, he was happy to let fortune take its course. It was likely that a good pile of their seeds would go to waste – a twinge of guilt skimmed through him at the prospect. But who could tell for certain? Maybe Joyce could concentrate for long enough to get it right.

He watched them every moment of the way, the tractor going up and down and up and down, Joyce riding the corn drill, the harrow making clouds out of the dirt. When they neared the final furrow, he went back to check their work. The field was scuffed and barkish-brown and orderly. He checked the spread of seeds under his feet, the coverage. He eyed the ground for inconsistencies. But strike him down with lightning, it looked good.

'So,' said Florence, like a shadow in the space behind him. 'How'd they do?'

He dusted off his hands. 'It's not the worst attempt.'

She gave him that shrewd smile of hers. 'A thumbs up will do fine.'

'Today was good, I'll give them that.'

'A bit of confidence in people can do wonders, can't it?' She was staring now into the distance, at a twist of starlings in the sky. 'Just like Mr Mayhood has been telling me.'

'They did all right. For once. Let's see how they get on next time of asking.'

Florence turned. She nudged his shoulder as she headed back towards the porch. 'Who said I was talking about *them*?'

He couldn't think of what to say to her, so he just scratched his jaw and let her go. The starlings made their senseless patterns overhead. Eventually, the tractor came to rest in the far corner of the field and he heard its engine rumbling out. By the time he reached the corn drill, Joyce and Charlie had a perch at either end, dangling their legs from it like two daft infants on a swing. 'Job's not finished yet,' he told them. 'We've to get all these machines back in the yard and clean them off.'

'Mr Mayhood wants us in the draughting room by one,' said Charlie, hopping down.

'You'd better crank the motor up, then, hadn't you? Relaxing time is over.'

They looked at one another, mute but sneering. 'Aye aye, captain,' Joyce said, giving a salute. So, there it was: her attitude was still the same. The honest-grafter act was for the Mayhoods' benefit. But when they weren't around to watch her, it was whinging and sarcasm all the way. He knew that it was going to be like this, week after week, one petty incident after the next. It'd be her word they favoured over his, whenever there were sulks or quarrels. In their minds, she was still young, a work in progress, someone worth their kindness and investment. They'd let her live in their warm house and eat their food and learn their trade, while he'd forever be their hired skivvy. An old man brought in from the outside for low wages. Replaceable and easy to forget. That was how things were for him, and how they'd always be.

'Who d'you think you're talking to?' he said.

She flapped her hand against her breastbone. 'What? Did I speak out of turn?'

'Leave it, Joy,' her brother said. 'Don't start.'

He told her straight: 'It's time you did more listening and less bleating. Both of you.'

'Charlie's not done anything. Get off his case.'

'The both of you could learn a thing or two, believe me.'

'Not from you, Geoff Hollis,' she said. 'You're no better than we are, just older by a hundred years – and you've been drunk for most of those.' She skipped down from the corn drill, wiped her nose upon her wrist. 'You'd best watch how you order me about, unless you want the Mayhoods knowing how you treat us. Anyone'd think you were snow white, but we've all seen the filth that washes off you on Sundays – takes a pile of Ajax just to clean you off our tub, you dirty sod.'

It'd been a while since he'd known brass like hers. He might've handled himself better, but she'd made him so irate. He kicked a lump of earth at her and specks of it went in her eye. 'You'll mind your manners now,' he said, and she came rushing at him. Charlie tried to collar her, but couldn't hold her, saying, 'Leave it, Joy. Just leave it.' Then there was a mighty whistle from behind them, stopping Tweedledum cold in her tracks. It was Florence, running over, jumping furrows on the

95

way. 'What's going *on* here, Mr Hollis?' she said, really scolding him this time. 'Did I just see you kicking dirt?'

'An accident. I never meant for it to go that far.' He couldn't bear to look at her, so watched the starlings for a moment while he caught his breath.

'What's all this about?' she said.

'A little disagreement over what needs doing. But we're past it now, don't worry.'

'Is that right?' she said, and took Joyce by the arm. 'Is that right, Joy?'

'She didn't understand, that's all,' said Charlie meekly.

'Just a quarrel, miss,' was Tweedledum's reply. 'It's nothing really.'

'I suppose I might've got myself a bit too hot under the collar,' he put in, to soften out the situation. He was suddenly aware of his own stench.

'Well, that had better be the end of it. Come on – shake hands and calm yourselves, before my husband sees you. It'll break his heart to know you're at each other's throats like this.'

The rightful thing to do was offer up his hand and say, 'That's that.'

'That's that,' Joyce said.

'So can we get this tractor in the yard and rinse it off now?'

'Fine by me.'

'No trouble, Mr Hollis,' Charlie said, and climbed up quick to start the motor.

There wasn't any bother after that, but still: he'd had a glimpse of his own future and he didn't care much for the view. By the close of day, above the normal aches and pains that plagued him, he could feel a sourness in his belly. A dismal mood came over him as he was leaving Leventree, and the drizzle soaked his woollens as he walked. Perhaps he wouldn't stick it out as long as he'd first thought. He was prepared to wait until the seed had taken and the rye was coming through – no more than that. He wouldn't stay somewhere that gave him headaches every time there was a field that needed ploughing.

As he came towards the far end of the drive, he spotted something in the corner of his eye. The passage of a body through the copse. It could've been a deer, or something smaller. Possibly a sheep had wriggled through the neighbour's fence and gone a-wander. Or it could've been their trespasser was still about. It hadn't made a noise. A flash of movement, nothing more, but it was something. He stepped over the verge to see what he could gather.

The copse was quiet. Empty. Not a stirring of a leaf that didn't have a reason to be stirring. Just the daylight breaking through the canopy of trees. Birds cheeping and pecking at the earth. He walked into the clearing where the air was thin and cooler, sweetened by the scent of plums and damsons left ungathered. There was a mighty hornbeam with a twisted trunk, a spuming head of branches. By its roots, he noticed a large rock, the sort he used to heave out of the ground all day when he was digging trenches overseas. The dirt beside it was imprinted with the tread of someone's boot, and, from the size of it, he reasoned it was Tweedledum's. Lifting up the rock, he found a little hollow underneath it, packed with insects. A perfect circle pressed there in the soil. It was unnatural, but not exactly untoward.

He set the rock back down and looked about him. Nothing. Not a sight or sound that gave him pause. Tomorrow, he'd tell Mr Mayhood that he'd spied some movement in the copse and pester him again about a German shepherd. But there wasn't any cause to go back up there now and interrupt his work. One dose of aggravation for the day was quite enough for everyone.

A thirst came over Hollis, then, and not the sort that could be quenched by water. He would've stopped into the Barley Mow, but his last ten bob was pissed away on wrong'uns at the weekend, more fool him. Even the few shillings he'd been saving from his wages every week to get himself a motorbike had gone now, too. At this rate, he'd be walking everywhere until the spring.

At least he had his little caravan – he'd never give that up. A fella who had known his brother years ago bequeathed it in his will, together with the slip of meadow where it sat today on Hungry Hill Lane. It was such a lovely thing, a Winchester with leaded windows and two skylights and a glossy wood interior, nestled in high grass and sheltered by a line of oak trees. He took proper care of it, revarnished it and painted it, and scraped off all the scum and moss that gathered on the roof. When his brother had moved down to Devon, he'd left the keys for him and said, 'It's all yours, Geoff. I've got no use for it no more,' and ever since they'd had their falling-out there'd been no mention of evicting him. Perhaps some day he'd find it missing from the meadow, towed away to Devon. But not yet.

The meadowgrass was flattened in a channel winding up to the front door. He dug the keys out of his pocket, hooked his sopping sunhat on the nail he'd hammered in above the window. It was days like this, when he was feeling low and sore all over, that he wished he had a pet – a cat to rub itself against his ankles, or maybe just a goldfish who could press its lips up to the tank. But as he sat and pulled his boots off on the step, he thought of Maureen Bull, imagining her plating up her husband's supper about now, bringing him his pipe and slippers. What a waste of a good woman. He went inside and let the coolness of the lino soothe his bunions.

There was water in the kettle, flakes of limescale. While it boiled, he rummaged in his cupboards for the pint of knock-off whisky he'd mislaid – there had to be one bottle lurking somewhere in the place that he could finish off – but all he found were cans of soup and pilchards. He rolled a cigarette and lit it on the stove. He leaned against the door frame, trying to remember to be grateful for the things he had.

From where he stood, there wasn't much to look at. A quaking of the drizzle as the wind got up. The swirl of branches miles away. He drank his tea and savoured it. A peace began to find him, spreading through the tightness in his back. He doused his ciggie in the sink and went to fold the table down to make room for his bed. If he couldn't drink, then he could sleep. As he was laying out the cushions on the boards, he heard a noise behind him. Heavy. The whole floor seemed to wobble, creaking. Before he'd even turned to look, he felt the knowing in him. His bones went soft with it. The blood sunk to his feet.

He recognized the fella, the enormous frame of him, the jelly gut, the messy beard. So then. All this time, his intuition had been off, distracted by the youngsters. He was cornered now, and helpless, calling, 'Piss off! What in God's name d'you think you're doing? You can't just barge in here –' He barrelled on, in the hope that he might hold off what was coming to him. But he couldn't keep the fright from weakening his voice.

The stranger put a finger to his lips. He was wearing winter gloves. 'Save your breath,' he said, almost a whisper. 'Rumour has it you've been nosing round in things you shouldn't.' He could barely stand up straight inside the caravan. His bald head grazed the ceiling as he took a forward stride. Looking round the place, he said, 'It's nice in here. You keep it neat and tidy, don't you? Shame you didn't park it fifty miles away.' There was a wire hanger in his fist. *Tap, tap, tap* it went against his open palm, and Hollis knew.

October 1933

She'd seen him on her way into the building: a solemn-looking boy in a serge suit, standing by the railings on the corner of the square. He'd been finishing a cigarette that smelled like tarmacadam, hair made flat and moist around his temples from the pressure of a hat, which he was dangling by his knee. It was an odd thing to be doing, just lurking there with his head tilted at the sky. Was he expecting somebody to throw down a rope ladder from the roof? Had he sighted a rare bird? He'd seemed a touch ridiculous – but also handsome, self-assured in his plain disregard for passers-by, the students constellated on the paving stones of Abercromby Square. Later, when they met in studio, across an empty draughting table in Architectural Design, she could think of little else but that first glimpse of him outside; because she had an inkling it would be the last time that she ever viewed him as a stranger.

Throughout her first class of the term, while their instructor, Mr Lundy, drifted between tables and extolled the wonders of his syllabus, she gave his words the fixity of concentration she'd resolved to bring to every aspect of her studies. There would be no greater failure, she'd decided in the summer, than to earn her place at Liverpool among the men and let herself become distracted by the admiration of someone in their ranks. She hadn't chosen to detach herself from everyone she knew to end up in the sort of ten-a-penny romance she could've found back home – knock on any door in Ockham and there'd be a fellow willing to go out to dinner. No, the reason she'd moved north was to achieve her architect's diploma, and she wouldn't leave until she had it. But there she was, in her first session of a five-year course, presented with a face she couldn't keep from staring at. Already, she was failing. Arthur Mayhood was his name. He'd spoken only once so far, to answer during registration. 'Present, sir,' he'd said. What a settled way he had with his surroundings, a subdued energy.

At the end of studio, when Mr Lundy told the class to pack their double-elephants away, Arthur sat there with his drawing on the table while she put hers carefully into her case. Before she could do up the clasps, he said, 'Excuse me, would you mind?' He was worrying the edges of his paper. 'I know we're meant to have our own portfolios by now, but the Stationery Office had none left and they were meant to have one for me yesterday, but –'

'By all means,' she said. 'And I won't even charge you.'

The straight line of his mouth began to curl. 'How kind.'

She opened out the case for him and watched him slide his paper into it with no regard for its condition. His drawing was, by contrast, conscientious and precise. Mr Lundy had instructed them to start work on a 'parti' – a basic concept in response to the dull brief he'd set them: to design a public building in the classical style. She'd struggled to imagine anything except a shameless replica of a church crypt she'd once visited in London. But Arthur Mayhood's parti was more abstract, a strange union of overlapping triangles and squares and semicircles, out of which a form revealed itself almost in negative. She didn't know if it conformed to the Beaux Arts values Mr Lundy had been trying to impart; still, when she looked at it, her breath stuck in her throat. Arthur didn't ask for her opinion, and she didn't give it, closing her portfolio and saying, 'Aren't you going to carry on with it?'

This wasn't taken in the spirit she'd intended. 'You're right, I know,' he said, 'it's ordinary. I'd like another go at it, to tell the truth, but you can mind it for me till I'm ready to set eyes on it again.' He spoke with the same pleasant drawl as all the locals she'd heard chatting on the trams, in greengrocers' and tea shops and outdoor markets – that long-vowelled, soft-edged Liverpudlian that seemed to her a blend of Welsh and Irish. 'If I need it back, I'll find you before Structural Mechanics.'

In her head, she was reviewing her timetable. 'That's on Thursday.'

'Well, let's hope your magic will rub off on it by then.' He tapped the table, saying, 'I appreciate it. Thank you,' and then headed for the door.

'Just a minute,' she said, causing him to turn and catch her eye. 'I was wondering . . . What exactly was it you were looking at out there, before?'

'I don't know what you mean.' He blinked, a little coldly.

'Earlier. I saw you staring up towards the roof. Just after eight. On Bedford Street. You had your head like this –' She mimed it for him, doing an impression of the way he smoked. Eventually, he smiled, displaying a row of teeth as neat as they were yellow.

'Oh, right, that was me,' he said. 'Those windows on the corner are bricked up. I suppose there has to be a reason for it, engineering-wise, but I quite like the way it looks. There's something, I don't know, *poetic* about how they've left it. Finished but unfinished.'

She hadn't noticed it, and told him so.

'You will now, every time.' He eyed the door. 'Well, cheerio, Miss Greaves.'

'It's Florence.'

'Arthur,' he said, pointing at his chin.

'I know.'

'Ta-ra, then.'

She left it half an hour or so, hovering in the corridors downstairs, lurking in the common room, before she went outside to see this touch of poetry that he'd been so enthralled by. He was right – as she'd suspected he'd be right – about the fenestration. There were ghosts of windows on the west side of the building, all three storeys walled off with the same red brick, and they were strangely beautiful.

After that, she saw him several times a week. In studio, they carried on with their designs for Mr Lundy and absorbed the principles of composition. In History and Theory lectures, she sat and gazed at Arthur's head among the others in the rows before her. He was lively in Construction classes on a Tuesday, asking their instructor, Mr Flynn, a raft of questions about concrete and its applications. She could tell that he respected working architects like Lundy but was less inspired by academic types (McKenna, Flynn and Dawson), who seemed to preach more than they practised.

In Sciagraphy – her favourite class – they sat a fair distance apart. But, one afternoon, the group was told to put their pencils down and gather round her table for a sudden crit. Old Dawson said, 'Could someone please inform Miss Greaves what's wrong with her approach so far?' The others squinted at the drawing she'd produced. It was supposed to represent a flight of stone steps in a concourse, sinking to a basement somewhere off the page. She was proud of how she'd shaded it and thought it looked authentic. Her fellow students muttered to each other, speculating on its flaws; one of them put up his hand and claimed the lower shadows didn't correspond to the same vanishing point as the rest. Dawson shook his head: 'No. Anybody else?' At this, Arthur raised an arm. 'Go on, Mayhood, out with it.'

'Well, sir, if the shadows are the main point of the exercise,' he said, 'it seems to me she's done them perfectly. It's just that she's forgotten to include a doorway. You said that if we drew a set of steps, they had to lead up to a doorway. So, Miss Greaves has gone a bit off-brief, that's all.'

'Glad to know that *somebody* was listening,' Dawson said.

She felt impossibly small. Her teeth hurt for some reason. How could she have overlooked that basic piece of information?

'But the shadows are the most important thing,' Arthur carried on. 'And she got those right.'

'Your gallantry is noted, Mayhood. And I'm sure Miss Greaves appreciates it.' Everybody laughed. She flushed, and so did Arthur. 'But I'm afraid the brief is unequivocal – you'll be assessed by it as long as you are here, and you'll be held to it as long as you're *out there*. If you learn bad habits now, you'll have them for the rest of your careers.'

She had to start again.

Leaving studio that afternoon, deflated, she found Arthur on the entrance steps. Gone was the serge suit of his first days, when he'd been trying not to disrespect the school by dressing too informally. Now he wore a shirt and pullover with flannel trousers like the others, with a docker's overcoat and the old hat, which he appeared to favour carrying like some exotic pet. He flicked ash off his cigarette. 'Miss Greaves, just a mo,' he called, and stubbed it out upon the railing. As she went past, he vaulted down from the top step with his portfolio above his head as parachute. He landed but a yard away from her, his shoes smacking the flagstones. 'I was hoping I could walk with you,' he said.

'Where to?'

'Wherever it is you're going.' His eyes were halfway down the street already, where the momentary calmness of the square gave way to real life: soot-blacked buildings, wagons at the junction loaded up with crates, women slogging into town with cases full of things to sell or fix or dump. 'I wanted to apologize,' he said, 'if I embarrassed you in there. I should've kept my mouth shut. But I've known too many Mr Dawsons in my time to let him get away with it.'

'He's just a pedant,' she said. 'No harm done.' The sting of the humiliation hadn't faded, though, and it was sure to last the year.

'Pedantry lives right next door to misery, if you ask me.' He gestured down the road with his portfolio. 'Shall we walk?'

'I've got something to do.'

'I'll help.'

'You're going to help me pay a cheque into the bank? I'll manage, thank you.'

'Which bank?'

'Martins,' she said, 'not that you have any business knowing.'

'Oh, that's my bank. The closest branch is Brunswick Street. I'll show you the best way to go.'

'What makes you think I don't know where I'm going?'

'Miss Greaves –'

'*Florence.*'

He nodded. 'Florence, I should think that you could find your way from here to Argentina without help from anyone. But I've lived here all my life – well, give or take – and I was going to show you a few secrets of the city.'

She let him roast a moment in his disappointment, then craned her head to say, 'Come on, then – guide me, if you must. I was going to catch a tram, but I suppose the weather's fair enough to go on foot.'

And so they went down Oxford Street in what passed for a fine day in Liverpool – a low sun stranded in a gauze of cloud above the rooftops as far as she could see; a sudden drop in temperature whenever they stepped through the dappled shade of trees; that scouring wind she'd grown accustomed to, now absent. The road withheld a slow procession of delivery vans and hooded trailers; here and there, the backsides of cart-horses flashed their tails. Everywhere, the cry of gulls, the brackish tincture of the sea and some pervasive scent like fruit-cake left for too long in the oven.

'You were born and raised here, then?' she said, while Arthur paced beside her. It was more of a determination than a question.

'Bootle, mostly.'

'The city has so many parts. I can't tell which is which.'

'Some of them are best avoided. Trust me.'

She didn't rise to this.

'Where'd they put you up this year – at Rankin Hall?' he said.

'Yes, I rather like it.'

'Nice out there. You're right next to the park.'

'I do feel spoiled. Although we have a warden who's more like a sergeant major.'

He went quiet for a good few seconds. 'Have you been to the cathedral yet?'

'Of course. The first place on my list.'

'Not bad, eh? As cathedrals go.'

'Not bad at all.'

'You think you'll ever get to build one?'

She gave him a slow, sidelong look. 'I imagine it's the sort of thing I'd do eventually. After I've retired from building concert halls and opera houses.' His laugh was like a parent's admonition: *tsk*. 'Is that your grand ambition? A cathedral?' They had reached Mount Pleasant and her shoes were rubbing on her heels.

'I think you've got to be religious, don't you? Well, to do it right. And if you're asking me, the Lord's got twice as many houses as he needs. I'd rather build for those who serve him.'

'Schools and hospitals,' she said. 'That's what I'd like to do.'

'I'll come and join that practice, any time you like.'

'Well, that's our future organized. The rest is easy.' Her feet were really aching now. 'Roughly how much further?'

He pointed west. 'About five minutes over there.'

The conversation lulled and she could hear his strides had syncopated with her own. He was nice to talk to, better than most men she knew: not because he always had the words to interest her or coax out her opinions, but because he let her speak exactly when she wanted to and didn't take her silences for lack of depth, as others had before. 'You said *give or take*. Which means there was a time you weren't in Liverpool.'

'If I respond to that, you mightn't talk to me again,' he said.

'Why not?'

'Because you'll think the worst of me.'

'Oh.' She couldn't look at him. 'I'm sure I wouldn't.' But she understood his meaning – the rumours had already passed her way, and now she felt somehow complicit in the gossip, angry at herself for leading him into the topic.

It had been an act of spite – that's how she'd come to hear of it. There was a fellow on the table next to hers in studio, Bill Embry, who'd asked her early in the term if she'd go with him to the theatre, and he'd done so rather pushily; when she'd declined, his face had purpled but he'd said, 'Oh, shame,' and edged away. Then, turning with a look of bitterness, he'd said, 'Fair warning, though, Miss Greaves. I wouldn't get too sweet on Mayhood. I can see the way you are with him. He draws well, there's no doubt, but no one's going to hire him if he ever qualifies. The chap's a thief. They put him in a borstal, and he's not been out that long. It's only fair that you should know. I have it all on good authority.' Right away, she'd told Bill Embry that if he concentrated less on slandering his fellow students and more on learning how to make his sketches look as though an adult drew them, he'd be so much better off – at least, that's what she'd tried to say by scowling back at him. What she'd really said was, 'Don't presume to tell me whose affections I can favour, Mr Embry. I'm sure you'll find somebody else to go with you.' That had spared the akwardness next time they saw each other. But she'd known the lint in Arthur's pockets had more goodness than Bill Embry would ever gather in his lifetime.

'I don't want to put you off me,' Arthur said now. 'Seeing as we're getting on so well. Besides, there are a million other things to talk about.'

She was content to let him change the subject. 'Such as what?'

'There's Martins bank, for one. I feel as though I ought to have a dinner jacket on when I go in there. I'll just drop you at the door, if that's all right.'

★

Of all the basic aspects of his training, Arthur was alarmed to find he struggled most with lettering. He'd practised through the Christmas break, copying the Roman capitals, half-uncials and small italics from the Johnston book and Graily Hewitt, trying to master the techniques. His basic handwriting was messy, even juvenile, so when it came to lettering he felt as though he'd gone right back to infant school to learn his alphabet with chalk and slate. Legibility was one thing, personality was another. He wanted to establish a distinctive style to complement his drawings. It frustrated him that something so routine, so incidental to his work, should occupy so much of his attention. When he saw how quickly other students in his group had learned the skill – those grammar-schooled, smart-collared boys with their safe, competent designs so ably lettered in the bottom margins – well, it was a reminder of how far behind the line he'd started in the race with them. And it *was* a type of race. For every ten men in his group, there was perhaps one opportunity for an assistantship at a good firm, and no one else would have to give an explanation for a two-year stretch at Feltham Institution in his application letter.

He wondered if this sense of otherness he felt was obvious in his behaviour. Sometimes, he was sure the only reason

Florence could abide his company was that it helped to keep the beam of scrutiny away from her occasionally. At least no one could see his difference just by looking at him. The instructors' attitude to her was plain dismissive. A faction of the boys were so concerned at being overshadowed by her, they were making smart remarks at crits: 'Don't mind what the tutors say, Miss Greaves. You won't need architecture to survive. I'll marry you right now.' She was either wrongly scrutinized or wholly disregarded, and that made them an alliance of a sort. How she bore the strain of it with so much positivity, he didn't know, but he admired her for it more and more each day.

Meanwhile, it was all that he could do to keep attending lectures, getting through the sessions in studio without succumbing to the feeling he'd arrived somewhere he wasn't meant to be. Every day, he recognized the contradiction of his training and his aspirations. He feared that he was being marshalled into line with all the rest of them. The syllabus was so constraining. He wanted to begin producing schemes for social housing – buildings that would benefit real working people – but the first-year briefs were all about adherence to the classical. Modillions. Acanthus leaves. Entablatures of stone. If it didn't have the facets of a mausoleum, it was unacceptable.

He understood that some of his ideals would have to be abandoned, over time. There were many years of nice-making and deference to come. He would have to bear the ugliness of privilege and overlook it, swallow down the small pills of disquiet, smooth out every dint his pride took on the way. And he could do that. For the sake of his own livelihood. Or so he thought. The first step was accepting the support where it was offered – an Entrance Scholarship that came with a good stipend and a weight of expectation. Getting his diploma was step two. Next, a paid assistantship at any firm that granted him a chance. And, after that, a practice of his own – even if he had to run it from the back room of a butcher's and live hand to mouth for ever, he would do it to make sure his work had meaning, value to the world. Until last year, he could envision all of it. Then Florence Greaves had come along and he'd begun to change his view.

He couldn't say that he regretted their discussion in the autumn, but the things he'd left unsaid had gathered so much weight they'd now become an obstacle. Every time they'd seen each other since, they'd had to step around it. One morning in December, he'd been browsing samples of cement in the materials gallery, and she'd entered, feigned some interest in a brick display and left without a word – later, she'd insisted that she hadn't seen him, but he had his doubts. An awkwardness had already fomented. The insecurity was there.

Not long after, she'd approached him as he smoked between the bay trees in the central court and they'd exchanged some pleasantries about their projects. She'd let him take her to the union refectory for lunch: they'd both had onion soup and hadn't finished it. Conversation wasn't only stilted, it was flat. The next day, she'd brought in a biscuit tin of corned-beef sandwiches and sat beside him on a park bench in the square, giving him the greater portion, saying she hadn't made them with herself in mind. On each of these occasions, he'd wished that he could simply talk about it – tell her where he'd come from, what he'd been through – but the subject hung around them like the heaviest of weather. How could he be frightened of destroying something that was not yet formed? And what relationship had ever been improved by smothering the truth? He was failing with her in the same way he was failing at his lettering: so anxious to progress that he was getting worse at each attempt.

Throughout the Christmas break, he'd thought about her constantly. He'd spent the last few weeks entombed in his damp room on Prescot Road, awakened every morning by the clamour of the bakery below at five a.m., the scent of bread advancing from the gaps between his floorboards. He'd completed his assignments by the light of gas lamps, wrapped himself in every blanket that he owned, reliant on the kettle for enough hot water every night to wash and shave. All those hours he'd studied Johnston's pages, trying to reproduce the elegance and deftness of the serifs, she'd been on his mind. A welcome apparition. Florence Greaves – her face kept visiting, disrupting him – Florence Greaves – the deep wave in her hair, its shine – Florence Greaves – the freckle pattern rambling across her nose, the two front teeth that rested on her lip when she was thinking – Florence Greaves – the quickness of her pencil marks, their gentleness, and the conviction she applied to everything: her speech, her art, her education, her deportment – Florence Greaves – the hyacinth and cherry blossom of her body passing through the studio – Florence – how she looked at him, as though she wanted to be haunted in return.

★

'I've got something for you,' he told her, as she settled in the space beside him. 'I should've given it to you before you left but, well, it took me most of Christmas to get right.'

She had no gift for him, although she'd almost bought a pullover in Lewis's and left it on the cashier's counter, deeming it presumptuous and foolish. (A pullover? What sort of message would it send? She might as well have given him a bar of soap or breath mints.) Their lecture hadn't started yet, but Mr Flynn was waiting at the blackboard, shuffling his papers. She'd overslept and missed her tram, arriving fifteen minutes later than she wanted to – which meant she wasn't fifteen minutes early for a change. There'd been an empty seat on the front row, reserved for her by Arthur. 'Happy New Year,' he said brightly. 'It doesn't feel much different from the last one so far.'

'Happy New Year, Arthur,' she said. 'I do hope you had a

pleasant holiday.' Could she have sounded any more impassive? She straightened out her skirt, pleated her hands across her lap. 'I had a card for you and I forgot to leave it by your desk. I'm sorry.' The truth was, it was still in the back sleeve of her portfolio, untouched, because she hadn't had the courage to deliver it. She'd thought it better to stand firm, await a card from him and then reciprocate. But nothing came. For the past few weeks, she'd fretted about what to do when she returned to Liverpool, admonishing herself for her mistakes last term. Like a fool, she'd tried to mother him with corned-beef sandwiches. She'd played silly schoolgirl games, pretending not to see him, being aloof. It hadn't worked.

'It's all right,' he said. 'I've got no mantelpiece to put it on at any rate.' He smiled his winsome smile and her hopes lifted.

After they'd withstood two hours of Mr Flynn expounding on the convolutions of Hooke's Law, everybody was released. They filed out of the lecture hall as though a funeral had ended. In the crowded corridor, Arthur waved to her. 'Come and see your gift.'

As she followed him upstairs, she saw the wobbly stitches in the elbows of his jumper where he'd darned them, and felt worse about herself. It turned out that he'd organized a wooden locker on the first floor – one drawer of a plan chest with a little key. 'I thought you'd like to share this with me,' he said. 'Useful when it's raining and you've got that big portfolio to lug around. I'll get you a key copied.'

She'd tried to get a locker months ago, but there'd been none available, and she'd not put her name down on the waiting list. Had she told him this, or had he just intuited the fact? 'It's very thoughtful, Arthur. Thank you. You must let me pay my share of the deposit, though.'

'Don't be daft. I'll get it back when we're both finished here.'

The key clunked in the lock and he pulled out the drawer.

Then, with a delicacy he'd never shown for handling his work before, he lifted up the single sheet that was inside. It was a square of heavy Whatman paper on to which he'd illustrated her initials in tall, serifed letters, the F entangled by what looked like ivy, the G by a climbing rose. 'I was practising,' he said, 'and I got tired of writing my own name. So, happy Christmas.'

'What a lovely thing. It's beautiful.'

'You really think so?'

'Yes. It must've taken ages.'

'Near enough a month,' he said. 'But if a job's worth doing . . . You can leave it in there, if you like. Don't feel obliged to take it home with you.'

'Nonsense. I can pick out a nice frame for it in town.'

'I'm glad you like it. Truly.'

She set her case upon the plan chest, slid the illustration into it. All the while, she was aware of his proximity, the passage of his shoulder next to hers, their hips barely an inch apart – and, in that space, the most unnerving static, a crackle she felt spreading through her blood. He must've known it, too, because he asked abruptly, 'Did you fetch your programme yet? I didn't get a chance on the way in. Come with me?'

Mr Lundy kept them in the pigeonhole outside the staff-room. Once a fortnight, he'd ascribe a building programme to the group and leave it for collection on a Thursday morning. They would have until that evening – a minute before nine p.m. – to submit a set of sketches in response to his conditions. If they were a second late, they couldn't get their pages stamped and would incur a fail grade. So far, none of the assignments had ignited her imagination.

She'd planned to go back to her room to work on her designs. At Rankin Hall, she had a draughting board set up beside her window on the top floor, overlooking Sefton Park. The afternoons were always peaceful there and she could put the wireless on and listen to the violin recitals and the military bands while she was sketching. But that kind of solitude seemed less appealing to her now. Instead, she went with Arthur to collect his copy of the programme, then stood there watching him flick through it with his brow sloped downward in examination of the brief. And when he looked at her, in search of her opinion, she said, 'Arts and Crafts – I'm happy. If I never have to shade another Doric column, it'll be too soon. And I happen to like Webb and Voysey quite a bit. Would you rather it were something different?'

'Honestly,' he said, 'I've had to read so much these past few months to catch up with the others – I haven't even started on the Ruskin yet. I don't know Arts and Crafts at all.'

'That's what the library's for,' she said. 'We'll catch them before lunch hour.'

His face reanimated. 'We?'

*

Every time they were alone, he noticed something new about her. In the library, she hushed her voice into a higher pitch. She fussed with the stray pin curls round her ears, patted at her breastbone in the throes of speaking, thumbed the fabric of her blouse above her clavicle. He hadn't even thought that she would stay there with him, but she did. It seemed there wasn't much she didn't know about the Arts and Crafts movement. She put him at a desk with several books held open at the glossy centre pages, showing photographs of houses built by Philip Webb. The mannered, partly rendered details that he studied – timber rafters, cone-roofed wells – were elegant yet rustic, and he admired them a good deal. She kept returning from the shelves with other texts, on Voysey, Lethaby, Mackmurdo, William Morris, skimming through them, muttering her quick tutorials while he listened and appraised the drawings. Before the library shut, he went to borrow his allowance of the books, and Florence let him put the rest on her own card. 'Don't leave town,' she said. He asked if she would join him in the park so they might keep on studying in the fresh air, but she had somewhere else to be. 'I think a bit of rain is on the way,' she said, examining the distance. 'Besides, I've got a meeting at my residence. Someone on my floor keeps breaking curfew and the warden isn't happy.'

If only to retain her company a little longer, he said, 'Maybe when we've got our drawings in for Lundy, I might take you for a bite to eat? I mean, to thank you.' She didn't give an answer right away. He watched the backward motion of her shoulders, bracing to return the disappointing news, and tried to intervene before she voiced it: 'Not the union. Somewhere nicer. There's a place in Chinatown – the people sort of know me there. I thought you'd like to see it.' And he couldn't quite believe it when she told him, 'Yes, I'd like that.'

Afterwards, he traipsed into the square and found the only bench that wasn't caked in droppings. Grey clouds trawled the sky. The light was dwindling. He felt her absence strongly and he did his best to deaden it with reading. When specks of rain began to fall, he gathered all his books and his portfolio and went to sit in the refectory to sketch. But the only visions he could summon were of her somewhere without him, and he'd never been in such a hurry to complete his work or so indifferent to its standard.

★

The Wah Yuen restaurant was small and noisy. She had to concentrate on listening. There wasn't just the clatter of the kitchen and the bellowed conversations in Chinese to overcome; there was a vendor on the street outside enticing folk to buy his fruit. Arthur ordered what he knew was good by pointing at the numbers on a blackboard hanging by the door. There weren't a lot of tables, so they sat beside each other on a low bench near the window. The owner, Mr Peng, brought out their dishes on a tray. Fried rice, noodles, medleys of green vegetables, char siu and strips of beef in a dark sauce.

'How long have you been coming here?' she asked.

'A while,' he said. 'Until last summer, I was washing pots for them. The weekend shift. It didn't pay well, but I'd get a proper feed at closing time.'

The meal was special – rich and flavoursome and filling – and she told him so. She'd never tried its kind before.

'I'm glad you like it. We'll come every week, then, since you're keen.' His voice softened as he smiled.

'Do you live nearby?'

He shook his head. 'I live in Fairfield. I've a room above a bakery.'

'That sounds nice to me.'

'It has its charms. I've grown a bit attached to it.'

'You didn't want to be in halls?'

'Not me, no. They're far too – let's just say, I didn't want to be cooped up.' He hurried on, as though she might've been offended: 'What I mean is, I prefer it on my own. And if I lived in halls, I'd get distracted. There's a chance I'd start forgetting where I came from. Once that happens, I'll be done for.'

'*Done for?*' she said. 'How'd you mean?'

He squared his eyes at her. 'Well, let me put it this way: did you always want to be an architect?'

'I think so. But I never thought I'd get this far.'

'Why not?'

'My father wanted me to be a nurse. Or rather, he expected it.'

'I never would've pegged you for a disappointment.'

'He'll get over it, I'm sure. It's not as though I didn't make it obvious.'

Somehow, when her own life was the object of the conversation, she began to wilt before him, feeling studied – which was wrong of her, because he was the least judgemental man she'd ever met. Perhaps it was a symptom of the fact that every time she told someone of her ambitions, they only seemed remote and unattainable, and she felt pathetic for pursuing them. If she talked about the creativity that had been encouraged in her as a child, it always sounded juvenile – the models she would make from dry grass in their meadow, oil paintings she would do of Monk the family dog, the schemes she used to draw for the arrangement of her bedroom furniture, the charcoal sketches of their house. But Arthur only smiled at her and said, 'I used to do the same. Drawing on my uncle's wall with bits of coal.'

The hardest part was getting past the mention of her mother without lapsing into tears. It was her mother who'd escorted her through London on their visits, pointing out the features of the skyline changing every year; who'd shared her interest in the galleries and museums and libraries; who'd told her, 'You should aim for a profession other than just being married to a man who has one – and it doesn't matter how well paid it is.' This advice had stuck with her, not least because it came towards the latter stages of her mother's life, a month or two before she got so poorly. An infection in her kidneys. Come next April, it would be four years without her.

'Well, I reckon she'd be proud,' he said, 'to know you're here.'

'I hope you're right.' She finished off the last of the green vegetables, which Arthur seemed to have ignored. 'One thing I know is, if she hadn't passed away, I'd never have found the strength for all of this. It's focused me – I'm doing this for her.'

'And what about your father? Does he mind you being here?'

She looked away. The vendor with the stack of crates was yelling out the prices of his fruit again. 'He's paying forty pounds a year for me. That's more than I expected he would do. I'm choosing to be grateful for his generosity.'

'You can pay him back when your cathedral fees come in.'

'I'm sure he's counting on it. First commission, he'll be asking for his share.'

'And don't forget the taxman,' Arthur said. He took the cigarettes from his coat pocket and lit one up. 'You didn't want to stay down south, then? Study there, I mean.'

'No. Liverpool's supposed to be the best.'

'Is that what people say?'

'Yes, from what I've read. You don't agree?'

'It seems all right. But I'm not sure if I could name another school. There must be plenty down in London, are there? Good ones, I suppose.'

Just when she believed that she was close to understanding him entirely, he'd surprise her with another layer he'd been withholding. 'Didn't you apply elsewhere?'

'That's what I was getting at before. I've never had a big desire to be an architect, but people think I've got a skill for it. Perhaps they're wrong – and I suppose I'll find that out. But the only way I'd want to be an architect is if it's all about the work itself – to see if I can't change something about the way things are, conditions people have to live in nowadays. It seems most fellas in our group are happy just to join the ranks, you know, and make a shilling. Fair enough, there's nothing wrong with earning, but I couldn't be content with just *maintaining* things as they are now. Don't see much good in that, do you?'

'Not really, no.' She found it wasn't difficult to stare at him when he was speaking. They were close enough that she could see a tiny trail of whiskers on his jaw, missed by the razor, and a splinter of char siu caught in his teeth. He was like those bricked-up windows on the side of the school building: attractively imperfect.

'At any rate,' he said, 'I'm only here because somebody vouched for me. I can't afford to let him down.'

'Why not?'

'Because. The likes of me don't get too many second chances.' He pinched the flesh around his nose. There was tiredness about his eyelids now. 'I have a – well, it's hard to say out loud. I have a record. Criminal, I mean. I'm none too proud of it. I'm not ashamed of it exactly neither. Just, you know – that's how it is. I didn't have things easy, growing up. Don't really like to speak about it much. And, well, I meant to tell you all of this before. I'm sorry if it shocks you, but –'

She reached and took his hand. 'I heard a rumour that you went to borstal. But I got that from Bill Embry and I'd rather hear the rest of it from you.'

'Embry? Jesus. Who'd *he* get it from?'

'He didn't say. I didn't ask.' There was a kind of panic in his squinting eyes, a moist heat to his palm, but he allowed her to keep hold.

*

He'd never shared so much about himself without a spit and polish on the tale to make it more respectable. But he gave Florence the entire, unburnished truth. Because he'd never been in a position where, by talking of it, he could feel as though another person wanted to appreciate his past for what it was: the makings of the person he was trying to become.

There were things he told her that he'd never let escape his mouth before. Such as the scrap of information he'd picked up about his father – that he'd served aboard a merchant navy training ship berthed at the Sloyne. Not once had he cared to check if this was true or not – he wouldn't give the coward the satisfaction of believing he existed – but he told Florence of it nonetheless. And he even spoke with honesty about his mother. Where usually he'd say to people that she'd had tuber-culosis or pneumonia to avoid a raft of questions on the matter, he didn't hide the facts this time: she'd died from los-ing too much blood in labour and had never even held him in her arms.

He wanted to give Florence everything. She asked where he'd grown up, who'd raised him, so he told her plainly: his great-uncle Patrick Leventree had spared him from the orphan-age. She sat there listening and nodding, sipping tea, while he accounted for his troubles in the only way he could make sense of them.

'I called him Uncle Patrick, but most people called him Lev. He used to push a handcart. Made the thing himself from scrap. He was industrious like that. He'd take it down the docks and back a hundred times a week. The folk who came in off the ships would pay him and he'd cart their wares back home – their kit-bags, furniture, big joints of meat and palliasses, all kinds. He'd been doing it for years and it was all he really knew. He never spoke a bitter word to anyone, my uncle Patrick. He'd be there for people if they needed help. *Ask Lev*, they'd say. *Old Lev won't mind.* But times have been especially hard on everyone round here. And circumstances change the way you've got to think. Came to a point when Uncle Patrick couldn't use his handcart like he used to any more. The ships weren't coming into dock and cargo wasn't moving anywhere, so all the men were gather-ing on the corners, asking after jobs – but there was nothing going. Just a bit of money from the government to live off, and it barely got you anything. A loaf or two. Everybody was on tick with every shop in town. My uncle had gone knocking on a thousand doors, looking for work, and he got sick of it. He wasn't in the best of health. And we were living off potatoes and fresh air. He could've dragged me out of school and sent me off somewhere to scrounge a wage – he didn't, though. He knew that I was better off in class. But still, he got me helping him on evenings and weekends.

'He started totting with his handcart, collecting empty jam jars. He knew a fella at the Hartley's factory who'd buy them back, a ha'penny for ten. That kept us going for a time. But it wasn't quite enough to stop the rent man banging on the door. My uncle had a lot of pain by then and he was really showing his age – his knees were shot. He couldn't walk, most days, and couldn't do the totting any more. So he sent me off to see a bloke he knew called Stanley Hoult – he was a runner for a local bookie. Stan said he had things that needed moving with the handcart later and he'd pay me half a crown to do it. Well, I knew what I was getting into – for that kind of money, it was obvious – but I reasoned we were desperate for it or my uncle would've told me not to do it.

'Anyway, that night, I hauled the cart to where Stan said I had to go – a house on Bedford Road, right on the corner, and I waited. Stan comes out the door with an enormous roll of fabric underneath his arm. He goes inside again and comes back with another, and another, and another. Once he's loaded up the cart with six of them, I heave it down to someone's shed on Derby Road and leave the fabric with some fella. And that's how it starts. Before too long, I'm coming home from school most days and hauling stuff for Stan at night. Beer barrels. Crates of whisky. Tea chests full of God knows what. Sacks of flour. Sacks of coal. That stuff was the easiest to hide. My uncle's happy with the money coming in and everything seems rosy for a while. But then Stan tells me I'm to go down to the shed and fetch some things for him. I get there and a fella starts to load the crates on to the cart. They're filled with bars of Battleaxe tobacco – really heavy stuff for pipes. I'm meant to take them over to a pub, the Washington, and see a bloke who runs the cellar. So I do. But when I get there, about eight or nine, I find a copper meddling with his bike chain on the kerb outside. And I suppose he hears the clatter of the cart along the street, because he looks right at me. I try and edge away – I know he's got me, though. A smarmy grin is on his face. He calls to me, *You'd best wait where you are, boy.* And I should've run, if I'd been thinking straight. But I just stood there. He walks over, has a peek what's in the cart. He says, *Ah, you like a pipe, do you? I like a pipe myself.* I'm thinking, maybe he's just after some for free. I might get out of this if I can let him have a bar or two. But no. He says, *I wouldn't touch the bar tobacco, mind. It's too much bother, cutting it. Where'd all this come from?* I don't give an answer. *Magic, was it? Miracle?* He looks towards the pub. *I don't suppose you've got a bill of sale or something you can show me?* That's when I decide to run. Forgetting that the copper's got his bike. I'm panting down the lane. He catches up with me in no time. And he puts me in the handcuffs, *Just in case you try and scarper on the way.* He walks me down to Bootle station. Happy with himself, he was, though I was crying like a baby. That was that. They charged me, sent me to the magistrate the morning after, and suddenly I was in the cells with proper criminals at Walton on remand. I never even got to see my uncle till he showed up at the Court of Sessions for my hearing. Feltham borstal's where they sent me – just about two years – and in the end it didn't turn out to be all that bad, considering where I might've ended up. At any rate, I think I've probably scared you off by now. I wouldn't blame you if you want to leave . . .'

But she didn't move at all. She stayed beside him, breathing slowly with a glassiness about her eyes. She hadn't interrupted once or glanced towards the door. 'And are you still in touch?' she asked him. 'You and Uncle Patrick?'

'No. It's like I said, he wasn't in good health, and he was never one for sending letters. It was only five months after I went in that he passed on. They told me that he got cremated, but I don't know where. I didn't even hear about the service. I suppose somebody somewhere's got his ashes in a box.'

She squeezed his hand again. 'Oh, Arthur, I'm so sorry,' and it seemed as though a valve had loosened in his heart.

'Well, there's nothing to be done about it now. Besides, he knew how much I cared about him. He was shy about his feelings, but I never was.' He lit another Woodbine, drank the leavings in the teapot. 'Would you like some pudding?'

'No. I think I'm full.'

'All right. Let me have a word with Mr Peng about the bill, see how many pots I'll need to wash.' He was glad to hear her laughter.

'Arthur, I can get this.'

'Don't be daft.'

He settled up with Mr Peng and promised he'd return before too long – and, yes, he hoped to bring the lady with him. There was something different in her manner when he got back to the table with their coats. A peaceful resignation in the way she looked at him, a fondness she'd stopped trying to conceal. 'I don't think I've ever talked so much in all my life,' he said. 'It's funny – if you asked me now, I feel as though I'd tell you anything.'

'Careful,' she said, 'or I just might do it.'

'You're a lovely girl to talk to, Florence. I do mean that.'

'All I did was listen.'

'Well, you make an art of it. Most people would've run a mile by now.' He opened out her coat for her and she slid into it; his fingers glanced her neck as they released the collar. And he realized there was something different, too, about himself.

Walking with her in the dark, he thought she might be frightened, wandering the city's lesser-taken paths. But as soon as they'd come out, she'd linked her arm with his, and when they reached the brighter avenues, they didn't separate. He'd never walked out with a girl for so long, hitched this way, and it was dizzying. Even in the heart of Chinatown, on Pitt Street, where the chimneys huffed out smoke as thick as eiderdown and viscous mud ran through the gutters, she looked at ease, composed.

'How will you get home?' he asked.

'A taxi, I suppose.'

'I'll ride with you. It's too late to be travelling alone.' But this was only half the reason: he was not prepared to say goodnight to her.

'All right,' she said. 'As long as you don't try to pay the fare, as well.'

They had to walk as far as Kent Street for a cab. The roads were calm and traffic sparse. He sat with her on the back seat, her hand enclosed in his. The street lamps yellowed her complexion, slid away. She had such open, active eyes. Those minutes, going southwards, seemed to pass by in a blink. The cab rolled on to Ullet Street and found the kerb outside her residence. He asked the driver to hang on until he'd walked her to the door. 'Better not,' she said. 'The warden never sleeps. She'll get the wrong impression, and I'll get my marching orders.' He sighed too heavily. 'But thank you, Arthur, for today. Tonight. For all of it. I'll not forget it in a hurry.' Her smile was a brief cinching of her lips, apologetic. He was going to mutter back some platitude – *the pleasure was all mine, you're welcome, till we meet again* – but she leaned her forehead on his temple and he felt the soft bulb of her nose against his ear. Then, with a conviction that elated him, she kissed his cheek and slipped away, towards the porch light.

PART TWO

The Savigears

October 1952

Joyce was staggered by how fast the rye came through. Already the north field was flecked with little purple shoots, and the soil had a chalky, sprouting look that made her think back to the one and only time she'd visited the make-up counter at the big department store in Maidstone (they'd given her a magnifying mirror and let her see the damage that her two-bit soap had wreaked on her poor skin). It had only been a fortnight since the seeds were sown, and having never grown a thing before except a pot of cress at infant school, she'd thought it would be months before they noticed any signs of life emerging. But from the window of her room, she had a perfect view over the field, and it surprised her how invested she'd become in its success.

Maybe it was stupid to get so attached – the rye would never know how much she thought about it, after all – and yet she couldn't stop herself from fretting over it each morning, going out to kneel in the dirt sometimes and touch it with the soft part of her hand. She supposed it was a consequence of how things were now. Mr Hollis had been gone for weeks, and this was what remained of him: a field of shoots that would eventually be mown and ploughed again and sown with something else. If she couldn't change what had been done to him, or speak of it, then she could take care of the things he'd left behind.

She didn't know for sure that he was dead – not yet – and she was clinging on to that uncertainty. Until she got the say-so, there was nothing else to do but carry on her normal ways of

127

being. If she took each day a minute at a time, she could stop the fright from leaking out of her in conversations. That was how she'd managed it before, when things had started spoiling. First, she would convince herself that she was fine and then she could persuade the world.

It meant she'd have to go on acting all polite with Mr Mayhood, even when he nit-picked over tiny details in her drawings. Offer no complaints about the rota when it came to chores about the place. Keep on working hard (but not *too* hard) to get the root cellar built, then complete her set of elevations for the greenhouse (in her own good time) and finish all the odds and ends of carpentry that she'd been putting off for weeks (but not in such a rush that it would draw attention). Stick to hassling her brother if she caught him staring with those dewy eyes at Mrs Mayhood from across the room and telling him that he was subtle as a dog outside a butcher's window. Be as late as usual to meet her supervising officer when he paid his visits, answering his list of questions in her standard tone, making the same faces, giving him the usual smart-alec comments. Everything she'd done before, she had to keep on doing. Or else she'd end up back in Aylesbury – even worse, a women's prison with a crowd of revokes, hard of heart, and not a hope in hell of going out on licence for another eighteen months. And Charlie – this would snuff out any last breath of forgiveness he had left to give, and that's what scared her most. But it was starting to exhaust her, thinking over every movement that she made, sieving out her words for hitches every time she had to speak. Her stomach was a shank knot, getting tighter by the hour.

This morning was the worst she'd felt in years. The shudders had set in. Her teeth were chattering so much she had to bite down on her sleeve to calm them. Since she couldn't sleep, she hadn't bothered getting into bed, and she'd been standing at her window fully dressed for ages, waiting for the sky to lose its pink. She didn't want the day to start, but there was nothing she could do to ward it off, and when the rumble of her brother pissing in the toilet carried down the hallway, she accepted that the time had come.

She went downstairs for breakfast, making small talk with the Mayhoods as they passed the toast rack back and forth, eating with her eyes down on the cartoons in the newspaper. Later, Charlie took a seat and pestered her about her drawings for the greenhouse; she satisfied him by insisting she would work on them all night to get them ready, at which point Mr Mayhood said, 'That's fine by me. Don't rush it.' Florence ate her usual three rounds of toast and jam, drank her pot of tea and cleared their plates. And the first time anybody mentioned the old man was after they'd wiped off the dishes, in the lull when they were sitting at the kitchen table waiting for the whistle of the kettle.

'Honestly, I'm still not sure if we should carry on the greenhouse plans with Mr Hollis out of reach like this,' Florence called in from the pantry. 'It was his idea, and God knows he had *very* strong opinions on the way it should be built.' She stepped out with a Mason jar of flour and her book of recipes. 'Perhaps we ought to leave it till he's back.'

Charlie said, 'What makes you think he's coming back?'

'Just a feeling, I suppose.'

'I wouldn't bank on it, if I were you, miss.'

Joyce said nothing, wringing out the dishcloth in the silence, but she worried that her thoughts were loud enough to hear. When she swallowed, it was like a boulder rolling down her throat, but nobody looked sideways at her or said, 'You've gone quiet, Joyce. Why's that? A guilty conscience?' which is how it would've happened in a Zane Grey book, causing some hot-tempered horseman to draw out his gun. Her little altercation in the field with Mr Hollis hadn't been forgotten and she sensed an undertone of blame whenever they discussed the matter. It was better to stay mute about all that. Instead, she let her brother prattle on, the way he liked to do. She could always hide behind his talk, even though what Charlie knew about the situation could be written on a grain of salt.

By their account of things, the Mayhoods hadn't found too many answers in their search for Hollis either. They'd been asking round the village for a while and nobody was shocked to learn he'd flown the coop. The old man was renowned for being a fickle sort, and no one ever paid too much attention to his whereabouts. He wasn't married, had no children, no old friends to phone or visit. The barmaid at the Barley Mow had said he'd long had problems with the drink: he'd fallen foul of everyone who'd ever trusted him, including his own brother, and he'd got the boot from the last farm he'd worked because of it (she knew, because her cousin was the one who'd sacked him). From the barmaid, they'd got word of where old Hollis parked his caravan and Mr Mayhood had gone down to have a look around. Well, that had been a frantic hour for everyone. Joyce had waited on the landing for the sight of him returning in the flatbed lorry, polishing the windowsills and skirting boards up there until they shone as well as any mirror in the house. She'd earwigged from the banister above when he'd come back: 'Nothing – not a sign,' he'd said to Florence in the hall. Thank Christ for that. 'The door was padlocked. Floor's been mopped inside and everything's been tidied. Nothing but some folded sheets and blankets on the bench, as far as I could see. He's not gone in a hurry, that's for sure. He's had this planned.' With every other day that passed, the more resigned the Mayhoods seemed to that idea.

Charlie was reminding everyone about this now. 'I'm saying, if you're gonna do a runner overnight, why stop and fold your linen? He's had it in his mind to go for ages, and he didn't even think to let you know.' She'd always thought her brother would've made a decent copper: he liked to press his nose in other people's business and complain about the smell. But she couldn't tell him he was wrong this time.

'Even if that's true –' Florence leafed the pages in her book of recipes – 'I still think we ought to hold on for a week or two. It's not an urgent job.'

'He's left us in the lurch. Who cares what *he* thinks any more?'

'Really, there's no point in holding grudges. He must have his reasons.'

'You're too sweet by half, miss, that's your trouble,' Charlie said.

'And you're a charmer.' Florence handed him the book, tapping her forefinger on the page. 'Here's what I suggest you cook for supper. Corned-beef hash. Go easy on the butter when you fry the onions and potatoes. It's as simple as it gets.'

'All right. If you say so.'

Too sweet by half, miss, that's your trouble. Joyce would tease him for this later. Twenty months in borstal with no pretty face to look upon had clogged him up with yearnings – it was natural, she supposed, and she hadn't said a thing about the crusted egg-white stains she'd noticed on his sheets when she did laundry duties. But just because the first nice skirt that wandered by belonged to Florence Mayhood, well, it didn't mean he had to latch on to it. He was in for quite a heartache there, and it would ruin his relationship with Mr Mayhood – not to mention how it added complications to her own life she could do without. She goaded him about it every chance she got, because the only way she'd ever known to make her brother drop a habit was to give him the idea that everyone was laughing at him for it.

'That's me finished, miss,' she said now, draping the tea towel on the range's handle. 'If there's anything that you want posting, I'd be glad to stretch my legs.'

'Yes, thank you, Joy. I think there are a few things in the drawer.'

'Pick me up some ciggies while you're at it,' Charlie said. 'I'll pay you back.'

'Shut up, mouse. I'm only going up the road.'

It had taken time to work out the right method – something so routine and innocent that nobody would ever think to question her behaviour – and, once she had things sorted in her mind, it wasn't hard to put them into practice. She went to the hall and fetched the letters from the console table. There were seven envelopes inside the drawer with fresh green stamps showing the Queen at her most beautiful: this would mean no queuing at the counter for the postage, but it robbed her of a decent reason to be late returning. She put the letters in the outer pocket of her coat and made sure that her headscarf was still tucked inside the sleeve. When it was warmer out, she didn't wear more than a pullover in case it looked unusual, but today was overcast and there was a good October chill. Taking the letters had become her daily errand. No one ever asked her why. They trusted her. It hurt how much they trusted her.

She passed through the front yard, checking on the rye shoots in the field with squinting eyes. A stiff wind brushed the treetops as she came along the driveway and the dirt blew now and then above the ankles of her boots. She closed the gate behind her, crossed the road and went down Alms Heath with no urgency at all, though she was sweating underneath her coat already. At the junction, where the postbox stood enclosed within a wall of bricks, she dropped the letters through the slot. The shudders were still with her, tracking down her arms, and it was quite a battle to dig out the headscarf from her sleeve. She tied it round her hair and felt a hundred years older.

Across the road, the empty phone box waited, all its little windowpanes tinged white with condensation, putting her in mind of Christmas. A car turned down the lane before she reached the other side and she was careful not to show her face. Inside, the booth was cold and musty as a cellar. The dial seemed to go on ratcheting for ever when she put the number in – she had it memorized by now, but it had taken a few days to stick – and she was under orders to speak first. When the line connected and she dropped her pennies in, she said what she'd been told to say: 'Another lovely morning in the country.' That was how Mal knew it was all right to talk – a cautionary measure, on account of all the people who were after him.

Eventually, she heard his heavy breath in the receiver. 'Half an hour late, aren't you?'

'Sorry, it's not easy getting out the house. My brother's always nosing.'

'If your Charlie's causing trouble –'

'No, I didn't say that.' The shudders reached her fingers and she had to squeeze the dangling cable. 'He's no bother, Mal. You know that I can manage him.'

There was an awful pause. She imagined he was scratching at his beard, the way he did when he was sizing up a problem. 'Next time, phone me when I say to phone me. I've got better things to do than wait around for you all day.'

She wanted to reply, *Like what exactly?* For as long as she'd known Mal, he'd had no pressing obligations or appointments, except to drop a car off at some backstreet garage or to sling some bit of gear down at the pawnbroker's in town. But she wasn't daft enough to start that conversation with him now. 'All right. OK. I'm sorry.'

When he cleared his throat, the sound was so distinctive

and familiar: a slow warble in his nose that ended with a crack of phlegm, a spit. She used to hear it often, waking up beside him on the pull-out in her flat. Mal had changed a lot since she first met him as a girl – he must've piled on six or seven stone over the years, and lost most of the hair above his forehead – but his habits were no different, or his manner. She'd never been entirely sure how old he was, because she'd always been afraid to ask – in those early days they were together, nothing could've mattered to her less. She imagined he was in his thirties now; maybe with a shave and better-fitting clothes, he could've passed for younger. 'I've got another parcel for you,' he said. 'Same place as the last one. Go and fetch it, would you?'

She covered up the mouthpiece so he wouldn't hear her seething. 'Fine, I'll go, but –'

'Don't start yapping, Joy. Get on with it.'

'How much longer do I have to keep on doing this? I'm running out of hiding places.'

'You'll think of something, clever girl like you.'

She could tell that he was sneering as he said it. His normal voice was never so alive. 'Don't I even get to know what's in them?'

'No chance.'

'Why not? I've a right to –'

'Put the phone down, Joyce, before I lose my rag with you.'

And she was just about to press the hook, as biddable as ever, when she felt a nick of anger at herself. How had she allowed all this to happen? She'd sworn she wouldn't let Mal Duggan back into her life, now here she was again, the stupid donkey that went trudging forward every time he whipped the birch. 'Listen, I'm not going to cry about some drunk old man who hated me,' she said, before the instinct left her. 'But he must've meant something to *someone* out there, mustn't he, and it's not right he's come to harm.' There was a faint hiss on the line, though it was still connected. 'If he's gone for good, you'd better say so. I can't keep this up much longer. I'm a nervous wreck.'

'You'll keep it up all right,' he said, 'because you know what happens otherwise.'

'I've done everything you wanted, haven't I?'

'So far. I'm not finished with you yet.'

'But why'd you have to go and hurt him? It was nothing that I couldn't handle.' A lorry with a trailer was approaching the main road. She watched it pass beyond her shoulder, vanish down the lane.

'Listen how you're talking to me,' Mal said, biting every word. *That's why*. You've been in the clink so long your head's turned funny. Don't go thinking you and me are square already. I'm the one who's making the decisions. You just let that old man be your warning.'

'Yeah, but, Mal –'

'No ifs or buts about it, girl. It's me you work for – not those two up in that house.'

'I know, I know.' She let it drop. Resistance had the same stink as disloyalty the longer it went on, and Mal could always sniff it on her – surely it would carry down the wires. Next thing, she'd be walking up the street and feel a hard tap on her shoulder, and he'd be there leering at her with his bloodshot eyes and cracking his fat knuckles.

It was just as well she hadn't needled him again, because he said, 'He saw you with that parcel, didn't he? The fella had to go. It's done with now. He won't be sniffing round again. And if you didn't want him hurt, you should've kept it to yourself. Your fault, not mine.'

She couldn't answer him, at first – the words snagged in her gullet.

'Right, are we done yapping yet?' he said. 'You're starting to annoy me.'

'Yeah,' she managed. 'Sorry. I'll go down and fetch it now.'

'Good. Same time tomorrow, then.'

'OK.'

A loud click in her ear and he was gone.

*

For a short time, she'd convinced herself that she was free of him. Those first six months in borstal, not a letter, not a word, had given her the notion that he wasn't thinking of her – perhaps he didn't even know where she'd been sent. She hadn't written to a soul except her brother, who kept writing back with cheerful news of books he'd read and friendships he was making with the other boys. Meanwhile, she'd slogged through her duties in the ordinary grade: cleaning floors and ironing and laundering, drills on the parade ground after dawn, cooking lessons and arithmetic. Hobby hours spent watercolour painting and embroidering – stuff they reckoned would prepare a woman for an honest life outside and make her happy. It seemed to her they'd got it backwards. They were training her for service as a wife, a housekeeper, a factory hand, which was everything that girls like her went thieving to avoid. What they should've done was teach her what her brother got to learn at Huntercombe: carpentry, mechanics, bricklaying and such. If they'd given her a chance to take a draughtsman's class like him, she'd would've understood the proper way to use a T-square long before she got to working for the Mayhoods and she wouldn't be the only person in the house who couldn't get a simple elevation right. She'd been good at watercolour painting in those hobby hours, which she put down to an inheritance from her father, given how he'd made his living with a brush – there were shopfronts all round Kent that bore his careful handiwork. Cartoons of the trees and birds and flowers, little scenes with people in them – she'd do these for fun sometimes. But architecture was so technical and stuffy and she couldn't get accustomed to it.

Anyway, the longer that Mal's silence had continued, the more she'd hoped that he'd forgotten her. Perhaps he'd got in bother with the law himself, or somebody he owed. She'd passed the hours in her dormitory at night, imagining his ending. Throat slit in a doorway by a fence he'd cheated. Body thrown into the Medway by some young girl's father. Skull crushed by the hooves of a police horse. But then, one morning of her seventh month at Aylesbury, she'd received an envelope addressed in a dull scribble. Mal had written very little:

Dear Joy

I bet your sick of borstal grub allready arent you but you got off easy as I see it. Keep your chin up and your mouth shut youll do fine.
Dont be a stranger.

M

Once that old connection was restored, the charge it carried was as strong as ever. She couldn't say that she was cursed with an obedient nature, but, for Mal, she had a heart of putty.

They'd met when she was sixteen, on a dreary afternoon in Maidstone, middle of the week. She'd been on lunch break, smoking round the back of E. H. Lacey's store, and he'd been sitting in a Daimler parked up in the alley, blocking the goods entrance with his bonnet. Her first thought had been: *Fancy motor. Must be rich, this fella.* She hadn't given much consideration to the way he looked, all slouched and rumple-shirted, messing with the dial on the radio. There'd been muffled squeals as he'd gone searching for the frequency he wanted; then a crackly commentator's voice had risen from the fuzz and he'd turned up the volume. The tail end of a horse race had played out. She'd watched his growing pleasure as the commentary got louder and more frantic, and eventually he'd drummed his fingers on the steering wheel and whooped, pumping his fists. Their eyes had hooked together for a moment, through the glass.

No boy had ever ogled her the way Mal did, as though he'd noticed some rare object on a rag-and-bone man's cart and wanted to possess it. At school, they'd called her names like Lumberjack and Elephant. But there he'd been, this grown man in his Daimler, giving her the up-and-down. She'd felt a hum go through her, like that time she'd touched the frayed wire of her aunty's hairdryer. Maybe if she hadn't smiled back at him, he would've left her well alone. Instead, he'd leaned across to scroll the window down. 'Oi there, listen – what's your name?' he'd called. 'You fancy going for a ride some-where? I just got ten quid richer and I want to spend it all before the sun goes down. You interested?'

'Sorry, can't,' she'd said. 'My shift's not done till six.'

'You can always find another place to work. There's plenty more shops in the sea.' He'd scratched his beard. 'Or, better yet, give up the working life for ever. It does wonders for the soul, believe me.'

'Nah,' she'd said. 'I've rent to pay. Thanks for the offer, though.'

'Well, maybe next time? Seems I know your place of work, so I can come and find you when I'm in the mood.'

'You can try.' She'd given him a nervous laugh.

'I will.' He'd rolled the window up again and leaned away.

By the time they'd finished talking, there was ash all down the front of her best blouse. Her sandwiches were still inside her bag. A little disappointment had begun to stab at her. Four more hours of drudgery indoors were her reward for being good. Was this how it was going to be for ever? Wrapping things for customers in womenswear, no conversation. Polishing the counters so her face reflected in the brass and sweeping floors at closing time until the boss said she could leave. How much worse off would she be if she went driving with a stranger for a while? It didn't seem that she'd be losing anything.

But she hadn't got the chance to change her mind, because the Daimler's engine wouldn't go when Mal had tried to fire it up again – she'd listened to the scratch and wheeze each time he pressed the starter. Eventually, he'd given up and stepped into the alley. 'What's the matter with your motor?' she'd said, as he'd walked around the back end, looking sheepish. It was rare to find a man so tall she couldn't see the top part of his scalp from yards away.

'Gone and drained the battery, I think,' he'd said. 'Ah, well. It was a nice one, too.'

For a second, she'd been puzzled, wondering what made one battery any nicer than another. Then she'd watched him open up the boot. He'd tossed the key with its big leather fob inside and slammed the lid. Turning slowly, he'd approached her. His enormous rubber soles had made no sound at all. He'd held his finger to his lips and shushed. 'I never got your name, but that's all right, I trust you.' With a wink, he'd backed away and strolled along the alley.

No young girl would ever look upon Mal Duggan as a picture worthy of a frame, but his appeal was in his attitude to life. He seemed to drift along without the worries that tied other people down and buried them. One day's graft after the next was not Mal's style. He was spontaneous, which made him unpredictable and dizzying. His confidence was like a tonic she'd been given to forget the fears that were ingrained in her – all those notions that she'd wind up miserable, a failure, on her own for good. So what if there was menace in him, too? A little danger meant excitement, didn't it? And if she'd wanted boredom she'd have stayed in school and lived the drab existence that her aunty wanted her to have in Borough Green. Church on Sundays. Married off to some God-fearing member of the congregation no one else would have, ironing his smalls throughout the week and cooking him two different kinds of gravy for his roast. No, thank you.

That was why she'd moved to Maidstone in the first place: to escape. She'd left with hopes of finding a nice boarding house beside the river, but it hadn't quite turned out that way. The only room she could afford to lodge in was a long walk from the water and there hadn't been enough space for a proper bedstead, let alone for Charlie to come visiting on weekends. She'd had to make do with a mattress propped up on a sheet of ply and bricks. No heating. No one else to blame for where she was, only herself.

She'd made the choice to leave her brother back in Borough Green until she could provide for him. Her aunty wanted him to stay put till he turned eighteen and maybe they'd have come to some arrangement if there hadn't been so much resentment lingering. Aunty Helen, as they called her, was really just their father's second cousin. She'd been widowed years before the war – her husband used to work for ICI and had some sort of illness they weren't ever meant to ask about – and it had turned her pious and unforgiving. All that Bible worship must've made a husk out of her brain, because she thought a bit of devilment on Joyce's part (or any girl's) was something only scorn and judgement could resolve. Compassion was a pantomime she'd put on for the vicar. She reserved her better side for Charlie – all her patience and soft-soaping – but, even then, she shovelled on her kindness till it cloyed and smothered him and made him tense.

There was never any tolerance for Joyce. No leeway had been granted for the fact that she was young and still in mourning. It had been as though her grief was an unpleasant incident she had to put behind her. And perhaps Aunt Helen hadn't bargained for the difficulties of raising them, but that was no excuse for the contempt with which she'd spit out Joyce's name at church, or when she visited the school to speak to her headmistress. At the dinner table, if her brother had a question, she would say, 'Well, don't be asking *Joyce*. You'll never get a true word out of her mouth. It's just her nature.' Day by day, Aunt Helen had done everything she could to raise a cordon in between them. She'd finagled her way into every aspect of his life and tried to elbow Joyce away – but Joyce hadn't surrendered.

When she'd been expelled from school a second time (for nothing more than wheeling round the village on her English teacher's bike and bending up the handlebars), her aunty had got holier-than-thou and forced her to find daytime work and take up evening classes till she finished her diploma. Nobody would hire her locally, which had made her sour about the place. The registration for the night school had been sorted, but she'd only shown up once. A short while after that, the next-door neighbours had come knocking with their accusations about missing pearls, and Aunty Helen took their side. 'I'm telling you, if you don't give that necklace back before the day is out, you're going to have to find another place to live. I mean *tomorrow*, you'll be on your ear. I wish I knew what made you do it, Joyce. Am I not good to you? I really thought that I was doing right, putting a roof over your head. But this is all the thanks I get for it . . .' Well, those pearls weren't worth as much as she'd expected, but they'd covered room and board in

Maidstone for a week or two. Then E. H. Lacey's hired her and she'd started saving what she could for a deposit on a flat.

After that first meeting in the alley, it had taken Mal another week to pay a visit to the shop. As brazen as you like, he'd stepped up to the counter with a ladies' raincoat folded in his hands, the tag still on it. 'Nice to see your face again,' he'd said, his voice gone plummy. 'Would you kindly wrap this up for me, all neat and tidy?' She'd made a gesture to her mouth to let him know she wasn't meant to speak to customers. Then her supervisor had come over, saying, 'Excuse me, sir, you need to pay for that before it can be wrapped.'

'Oh, really. Where's the fun in that?' he'd said.

'Well, I don't – I'm not sure I understand, sir.'

Joyce had beamed at him. Her supervisor had gone pale.

'Never mind,' he'd said. 'It's not my colour, anyway. I'll leave it.'

'I believe it comes in navy, too. And powder blue . . .'

'No, it's fine. I'll put it back.' He'd pointed through the entrance doors, towards the street outside. 'My car's parked there, you see – that nice green Morris – and I think I left the handbrake off.' He'd been looking at her supervisor all the while, but Joyce had got the message. 'Have a pleasant afternoon. I know I'm going to.'

She'd left it ten or fifteen minutes – maybe even less than that – before she'd asked to be excused so she could use the ladies. Slipping out the service door and round the back, there'd been a fizz of energy inside her, knowing she was risking everything. But there'd been no real thought of backing out. The Morris had still been there, parked over the road, and she'd hurried down the street to knock upon the window.

Mal had hardly blinked. 'It's open, girl,' he'd said, and she'd climbed in. 'I'm glad you came.'

'I shouldn't have.'

'My mother used to say that when she'd eaten too much cake. It never stopped her baking, though.' He'd clutched her fingertips and pecked her on the hand. 'I'm Mal.' His beard was softer than she'd guessed it would be. 'And what should I call *you*?'

'I'm Joyce. But Joy will do.' She'd seen a roadmap folded on the dashboard, with a circle drawn beside the crease. 'Where we going?'

'Anywhere you fancy.'

'Anywhere?'

He'd turned the engine on. 'The weather's holding. Sun might just come out eventually. Let's make the most of it. A picnic, or a nice walk on the beach.'

'Well, I've always meant to see the zoo but never had the chance.'

'The zoo it is, then. Hold on tight.'

She'd talked in nervous bursts the whole way there, watching as he'd steered with a loose grip upon the wheel, an elbow on the door ledge. By the time they'd reached the car park, Mal knew all about her aunty and the neighbours and the stolen pearls; they'd even broached the subject of the bombs that landed on her parents' house, and he'd told half a story of his service as an army cook in Borneo. At the zoo, he'd paid for everything – the tickets, two big helpings of ice cream, the picture she'd had taken riding the stuffed lion, which was really meant to be for kiddies only but he'd slipped a few bob in the pocket of the old photographer. Once they'd seen most of the animals and had some fish and chips in the canteen, the rain had started teeming, so they'd walked back to the car.

'Well, you can cross it off your list now, can't you?' Mal had said. 'To think you could've wasted a whole day at work instead of having fun with me and all the animals.'

There was no doubt it had been a happy, carefree afternoon,

and it had given her a flavour of what life with Mal could be like, always: no responsibility to anyone besides themselves. But then, on the drive home, she'd thought about her brother, wondering what he'd have made of all those strange hyenas, leopards, kangaroos and talking parrots. She'd imagined the expression of amazement on his face and felt a sad detachment from him. Recovering the photo from her bag, she'd seen her silly image: a giant, grinning jockey on the back of a dead lion. What a picture! Maybe she could send it off to Charlie so the lad could have a proper laugh at her expense.

'You've gone quiet,' Mal had said. 'What happened to that smile, eh?'

'Just been thinking.'

'What about?'

'Tomorrow. Have to find another job now, don't I?'

He'd turned his head to frown at her. 'And here's me thinking that I'd taught you something.' The car had slowed down, coming to a standstill on the muddy apron of the road. They'd sat there for a moment with the engine idling and traffic smudging past Mal's head. He'd gazed out of the rainy windscreen, saying, 'Now or never, Joy. It's either you go back to living like the ordinary folk, standing at a counter till your feet are sore and saving up your pennies for a pretty dress from Kay's at Christmas time. Or else –' He'd put his hand upon her shoulder. 'Or else, you'll follow my advice and sod the lot of 'em. Look at me, I'm serious. I've never had a debt I couldn't settle in my life. There's money to be made a thousand times a day, as long as you've got eyes for it, and I don't mind partaking – *you* know what I'm saying. Like you stole those pearls and pawned them when you needed to. That's called being sharper than the rest, if you ask me. No matter what they try and drum into your head at school about what's wrong and right. I learned that quick in Borneo: look after number one, 'cause no one else is going to do it, and regrets go with you to the grave. That's why, in the morning, all you've got to do is have a long lie-in and listen to the wireless. Malcolm's orders.'

She'd allowed his hand to travel to her forearm. 'Oh yeah?' she'd said, giving him the smile that he'd been wanting. 'Then what? You'll probably meet some lady and get married, and it's goodbye, Joyce, good luck.'

He'd scrunched his face up. 'Christ almighty, I've no interest in all that. Were you not listening?'

'No, I was, but I don't think I've got a choice. I'm not like you.'

'Of course you are. You wouldn't be here if you weren't.'

She'd wanted to object, but didn't know how best to word it.

'Listen, I've got something going, if you're interested,' he'd said. 'It'll only take an hour, but it'll pay you well. And you're the perfect woman for the job.'

'I don't know, Mal. I'll just get the paper, have a look what's doing. Must be something out there.'

'Trust me, it's the easiest few quid you'll ever make with all your clothes on.' He'd put the Morris into gear and edged them back on to the road. 'Where d'you want to be dropped off? I've got to get this car to someone in an hour or two.'

That was how it had begun. The speech he'd made had weakened her and then he'd kept on chiselling away. On the kerb outside her boarding house, he'd peered up at the building from the driver's seat and said, 'Well, this won't do you in the long run, will it? No, you're going to need a little flat to call your own. I know some people. Leave it with me.'

'Really?'

'Yeah, I'll sort you out.'

'You needn't go to any trouble, Mal. I'm comfortable enough.'

'No trouble whatsoever.' He'd licked the corner of his

mouth. 'I was hoping to drop by again tomorrow evening. How's that sound to you?'

'All right.'

'I'll have a different motor. Listen for the horn. Round sevenish?'

'Yeah, fine.'

'Let's have it, then,' he'd said, and pointed to the fleshy section of his cheek. It hadn't felt polite to turn him down. She'd leaned across and kissed him there. 'See you soon, girl.'

'Bye, Mal. Thanks for everything.'

He'd had her spinning like a pony on a carousel from the beginning, and she hadn't even heard the music playing.

*

Now there was a dial tone bleating in the earpiece. She slammed the phone down on its cradle, wishing the entire booth would sink into the ground and swallow her for ever. Through the misty glass, she checked for movement in the doorway of the post office, but no one came. The shudders hadn't faded, so she got her ciggies out and lit one. She stuffed the headscarf up her sleeve again and went outside.

Coming back down Alms Heath, worries landed in her mind like birds; she had to think of an old song to make them disappear. *By the old mill stream I'm dreaming, Nellie Dean* . . . It was something that her mother used to sing to help her fall asleep, to calm her if she knocked her head upon a table's edge, or if her brother woke up wailing in the night. *Dreaming of your bright eyes gleaming, Nellie Dean* . . . And she couldn't separate her mother's voice from the sweet melody, which quieted her mind enough for her to carry on and do what needed doing. *As they used to fondly glow, when we sat there long ago* . . . She dumped her cigarette, unlatched the gate. The wind swelled, wetting her eyes. Twenty paces up the drive, there was a thin division in the hedge for her to cut through. *Listening to the waters flow, Nellie Dean* . . .

She veered off when she got there, hurdling the verges of the track and pushing through the spindly arms of shrubs. Deeper in the copse, the ground was soft and padded with damp leaves. A little further on, there was a tree with pale grey bark – a hornbeam was the name for it, or so Mal claimed. It had a mighty trunk that twisted up into a whirligig of branches. At its base, there was a good-sized rock the shape of a clenched fist. She crouched and tilted it, watching as the woodlice scuttled in the flat space underneath. Then she dug, scooping up the cold earth till her fingers met the edge of something.

The first three parcels she'd collected had the same light feeling in her hand. They'd been round, like tubs of Pond's cream, sealed up tight with loops of packing tape. When she'd shaken them, they'd made no sound at all. But this one was much different – thinner, longer, and it rattled. It was bundled in a square of shammy, tied with string. The way it was presented – just a loose knot to untangle – must've been some kind of test of her devotion. Mal was tempting her to open it. With nobody around to check on her, she couldn't stop herself.

The string unravelled easily. The shammy flopped apart. There was a jeweller's box inside, the sort a bracelet comes in or a lady's watch. It was banded round the middle with brown tape – not so much she couldn't slice it open, but she'd have to use the nail scissors in her room to make a proper job of it. She bundled it all up again and shoved it in her pocket, filled the hole in, put the rock back where she'd found it. Off she went, through all the leaves and briar, until she found the driveway.

Her mother's song escaped her now – she'd lost the next few verses. All that she could think about, as she came down the track towards the house, was how to keep her worries out of sight. The Mayhoods didn't know her well enough to notice when she took an extra breath before she spoke or when she failed to blink, but all these things were signals that her brother had tuned into down the years. It didn't help that Charlie was so curious about the world – every passing cloud, each crawling bug was fascinating to him in a way she couldn't fathom – and it was getting harder to distract him from the truth. When he was little, she could call him names, pick fights with him about all kinds of nonsense; and, if that didn't work, she'd pinch him underneath the ribs until he squealed and ran off, crying to their aunty. But he was a man now, full of questions all the time. Some day soon, he'd wise up to the lies that he'd been fed: *No, mouse, I'm telling you, I haven't seen him. Just how stupid do you think I am? I haven't heard a thing. I only hope to God he's fallen off a cliff somewhere and no one ever finds him. And I hope that it was long and painful at the end. Is that all right with you?*

*

She'd written back to Mal because she was afraid of what he'd do if she ignored him. In his mind, there was no difference between silence and a snub. So she'd begged a sheet of paper from a prefect and begun exchanging letters. Once a month, at first, reporting things that happened in her days, small wonderings she'd had about the future. Then every fortnight, with her vague apologies for disappointing him and making his life difficult with her mistakes. He'd written back with: *You can make it up to me when you get out.* And: *You can square it with me soon.* Those days of zoos and ice-cream cones were long gone, but she'd carried on believing that they meant something. In borstal, she'd returned to the idea that what she had with Mal was special, a relationship too individual for anyone but them to understand.

Over time, he'd put the squeeze on her, determined where she went, and what she did, and who she was allowed to have a conversation with. It had started with that night he came to beep his horn outside her window. Two minutes after seven, as he'd promised. In a blue Ford Anglia, from which he'd given a salute as she'd walked up the path. His hair had been combed flat. He'd worn a shirt and tie, a nice grey pullover. 'Here,' he'd said, once they'd begun to drive. 'You'll need to put this on.' He'd reached to the back seat and handed her a blazer – it was tweed with elbow patches, just the sort her aunty would've gone to church in. When she'd slipped it on, she'd found two little bags of lavender inside the pockets.

'Why've I got to wear this ugly thing?' she'd said, dumping the bags in the footwell.

'Because. It's all about the first impression. How you let folk read you. Some jobs, it's important. Others, not at all. Tonight, it is.'

'I thought you were taking me somewhere.'

'I am.'

'I meant the pictures or a show. I didn't think the job would be *tonight*.'

'Well, it's not my fault if you forgot. We talked about it, didn't we?'

'Yeah, I know, but –'

'It looks good on you. The jacket.'

'It's a blazer.'

'Doesn't matter what it's called, as long as it looks right.' He'd wound the window down, clearing his throat and spitting on the tarmacadam. The air was cold and blasting. 'Let me tell you how we're going to play it. If you're still not clear on anything, you'd better ask me now, before we get there. Understand? It won't be in-and-out tonight, but it'll be a simple one if you keep up your end of it.'

She'd been surprised how simple it had been, in fact.

They'd driven a few miles to Chatham and arrived outside the gate of a three-storey house close to the cemetery. Stained-glass panels glowing blue and red around the doorway. Leaded windows and a tall brick chimney. Lush and tidy lawns. A vision. 'Remember now,' he'd told her, 'be as loud and tuneless as you can. The more noise you can make for me in there, the better.' She'd followed Mal along the path as he'd gone up to ring the bell. Just as he'd described it, the old widow had come out to let them in. Mal had made the introductions in the hall-way: 'Mrs Abner, here's the girl I mentioned on the phone – my cousin Sadie. I hope that you can work your magic on her. She needs a boost of confidence before we let her join the choir.'

The old widow had invited them into the living room, where the grand piano stood. It was a daunting space, but elegant, lit by an arrangement of tall lamps. 'Come and stand here at the mirror, Sadie,' the old lady had instructed her. 'Before you sing a note, I should like to see how you are breathing – and I should also like you to observe yourself. Most beginners sing from *here*, in the throat. The first good habit to acquire is how to sing from *here*, the diaphragm.' Well, that poor widow hadn't known how bad a song could sound until that night.

As soon as Mrs Abner had sat down at the piano, Mal had said, 'You're in the best of hands now, Sadie. Pick you up at eight fifteen. Be good.' Mrs Abner had begun to move. 'No, please don't get up, dear – no need to show me out,' he'd told her. His plan had been to leave the night-latch open on his way outside. 'There's a little nib you press to stop it closing,' he'd explained to her ahead of time. 'It's as if they *want* you walking in and taking everything.' So that's how it had gone. He'd strolled back to the car and made a show of driving off, flash-ing the headlights through the window. Her singing lesson had continued. Tone-deaf Sadie had got worse and worse – it hadn't taken any effort to act out her part. She'd whined her way through 'Bread of Heaven' and 'Jerusalem' for half an hour, as loud as she could manage. The widow had grown more and more exasperated, but she'd stayed at the piano. Meanwhile, Mal had parked the car around the block, crept back into the house and rummaged in her study for the treasure he was after. At eight fifteen, he'd rung the door bell. Mrs Abner had sprung up and said, 'Oh, what a shame. We'd only just begun . . .' There'd hardly been a wrinkle of concern in Mal's expression as he'd forked out twelve and six on to the widow's palm and said goodnight – he'd even waved to the old lady from the car before they'd driven off. 'Sadie, my dear girl,' he'd said, through smiling teeth, 'that went like bloomin' clockwork.' As soon as they were on the road and out of sight, he'd shared the take with her. 'First prize,' he'd said, dangling a set of keys above the dash. There was a massive chunk of cork attached to them by wire.

'Next time, you can pay me twelve and six instead,' she'd said. 'It wasn't worth it.'

'Shows what you know.' He'd snatched them from her grip. 'They're for a cuddy boat. Her old man's pride and joy, or so they tell me. It's not left its moorings since he croaked.'

'So *who* tells you?'

'Folk I know.' He'd tapped his nose. 'Loose lips sink ships.'

'Well, how much do you think it's worth?'

'Enough that we can put our feet up for a while. As soon as I can get the thing upriver, anyway.' He'd reached across to squeeze her hand and she'd squeezed back. 'Don't tell me that you didn't get a little thrill from all of this. The blood is pumping, isn't it? You've got a flutter in your heart, I know it. You're a natural.'

'I suppose it was all right.'

When a job had gone to plan, small flickers of Mal Duggan's

kindness would show through. His mood would sweeten for the next few days and she'd feel lifted by him. 'There she is,' he'd say, when she'd approach him from across the room, 'my young accomplice.' There'd be compliments on her appearance – 'Got to say, Joy, you don't half look gorgeous with your hair done that way' – and praise for her abilities. He'd rabbit on about how different she was from all the older women in his life, who'd only wanted to get married quick and fill the house with babies and complain about their figures. How much fun she was to be around compared to them. How much he relied on her. 'I swear, it's like we see the world with the same eyes,' he'd say. 'A proper understanding, you and me have got, Joy, don't we?' True affection wasn't in his nature, but she could take these little things he said and make them fill the empty space.

His good intentions, when he showed them, always had a faulty seam, like every knock-off pair of stockings that she'd ever bought. The flat he'd 'sorted out' for her on Kingsley Road had been her first real measure of this fact. On the afternoon they'd gone to look at it, the skinny tenant who was living there had answered in his tatty woollen vest – there'd been a yellow swelling round his eye, a sling over his elbow, and he'd cowered at the sight of them: 'Oh heck. I'm sorry, Mal, I hope you've not been waiting long. I didn't hear a knock – my ear's been giving me some gyp.' She should've read her fortune in that man's behaviour. Instead, she'd moved into his flat, repainted all the walls and skirting boards, and thought she'd scrubbed him out of memory. She'd been very pleased when Mal had driven over with a vanload of good furniture he claimed was second-hand, and she'd arranged those new belongings with a sense of pride in her adulthood. Before they'd lugged it up the stairs, she'd never known that such a thing existed as a pull-out sofa bed, but it became a fixture in her life. With every gift like this that she accepted, she was deepening her debt. In time, the noises of that sofa bed would turn her stomach.

There were skills she'd learned from him that she would not forget – in that sense, he achieved more than her teachers ever could. Except when Mal passed down his knowledge, it was always with a view towards the benefits. So yes, he might've shown her how to drive by doing circuits in an empty car park till the wheels stopped bouncing; and he might've introduced her to the game of euchre and explained its strategies; and he might've given her a rundown of the boxing moves he'd picked up in the army; but his real purpose would be borne out later and seem accidental. That's how she became the driver on his so-called 'missions', scouting hotels in the country, sitting lookout for him, ferrying him home in darkness. That's how he prepared her for those Thursday nights down at the pub with factory women, cheating them at euchre for 'a bit of petrol money'. That's how he persuaded her to keep on practising her jab-jab-cross and other combinations while he pressed his crotch against her from behind and held her arms. She'd had no possible excuse to shut the door when he appeared one night in the small hours, saying he'd be sleeping on the pull-out for a while until a 'little disagreement' with his landlord had blown over. And once she'd let him in, he'd taken up residence.

Mal Duggan wasn't dim: he'd waited a long while before he'd laid a hand on her. First of all, he'd got her used to staying up past midnight with him, swigging from his Pusser's bottle, listening to jazz band records on the radiogram he'd brought in on her birthday saying, 'Nightio, my girl,' as she'd gone off to sleep in her own room. Then he'd made sure she invited Charlie for his visits, so her brother would take up her bed and she would have to share the pull-out. Two weekends had passed without a touch; they'd both slept fully clothed, with towels and a dressing gown rolled up between them. On the third, she'd had a head full of Jamaica rum, and felt the mattress shift, his fingers drawing up her skirt. 'Shhh, don't wake the lad,' he'd told her. 'I'll be gentle.' And he'd climbed on top of her and peeled her knickers off.

'No, Mal, please.'

'We're in the same bed, aren't we? And we like each other.'

'Please don't.'

'What are you, expecting to be married first?'

'No, I just –'

'Come on, I see the way you look at me. It's not fair acting coy about it now.'

She hadn't wanted it to happen this way, but she was bleary with the drink and couldn't get her thoughts in a straight line. 'Please just take it out before you –'

'I'm not even going to put it in you. Stay there, on your front.' For a long, strange moment, he'd just knelt behind her, tugging at himself until he'd spilled over her rear. Then he'd gone to fetch the dirty tea towel from the oven door to wipe her off, and that was it. 'No danger this way, is there?' he'd said. Nearly every night thereafter, they'd enacted this routine, apart from when she'd put him in her hand so he would finish sooner. She'd become so used to it that she would put a clean white flannel underneath her pillow when she made the bed up of an evening, and a pot of Vaseline.

*

She was thinking of this now, the shame of it, as she approached the north field in the wind. From this end of the yard, the buds of rye looked greener in the light, which she assumed to be a sign of their good health – it wasn't much, but she was glad of it. The parcel's edge was sticking out of her coat pocket. Before she left the yard, she took the chance to tuck it in the waistband of her trousers, hiding it beneath the tails of her blouse. She wiped her mucky fingers on the grass. No sooner had she hung her coat up in the hallway, she heard footsteps coming down the stairs. 'I hate to rush you, Joyce, but we've got plenty to be getting on with . . .' It was Mr Mayhood, passing through. His eyes were on the pages of a ledger, which was resting in his hand the way a vicar holds a Bible.

'Won't be long,' she said. 'I stepped right in a puddle, so I'd better change my trousers.'

'Well, go on – be quick.' He went off with the ledger, calling back, 'Your brother's at his desk already.'

She managed to get straight up to her room and shut the door. The only hiding place that she could think of was inside the lining of her suitcase. She'd tried to fit the other parcels in it, weeks ago, but they'd made too big a bulge. The case was stowed above her wardrobe. Its silky fabric had gone baggy underneath the lid and she'd already worked a hole into the pouch on the outside. When she slid the parcel in, it sank down well enough that nobody would see its shape. She was halfway out the door before she realized she hadn't changed her trousers and she had to pull a crumpled pair out of the laundry basket.

If she'd had a bit of foresight, she'd have thought to build a false back in a cabinet or a panel she could slide out of a drawer. But when she'd made the plans to renovate her bedroom, back in August, she hadn't known what would be needed. Instead, she'd had a vision of a dressing table with a nice round mirror and a green felt pad to put her hairbrush on – she'd drawn a sketch and Mr Mayhood had been helping her to make it ever since. He'd shown her how to use the lathe out in the shed to turn the legs, which she'd enjoyed a lot. Even Charlie had pitched in, sanding down the tabletop and hack-sawing a dove-tail joint or two. It was mostly done now, clamped in pieces on the workbench while they waited for the glue to set. She could see herself becoming skilled in making furniture – as in really taking time to get the measure of the tools. For now, the only thing she dreamed of making was a tall wood box to put Mal Duggan in the ground.

In the draughting room, she found the Mayhoods and her brother standing by the window, sipping coffee. They were in the throes of conversation – about what, she couldn't tell. Mr Mayhood was saying, 'If it's eight by eight, we'll save a fraction on materials. But, in time, I think we'll need more space than that. He always took a long old view on things, did Hollis, and I still can't disagree with him. What do you think, Charlie? Do we stick to ten by ten?'

'All the same to me.' Her brother heard her close the door and craned his head in her direction. 'But maybe having extra room makes sense. I mean, there's nothing lost by keeping it half-empty for a while.'

'Yes, good lad. You're seeing it right.'

When she went to stand with them, she saw that Charlie's careful drawings for the root cellar had been laid out on the plan chest.

'Nice of you to join us,' Florence said. 'We're just consulting on dimensions. For the final time, I hope.'

'You're late again,' her brother said.

She whispered, 'Women's trouble. Shush.'

Mr Mayhood was still pondering his answer. 'All right, then, decision made. Let's stick with ten by ten. I'll take on more surveying work if need be, to offset the costs.'

'Good. I'll phone the fellow with the digger. You never know, he mightn't charge us much. I'd like to start the ground-work in a day or so.' Florence lifted up the drawing and was carrying it away towards her desk when Mr Mayhood stopped her. 'Hold on. We should have him do a negative of that, I think,' he said. 'The lad could use the practice.'

'Right you are.' She went and placed it next to Charlie's board instead.

'You'll need to watch this, Joyce, for future reference.' Mr Mayhood clicked his fingers, pointing at the plan chest. 'There's good tracing paper in the bottom drawer, there. Standard size.'

As her brother took it over to his desk, it made a pleasant, rippling sound. He was told to stick it carefully on to his board and smooth it flat. 'The lazy draughtsman would trace over the original. I always say it's better to redraw. That way, you can spot mistakes before they cost you anything. If you want to, you can borrow my good pens to ink it later on.'

'You mean he's got to do it all again from scratch?' She went and slapped her brother in between the shoulder blades. 'Ha ha. Unlucky, mouse.'

'I don't mind,' her brother said. 'I've got to learn this stuff.'

Mr Mayhood took the last slurp of his coffee. 'Well, be glad it's just a root cellar. Wait until you're doing masters for a concert hall. You'll want to delegate the task to some assistants of your own. Now, here we go – let's get a north point on it and a scale . . .'

She was relieved to stand behind her brother for a while, doing nothing except watching him put lines precisely on a sheet, clicking the mechanics of his pencil when his lead wore down. He had powers of concentration that she wasn't born with. He made the job of draughting look as simple as a sneeze. Every mark he put down seemed to slide like butter on the surface of the tracing paper – it was gentle, measured and exact – and his skilfulness brought out approving nods from Mr Mayhood, who kept lifting his specs up and down to study what was forming. It wasn't long before the ground plan was drawn out and he was starting on the elevations. Mr Mayhood took a breath and said, 'Keep going, Charlie. Looking good,' and walked off to his table.

If she'd had only a quarter of the talent God had blessed her brother with, then maybe she'd have found it easier to see a brighter future coming for her, too. But she could barely muster any interest in the progress of her work, because she knew – no matter how much effort she put into it – she'd never meet the standards of a real architect. At the moment, she was coasting on the Mayhoods' faith and patience. 'Don't get flustered. You'll soon get the knack – it's tricky,' Florence kept on saying. And, to his credit, Mr Mayhood might've been particular about the way he liked things done, but he hadn't once got angry at her clumsiness or irritated by her blunders. It was as though, to him, the signs of failure were like pimples on her face – a dreadful sight, but temporary.

He'd given her the greenhouse project to complete and she was doing what she could to satisfy him. Maybe, by his thinking, if she managed to produce a single line worth praising, it would feel like progress to them both. But even though it was a very basic structure – an even-span design that he'd sketched out for her with help from Mr Hollis – she couldn't get her mind to focus. Three different views were needed – front, side, rear – and drawing elevations was a fussy job, more like geometry than painting. Mr Mayhood had typed up a sheet of information to explain dimensions and materials. So, while her brother got on with the root cellar, she was left to make her drawings, slowly, with the constant sense that she was going backwards. She'd already burned her way through an eraser and a lump of India rubber. By now, the paper on her board looked grey and craggy.

When she turned her lamp on, there was nothing under the warm light she hadn't seen before – no impressive parts within the drawing that she might've undervalued. It was every bit as poor as it was yesterday. The shudders worsened as she sat down on her stool. She tried to lift her pencil, but her right hand shook so much she had to press her wrist against the table. The only thing that she could think to do was sit there with her eyes shut, letting it wash over her. This was all her fault for listening to Mal Duggan. She should've torn up every letter that he'd sent her.

Your not going about this right, the way I see it. In Borneo I had another private peel the spuds for me so I could get some kip. He did it for two packets a week at first and then just cos I told him to. Thats what you need. Another private who can do it for you.

She'd taken this advice because it offered hope, no matter how unpleasant.

The announcement of the borstal drawing competition had come directly from the governor. They'd all been herded into the association hall, where they'd stood in rank and file, arranged by houses. 'Now the boys' part of the contest has been won, the architects are looking to appoint –' There'd been sniggers from a few in line at hearing 'boys' part', and someone in the row behind had done a funny whistle. 'All right, settle down, behave . . . As I was saying, the architects are looking to appoint a pair of young apprentices: one boy, one girl. This means, in effect, a place has been reserved for someone in this room. So, even if you've never thought much of your drawing skills before, I hope you'll have a go – year on year, an Aylesbury girl discovers talents that she never knew she had before she got here. As for those in Mrs Graham's hobby hour, I trust that you're already thinking of your contributions . . .'

At first, she hadn't been remotely interested, and neither had the other girls in laundry party (some of them had even wondered if a woman was *allowed* to be an architect). Like most, she'd had a plan set in her mind for what to do when she got out, and she'd passed the long hours while she scrubbed and rinsed and hung up uniforms imagining the day they let her out.

She was going to borrow cash from Mal to buy herself a van and start up as a signpainter. Her grand idea was that she'd use her father's name, J. Savigear, and go round all the pubs and shops and restaurants in Gillingham with photos of the work he'd done as proof of her experience. Once she'd got established, they'd be comfortable again. Her brother would have better options then. Either he could stay with her until he got a decent job, or else he'd join her in the family business and they'd share a house until he found a girl to marry. She'd been practising her lettering in readiness, by writing her own name a thousand times in different styles on watercolour paper. It was such a solid plan that she'd begun to dream on the foundations of it, seeing the nice two-up two-down they'd buy eventually, around the corner from the graveyard where her parents were at rest, and the sleek white van emblazoned with J. SAVIGEAR & CO. But then:

Dear Joy,

Are you all right? Did you not get my last few letters? You haven't answered for a bit. So if your letters cross with this one, sorry, but I couldn't wait to tell you my good news.

There's been a drawing competition going on here for the past few months. Not just for lads at Huntercombe but all the other borstals too. At any rate we had to make a sketch of either an entire building or just a little piece of one in detail. I chose to do two different kinds with a bridge to join them up. I don't know why. I thought it would be something different. Anyway the first one that I drew was of the chapel I can see from out my window, except I made it look as if a bomb had hit it! Then I did another building right out of my head. I wanted it to look like something from 100 years off in the future.

Well, they must have really liked it after all because today I heard from my housemaster that I've only gone and won it! And wait until

*you hear the best part of it. First prize is an apprenticeship. It's with
a proper firm of architects. So once I've done my time in here they're
going to put me up in digs with them in Surrey where they work and
guess what else? They'll even pay me. A pound and fifteen shillings a
week! And that's supposed to go up every year, if I . . .*

His excitement had spread on to three more pages.

After this, the modest plans she'd made seemed more like
obstacles to Charlie's progress. She was thrilled for him, and
wrote back saying so; but it had crept in slowly, the despair of
what she'd do without him. If she didn't have her brother to
look after on the outside, she'd have no ground beneath her
feet, no sense of purpose or direction. She'd end up thieving,
back in borstal as a revoke, time and time again. Her prospects
would amount to nil. The only signs she'd get to paint would
be the ones she daubed on bits of cardboard saying, SPARE
CHANGE PLEASE and HOMELESS HELP ME. So, the next time she
heard Mrs Graham asking other girls in hobby hour about
their competition pieces, she'd raised her hand and said, 'Am I
too late to enter something, miss?'

She'd tried to win it fairly. Every minute that she'd had to
spare – before lights out, before the morning call to the parade
ground – she'd drawn and drawn. But the pictures that she'd
made had no sophistication. All her buildings had the look of
gingerbread. She couldn't get her roof to slant away into the
distance at the proper angle, or space her windows evenly as
they got smaller. Her big mistake was telling Mal of her frus-
trations in a letter, thinking he would write back with a dose of
bluster to inspire her confidence. Instead, he'd given her a
cheat's solution.

There was a girl in laundry party, Irma Dale, who was shy
and thin and looked no older than eleven, and Joyce had always
tried to stop the mouthy bunch from North House giving her

more aggravation than was fair. Of all the things to get in trouble over, Irma had been nicked for throwing rocks at her school's window, which she reckoned someone else had smashed before she even got there. They'd done hobby hour together for a week or two, long enough for Joyce to see she had a way of getting details in a watercolour no one else could paint – tiny broken branches in the treetops, balls of mistletoe and drifting puffs of clouds on the horizon. But Irma had swapped into rug-making with Mrs Frost quite early on – there was some logic to it, as her father ran a carpet shop in Manchester and she was keen on being more useful to him after she got out. As far as Joyce could tell, the girl had no designs on entering the competition, anyway. It hadn't been too difficult to start a conversation with her: 'Oi, Irma, what d'you think's best – Gold Flake or Player's?' They'd been side by side at the long basin in the scullery, soaking uniforms in soapy water.

'Don't mind, really. Capstans, if I had to pick.'

'Too weak for me.'

'I like the flavour. Why? You got some?'

'No, but I can get them,' she'd said, shifting closer, 'if you want.'

Irma had chewed on her lip. 'I gave them up for Lent.'

'Yeah, me too. I do it every year.' She'd smirked, dunking another uniform below the suds. 'How many rugs have you lot made with Mrs Frost so far, then?'

'One. A small one. And it wrecked my fingers. Wool burns something awful when you feed it through the loom.'

'Is she all right with you?'

'Yeah, she's nice. We like her.'

'Sounds like you're not coming back to watercolours, then.'

'Don't have a choice. My dad says it's a waste of time.'

'Well, no one's going to pay for any pictures I make, that's for sure.' Feeling Irma's stance begin to soften, she'd hurried on: 'A shame for you to give it up, though. With the eye you've got for it. Those sketches that you used to do – well, Mrs Graham used to sing your praises, didn't she? You'd win that drawing competition easy.'

'I dunno.' Irma had looked up, her hands still plunging in the soapy water. 'I'm not fussed about it, really. There's a good job waiting once I'm out of here. And if I let my dad down this time, he'll be finished with me.'

'Do you think that you could teach me? How to draw well?' If she'd had a mirror to reflect her own expression in that moment, she would probably have seen how much it owed to Mal – that varnish of pure innocence, that gently bended brow.

'Suppose I could.' Irma's voice had been a little pained. The sting of the detergent gave their hands a sunburnt feeling after a few hours. 'How many ciggies would I get for it?'

'As many as you like – I know a girl. They're Gold Flakes, mind.'

'They'll do for me.'

For most of that November week, they'd spent their meagre recreation time together in the library. She'd put the thought in Irma's head – 'Why don't you draw a version of your own, while I do mine? Then you can sort of guide me through it' – and the rest had been a matter of persuasion. On the Religion shelf, she'd found a book with glossy photographs of British churches and one had caught her interest. It had showed only a corner of a building. Viewed from an angle. Great stone arms sloping down from the walls like banister rails. *Flying buttresses at Lincoln Cathedral*, said the caption. She'd given it to Irma, who'd begun to sketch it, whispering instructions about which line to put where, and how to sweep the pencil to create the perfect arc, and saying after, 'Your turn, Joy. Come on.' Day by day, their sketches had developed – one so stylish and pristine they could've hung it in a gallery, the other so unbalanced it was hardly recognizable as the same building. 'You should be proud of it. I would be,' Irma had insisted. 'I reckon you've as good a chance as anybody else.' The library had been closing for the day. A screw had shuffled over from the doorway, warning them that they'd be late for cleaning duty if they didn't quicken up the pace.

'Well, I never would've got this far without you. Thanks for all your help.' She'd packed her drawing into the big envelope that Mrs Graham had given her.

'I didn't do much. Thanks for all the *you know whats*. I'm trying to make them last.' Irma had begun to scroll her paper up.

'You going to give that to your dad?'

'Nah. He wouldn't want it.'

'When's he visiting again?'

'Not really sure.'

'I'll buy it off you, then.'

'Shut up.'

She'd placed her hand on Irma's. There were certain habits she'd acquired that she no longer recognized for what they were: plain trickery. 'Honestly, I'd give you a few bob for it. I've nothing on my wall to look at. It'd cheer me up, to see that every day.'

'*Dale!*' the screw had called. 'Ten seconds. Get a move on.'

'You're on,' Irma had told her, letting the paper unravel on the table.

'I'll owe it you.'

'Suits me.'

The screw had clapped. 'That means you, too, Savigear! Stop the nattering.'

'We're coming, sir!' She'd slipped the picture in her envelope and hurried off to stash it in her cubicle, below her bed. The next morning, after drills were over and the other girls were still emerging from the baths, she'd taken it along to the house-master's office. She'd filled her name out on the entry form and watched as it was paper-clipped to Irma's drawing and slotted into a thick folder. Ever since that day, she'd been expecting somebody to grab her by the elbow and escort her down to solitary – but no one came. And still she hadn't posted Irma Dale a penny.

'Are you all right, Joyce?' came a voice behind her now, subdued and kindly. It was Mr Mayhood, calling to her from his desk. 'You've been staring at your board there for a good few minutes. Is your pencil broken?'

'No, I just – my stomach is a bit upset,' she said. 'I'll be OK.'

'Hope I didn't undercook those eggs this morning.'

'I don't think so.'

Mr Mayhood wandered over. 'If you're not feeling well, perhaps you'd better go and lie down for a bit.'

'I need to get these drawings done for you.'

'Well, speaking as your client, I reckon they can wait a day or two.'

'I'll be all right,' she said, but when she moved her arm up to the board, it shook again.

'You're shivering,' he said. 'You must've caught a bug.'

Florence was approaching now, her face creased with concern. 'You *do* look pale. I'll make some honey lemon. Nice and warming – soothes the stomach, too. Go over by the fire and put your feet up.'

'Look, if neither of you mind,' she said, 'I might just go up to my room.'

'Please,' said Mr Mayhood. 'Rest.'

As she stood up, blinking, sighing, putting on the poorly act, she noticed that her brother hadn't moved from his position at the draughting board. He was peering over his shoulder with his mouth all pursed and cornered, as if sucking on a mint. But as soon as their eyes met, he turned away, picked up a set square from the tabletop and carried on his drawing.

'I'll bring you up that honey lemon,' Florence said.

'Thanks, miss. Kind of you.' She went upstairs and kicked her shoes off, put a second jumper on, although she wasn't cold. For appearances, she scruffed the counterpane and pressed a head-sized dint into her pillow. There was no chance she could keep this up for ever. Once or twice play-acting illness was a good solution, but any more than that and it became suspicious.

After a short while, there was a knock. 'May I come in?'

'It's open.'

Florence had a cup and saucer in her hand. She stepped in, timidly. 'Make sure to let it cool a bit before you drink it, eh? Don't want you burned as well as sick. I'll leave it here.' But once she'd placed it on the ottoman, she hovered at the window. Arms crossed, with her pretty freckled head sloped to the side. 'Listen, if you've got your monthly, I can bring you a hot-water bottle.'

'It's not that. I'm just a bit under the weather. Don't know why.'

'Well, I should probably take your temperature, then.'

'No, I'll be fine.'

'What about more blankets?'

'No, miss. This is too much fuss already.'

'You're right. It's peace and quiet you'll be needing.' This caring manner Florence had was sweet but inconvenient. It wasn't mothering, though it was something similar. 'Keep warm. We'll see you later on – for lunch maybe?'

'I think so, yeah.'

'Do you want this closed or open?'

'Closed, miss.'

'All right. Get well soon.'

'I'll try.'

The door clacked shut. She listened for the noise of foot-steps treading down the stairs. When she was sure she wouldn't be disturbed, she dumped her extra jumper on the bed. The fragrance of the honey lemon was so strong and sharp it made her want to retch. It had the tang of borstal disinfectant. She opened up her window sash and threw the contents of the cup as far as she could make them go. After a few breaths of air, the trembling in her arms began to ease a bit.

She rummaged in the top drawer of her little cabinet and found her nail scissors. It took her a few tries to jimmy out the parcel from the suitcase, as it snagged on something deep within the lining, but eventually she had it in her hands. When it was stripped of all its string and shammy and put flat upon her desk, it looked stranger than she'd realized. Grubby at the edges. Damp. The flimsy seal of tape already peeling. An earth and iron smell. It wasn't right. She put the scissor blades up to the tape, but something stopped her pushing.

D'you really think I've not gone down and done a recce, Joy? A nice big farmhouse they've got there. Access front and back. Huge master bedroom on the top floor, office on the ground. A fancy living room. No dog to bother you when you get close – it's odd, that, for a house out in the sticks. They usually keep a dog, but all they've got is hens . . .

Fourteen days was all she'd had. Fourteen unspoiled days in Ockham with her brother, thinking that she'd finally stumbled into some good fortune. The supervising officer had been over to the house to check how they were settling in, running through his questions, making her aware of her responsibilities to herself, her brother and the Mayhoods. He had a briefcase full of forms and always wore the same grey suit. He'd warned her of the penalties for breaking her probation terms and ram-bled on at her like they were best of chums. 'You're lucky that you've got a stable base here,' he had told her. 'People who believe in you, who'll help you get your life on track again.' And it was true – those fourteen days, she'd been in clover.

But on her second Friday, she'd received her first wage packet. Quite the thrill, to open up that little envelope and see the cash inside – for doing what? Cooking a few meals and drawing a few wonky pictures? Not the easiest money of her life, but close. Next morning, after chores were done, she'd walked into the village with her brother. There'd been near enough two pounds inside her pocket and she'd had the notion that she'd squander some of it on things she'd craved the most in borstal: Player's, *Eagle* comics and either chocolate or the sort of toffee that'd make the paper bag go see-through, maybe some cold bottles of that fizzy yellow pop. Charlie had been less enthusiastic, saying, 'Don't you think that you should save it? I was thinking I'd ask Mr Mayhood if he'd hold most of it back – you know, ten bob a week in hand for spending, and the rest kept in the bank for when I need it.' But she'd batted that idea away: 'Do what you like with yours. I'm going to live a bit.'

In East Horsley, when they'd reached the quaint parade of shops, she'd been intent on going straight to the tobacconist's, but her brother wouldn't follow. 'I'll catch up with you later on,' he'd said. 'I'm going to take the bus to Guildford, see if I can get myself a library card.'

She'd rolled her eyes at him. 'Since when did you become so boring?'

'I dunno.' He'd dug her in the arm. 'Since I was born. But you go on. Enjoy your sweets and pop.'

'I bloody will.'

'Don't get yourself in any scrapes.'

'As if I would.'

'I mean it, Joy – I really like it here.'

'Who'd you think I'm going to bother? There's more sheep round here than people.'

'Yeah, and that's the trouble.'

'Leave it out.'

Her brother must've realized he'd stung her. 'Should we meet in a few hours, then?'

'No, thanks. I don't need your pity. I'll find a bench somewhere and read my comics.'

'Fine. I'll see you back at Leventree.'

'We're calling it that now, are we? *Leventree*.'

'Yeah. That's what it's called.'

She'd tried to wound him in return. 'Well, it didn't take you too long, did it? You'll be asking me to call you Charles before the year is out. And if you think I haven't noticed all your swooning over Florence, blimey – it's embarrassing.'

He'd looked away, towards the road, but she could see his neck was reddening. 'I'm going to the library now,' he'd said, and walked off, hands in pockets, to the bus stop. That was how he'd always ended disagreements with her, even when he was a littl'un. He'd just tell her calmly what he was about to do and then he'd do it. There was nobody more precious or infuriating to her.

Waiting in the queue at the tobacconist's, she'd studied the confectionery in the glass display. They'd had the toffee she liked best, with chips of hazelnuts in it, and there were so many varieties of chocolate – she hadn't known which way to use her ration up. When she'd heard the tinkle of the bell behind her, she'd thought nothing of it – just another customer arriving for his ten-a-day, no doubt. But then the old bloke paying at the till had carried off his things and the tobacconist had asked her what she wanted. 'A pound of treacle toffee and two packets of Player's,' someone else had answered for her. She'd spun round and there was Mal. Much fatter in the face and balder than he'd ever been, and still as badly groomed. He hadn't smiled or said hello. He'd only stood there.

The tobacconist had chided him. 'The lady was the first in line, I think.'

'Of course. I'll wait my turn,' came Mal's reply.

'Young lady? Is there something I can get you?'

It had rattled her so much she'd left with twenty Capstans and eight ounces of humbugs. She hadn't known where else to go but round the corner, in the opposite direction from the bus stop. But no sooner had she made it on to Kingston Avenue, he'd bounded after her. He'd matched her pace and got her by the sleeve. 'Follow me,' he'd told her. 'I've a car just up the way.'

'What are you doing here? You said you'd give me notice if you ever paid a visit . . .'

'It's right there, look. The blue one.'

'I'm not coming, Mal.'

'You are.' He'd twisted at the fabric. 'We've got things to talk about.'

'My brother's here. I'm meant to meet him.'

'No, you aren't. He's gone off to the library.'

She'd stopped. 'Have you been following me round?'

'Pipe down. I don't know why you're acting so surprised about it.' He'd steered her to the car, opened the door for her. 'Get in.'

'No.'

'Well, we can have the conversation in the open, if you want. But I don't think it's wise to be cavorting with the likes of me in plain view of the world now, is it? Seeing as you're on probation.'

There'd been a mess inside the car: balls of old chip papers on the seats and empty bottles cloudy with the residue of milk. The upholstery was ripped, the ceiling tarred and kippered by the owner's smoking. She'd made the big mistake of saying, 'Below your normal standards, this one.'

'Do yourself a favour, Joy,' he'd said, 'and shut your fucking trap.'

They'd driven all the way down Kingston Avenue until it turned to fields and hedges on both sides. He'd pulled into a shaded spot where there was no kerb, just a patch of stones and grass. In the quiet after he'd shut off the engine, she'd been able to make out the bleating of the sheep. He'd told her, 'I'm in twenty different kinds of trouble. You don't even realize the mess you and your brother got me into. I've been scrambling round just trying to keep folk satisfied since you were put away. So now it's time you paid me back.'

'I never got you into *anything*.'

'A lot was riding on that job. You ballsed it up. And more besides.'

'I did exactly what you told me to.'

'I don't remember telling you to get arrested.'

'Mal, the coppers *pulled us over*. They knew it wasn't mine.'

'You should've driven slower.'

'I never went above the limit for a second.'

'So you say. Five hundred quid you cost me. I was counting on that money.'

'At least I never grassed you up. I could've too.'

'You think that makes up for the grief you've caused me? Get your head out of your arse.' He'd twisted in his seat. Up close, the drying pimples by his mouth seemed more like coldsores. There was no part of his skin that didn't have a sheen of grease. 'If you ever want us to be square, you need to listen to me now. This can't go in one ear and out the other. No pissing about. You'll do exactly what I tell you, otherwise I'll have to *make* you do it. And I don't care what it takes. You hearing me?'

'Mal, come on.' She'd tried to sweeten him. 'I don't know what you're into, but it can't be worth this aggravation.'

He'd grabbed her by the wrist and throttled it. 'Are – you – fucking – *hearing* – me?'

'Yes, yes. Jesus Christ, I get it. *Ow.*'

He'd leaned back, then released her arm. For a time, he'd sat there, sucking air in through his teeth and huffing it back out. She'd forgotten this, how comfortable he was with cruelty, catching mice behind her kitchen skirting boards for sport and braining them with his enormous shoes. He'd said, 'I've got some gear I need you to look after. Not your normal thing. It's going to set me up for good – more money than I've ever made – but I can't have it on me any longer. You're going to take it off my hands for a few weeks. Or months. I don't know yet. I have to find a fence who'll take the gear.'

'What is it?'

'I'm not telling you.'

'All right. *Whose* is it?'

'You don't get to know that either.'

'God, Mal. What am I supposed to do with it?'

'Just stash it for me. Somewhere nobody will look. I'll have to give it you in bits. There's only so much I can move at once. They find me with it, I'm a goner.'

'This isn't sounding good to me.'

'I don't care how it sounds.' The sheep had gathered at the boundary to gaze at them. 'I've got a number you can reach me at. Remember it, then dump it. I don't want it getting passed around.' He'd riffled through the glovebox for a stubby pencil. Then he'd snatched a packet of the Capstans from her grip and started writing digits on the inside of the lid. 'Phone me in the morning. Eight o'clock. I'll have instructions for you. *Do not say your name.* Say something else that lets me know it's

172

you. Like, I don't know, *A lovely day out in the countryside*. If it's safe for me to speak, I will.'

'Is this a wind-up?'

'I don't know, Joy, have a look at me. What do you reckon?'

There'd been no lightness to his face at all. He'd seemed tired and raw and, maybe for the first time since she'd known him, beaten. It had set her heart to panicking. She'd tried protesting and it hadn't worked. So what else could she do but throw up a few crumbs of doubt and hope to God he swallowed them?

'And just how big is all this gear I'm meant to hide? I mean, there's hardly any space where I am now. I'm bunking with my brother. It's a tiny house and there are four of us – an old man comes to share our bath as well on Sundays. He's always got his eyes on what we're doing. Right nosy parker. I can't even use the pot at night without somebody waking up – it's too much of a risk. If Charlie doesn't catch me at it, someone will.'

Mal had sniffed a long breath in. He'd gathered his right fist inside his left, cracking the knuckles one by one. She'd thought that he was weighing up her information, considering another way. 'D'you really think I've not gone down and done a recce, Joy?' he'd said. 'A nice big farmhouse they've got there. Access front and back. Huge master bedroom on the top floor, office on the ground. A fancy living room. No dog to bother you when you get close – it's odd, that, for a house out in the sticks. They usually keep a dog, but all they've got is hens. I have to say, the woman is nice-looking, isn't she? Bright green eyes. And she can fill a blouse all right. She drives a lovely Austin into town, sometimes that old flatbed. And she tinkers in the garage with a tractor in the afternoons. Must be very handy round the place. Especially as *he's* only got the one. Poor bloke.

Spends ages in those fields, not doing much of anything, as far as I can tell. I spoke to him – he's friendly. Not the sort who'd trouble me. You know, who's got a bit of fight left in him. He'd probably kneel down for me and beg to have his throat cut. But you know that isn't how I'd do it. Far too messy. Nah. A simple fire'd do the job. The lights stay on downstairs till half past two sometimes. I'd wait it out till then. Bring that jerrycan back there. Four gallons, that one holds. Enough to get things cooking.' He'd glowered at her, dropped the ciggy packet on her lap. 'You get the picture. I am deadly fucking serious.'

There was no shame in admitting that she'd blubbed a bit, seeing the cold whites of his eyes, the malice in them. 'I wish I'd never met you, Mal. You make me sick.'

'Well, blimey, I don't blame you. Then again, I don't much care.'

'Can I get out now?'

He'd nodded.

Stepping out on to the muddy ground, she'd felt nothing in her legs, a numb wobble as she moved away. The greyness of the day had been too bright for her.

'Oi,' he'd called through the window. 'Just remember what I told you and there won't be any bother.'

The walk back to the house had been the worst trudge of her life. Worse than even that first noisy march in handcuffs through the corridors of Holloway when she was on remand. Worse than the slow creep along the aisle to view her parents' coffins in the funeral home – at least, back then, she hadn't felt responsible for what had happened, only cursed. This time, she'd had to shake the panic from her face, her voice, and go about pretending she was glad to be alive. She'd had to conjure an excuse for Charlie when he'd asked about the comics – 'Sold out. Not one copy left. It's typical' – and laugh and joke her way through supper, smiling at the Mayhoods with an awful sense of doom pinching her guts. It was still there now, that dread inside her. No amount of honey lemon drinks was going to fix it.

She took a breath.

Her fingers were so clammy on the scissors, jittering.

She remembered those fourteen days, how happy she'd once been.

She sliced the tape.

The box's lid was stiff. As she was lifting it, a few small pieces tumbled out and skittered on the floorboards. Pearls, she thought. But she was on her hands and knees before she noticed what they were. Loose teeth. She picked up six of them. Brown blood around their roots, still gluey. There were three more in the box. And where the padding had been stripped out of the base, a thatch of straw had been pushed in to fit – a short piece, plaited in a handsome pattern, fraying where the blade had sliced it. On the underside, there was a cotton strip attached, embroidered: *For my darling Geoffrey love Maureen*. She would've cried again, but there was nothing left. Her mind was dead. She couldn't even feel the shudders any more.

A square pit in the ground. It's eight feet deep and he is standing in it with his sister. There are scratchmarks in the earth behind them, clawed out by the backhoe. A wooden ladder leans against one side for entry and escape. They're laying blocks, cementing them. Trowels in hand and spirit levels. Two walls built so far, waist high. His sister's back is to the camera – she's furthest from the front – but he looks above the parapet and knocks the ash off what he's smoking. Jabs the handle of his trowel upon a block until it's sitting right. Wipes the sweat from his slick brow with his shirtsleeve. Gestures to the sky, as though a spell of rain might yet be coming. The camera pans. A smear of trees and hedges. Acres, stippled with emerging crops. A ditch. The north-west corner of the house. A brook of smoke ascending from the kitchen flue. Hens skipping in the yard. Slow pan round. Full circle. Joyce is coming down the ladder with a bucket of cement. Her face is moony, pale. A raindrop spots the lens. Another. Cut this.

November 1952

Charlie had determined months ago that it would do no good confiding in his supervising officer. There was something passive and officious about Mr Kimball that he couldn't trust, despite the man's attempts to cosy up to him. 'Anything you want me to report to the association, you just let me know, son,' he'd announced at their first meeting. 'If you're unhappy with the set-up here, I'll see what I can do to change it. That's my job. You shouldn't feel afraid of raising any problems, big or small. There might be some who think that Aftercare's about us keeping tabs on you, as if I'm sat here waiting for the first good opportunity to send you back to borstal. Nothing could be further from the truth. I'm here to make sure you succeed in life from this point on. So if you break your licence, well, it wouldn't just be you who'd failed now, would it? No, I take these matters very much to heart, believe you me.' The speech had rolled so easily off Mr Kimball's tongue it hadn't carried much conviction. Any man who had to advertise his motives so routinely wasn't selling you the truth, as far as Charlie was concerned. Since then, he hadn't felt inclined to talk much in their meetings, giving bare-bones answers to the questions, just enough to satisfy the basic needs of his report.

Today, he wasn't even in the mood to be polite. He couldn't listen to the man's dull recollections of his day at Farnborough Airshow or the rugby match he'd been to, or whatever subject happened to be buzzing in his bonnet when they both sat down to chat. There was only so much information Charlie could contain inside his head, and there was no space for the things that didn't matter. He was worried for his sister. He was worried for himself. He had a sense that she was drifting, but he didn't know to where. And he was sure that if he had to hear another bulletin from Mr Kimball on the progress of the roadworks outside Tolworth, he was going to catapult his chair across the room.

Two full days of rain had scuppered plans to finish off the root cellar, which had only made him irritable. He was supposed to be outdoors today with Joyce and Mr Mayhood, smoothing out the concrete on the roof. They'd built a timber form and nailed it to the walls already. The surround of bricks and all the rebar had been fitted, too. But when Tuesday's mizzle took a turn for the torrential, Florence had to ring the concrete company to stop the mixer coming. They'd put the whole thing off until tomorrow, when the forecast looked much brighter.

He'd spent this morning doing chores around the farm: collecting eggs and mucking out the henhouse, scrubbing down the porch steps, heaving shovel-loads of sodden leaves into the compost bin and trampling on them. Meanwhile, Joyce had gone off to survey the trees along the driveway with the Mayhoods, marking out the ones that needed lopping back or felling. 'Looks as if I drew the long straw for a change,' she'd boasted, passing through the yard, but he was glad to see her smiling. And besides, a bit of hard work with a shovel did him good – the muscles he'd developed in his stretch at Huntercombe were starting to get softer. When he was done out there, his armpits had an awful reek and there were specks of chicken muck and leaves stuck to his face. He'd gone to have a quick wash in the sink and smarten himself up for his appointment, combing through a bit of hair cream, putting on a collar and a tie.

As punctual as ever, Mr Kimball pulled into the drive at ten o'clock. It was funny how the Mayhoods always treated him as though he were the Duke of Edinburgh, coming to the door to shake his hand and ask about his wife and daughter, who was still in infant school. He was shown into the dining room, where Florence had set out a pot of tea for him beside a plate of home-made biscuits. She'd even put a little cushion on the chair, in case he made the same complaint as last time: 'Honestly, I've had such trouble with my back since I was in the army.' It had seemed to Charlie like a thin excuse to drop a mention of his service, but perhaps that was unfair. Any man who'd seen the front lines was deserving of some adulation, he supposed, and had the right to publicize it.

Well, as soon as Mr Kimball saw that cushion waiting there today, he almost teared up. 'Oh, that's very sweet of you to think of me,' he said. 'I never meant to trouble you.'

'Not at all,' she said. 'I only had to fetch it from upstairs.'

'Still, I do appreciate it.'

She glanced towards the mantel clock. 'I'll leave you gents alone. If there's something else you need, you only have to shout.'

'Thank you, Mrs Mayhood. We seem very well provided for.'

Charlie didn't care much for the way he talked to her, as though she were a housekeeper. Neither did he like the way his eyes trained on her when she turned and went, that subtle tilting of his head to watch her backside. But no matter what he thought of Mr Kimball, he was stuck with him for one more year, until he'd seen out the duration of his licence. In the short term, he would have to go on meeting him across the dining table every month and smiling at the man's half-hearted jokes. He'd have to carry on the rigmarole of putting on a collar and a tie to demonstrate his new sophistication. He'd have to keep on giving his thinned-out accounts of all the goings-on at

Leventree, skimming off the fat of everything that worried him and leaving only the nice underlayer of truth.

'Righto, then, Charlie, let's get started.' Mr Kimball was already wiping down his fountain pen – he kept an inky handkerchief inside his pocket for the job. 'Tell me, what've you been working on with Mr Mayhood since we saw each other last?'

'You mean *the Mayhoods*, sir.'

'Excuse me?'

'Well, it's not just Mr Mayhood who I work with, sir. It's both of them.'

'You're right. *The Mayhoods*. My mistake.' A note was jotted down on his pad. 'You know, you mustn't call me "sir", if you can help it, Charlie. I'd prefer you called me by my name.'

He would've said, *As long as you don't ever call me 'son' again*, but it was better not to air your grievances to men of a certain standing, as they only took offence. 'It's difficult,' he said instead. 'I've got so used to it.'

'I understand. But do your best.' Another flurry of the pen.

The most important thing about these conversations, Charlie knew, was that he put across the happiness he felt at Leventree. No matter how well he explained the methods he was learning in the draughting room, it all would get abridged in the report. It had been the same whenever he'd gone in to see the nurse at Huntercombe: he could rabbit on about his ailments, how they plagued him first thing of a morning, just what sort of sharp electric pain he was encountering, but the note he'd carry back to his housemaster would reduce it to *Charles Savigear has been experiencing some mild discomfort in his knees and shoulders. Recommend a day's exemption from his working party*. So he rattled through the past few weeks of happenings for Mr Kimball's benefit. First, an update on the progress of the root cellar, admitting he'd been proud to draw the negative and put his name on it: 'Well, it's a decent start. I hope I'll get to do more complicated ones in future.' Then he spoke about the dye-line prints they'd ordered from the special printers down in Guildford, and even went so far as to describe the thin white paper, soft as cotton in his hands, that he'd received a few days later in the post. As usual, he pitched his voice up loud to show enthusiasm. If he didn't do this, Mr Kimball would chime in with something like, 'You don't sound too convinced . . .' or 'Wasn't it as good as you were hoping?' Last of all, he talked about the visit to the Proctor house, taking care to leave his sister's part out of the story.

'Is it all right if I smoke?'

'It's fine by me. But, then again, it's not my house,' said Mr Kimball.

'Florence doesn't mind. And Mr Mayhood says it's fine as long as I don't do it in the draughting room.'

'You haven't asked before. I thought perhaps you'd given up.'

'Nah. They help me concentrate. I reckon I don't smoke as many as I used to, though. I'm in the draughting room so much these days.' He went over to the dresser for the nice ceramic ashtray he sometimes used at supper. 'See,' he said, presenting it. 'All above board.' He lit up and felt better right away. 'I can't remember where I left things now . . .'

'You were telling me about your visit to the site. An argument about the steel.'

'Oh yeah. Well, it wasn't quite an argument.'

'What was it, then?'

'I don't know what you'd call it. A debate, maybe.'

'A frank exchange of views.'

'Yeah, it was more like that.'

'And did it get resolved?'

'Of course. It had to.'

Being with the Mayhoods at the building site last week had felt like a rehearsal for the life he wanted. Even the short ride to Sunbury had been a pleasure, with Florence driving in the seat ahead of him, the scent of hyacinth inside the car and all the fresh temptations of her skin enlivened by the morning light. A glorious picture she had been. He could've gazed for ever at the little threads of hair upon her neck, so fair and plumy, which had come untangled from the metal pins beneath her curls – but too much staring made him feel transparent, not to mention seedy. Somehow, he could never pine for anyone without his sister getting wise to it; she'd been chipping at him with her snide remarks of late, in earshot of the Mayhoods – 'Wind your tongue in, mouse, or you'll trip over it' – and these embarrassments had bruised him slightly. That morning in the car, though, Joyce had been so quiet and disconnected. Her thigh had clattered on his knee with every bend along the road, reminding him that she was there. She'd looked hungover, pale, as though her face had been rubbed down with calamine. The light had seemed to injure her each time it passed across her brow. And when his sister's head was sore from drink, she didn't welcome company or interference. He'd learned this years ago, when they were kids – to leave her simmering until the poison boiled away. 'Joy, are you all right?' he'd whispered.

She'd laid her head down on the rim of the back seat, closed her eyes and put a finger to her lips. 'I've not been sleeping much,' she'd told him.

'If you say so.'

'It's the truth.'

'You've not been on the rum, then?'

'Shut up. I'm just trying to rest my eyes.'

He'd watched the passing scenery instead. The open fields dissolved into the suburbs, red-brick homes with tarmacadam drives and charmless gatherings of shops. They'd crossed over the Thames, the low sun flashing through the railings of the bridge, until they'd turned off the main road and driven up a shallow slope, pulling through a gate within a wall of temporary fencing. The Proctor house was being built there, on a square of muddy land – when it was done, it wouldn't so much overlook the river as stare hopefully in its direction, beyond the shoulders of the houses opposite. 'Nice how some folk get to live,' his sister had leaned in to say. She'd come alive all of a sudden. 'Who d'you suppose these Proctor people are?' He'd shrugged at her, and she'd concluded: 'Lawyers would be my guess. Can't be short of a few bob.'

By the time they'd parked up on the mud, the sun had dipped behind the clouds. Mr Mayhood had called back at them from the front seat, 'A lot of voices and opinions on a building site can get confusing, so resist the urge to chatter once we're out there, please. If there are things you want to know, just write them down and ask me later. With a bit of luck, we shouldn't be here longer than an hour.'

Together, they'd gone trudging over to the office of the clerk of works. It was only a small shed of corrugated iron with dirty windows and Charlie had the strangest sense that he was bunkering against the world again – its atmosphere was not much different from the Anderson in Aunty Helen's garden, only with a lot more room to stand up straight and pace around.

The clerk of works, whose name was Vernon Quinn, had taken off his cap to greet them, holding it across his heart as though he was about to sing the national anthem. 'Arthur, Flo, always a pleasure,' he'd said. 'Do you want to go and see about that steelwork right away? Or should I ease you in, one headache at a time?'

'Nice to see you, Vern. It's your decision. Take us where you need us most.'

'All right, then. I'll get my coat on.'

Mr Mayhood had stood back to let him through. 'Any other variations?'

'Not yet. But I reckon one's enough, don't you?'

'Amen to that.'

'How long can you stay today? 'Cause if I'm right about the steel, you'll need to fix the drawings and sign off on the VO.'

'We'd like to see the patient first, if you don't mind, before we do the amputation.'

Quinn had laughed at at this, although a bit uneasily. Fetching his jacket from the hooks beside the door, his eyes had shifted towards Charlie and his sister. 'Have a look at those fresh faces. They don't know the life of aggravation that awaits 'em, do they?'

'They'll know it by the time we're finished here.'

'Where's Tommy?' Florence had put in. 'I thought he'd have the kettle on for us already.'

'No, he's out there, doing what a foreman does. Standing round and pointing out the bleedin' obvious.' With a flourish, Quinn had straightened out the peak of his flat cap. 'Right then, lads and lasses – shall we?'

The ground floor of the Proctor house was almost done, or at least the outer shell. But Charlie hadn't got a proper measure of the builders' progress, given that so much of it was screened behind a layer of scaffolding. He knew how it was meant to look when it was finished. The Mayhoods had designed a low, wide house, with one long fascia and a taller section to the south, so that the bedroom had a view towards the river. The windows were supposed to rest upon a course of brickwork on all sides. Walls that didn't bear a load or brace the wind were going to be made of glass or board and batten. Mr Mayhood had explained the process, months ago, standing at the noticeboard with him and Joyce, examining the drawings as a means of teaching them approaches to construction. 'It's one of Wright's old tricks – he got it from the Japanese, I think,' he'd said. 'It's such a simple method really, everybody ought to do it, but you have to find the right contractor for the job. There'll be insulation issues, if the work's done badly . . .' Even then, to Charlie's untrained ears, it hadn't seemed a difficult technique to master. First, the builders had to make an inner section of the wall from plywood, skin it with a membrane to protect from damp. Next, they'd screw in battens on both sides to support the narrow boards of pine, all sanded down and oiled to show their grain. It'd give the house a rustic feeling, soften its impression on the landscape; but anyone who saw it would be bound to say how fresh it was, how modern.

Charlie hadn't understood the house, at first, or why it had to look so different from the normal type that most folk were content to live in. On the inside, there would be no carpet and no fancy Anaglypta, no dado rails, not even a partition wall. The downstairs would be open plan, with well-positioned corners that would hide the dining area from the living room, the kitchen from the hall. The floor line of the living space would spill on to a terrace. It wouldn't be like any house he'd ever stood in. But the more he'd studied the design on paper, the more he'd grown attached to it.

Then, one morning, Mr Mayhood had brought out the 3D model from the storeroom and they'd circled round the plan chest to appraise it from all sides, so Charlie and his sister understood 'the through-lines' of the building. 'Model-making's far too intricate for me these days. But there's a man we know in Hampstead. He's not cheap by half, because he does terrific work, as you can tell.' The roof had lifted off as though it were a doll's house and they'd seen the way the ground plan was supposed to flow from room to room. The fireplace was cut out of foam and sandpaper, the painted floorboards made from matchsticks. His sister had been awe-struck: 'Look at all that detail on the bricks! Your fella's eyes must be like magnifying glasses!' But it was only on the day that Charlie had been standing there on site, surrounded by the scaffold and the smell of oiled timber, that he'd really got a sense of what the building would become. His body had gone weightless at the thought.

The Mayhoods' satisfaction with it was much harder to determine. He'd tried to gauge it from the way they'd talked to Quinn, how often they'd both sighed and hummed and scratched their heads. At one point, eyeing up the intersection where the lower aspect of the roof was going to join the upper, Quinn had asked to borrow Joyce's notebook. 'Here, Flo, let me show you what I mean,' he'd said. 'This sort of thing is what I had in mind. A few rods here to suspend it. Flitch plates *here* on the one below,' and he'd scribbled a quick picture of the problem – he was certain that the timber beams were not enough to bear the weight, but Florence had said, 'Surely that'll *over*load it. You've just made a different problem.' Then Mr Mayhood had sketched out a version of his own on the reverse and argued that the cantilever would give plenty of support: 'You see it now? They'll hold each other, no two ways about it. I don't see the benefit of steelwork. It's redundant.' This back and forth had lasted for an hour. Charlie's toes had chilled from standing in one place so long and Joyce's dour mood had worsened by the minute. She'd grown bored and weary, singing in that quiet, tuneless way she often liked to do when she was waiting for a bus. After a while, she'd lowered herself on to a stack of pallets, crossed her arms and stared down at her feet. When he'd gone to sit beside her, she'd said, 'Wake me when it's over. I don't get why Mr Mayhood hasn't told this fella where to go yet.'

'You'd have thumped him in the mouth by now.'

'Too right I would've.'

'Yeah, and after that, you'd never work again.'

She'd scowled at him. 'What are you saying, mouse? I can't be trusted?'

'No. I'm saying Mr Mayhood has a different way of going about things.'

'Well, I'm glad he isn't gettting walked all over. But I wish he'd hurry up.'

'It's a big decision. Only right to hear the other side's opinion.'

'Christ, you've always got to be so bloody sensible,' she said. 'You must've been adopted.'

The fact was, he could see the merits of both arguments, although he didn't fully understand the explanations. Still, when Quinn had thrown his arms up in the end and said, 'That's settled, then. No bother. Fine by me,' he'd seen it as a victory. The more he'd walked around the site that day, the more his notebook had filled up with questions.

'Disputes must happen all the time. I've had run-ins with the building trade myself,' said Mr Kimball now. There was a trail of biscuit crumbs on his lapel, which Charlie wasn't minded to point out. 'But Mr Mayhood's very even-tempered, in my view. I'd imagine he knows how to weigh the pros and cons.'

'You're not wrong there.'

'Follow his example, you'll do very well in life.'

'I know, sir – Mr Kimball.'

'What about your sister?'

'What about her?'

'Do you think she sees the Mayhoods that way, too? As good examples.'

'I couldn't say. You'd have to ask her that yourself.'

'I will. I thought perhaps she might've said something to you about it.'

'Nah.' He let the smoke vent slowly from his nose. 'Joy doesn't tell me half of what's inside her head, and if she did, I'd put it back.'

He could sniff the bait on Kimball's questions when he fished for information on his sister. No doubt it was easier to get the knowledge second-hand than try and prise it out of Joyce himself. She was always guarded, always touchy – if anybody asked how tall she was, she'd say, 'Come over here and measure me, if you can reach that high' – so he had sympathy for Mr Kimball on that front. But still, he didn't like to be the door that other people came to knock on for a short cut to his sister's mind. His aunty used to do it, and his teachers used to do it, and the coppers had all done it, too. Ever since he could remember, he'd been answering for her behaviour, which wasn't meant to be a younger brother's job. It made him tense.

On the ride back from the building site that day, she'd been withdrawn, deflated. He'd tried everything he could to cover for her silence, running through the questions in his notebook, causing Mr Mayhood to twist round and say, 'My God, Charlie, if I ever need a good amanuensis, I'll know exactly who to come to.'

'Is that a good thing?'

'Doesn't matter.'

'Well, I thought you said we had to write things down . . . I'm sorry.'

'Don't apologize. I'm just impressed how much of it you managed to absorb.'

'It's somebody who takes a record of your conversations,' Joyce had said, from nowhere. She'd been gazing out of the window with the glummest look, and her voice had sounded winded, emptied out. 'I had one at my hearing, going *rat-a-tat* on her machine. You probably had one too, mouse.'

'Joyce is right – there's always a stenographer in court.' Mr

Mayhood had gazed back at them, a faint appreciation in his smile. 'Anyway, you did right, taking notes. I'm sorry for the wisecrack.'

Joyce had leaned away again and murmured, 'Told you,' following the motion of the traffic as it hurried by.

He couldn't pinpoint what it was, or when it happened, but he knew that somewhere in the past few months she'd got discouraged. Maybe it was all to do with Mr Hollis and their little quarrel in the field – that old bastard was so blunt with his commands and had no patience for her sense of humour. No one really blamed her for reacting as she'd done, and if the old man felt too mortified to show his face again, he didn't have enough resilience for the job. But it wouldn't be like Joyce to stew for ages over someone she'd insulted; wasting sympathy on gruff old men who barked at her all day was not her way. So maybe it was something Mr Mayhood had instructed her to do – the endless drawing of the greenhouse till it met his expectations, which she'd only just completed, after weeks of bungling the job. It couldn't have been Florence – she'd been kind and understanding from their first day in the house together, always making efforts to ensure that Joyce was praised when she deserved to be. Which just left *him*.

Was there anything he'd said or done to put her in this frame of mind? It was impossible to tell. With Joyce, a slight discouragement was like the slowest puncture to the heart, letting all the motivation out of her. He'd seen it time and time again. One scolding from a teacher and she'd stop attending school. One unthinking comment on her hairdo over breakfast and they'd find her at the bathroom mirror with the scissors. And, of course, there was that episode when he was twelve, when she'd brought home the lawnmower – things had never been the same between them since, not really. A splinter of mistrust had lingered after that and it was still embedded in him.

That broken mower had been waiting on their aunty's patio one Thursday afternoon when he'd got home from school. A tired old machine with all the green paint flaking off its hood and particles of grass stuck to its innards. 'Now you've something else to pull apart and tinker with,' she'd told him, seeing his bewilderment. 'Just watch your fingers on the blades – they're not as dull as they might look.' She had more heart than sense, his sister, and she hadn't meant to tangle herself up in trouble. All because she'd watched him stripping down his little traction engine toy so often in his room, filling it back up with kerosene so it would chug around the carpet – he'd taught himself to disassemble it and put it back together, telling anyone who'd listen of his plans to be an engineer or an inventor. She must've reasoned that a shabby mower would help him to achieve his dreams. He hadn't thought to ask where it had come from, only thanked her, kissed her cheek. She'd told him, 'Listen, if you clean it up and make it go again, you might start mowing lawns on weekends, earn yourself some money. Get yourself a bit of independence. Start here, in the close, and you'll have takers everywhere before too long.'

To begin with, Aunty Helen had allowed it. He'd spent hours in the garden at the weekend with the engine parts spread out on newspaper, wire-brushing them, discovering which pieces needed fixing, how to slot them all back into place. But then, at church that Sunday, his aunty had been pulled aside before the service by the vicar. It turned out that the padlock on the groundsman's shed had been sawn through on Wednesday night and several tools were missing. 'Plus a petrol mower that was always conking out. Nothing of much value, to be frank,' the vicar had explained, while Aunty Helen's face grew hot with shame, 'but they're going to need replacing. So I thought perhaps you might get word out to the congregation, see if anyone has any spare equipment we could borrow.' His sister hadn't taken kindly to the accusations when they'd got back home. 'You can bloody well piss off – you and that vicar *both*!' she'd yelled. 'I found it lying in the bushes. Halfway up the hill on Sandy Ridge. I didn't know someone had gone and robbed it, did I?' All her explanations had the gloss of salesmanship. On an ordinary day, she couldn't recollect what she'd put on her toast at breakfast, but ask her to explain her whereabouts when things got pinched and she could tell you to the nearest second. She'd always add one reasonable detail for you to orient yourself – a local landmark or familiar street – as if this certified her story.

In the end, their aunty had grown tired of confrontation. She'd given Charlie orders to pack all the parts into a box and carry them back to the church – it must've been over a mile on foot. As punishment, his sister had to drag the mower's rusty frame beside him, rattling like an empty can the whole way there. She wouldn't even look at him. She'd cursed their aunt. She'd said, 'I only wanted you to have something to do. I never stole the bloody thing – I *found it*. You believe me, right?' When he'd shrugged back at her and said, 'Dunno,' she'd made an injured noise, not quite a cough, not quite a laugh. 'Oh, so that's the way it is,' she'd said. 'You're on the other side now, too.'

The vicar had accepted her account of things, but said he'd have to notify the local constable in charge of the investigation. Early Monday evening, a young copper had come strolling up the front path, knocking on the door so hard that Aunty Helen flinched. He'd let Joyce off with just a caution: after all, there was no proof she'd stolen anything, only that she'd had the mower in her possession. But she'd had prior charges on her sheet – one of which had been for nothing more than snatching a few apples from the greengrocer's stand – and so the incident was put on record. After that, his sister never gave him anything again, except at Christmas and on birthdays, when her gift would be the same: a book with the receipt inside.

She'd always made it easier to doubt her goodness than believe it. Even now, he wasn't certain that she'd earned her place at Leventree the rightful way. There were things he knew about her that the Mayhoods didn't, and which no amount of ferreting in borstal files would show. For one, she'd never shown much interest or ability in drawing. Not as far as he could recollect, at least. She'd kept a diary as a girl and used to leave it on her windowsill – the cover was tattooed with doodles and cartoons she'd scribbled on, part-shaded, and perhaps it had been full of sketches and designs: he'd never dared to open it. He could half-recall an argument she'd had with Aunty Helen once about a school report, in which the only hint of praise had come from her art teacher. 'Of course you don't mind *art* – a dosser's subject if I ever heard of one,' their aunt had said. But he would never have imagined that his sister had been harbouring a talent for it down the years – not enough to win a competition with a hundred other girls. *Dear Mouse,* she'd written to him with the news about her entry being chosen, *I hope you're sitting down, I've something big to tell you . . .* and he'd recognized the careful method she'd applied to the delivery of the information, all the joints smoothed out, made water-tight and plausible. It put a dull ache in his gut just thinking of it. *I reckon it would make our old dad proud to know we got his knack for drawing. Both of us.* Well, who was he to question that idea or trample on it? *I must've learned a lot more from him than I ever realized. You won't remember it but me and him would sit out in the garden in the summer and draw pictures on the flags with chalk. He taught me loads and I suppose it all went in . . .* He knew much better than to challenge her or speak his doubts to anyone. He'd learned to bury his suspicions every time the subject was brought up, which only made a liar of him, too. But if anything accounted for her glumness lately, this was surely it. At Leventree, there were no cheats or workarounds to get things done, and she was finding out her limits.

The strangest part of it was that he owed his happiness to her. He could never have acquired it from the life his aunty had mapped out for him: a good job in the civil service and a bungalow just down the lane to raise his children. Safe from worry. Unexciting. Nothing ventured. Plain. It was a decent life for somebody, but not for him. He'd always hoped to be a person of invention, someone who inquired about the world and made a big impression on it. In her way, Joyce understood this – always had. It was why she'd wanted him to spend his weekends with her at the flat in Maidstone. It was why she hadn't let a day go by without a phone call to the house in Borough Green, even when their aunty warned her off: 'Can't you let the poor lad be? You're no good for him, Joy.' She'd tried to show him it was possible to function on his own. She'd told him not to be a ha'penny in other people's games, shoved back and forth to suit their needs – and he'd admired her for what she'd done, the way she'd lived, no judgement or constraints. While it was true he never should've been inside that car with her the night they were arrested, he was grateful now that it had happened. If she hadn't landed him in borstal, he would never have been *here*.

But all his time in the men's prison on remand, he'd wished that she were dead. Those weeks had petrified him, and he'd thought the dismal cell that he'd been put in would be where he'd stay for ever: half-stale bread and margarine for every meal, a constant threat of harm for speaking out of turn, excercises on the ring that turned to fist fights for no reason, shadows sloping past his door at night. His guts had twisted up and made him retch into the lavvy bowl most nights. He hadn't thought that borstal would provide relief, but he'd been treated right at Huntercombe. With a dozen others, he'd been transferred to its gates in a smart coach. It was as close to living as he could've hoped for: tree-lined paths outside and flower beds beneath his window, a library full of books, hot food that had a taste of home, a group of lads to talk to who had stories like his own, and some that made him grateful for his better fortune. At Huntercombe, he'd let himself start thinking of his sister's situation; and the more he'd thought of her, the more he'd missed her.

Now, Mr Kimball had his hankie out again – you had to give him credit for the upkeep of his instruments, but why he didn't use a pencil was a mystery. 'How about new friendships, then? Have you been socializing in the village?'

'There isn't much to do round here. It's probably for the best.'

'Why's that, Charlie? You're allowed to let your hair down now and then, you know.'

'Yeah, but I'm not one for drinking with a bunch of strangers. I prefer it where I am.'

'They're only strangers till you get to know them.'

'True,' he answered, thinking it was cheap advice he could've got from a machine in the arcade. Put a penny in a slot and pull the lever – *whump*, a little card would drop into the tray, all neatly stamped.

'Don't you want to meet new people?' Mr Kimball went on, simpering. 'Surely you must want to meet a girl and take her into town – or am I just old-fashioned?'

'Yes and no. I'm not in any hurry.'

'Come on now. There's nobody you've got your eye on? A farmer's daughter somewhere that you're keeping quiet?'

As far as Charlie was concerned, the problems of his heart were no one else's business, but he answered, 'Honestly, if any girl was sweet on me, I'd shout it from the rooftops.'

'Fair enough. I'm sure you'll have your pick one day . . .'

Every month, it seemed that Mr Kimball raised the topic of the local girls. It must've pleased a man like him – upstanding, middle-aged and bored – to imagine he was young again and free of burden, given one more chance to charm a pretty face and reach beneath her skirt. Charlie's skin was prickling at the mention of it. He stabbed his ciggie hard into the ashtray, letting thoughts go skittling through his mind again. Silk undergarments hanging on the pulley-rack inside the scullery. Metal hairpins clamped in her front teeth gone shiny with her spit. The tiny songbird pendant of her necklace resting in the shallow of her throat. He wondered if he shouldn't just release the pressure on himself and *say something*. His urges were not going away. They'd proved impossible to drown – he had a glut of them, each one a little thrill, indecent probably – and who else could he turn to for support? Not his sister, not his aunty. Definitely not Mr Mayhood. So, perhaps if he was careful with his words, he could explain the situation he was in, the curse of it. He could spin a story round his heartache to disguise it. He could say he'd met a woman on a trip to Guildford, someone nearly twice his age. He was in love with her but she would never know it. What occupation could he give her – a librarian? – and maybe she'd be in a long engagement with a decent man, someone heroic, like a fireman, or – well, it didn't matter, because he couldn't bring himself to tell the tale.

'You realize it's my duty to inquire about new friendships and the like,' said Mr Kimball, leafing through his files. 'We don't want you making any bad associations.'

'I understand.'

'I mean, it's very tough for boys on licence – readjusting to the outside world again, finding ways to motivate themselves. Seems to me, whenever lads go off the rails, there's only two clear reasons. It's because they're caught up in some sort of gang, or there's a girl involved. That's why I have to ask, you see.'

'All right.' He sighed. 'But that's not going to happen here, I promise.'

'And Joyce – has she been going out a lot?'

'She's not looking for a husband, trust me.'

'That isn't what I asked.'

'Well, look, you're seeing her next, aren't you? Find out.'

'Just a question, Charlie. I'm not trying to make a snitch of you.' But Mr Kimball's pen was scratching on the pad again.

'That's good,' he said, 'because I won't be that for you, *ever*,' and he fished another ciggie from the packet. 'There's not much worse than being a grass.' He was going to be a chain-smoker before this so-called Aftercare was done with. 'Anyway, she stays here every night, as far as I can tell. We like it here. Nobody bothers us or pokes their noses in. We work all day, we eat together, then we work some more and go to sleep. That's it. We read. She likes her cowboy books and comics. Me, I'm trying to get to grips with Ruskin at the moment. Do you know *The Stones of Venice*? You'd enjoy it. Very interesting. And we listen to the radio when we're in the mood. Sometimes we put records on and have a dance, a nip of brandy with the Mayhoods. Six o'clock, we're back out in the fields and start again. We're putting in the graft . . . So listen, I don't know about the other lads you've done this with, how hard they might've found it coping in the outside world, but this is just about a perfect situation, if you're asking me.'

'I'm very glad to hear it,' Mr Kimball said, although he didn't sound too pleased. He was dabbing ink from his shirtsleeve, tutting at himself. 'It sounds as though you've found yourself a home. And that's exactly what we want.'

'I hope I have.' He finally lit the ciggie he'd been worrying with his fingers.

'And what about your aunty – Helen, isn't it? The one you lived with.'

'Yes, sir. What about her?'

'Well, last I heard, you planned to phone her. Did you ever manage it?'

'No, I just – I couldn't. I suppose I couldn't face it. But I've written to her.'

'And she hasn't written back, I take it.'

'No, not yet. She probably won't.'

'Can I ask what you put in your letter?'

For a moment, he was back there, at the little table in his room upstairs. The breeze was whistling through the open sash and pushing at the edges of his paper. He was hearing the rabble of hens down in the yard below as Florence went into the coop to fetch their eggs, and thinking what a clear and pleasant sky it was out there, above the sway of trees, how alive the day seemed from his window and how dead he felt when he returned his pencil to the letter full of clichés he'd produced.

'Only that I've found a place I'm happy and I hope she's happy for me too,' he said. 'And that, you know – I'm sorry if I caused her any trouble.'

'I'm sure she would appreciate that sort of letter – anybody would.'

'Right, but you've not met my aunty Helen. She'd cut off her entire head to spite her face, I swear. It's hopeless. In her eyes, I made my choice – and I chose Joyce instead of her.'

'It can't be that straightforward, surely?'

'Well, she's said as much. She only wrote to me in borstal once – I got the message loud and clear. *It's your own damn fault. You should've listened. Now you'll see how tough the world is on your own.* As if I didn't know all that already. But I don't regret it.'

'Really?' Mr Kimball leaned away and crossed his arms. 'Surprised to hear you say that, Charlie.'

'No, I mean, I'm sorry that we took the car – that wasn't right. Of course that wasn't right. But I can't say I miss my aunty. Maybe at the start, the first few weeks inside. Remand was hard. But not right now. I know that makes me sound ungrateful, given how she took us in. Perhaps I *am* ungrateful. But I can't pretend I miss that house. The way she was. Bossing me about, as if I was her son – her *husband* even. And I don't like most of what she raised me up to think.'

'Such as?'

There was a small chip in the tabletop, he noticed, in the place his sister usually sat. It would need a bit of woodstain. 'You know, that high and mighty stuff. I don't have a problem with the Bible – I don't think about it much at all – and I don't mind what stories people want to put their faith in, honestly. But I don't think the church should be what gives your life its meaning. Keeping in good favour with the vicar. Putting money on a plate on Sunday so the weathervane can be replaced. Doing things for charity so you can get yourself a nice pat on the back. She thinks that's generosity, my aunty – doing jumble sales and baking cakes and giving all the proceeds to the church. *Nah*. That's all to make herself look good. Real generosity is putting other people's happiness ahead of yours. Like Joyce's, for a start. Like *mine*. She never saw it that way, really. Generosity is when you've only got two sticks to rub together and you give them both to someone else who needs them more. That's what I mean.' He didn't want his ciggie now – his mouth had gone all pasty – so he let it burn down in the ashtray. 'I didn't mean to rabbit on, I'm sorry. I suppose it's just been on my mind.'

'That's all right. It's what I'm here for – more or less.' Mr Kimball closed his file. 'You know, I'm sure she must've done her best. It's never easy. Difficult enough with kids when they're your own.'

'Yeah, well. I'll get round to phoning her – I will. Eventually.' He left the tabletop alone, looked up. 'But let me ask you something. If your daughter ever gets herself in trouble with the law, would you just wash your hands of her? That's what my aunty did.'

'Oh, blimey, that's a question . . .' Mr Kimball pulled his mouth into a knot. 'I'm going to decline to answer that, if you don't mind,' he said, and then a warm smile spread across his face.

*

He found his sister in the draughting room, ink-washing a section of the greenhouse she'd enlarged on to a sheet of heavy Whatman paper. Florence was beside her, settled on a wooden stool, saying, 'There, you're getting it, that's it. Now stop and bring it back. Apply a bit more pressure at the edge, yes, good . . . Lightly as you go from here. That's perfect. Lovely even tone.'

There was a spreading gloom outside, a failed spark about the day, but Joyce's paper was lit white beneath the angled lamp, slick wet, reflective. Her face was concentrated and more cheerful than he'd ever seen it in the throes of work before. When Florence turned to wave him over – 'Come and look at this. Your sister just got further in ten minutes than I managed in my first two years of architecture school. We'll make a Beaux Arts master of her yet' – he saw right through the cotton of her blouse, so that the form of her brassiere was obvious, the lie of it across her ribs. He flicked his eyes away and took in what his sister was creating: a section so exact and flawless, drawn in such an organized array of pencil lines, that he knew somebody else had made it for her. Still, the wash she'd done was excellent, a subtle layer of ink the colour of dishwater.

'A proper job, that, Joy,' he said. 'Much better than my effort.'

His sister kept on sweeping the thick sable brush across the paper, soaking it. 'You reckon?'

'Yeah. It's neater than my first go, anyway.'

'Thanks, mouse. I suppose I have my uses.'

Suddenly, there was a peal of laughter from behind him. He hadn't noticed Mr Mayhood in the wing chair by the fireplace – the telephone was in his fist, its cable ranging from the socket underneath his desk like a festoon. 'I swear, I would've given anything to be there when they told him! Ha, poor Miles! Can't win them all!' It didn't sound much like a work call.

'Well,' he told his sister, 'I don't want to interrupt your shining hour, but Kimball's ready for you now.'

'He'll keep.'

'Yeah, except you know how he'll report it. *Joyce was thirteen minutes and nine seconds late today for her appointment.*'

'Fine. I'm coming.' She wiped her brush down on the rag and set it on the table. Getting up, she reached back to undo her apron strings. 'Why in God's name did I do this up so tight?'

'Here, Joy, let me help you.' Florence took a while to pick apart the cord. 'You're right –you've really done a number on this thing.'

His sister stood there, gazing down at him. 'What sort of mood is Kimball in today – how chatty is he?'

'More than usual, I'd say.'

'Oh, give me strength.' At last, she slipped out of her apron, handing it to Florence. 'I'm running out of things to tell him. He knows everything about me now. He's my imaginary friend I can't get rid of.' She traipsed off. 'Wish me luck.'

'Enjoy yourself.'

'I will, son. Thanks.'

'Give over.'

He watched her ambling away, past Mr Mayhood by the fire,

still chuntering into the phone, and past the corner of the noticeboard where copies of his elevations for the root cellar had been pinned, beneath the label WORK IN PROGRESS. There was such a heaviness about the way she walked, heels clouting the parquet. And what faulty patch inside her brain had made it so she couldn't close a door behind her properly? It sprang open on its latch as she went down the hall, allowing in the draught.

Florence bundled up the apron, laid it on the table. She twisted off the lamp and the entire world seemed dimmer. When she sniffed the air in sharply, blinking, he wondered if he'd been too heavy-handed with the hair cream earlier.

'You'd better hope nobody hears you talk that way about your supervising officer,' she said.

'It's just a bit of fun. He's all right, Mr Kimball. Sometimes.'

'Well, you can call him fit to burn, for all I care – but do it privately. For everybody's sake.'

'You're right. I'm sorry.'

She nodded at the doorway. 'Go and shut that, would you? I can feel the cold around my feet already.'

'Is it all right if I go and make a pot of coffee?'

'If you want one. Mr Mayhood's due another cup by now.'

'I thought as much.'

'Bring in the Carnation too. I'll have a splash in mine.'

'OK.'

She faced the window, checking on the weather. 'Seems the rain is holding off. It bodes well for tomorrow. They're sending us the mixer bright and early.'

'That's good. I'll be ready. What about the old man? Any word?'

She took a stride towards him. The tendons of her neck were edged in daylight, long and tapering below the skin, as firm as tree roots. He could make a drawing of them some day.

An entire building. What a fool he must've seemed to her, in turn. A little boy dressed up in adult clothes, his hair all shined and parted.

She lowered her voice to say, 'Hollis has abandoned ship – I think that's clear to everyone by now. But we won't replace him till we're sure he doesn't want the job back. And we think he might be down in Devon with his brother. We're still trying for an address.'

'He doesn't want the job back. If he did, he would've stuck about.'

'Well, this is meant to be a place for second chances, isn't it? My husband won't give up on people easily.'

He couldn't argue with this point and he suspected that she knew it. 'I suppose that's how it's got to be, then. Mr Mayhood knows what's best.'

She cast her eyes across the room. 'Either way, it means we'll need to dig out our potatoes by ourselves. The carrots can be left all winter, but we ought to put a mulch on them in case the cellar can't be finished. Probably this weekend, he's been saying. I hope you two are ready for some backache.'

'You can always bring me down a cushion for my chair,' he said, and smiled.

She thinned her eyes. 'I didn't do that for *his* benefit, you know.' Her hands went to her hips. She sighed and shook her head at him. 'Next time, I can let him grumble on at you instead about his army days. Carrying the mortars and what have you.'

'Did you know a two-inch mortar weighs ten pounds?'

'Really, you don't say.' She giggled. 'That's the first I've heard of it.'

He loved to make her laugh. Just knowing he was liable for something that amused her – not by accident, or as the punch-line to his sister's smart remarks, but as the maker of a thought, a phrase – gave him more confidence, belief that in another time and place, another life . . .

'Yes, absolutely – only if you can. I wouldn't want to put you in a spot, Fred . . .' Mr Mayhood's voice cut through the quiet of the room. 'I'd be so grateful . . .' He was winding up his conversation, an elbow on the wing chair with the phone against his ear. He was saying, 'Possibly. What time? . . . The one in the West End? . . . Yes, fine. Count us in. If something changes . . . I was saying, if something changes, phone again . . . We'll find somewhere, don't worry . . . All right, Fred. We'll be there. Thanks again. Ta-ra for now . . .' And then he planted the receiver down and stared at it a moment. He stood up and went to shut the door. 'Who left this hanging open?'

'Have a guess,' said Florence. 'What did Fred want?'

'This and that – you know how Fred can be. It takes you half an hour to work out why he's calling.' Mr Mayhood seemed to float towards them in a daze. He sat on Joyce's chair and studied what she'd done. 'This is very good so far. Is she not going to finish it?'

'She's gone to her appointment.' It was like a nervous tic, this strange compulsion Charlie had to leap in and defend his sister. 'Mr Kimball gets all hot and bothered when she's late.' No doubt he'd still be doing it when they were in their dotage. One day, they'd be buried next to one another in the cemetery, and his epitaph would read: *Joyce didn't mean it.*

'Fair enough. Important that she stays in his good graces.'

'As it happens, she's a dab hand with a paintbrush,' Florence said. 'Early days, but if she keeps this up, I'd let her colour anything of mine.'

'I wonder if she'd take well to sciagraphy.' Mr Mayhood glanced towards the page again, then back at her. 'I think she learns much quicker when you teach her, Flo. It's something to consider.'

'Yes, I'll dig out my McGoodwin. Give her a few things to try.'

'For Charlie, too.'

'Of course.'

He'd come across that word before, *sciagraphy*, but he'd forgotten where. Perhaps in Ruskin. He was going to ask them to explain it, but then Florence said, 'I heard you making plans with Fred. Don't tell me he's got tickets for a show. You'll end up in an oyster bar somewhere until the morning, and he'll land you with the bill.'

'He's going to see a play tonight – but that's not where I'm taking you.'

'Please, don't drag me into it. I haven't got the energy.' She put her hands on Mr Mayhood's shoulders and began to straighten out the back of his shirt collar, which had formed a little kink over his tie. 'I love Fred, but he drinks too much, and so do you when you're together.'

'No, no – this is strictly business. And Fred's not going to be there. He's just setting up a meeting with a friend of his. He's given me a lead.'

Charlie wished he had a kink in his own collar. He'd make sure to put one there on purpose next time, lose a button for good measure.

'I thought we'd given up on all that nonsense,' she said. 'Fluttering our lashes for commissions.'

'This is different. I just want to get our name into the reckoning.'

'A competition?'

'Yes.'

'For what?'

'Battersea Poly. New halls of residence. They're planning an expansion, and a big one from the sounds of it.'

'Well, I didn't see it posted, and you know I check the trades,' she said.

'There's politics at play, as ever.' Mr Mayhood swivelled round and stood. He took her by the hand and kissed her on the forehead. 'Fred thinks if we meet this fella and his wife, turn on the charm, they'll put us on the list.'

'*Fred* thinks?'

'Yes. And he's the gospel when it comes to this. He knows this bloke from school – the chancellor. The Proctors know him, too, and they've already put a word in for us. It'll take a bit of toadying – and God knows I can't stand the toadying – but it's a major competition and we'd have a decent chance. What do you think?'

'We can't be out too late,' she said. 'The mixer's coming in the morning.'

'I'll be sure to get you home by midnight.'

'But I don't know what I'd wear. I'd have to get my dresses out of mothballs.'

'It never matters what you wear, my love. It's what you have to say that counts.'

She hummed at him. 'If that were true, we'd have the conversation on the phone. Where are we meeting them?'

'At Rules. Fred's organized a table.'

'Oh, terrific. Pastry all the way.'

In these moments, Charlie understood he was supposed to stand there and pretend he wasn't listening. He could manage it, up to a point, but there was only so long he could watch the tenderness between the Mayhoods without feeling sickened with himself – for sheltering so many urges in his head that were invisible. If either of them ever saw the picture show he played himself at night in bed, the visions of her that he put to use under his sheets, they'd ship him off so far from Leventree he'd have to learn a different language. He was thinking now of Florence sitting on her bedspread in a plain black dress, her legs in sheer tan stockings, crossed; and she was reaching down to slide her pointed foot into a spindly shoe, her songbird pendant hanging like a plumb bob, swaying.

'This list,' he said, with his eyes on the space between them, 'what will it mean if you get on it?'

Mr Mayhood said, 'A lot of work, potentially a lot of money.'

'It'll mean all hands on deck for a few weeks – or even months, depending on the deadline,' Florence said. 'A competition is a full commitment. You can't approach it any other way. And usually it's a perfect waste of time and effort. But then sometimes –'

'Sometimes, Charlie, you get lucky,' Mr Mayhood said. 'And even if you don't, the work's its own reward. There's no such thing as failure in this business, only disappointment.'

*

From his room, they watched the Austin's headlights beaming on the drive until it coasted out of sight. The darkness in the yard seemed thick as mud but there weren't any nightjars churring in the trees tonight – that noise he'd grown familiar with at Huntercombe, like broken radios that never find a frequency. There wasn't even time for him to lift the sash and have a smoke before his sister climbed the ladder to his bed and flopped down on it, saying, 'I should think we've got at least till half past twelve. Let's make the most of it. A bit of reading maybe, or perhaps I'll get on with some knitting . . .' She mumbled this last part towards the ceiling, with her skull pushed deep into his pillow – he'd probably be finding strands of her coarse hair entangled in the cotton until laundry day. '*Or*,' she said, quick-rolling her big melon of a head, so he could share in her delight, 'in the parlour there's a bottle of White Horse – it's the real thing, too. They keep it right back in the cupboard, and it's open but it's nearly full, so neither of them must be partial. Me, I wouldn't mind a glass or two. I've not had proper whisky for a while. Mix it with a bit of soda. Lovely.'

'How d'you know they aren't just saving it for something special?'

'I thought of that. I reckon if they were, they'd not have opened it at all.'

He couldn't really fault her logic. 'Nah, Joy. It's not worth it. I'd prefer a cup of cocoa.'

'Cocoa, he says. *Cocoa!*' She was laughing at him now.

'What's wrong with that?'

'You're eighteen, that's what. Come on, mouse, we never got to celebrate together on your birthday, did we?'

'No, but –'

'It'll be all right. They won't find out, and if they do, blame me.'

'I'd never do that.'

'Well, it's not as though they're going to mind. They left us here. They haven't asked somebody round to watch us, have they? And they *did* say make yourselves at home. They've said that from the start.'

Something had got into her. Here they were, alone for the first time – entrusted by the Mayhoods with their home, their practice, their belongings – and she was trying to take it as her opportunity to roam about in places where she had no business being. Only Joyce could turn a few hours' peace into an aggravation. 'Can't you leave it?' he said. It came out with added desperation. 'You'll get us into bother.'

'Jesus. You're no fun.' She levered herself upright, looked at him with an expression that he knew spelled trouble, all her features still except her mouth, which danced a little at the edges. 'If you won't have a drink with me, I'm going to have a nice, long bath.'

'Do what you like.'

She climbed down, jumping the last rung, and cocked her head at him. There was an attitude about her. Smirky. Teasing. Secretive. The Joy of the old days in Borough Green. He wasn't pleased to see it.

As she walked out, down the hall, across the landing – he could hear the moaning floorboards all the way – he straightened out the bedspread, fluffed his pillow and restored the ribbon in *The Stones of Venice* to the page he'd left it on (before she'd found the book left open on his desk and riffled through it, saying, 'Hardly any illustrations in this one'). An icy draught came in as he pulled up the sash. He tied a jumper round his shoulders, lit the final ciggie in his packet. The moon had put a silver polish on the clouds. He really had a hankering for cocoa, but he couldn't make it very well – his sister had a special way of doing it, whisking up evaporated milk on a low heat for sweetness, and no lumps or skin on top.

There was another movement on the landing. A door snapped shut somewhere. It must've been the draught. He dragged hard on his ciggie and it gave his thoughts a rush. They'd looked so smart and proper on their way to dinner: Mr Mayhood in his best blue three-piece and his false arm tucked inside the pocket of his greatcoat; and Florence, who'd been dressed in something very different from his daydreams, which he realized now were stitched together from weak memories of films he'd watched with Lana Turner and Joan Bennett. Instead, she'd worn a brown tweed jacket with a velvet collar that cinched tightly at her waist. A matching skirt with pleats that flowed down past her knees. Warm pink lipstick and pearl earrings. Leather gloves. A furry little hat. She wouldn't have looked out of place among his aunty's friends at church. And still she wasn't anything like them. Those women had no flesh beneath their clothes. No mystery or passion. They were grave-yard statues, vacant in the head and heart. But Florence had a spirit and a shape. Her mind was always in a state of motion. She had pretty eyes, all right – they didn't take much noticing – but it wasn't till he'd seen her on the station platform back in August that he'd understood how much a woman's eyes projected. Her nature, her desires – he could read them, even if he couldn't quite translate them into words. He'd never kissed a girl or even held one in his arms. He'd only seen one naked in a dirty book that older lads had passed round school. So how come he was certain that he'd know exactly what to do with Florence Mayhood if she ever stood before him in the dark and opened up her gown?

He flicked his fag end out of the window, shut the sash. There was a noise of bathtaps running, and the pipes were humming in the walls, but not nearby. He went and knocked upon their bathroom door, which hung ajar. 'You in there, Joy? I need the loo.' No answer. 'I'm coming in,' he said, shielding his brow. But there was no one in the room. The tub sat dry and empty while he stood there, pissing in the pot. 'Joy? Where are you?'

On the landing, he could hear the full gust of the taps, the tinkling of glassware. The Mayhoods' bedroom door was closed, but he knew that she was in there. So he took a breath and turned the handle. No lights on inside. The curtains had been drawn. But there was a venting yellow glow from the en suite, writhing with steam. As the taps went off, he made out Joyce's tuneless singing – '. . . *and you pinned a rose of red on my coat of blue and said . . .*' A rage began to swell within him. '. . . *that a soldier boy you'd wed, Nellie Dean.*'

He barged in, saying, 'What's the matter with you? You're not meant to be in here,' and, seeing him, she sank below the thick white bubbles, spread an arm across her chest, a hand above her nether regions.

'Sod off, Charlie! I'm just trying to relax.'

'We've got our own bath you can use.'

'Yeah, but this one's deeper. They've got bubbles. You can go in after me.'

'No chance. Why've you always got to do this?'

'What?'

'Mess about with things that don't belong to you. You've no respect.'

She leaned her head back, blinking at him. 'It's called living. You should try it.' Then, *'There's an old mill by the stream, Nellie Dean . . .'* She sighed. 'You'll cop an eyeful in a minute, if you plan on standing there. Get lost.'

'You're wrong in the head, you are,' he told her.

'Don't I know it.'

He made sure the latch closed properly behind him. But, presented with the lonely darkness of the Mayhoods' room, he felt the need to switch a light on. And, at once, he saw the double bed with Florence's possessions laid out neatly on the table at the pillow end: a carriage clock, a water glass, a novel she was reading called *My Cousin Rachel* and a jar of Nulon hand cream. He couldn't fight the urge to hold them all, which made a hypocrite of him, but who would know?

He wandered over, toeing the long vallance with his shoe, and pictured her asleep below him, beautiful, at peace. It didn't take too much consideration. Everything he'd charged his sister with came just as easily to him. *You've no respect.* He lifted up the counterpane, revealed the pillow's whiteness and its smears of grey and beige, and then he knelt right down and kissed it – more than that, he breathed in every trace of Florence that was present in the fabric. Hyacinths. A honeyed kind of shampoo that she used. Pond's cream, too. He wished he could've bottled up the scent for ever, but his memory would have to be enough.

The counterpane was easy to fold back; he smoothed it flat,

left no impressions. In the en suite, Joyce was splashing like an eel in a tank. He rummaged in the dressing table, found a load of curlers with hairs twisted in the joins. He plucked a couple off and put them in his mouth a moment. There were other things he wouldn't dare disturb for fear that he'd forget their places: many spools of thread and thimbles, scissors, tweezers, little brushes, make-up cases. On the chest of drawers beside the window, Florence had set out a browning picture in a frame, of handsome people old enough to be her parents, which he guessed they were – they had the same lean features – and a jewellery box he didn't want to open. In another frame, there was a square of paper with two initials rendered lovingly in ink. *FG.* He could tell who'd done this for her and it cooled his blood. He pulled the top drawer out and everything he hoped to find was in there. Slips and stockings. Shifts and nightshirts and pyjamas. Knickers – functional and basic mostly, but some fancy silken ones and lacy numbers. If a pair went missing, she'd be sure to notice, given she was thrifty and responsible. But what if he could hide some in the corner of the scullery, as though they'd fallen from the pulley-rack? He could sneak them to the privy in the yard and wrap them in his fist. And then what? Let his sticky mess dry on the silk and stow them somewhere? He couldn't think beyond the swelling in his crotch.

Joyce's voice was closer now. That jolly song about the old mill stream and Nellie Dean that she would sing inside the Anderson to grate on everybody's nerves. She must've stepped out of the bath. Her hand was buffetting the door, where she'd hung up a towel.

He closed the drawer and shut the lights off at the wall.

'You out there, mouse?' she called.

He hurried down the stairs, the softness of the knickers fading on his cheek. The little frill adornments round the legholes – he'd remember them tonight. No need to take what wasn't his.

For now, he'd have to let his thoughts run somewhere else: back to the biscuit crumbs on Mr Kimball's jacket, the stench of hen muck on his nails, the rim of greenish dirt the old man used to leave inside their bathtub after he'd been soaking in it. Nothing did the job. The strain between his legs was getting worse. He got a saucepan out and warmed some milk up on the range. The cocoa powder spilled when he took off the lid and he was wiping down the counter when he heard Joyce thudding through the hallway. Going where? To help herself to White Horse, if he had to guess. He tried to froth the milk, but he forgot to add a spoon of golden syrup, so he ended up with something watery and foul. It burned his tongue. The pressure in his crotch had eased, though, and he wouldn't have to worry that the bulge was showing any more. He dumped the panful down the sink. Perhaps a nip of whisky wasn't such a bad idea, after all.

He found his sister in the parlour. She was standing in the corner by the gramophone and fumbling to make it play. 'Did this thing break?' she said, not even turning round. The whisky bottle was already in her hand, the cap still on it.

'It was working a few nights ago,' he said.

'Well, come and have a look at it. Seems bust to me.' Her hair was damp and wiry from the towelling she'd given it. Her face was pink as bacon. She was in her dressing gown and slippers. 'I've wound it up and wound it up.'

'I know the feeling,' he said.

'Ha ha ha.'

'I hope you rinsed that tub out.'

'No, I left it nice and mucky for them. Talcum powder everywhere and loo roll.'

'What's got into you tonight?'

She shrugged. 'I'm happy, I suppose. There's no one breathing down my neck for once. Apart from you.' The gramophone was spinning now. 'Oh good, you fixed it.'

'Wasn't broken in the first place. The brake was set to manual. Have you not changed the stylus yet?'

'I didn't know I had to.'

'It's an old machine, you clod. I showed you this before.'

'OK. Well, you change it, then. I'm going to make myself a drink.' She gathered one of Mr Mayhood's cut-glass tumblers from the sideboard. Glugging out an inch of whisky, she added a few dashes of soda from the siphon. Then she jumped on to the sofa and draped herself in crocheted blankets with her legs sprawled out across the cushions. 'Come on, hurry up,' she said. 'I want my Benny Goodman.'

He hadn't seen her like this for a while – not since those long weekends at her flat in Maidstone, when she'd stay up drinking with that fella Malcolm, blasting their jazz music on the radiogram. Talk about a bad association. For a while, he'd thought she'd end up married to the fella, they were so entangled. Sometimes, she'd collect him at the bus stop on a Friday evening and Malcolm would be waiting at the flat to let them in; a sorry bunch of flowers would be laid out on the table for her, or a pot of jam or honey, or there'd be a packet from the butcher's on the counter full of sausages or chops, a bottle of the rum she liked. And Joyce's backbone would go soft on seeing what he'd brought, as though she would've danced with any man who'd trade his ration book for her affections. But Malcolm had more faces than a set of dice. On certain Friday nights, the fella would show up a few hours after supper, stinking of the pub; he'd throw his overcoat at Charlie and say, 'Hang that up. Good lad,' and he'd march over to the radiogram, switch off the quiz show they'd been listening to on the Home Service. 'How'd it go, Mal?' his sister would spring up and ask, and he'd say, 'Pour me a stiff drink. We're celebrating.' That'd end their plans together for the night – no dominoes and cocoa, after all. Charlie would be left to sit there on the sofa, watching her and Malcolm foxtrot round the room to Benny Goodman. They had clumsy, thumping feet, but they were eager. Their voices and their laughter and the music would go on all night, as he was trying to fall asleep in Joyce's room. He'd wake up and the phonogram would still be on and crackling with static. Malcolm would be standing at the kitchen counter in his manky shorts and vest, nursing a headache, while Joyce was folding up the pull-out. '*Shshh*, lad, will you? Stop your clattering,' he'd say. 'If you want to play the spoons, go somewhere else and do it.' In those moments, he'd looked middle-aged and sallow. Old enough to be his sister's teacher. Sweaty-faced and hairy at the chest and belly, morning breath like vinegar. What had she seen in him? He was always lurking round the place, pulling her to one side for a cuddle, whispering about things in a sort of code – 'My cousin's back in town. He wants to take a trip to Margate. Better count me out for supper' – and she would try to plead with him, 'Oh, can't it wait? I'm taking Charlie to the pictures. Come with us,' but he'd collect his coat and go. 'Sorry, I can't let my cousin down again.' That fella had so many cousins they could fill a corn exchange. Then Sunday evening would come round and he'd be there to make his customary joke: 'I'd offer you a lift home, Charles, but I can't drive.' For six or seven months, that's how things went. Until, one Friday, Malcolm wasn't at the flat and Joyce wouldn't explain the reasons why.

'Are you having some?' she asked him now, lifting up her glass. 'It's proper stuff. No bite to it at all.'

'I'll take a sip of yours.'

'You bloody won't.'

He drew the arm across and set the needle to the record. Summery piano chords, the jounce of clarinets, a skip-along old tune. It put his teeth on edge, but Joyce's feet began to dance below the blankets, left to right. Her fingers jumped against the glass in rhythm. After only a few minutes, it was over. She called, 'Put the other side on.'

'I'm not standing here all night, flipping your records. You can find another skivvy.'

'But you love it.'

'No, I don't.'

'You *do*. Remember that machine Aunt Helen had? You'd stand there all day with your head shoved in the speaker, putting on the lot she owned – and all she had was Florrie Forde. Anything mechanical, you wanted to be in charge of it.'

He'd forgotten about that. The warble of that woman's crooning and the rasp of the applause on the recordings. 'All right. Just this once. Have you got any ciggies on you?'

'No. I left them in my room.' She ruffled the ends of her hair. 'Aren't you going to smoke in here and keep me company?'

'I've better things to do.'

'Ah, so that's the way it is. Too busy for your own big sister. Shame.'

She had a pained expression that he'd seen before so often; it was three parts forgery to one part truth, but still. 'You're being soft,' he said. And then she drained the whisky in a few short gulps and poured another. 'Take it easy with that. We've an early start tomorrow. Mixer's coming.' Her second measure was at least a double and she even spared the soda.

Gawping at the oak beams overhead, she asked him, 'What've you been telling Kimball, by the way? He seems to think that I'm unhappy. *Not adjusting very well* – who put that in his head?'

'You think I'd grass you up? No chance.'

'Well, someone's given him the daft idea.'

'Maybe it's because you had a face on like a wet weekend. He isn't blind, you know.'

She slugged her whisky. 'He was on at me again about my lovelife.'

'Me and all.'

'He asked me, *Don't you want to find yourself a husband and have kids one day?* I mean, what sort of question's that? The cheek of it.'

'Well, don't you?'

'Yeah, but I've got ages for all that. You'd think I was fifty-eight, the way he was going on.'

'I suppose he's got to ask that sort of stuff. I hate it, too.'

'Only 'cause you can't say who you've really got the hots for.'

'Shut up, Joy.'

'If only Kimball knew how dopey your face goes at supper when she's next to you.'

'I mean it, Joy. Get lost. It isn't funny.'

'No, you're right, it's not.' She took in a big mouthful and it stung her throat. Wincing at him, coughing, she said, 'Anyway, in case you're wondering, I've got my eye on someone, too. This fella I bump into now and then. Works down the post office. He might be married, I don't know. He's very shy in speaking to me, that's for sure. But he's all right to look at. And there could be something in it, once I get him talking.'

'I just hope he's better than the last one.'

'Yeah, that wouldn't take much.' She gave a little sniff and shudder, pulled the blanket round her shoulders. 'Are you going to flip it, then, or aren't you?'

He turned the record over, cranked the handle. 'Now it all makes sense,' he said, setting the stylus to the shellac till it purred. 'No wonder you've been dying to post the letters every day.'

She raised her glass at him and winked. 'Don't breathe a word, you hear?'

'As if I would.' Here came the jangle of piano keys again, the bouncy clarinet. He liked this tune much better, but it didn't last as long. The problem with a ten-inch was no sooner had the music found its energy and flow, the track was over.

'Put that on again,' she said, 'before you leave.'

'I'll stay for a few more.'

'Good lad.'

He had a shuffle through the Mayhoods' stack of records on the shelf. 'What do you want to hear?'

'Anything but Florrie Forde.'

'Let's see . . . The Andrews Sisters?'

'They'll do fine.'

He put on 'Boogie Woogie Bugle Boy' and, after that, the B-side. While the music played, she sank into the sofa cushions with the whisky tumbler on her chest. She kept her eyelids shut and her feet dancing. Once or twice, she angled her head forward for another slurp. If she was sweet on someone and the feeling wasn't mutual, then maybe it accounted for her moods of late: her sullenness and sleeplessness, not to mention all the grief she'd given him about his pining over Florence, which he'd thought a bit extreme. Now he knew. She'd been distracting his attention from the stink of her own heartache. With his sister, there was always more to every story than she let you hear. She'd been wounded by someone, that much he understood. He'd have to drop into the post office tomorrow, have a good look at this fella she was smitten with. Joyce's heart was a grenade – there weren't too many he would trust with it. The last thing either of them needed was another chancer rattling through her life and disappearing.

After she'd been ditched by Malcolm, her entire attitude to life had spoiled. She'd been angry at the world again. Impulsive. Starting arguments with women at the chippie if they nudged her in the queue, saying, 'Watch your elbows, you fat cow,' and laughing on their way out to the street. Sitting on the railing of the bridge and spitting on the river boats that chugged below. Taking him to see a film and making them change seats five times, cackling at lines that weren't intended to be funny, booing actors she resented from their roles in other films. If she couldn't aim her anger at the person who had injured her, she'd dole it out to anyone who wandered by. She'd be quiet, preoccupied and dour one minute, giddy and belligerent the next. And he'd reached the point when, after a few weekends of endurance, he'd told her that he didn't want to visit her again: 'Not if this is how you're going to act – it's giving me an ulcer.' She'd thumbed away her tears before they'd spilled and said, 'OK, then, suit yourself.' The bus had rolled up to the shelter and she'd put him on it, waving at him from the pavement, glossy-eyed, until it moved. But the next weekend – his first in Borough Green for months – he couldn't bear his aunty's sanctimony, how she'd lingered on the threshold between rooms observing him, as though he were a trophy earned by perseverance; and the way that she'd paraded him round church on Sunday morning with her gloved hand pulling at his elbow, basking in the admiration of her friends, who'd said, 'It's nice to see you back where you belong,' and 'Well done, Helen, bringing this one home,' and 'Don't you make a handsome pair?' Worse than that, she'd told the vicar, 'Yes, we knew it wouldn't take him long to see the light.' That 'we' had riled him. He'd ducked out of the service early, claiming nature's call, and gone down to the phone box at the far end of the lane to reach his sister. Right away, he'd said, 'You know what? Come to think of it, I'd rather have an ulcer.' She'd laughed. 'Next Friday, then?' she'd said. 'Next Friday,' he'd replied, and put the phone down.

Looking at her now, he couldn't tell if she was still awake. He cued up an orchestral record Mr Mayhood liked. 'Carissima'. No movement from his sister. Not a word. The music was so soothing and melodious. He went and took the tumbler from her clutches.

'Oi,' she said, 'I'm not done yet,' but her grip was very loose and she turned over, nestling into the cushions. 'Play this one again. It feels as though I'm in a film.'

'Yeah,' he said, 'a proper weepy.'

She was shivering a bit, so wrapped herself more tightly in the blanket. 'I do feel bad for him, you know.'

'Who?'

'Mr Kimball.'

'Why?'

'He thinks that I don't like him.'

'You don't have to. He's not meant to be your pal.'

'I shouldn't give him such a hard time, though.'

'I didn't know you did.'

She rolled on to her other side. 'Do *you* like him?'

'Not much.'

'He's all right if you get the stick out of his arse.'

'Yeah, maybe.'

'It's always men like Hollis who I give the hardest time,' she said. 'Why is that?'

'You mean Kimball.'

'What did I say?'

'Hollis.'

'Oh. Well, that's the whisky kicking in.'

'You shouldn't take the blame for that, you know,' he said. 'The old man would've jumped without you nudging him. He didn't care for me much neither. Angry at the whole wide world, if you ask me. I'm sort of glad he's gone.'

His sister didn't seem to recognize that he was trying to reassure her. She answered in her gently mocking voice, 'Too sweet by half, miss, that's your problem.'

'Piss off, Joy.'

'And you're a charmer.'

'Hurry up and sleep that whisky off before they get back home.'

'Pipe down,' she slurred. 'I'm trying to listen . . .'

When the record finished, he reset the needle to the start. She was snoring piggishly next time he checked, her mouth gone slack and drooling. So he carried out the White Horse bottle to the kitchen and refilled it at the tap. He drank the dregs left in the tumbler, washed and dried it to a gleam. And then he took them back into the parlour, wondering if he should leave his sister there. The Mayhoods would be out till after midnight. She would keep for a few hours yet.

Upstairs, in his room, he searched his ashtray for a worthy dog-end, but none of them had anything to give. He patted down each pocket hanging in his wardrobe, just in case there was a stray that he'd forgotten. Nothing there. Instead, the feeling of the fabric in the dark made him remember Florence's pyjamas, and those knickers with the frilly trim. He could go and fetch them, hold them to his face again – nobody would know or try to stop him – but the guilt still weighed too heavily inside his chest. So he fell back on his bed and buttoned down his fly. He put one arm across his eyes, so he could see her better. In the floodlights of the garage. Underneath the tractor. On her back. Knees bent, apart. The gather of the overalls between her legs, just for a moment. Now he had a picture of what she wore beneath. His lips had been there and his tongue had licked the cotton . . .

Every time, his pleasure was short-lived and it was weakening the more he did it. He wiped his stomach with his vest, disgusted at himself. He couldn't help imagining her disappointment in him. Things had been much easier in borstal: every boy was at it. After lights out, there'd be bedsprings squealing in the dormitory, fleshy noises from the other

222

cubicles. It was practically expected. But even then, without the shame attached, his mind was like a clock that ticked too loudly. He could never get enough relief. His body was tensed up with urges. And the only way to ease it was to smoke, a habit which had left him feather-mouthed and yellow-fingered by the age of seventeen.

He headed for his sister's room to scrounge for cigarettes.

The lampshade gave a meagre orange light. She hadn't drawn the curtain on one side. Her bed was made so tidily you could've skated on it, but her bath towel had been left in a wet heap upon the floor. He couldn't find her cigarettes. He checked the windowsill, the ottoman, the desk. In the coat behind the door, he found a packet stuffed in the breast pocket. They were Capstans, but they'd have to do. He tipped one out, and then another, and another. Four was probably too many. As he put the last one back, he noticed something on the inside of the lid. Written in blunt pencil. Clumsy and a little smeared.

WO59264

A phone number perhaps? He didn't recognize the area code, but he could look it up in the directory. Something deep within him knew. Wherever Joyce's head had been of late, this had to be a part of it.

He went downstairs again and craned his head in through the parlour door. She was passed out on the sofa, snorting in her sleep. The gramophone had lost its spin. He left her well alone and took himself along the hall, into the draughting room, to sit at Mr Mayhood's desk. In a tray beside the phone, there was a small black book in which they kept important numbers – for clients and contractors and the like; the front page had a list of area codes. He ran his finger down the alphabet and saw it: WO5 for Woldingham. That wasn't far from here. A little further east. Halfway to Kent. What time was it by now? The clock said twenty-five to ten or thereabouts. Too late to phone a stranger. But he dialled. It rang and rang. Nobody home. And then, at last, connection.

All he heard was breathing.

'Is this Woldingham 9266?' he asked, keeping his tone good and friendly.

Breathing.

'Sorry, is this Woldingham 9266? I hate to call so late.' Breathing and more breathing. 'The operator put me through. I hope she hasn't patched me a wrong number. I'm looking for a Mrs –' *Click*. The line went dead. He phoned straight back and no one answered.

The carrot tops are lush in the east field. Florence is bent double with a burlap sack between her knees. She's shaking off the soil and tossing out the duds. The good roots are as long as tablespoons; she puts these in the sack. There he is, one row behind her. Working at a slower rate. A small part of an acre still to go. He looks up. Waves a nosegay he has made from carrots. Florence straightens up and stretches out her back. A face of agony. Then Joyce comes ghosting through the frame. An ursine shadow briefly in the distance with a sack half-full. Zoom out. Cut this. Now they're putting cabbages on the conveyor. He and Joyce are loading at one end. Florence crouches on a trailer stacked with empty crates. The cabbages drop off the belt into a rusty tub in front of her; she packs the best ones. Cut this, too. A static shot. The root cellar in all its glory. Simple, ordinary, finished. It's no more than an ingress to a mound of earth, grassed over. He emerges, bounding up the steps, a sack draped round his shoulders. Gives a thumbs up for the camera, satisfied. Opens out the burlap sack to prove it's empty. Keep it.

December 1952

The car was waiting for her on this lane somewhere, but it was dark by now and there weren't any street lamps. Just a long, straight, narrow road between a grid of fields that looked the same as all the others. She could tell why Mal had chosen it. Any slight misstep and she would end up face down in the ditch and nobody would find her until morning. She was sweating in her winter coat again and dolled up underneath it. When she'd come up with her plan, she hadn't thought about the fuss and primping it entailed. Now, all night, she'd have to wear a skirt that bit her waist as soon as she sat down and chafed her knees as she was walking, not to mention the stiff Woolies bra that seemed to shrink a bit each time she washed it. Perfume, too. At least she'd worn a proper pair of shoes. Earlier, as she'd been pulling on her coat to leave, she'd heard a voice behind her say, 'My goodness, Joyce, don't you look nice.' Florence had been in the dining room. She'd come out with a copy of some journal rolled up in her fist. 'So where's he taking you, this fellow?'

'Only to the pub. It's nothing fancy.'

'Well, I hope he knows how fortunate he is.'

'He will, miss, by tomorrow. How's my hair look?'

'Very pretty. Except – may I?' Florence had come over, re-arranged her fringe and plumped her curls. 'There you are. You're perfect now.'

'By the time I get there it'll all be flattened out again.'

'Why don't you let me drop you in the village?'

'No, miss. Thanks. He's going to pick me up outside the

gate – slight change of plan. Besides, a bit of air will calm me down. I've got the butterflies.' These lies had felt no worse than all the others she had told before, but it was never any less than torment, knowing she'd accepted someone else's kindness without giving back a single honest word. If she'd been asked to open up her handbag then, she would've had no explanation for the contents. The packages weren't heavy, but they bulked the leather at the middle and she'd had to swing the bag low by her knees so it would go unnoticed.

Soon enough, her brother had come down the stairs and leaned one hand upon the newel post, saying, 'Off already, are you?'

'Yeah.'

'You've done your hair up nice,' he'd said.

'Thanks, mouse.'

'All that perfume, too. You must be keen on this one.'

'Stop it. I'm a bag of nerves.'

'Which pub is it you're going to?'

'The Duke of Wellington, I think.'

'And then what?'

'How'd you mean?'

'No dancing afterwards?'

'Well, I don't bloody know. Depends how much he likes me, doesn't it?' she'd told him. 'Shut up now. You're getting me worked up. My lip's all sweaty . . .'

His thick brow had scrunched. 'All right. Have a good time, then. Don't talk his ear off.' And he'd traipsed along the hallway to the draughting room.

'There's no reason to be nervous,' Florence had put in. 'Just be yourself.'

'It's much too soon for that, miss.'

'Well, at least make sure he foots the bill.'

'I'll do my best. I should be home about eleven.'

'There's no curfew. You enjoy your evening.' Florence had a smile that somehow made her look both wiser and more childish. She'd tapped her breastbone with the rolled-up journal. 'Still, it's nice to hear you call this home.'

These sentiments had left a mark on her, but there was nothing she could do with them. She'd wandered up the driveway, out the gate, with Mal's instructions circling in her head. *I'll have a car for you, don't worry.* She'd come to hate the grousing of his voice so much. It was a pain that wouldn't fade. *Just take a walk down Hungry Hill Lane till you reach the bend. I'll park it on the verge a few yards after that.* Well, she was pacing through the darkness now and following the tarmacadam, looking for that bend, but she'd been going for a while and the road had barely turned. *A Vanguard, it'll be. Mint green, but that's not so important – you won't see the colour.* And she didn't even have a torch, in case it drew attention. But she'd brought some matches, fearing she might wind up lost and freezing in the woods. There was an engine ticking over somewhere in the black, a distant shush of wheels. *I'll leave the keys inside the glovebox with a map. You'll need to drive to Streatham Vale.* She hadn't got the chance to argue with him. *I'll put a cross where you're to meet me after.*

For the past two months, there'd been a sort of peace between them – fragile and uneasy – and she'd carried the lead weight of fear inside her belly all that time. She'd smothered it with attitude so nobody would see. She'd dulled the sting of it with labour on the farm. She'd started drinking Mr Mayhood's brandy in the night, to blunt the edge of it enough that she could sleep; and when she had, she'd dreamed of him, Mal Duggan, with an ice cream dripping on his knuckles, a stuffed lion underneath his arm, missing a paw; or she'd dreamed of Mr Hollis in his straw hat, dropping rye seeds on a pure white bedsheet, only when she scooped her fingers in the fallen grain, it was a heap of teeth.

There hadn't been another package since the last one, which she'd taken as a mercy. She and Mal had barely spoken. At the start of every week, she'd made her calls. 'A lovely morning in the countryside again,' she'd said, while sleet had struck the phone box, hard diagonal rain, and one day, out of nowhere, hailstones the size of peppercorns had rapped against the glass. 'Nothing doing yet. Ring back on Tuesday,' Mal had told her. So she had, five Tuesdays in a row. The only information she'd been given was, 'I'm working on a fence, that's all. I wouldn't bother getting shirty with me, Joy, if you've got any sense left in you.' All the while, she'd wondered just what sort of gear could be so hot no fence would touch it. Something wasn't right, and Mal had sounded more and more beleaguered.

She'd thought of going to the coppers with the packages, but they weren't likely to believe her. A history of thieving was a drawback when you needed to be taken at your word. It was the teeth that were the problem. She'd been euchred by those teeth. The bastard knew the game that he was playing. She'd considered dumping them into the compost, scattering the lot of them across the east field while she pulled up carrots, burying the box so far away that nobody could ever dig it up. But there was too much risk with that: she'd hang for it if she got caught. Everyone would think she'd been responsible for what had happened. Mal was always dealing her a crooked hand. He'd played a bower with those teeth, all right. That awful strip of hat inside, just so she'd know whose head they'd come from. Bastard. Worthless bloody bastard. He'd been sending her a message to go with it: *Follow orders and keep quiet. Remember what'll happen if you don't.*

One night, shy of sleep, she'd come up with the bright idea to open all the other parcels. Maybe they might give her the advantage back: if not a joker, then a jack she could lay down to change the pattern of the game. They were underneath her bedpost on the far side, by the wall. She'd heaved the frame back, where the shortest piece of floorboard lifted with a bit of jimmying – the blade of a butter knife worked best and she kept one in her desk drawer for the task. It had served her well, this hidey-hole she'd made – big enough to hold the packages and hard to spot. Removing one, she'd started picking at the tape, but hadn't gone much further. There was nothing to be gained by knowing, she'd decided, and everything to lose. If she kept those packages intact for Mal, as promised, and delivered them to where he needed, maybe he'd release her when the job was done.

There'd been no trace of sunshine in the sky when she'd phoned through to him this morning. Still, 'A fine day in the countryside again,' she'd said.

'Can't argue with you there.'

She hadn't been expecting this, or the contentment in his tone.

'I've got instructions for you, finally,' he'd said. 'We're nearly out the woods.'

'You found a fence?'

'Not quite. A middleman. The buyer trusts him.'

'Jesus. What does that make me, then?'

'Nothing that you weren't before. A go-between.'

'You know this bloke – the middleman?'

'I trust him. We've done bits and pieces down the years.' There'd been a momentary rustle, then his voice had softened. 'Listen here, I'm banking on you, Joy. If this goes wrong for me, I'm going to wind up dead or something worse. And they'll not spare you either.'

'Worse than being dead?' she'd said. 'How's that?'

'Let's hope you don't find out.'

That part had shaken her. A fella with a walking stick had shuffled down the lane to post a letter. He'd looked across the road, towards her in the box, and she'd glared back. The moisture in her mouth had gone. She'd felt a flutter in her bladder. But a robin redbreast had flapped down and landed on the grass outside and she'd relaxed again. As soon as it had darted off, the man had gone away.

'You still there, or what, Joy?'

'Yeah,' she'd said, 'just someone passing by.'

'Well, look, it's happening tonight. You'd best be ready.'

'What d'you mean *tonight*? Am I supposed to just –'

'It's not my problem. Work it out. You'll need the first three parcels. Leave the last one where it is for now.'

'Why not the other one?' she'd said, pretending ignorance.

'Because I say so.'

'All right, Mal. It's just a question.'

'Well, I'm getting tired of them.' He'd huffed. 'You'll need to drive to Streatham Vale.'

'In what?'

'I'll have a car for you, don't worry.'

'Where?'

'Can you just bloody listen for a change instead of badgering?' His voice had fuzzed inside her ear. 'Here's what you're going to do . . .'

Now she could see it, up ahead. The shape of it, at least. A Vanguard parked around the bend. Her fingertips were numb, no matter how much air she blew on them or rubbed. Her handbag beat against her hip like stirrup leather as she walked. The mulch smell of the fields was neither sweet nor sour and not exactly foul. In the stillness of the night, she felt as though she were the only thing alive for miles. Her panting breaths, her footsteps – there was nothing else to hear except her own mad rhythm.

When she reached the car, she touched the bonnet and the radiator grille – a simple test she'd learned from Mal to check how long it had been sitting idle – and she found them tepid. He must've left the car here, slanted on the verge, no longer than an hour ago. She panned her eyes across the distance, thinking she might catch his bald scalp dipping underneath the hedgerows. But there was just a waxing moon, a spread of clouded-over stars, and bony silhouettes of trees, unmoving, far away. One thing Mal was wrong about: the pale green paint-work of the car was obvious up close, reminding her of bathroom suites she'd seen in magazines, the better brands of soap and tooth powder. It wasn't what you'd call discreet, but she was lumbered with it.

The door came open for her nice and easy, and she dropped into the driver's seat, jamming her fat handbag in the space beside her. She rummaged blindly in the glovebox, reaching till her fingers found the keys. And there they were – a pair of them, connected on a ring. The big one turned in the ignition. She switched the headlamps on. The tarmac glazed before her and the tall grass on the verge went blue. She checked the map, where Mal had charted out the route in pencil. It'd take the best part of an hour to get to Streatham Vale, another hour to the meeting point in – where exactly was that? – Oxted? It looked as though she'd have to do a loop round the east end of Surrey, taking in a bit of south-west London. She'd be on the road most of the night. No curfew was a blessing, after all. She tied the headscarf underneath her chin. The tyres skidded on the grass as she pulled off the verge, turning back in the direction she'd just walked.

At the junction, there was nothing coming at first glance; but then, as she steered right, she saw a car was heading down the road without its headlights. She would've hit the horn but didn't want to get into a confrontation, so she hurried out ahead of it. Passing by, she bowed her head from view. Until she was a few miles out of Ockham, she was going to have to keep the headscarf on and make sure that her face was never seen. The more she drove, the more she sweated in the seat. Everything beneath her coat was hot and clammy, while the outer parts were chilled to goose pimples. She wished she'd put on nylons. Snot was pooling at her nose. As she drove, she didn't give much thought to her direction, but she wondered how things might've been if only half the lies she'd told her brother and the Mayhoods had been true.

What might it have been like to meet a kind man at the post office and have him take you for a drink? A fella with brown hair and specs who wore a lovely worsted blazer: that was the description she'd fed Charlie. It didn't sound too bad. She'd always hoped to find herself a Lassiter from *Riders of the Purple Sage* – gentle-natured, brooding, with a hard-set jaw and eyes that withered you right where you stood – but men like him were no more real than any of the fakes who she'd invented. 'I'm not sure what hours he works. He's area manager,' she'd told her brother. 'They've got him going up and down to branches everywhere for miles, and there's hardly any rhyme or reason to it. I'm lucky if I ever see him. I just go there every day and hope that I'll bump into him.' Well, she and her imaginary fella wouldn't have a future after she'd got through with things tonight. He'd get a call to national service or he'd land himself employment overseas. She was going to be out of love again; and, even though it hadn't been a true love, she would miss it.

These country lanes were slim and hard to navigate. The empty arms of trees spanned one side to the other. Headlamps wobbled in the mirror, far behind. The overgrowth of hedges whipped the bonnet as she passed. She kept her speed exactly at the limit. Once she reached the carriageway, she could unwind. Settle in with all the traffic, put her foot down, coast. But for a good few miles, she only had her thoughts for company, which wasn't any company at all.

She didn't know the buyer's name. That didn't trouble her. Sometimes, it was better not to have the information, as it only put her in a weary state, anticipating faces in the room that matched the pictures in her head. Besides, the buyer wouldn't be there. Once she got to Streatham Vale, she'd come across a lighting and repair shop, big gold letters on the window saying: G. G. WILSON'S.

'You can't miss it,' Mal had told her. 'Fella keeps the lamps on overnight so folk can see his wares. The place is lit up like the end of Margate pier. Wilson is the one you're meeting. Don't try walking in the front. Go round the back and knock.'

'Wilson? What is he, a Scot?'

'A Welshman.'

'Well, he'd better know I'm coming.'

'What d'you want, the kettle on? A tray of sandwiches? Just get there for nine thirty.'

'What am I supposed to tell him?'

'Nothing. We've already spoken on the phone. I've made things nice and simple for you, Joy – I know that's how you like it. Go inside and hand him what you've got. He'll give you something in return, then you hop back in the car and drive it straight to me. That's it.'

'And then what?'

'Then we'll see.'

'We'd best be square. I'm done with all this carry-on.'

'You'll do the job right, first. Exactly like I told you.'

'Yeah, the last time I did that it got me nicked, remember.'

'Lightning won't strike twice. You're older now and wiser.'

If only that were true. She might've aged, but all she'd learned in borstal were new ways to make the same mistakes. Here she was again, behind the wheel. Another stolen car. Another lawless errand she was running just to keep him satisfied and tamed. Mal Duggan on her mind from dawn till dusk.

Her own needs pushed aside for his. She might as well have scrubbed the gussets of his long johns, too, and combed his beard and emptied out his chamber pot. She might as well have baked him pies and lain with him at night and borne his grubby children. Even if she could be rid of him some day, he'd always be the rot that plagued her bones, the reason she could never see the permanence of things. He'd spoil the goodness of the air when he was six feet under.

If she tried, she could account for every single car she'd moved for Mal over the years but she could hardly think of any use she'd put the money to, except for the electric bill, the gas and water, telephone, her monthly groceries, some clothes and a few records, tickets for the flicks. Her first delivery had been a Morris, then it was a black Ford Anglia, two Standards and a Singer; then came four of those dull Vauxhall Wyverns and a Velox. She'd done these jobs on weeknights only, so her brother wouldn't have to know. For some of them, Mal had a way of jamming a flat-headed screwdriver into the ignition. For the others, he relied on trickery and wits. In quiet country pubs, he'd steal the keys right out of boozy fellas' pockets while they stood at the urinals or the cigarette machines. In hotel bars, he'd charm old men and slip a blue into their cognac, filch the car keys out their jackets, drive off in their Daimlers and Lagondas after they'd passed out. He'd be up and down the country all week long on visits, never in the same place twice, varying the counties that he worked as though he were rotating crops. For the flashiest cars, he'd always have a fence he could rely on, whether it was somebody in Devon or the Yorkshire Dales. He'd keep his business on the fringes of the cities, which were other people's territory, belonging to the sorts of gangs you didn't want to know your face. But when the car was ordinary, he'd always use the same two fences – one who had a garage out in Sevenoaks, another out in Sittingbourne – and he'd give her the responsibility. 'A wholesome-looking girl like you behind the wheel and no one bats an eye. You won't have any bother in a family car. Just get a bag and fill it up with fruit and veg, make sure it's on the seat beside you. Have a picnic blanket in the back. Dress up nice and get your hair done.' He'd appear at the flat by night, waking her sometimes or finding her halfway through clearing supper. 'Got one for you. Parked it three streets down, by number 57. *Here.*' He'd throw the keys and tell her where she had to go. 'Well, hurry up, girl. Blimey.' And she'd drive for half an hour to Sevenoaks, where, under lantern light, a bloked called Oz would swing his garage doors back for the car, no pleasantries exchanged; or further out, to Sittingbourne, where a white-haired bloke called Munce would do the same. 'You want to stay and have a drink with me this time?' old Munce would ask, a quart of Pusser's springing from his overalls, and she'd refuse. 'All right, darling. More for me.' With that, she'd fetch her blanket and her bag of groceries and catch the late bus home.

All of this, she'd done while she and Mal were still attached; and now that she thought back on it, she'd carried out these jobs because she liked the home she'd fashioned for herself, the little one-bed flat with its neat kitchenette and the magnolia in the neighbour's garden she could gaze at all day from her window if she cared to; and, above all else, the easiness of waking in the morning at no given hour, to wear no uniform, appease no customers, hold no panic as to what the boss would think of her attempts to please or how the other women at the counter felt about her manner with the men returning items for their wives. She'd had a certain kind of life that fitted her, and Mal had made it possible – for this, she'd felt an obligation to the man, which she'd confused with tenderness. Until, one afternoon, he'd phoned to say that he was changing their arrangement. 'Look, it's best you hear this now: I'm tired of living in each other's pockets like we're doing. I've sorted out another place to live and that's where I'll be staying from this point on.' In fact, it must've been approaching evening, as *Mrs Dale's Diary* was on the Light Programme and she'd not long got out of the bath. She could remember how his words had failed to register at first, as though it was somebody else's conversation she'd tuned into, passing by a doorway. 'You can stay put where you are,' he'd said. 'The rent's no bother, and it's handy knowing where to reach you. Hope you understand. It's nothing personal. Just think we've had our run.'

'You're ditching me. By telephone,' she'd said. 'I never pegged you for a coward.'

'Leave it out. Nobody's *ditching* you. I'm changing our arrangement, that's all.'

'You don't want to sleep here any more. That it?'

'I reckon that's about the gist of it.' He'd coughed. 'I only want to make things simpler for the two of us. More work, less play.'

'Simpler for *you*, you mean.' She'd had to sit down on the carpet for a moment with the phone receiver hanging from the wall. Heaving herself up again, she'd said, 'All right, then. Who's going after me? I hope she likes it on her front.'

'Come on, Joy. Don't be that way.'

'You're welcome to each other. Honest. I don't care.'

He'd said, 'You want to keep the flat or don't you?'

'Piss off, Mal,' she'd barked at him. 'You know I do. Where else am I supposed to go?'

'Well, I can see you're not in the best state to talk. I'll give you a few days to get yourself in order.'

'I suppose she doesn't know you're phoning me. Poor girl.'

He'd let this pass and fade. 'OK, then. A few *weeks*, if you need. I'll be in touch.'

For some time afterwards, she couldn't reconcile the hurt

with the relief. She'd felt slighted and rejected, and she couldn't stand it, even though what Mal had given her was what she wanted – a reprieve. It hadn't mattered who the other woman was. Whether he was teaching army boxing combinations to some silly-headed girl like her, if she was prettier or more amenable. Whether it was someone older, a dim tart with lipstick on her teeth who'd open up her legs to keep him satisfied in trade for company, a few bob for the meter. What had devilled her the most was being abandoned. After all the effort she'd put in, the months and months of sufferance. To be ditched the same way he'd once left that Daimler in the alley, with its battery drained, made useless – that type of agony was too familiar, and it hurt her double.

On the weekends when her brother came to Maidstone, she'd put on her most shrugging attitude to ward him off. But Charlie always knew when she'd been crying or when her heart was limping. Now and then, he'd raised Mal's name in conversation and she'd batted it away. 'Some things don't turn out as you were hoping, do they?' she'd said, pleasantly enough. 'It wasn't meant to be.' These words had been accepted for exactly what they were, a means of skirting round the problem. But she'd lost control over her temper sometimes, snapping at him, getting irked by strangers for the slightest look. She'd drunk more than she should've, too. She'd got them kicked out of the cinema for reasons she could scarcely call to mind a few hours after, which had spooked the lad. One Sunday he'd gone home to Aunt Helen early and the next weekend he'd said he wasn't going to visit any more. Well, that had given her a jolt. She'd glimpsed her future days without him and it horrified her. Lying in the gutter with a sluice of rain and horse shit, begging for spare pennies from the passers-by. Her brother all grown up and far away, with better people in his life to love. She'd got herself in order, after that.

There were bills she'd been ignoring – first thing that she'd done was pay them off. Any shops that had her name on tick, she'd settled with them, too. What little she had left, she'd put to cleaning all her pillowslips and bedsheets at the bagwash. And she'd allowed Mal in the flat the next time he'd come knocking in the night with something for her. 'Glad you're feeling better now,' he'd said. 'You know I'll always see you right, Joy, don't you? It's going to work out for the best.' His left hand had been wrapped up in a bandage, with a blurry disc of blood there, on the knuckle side.

'What bit you? Guard dog?'

He'd studied it, as though he'd clean forgotten. 'Nah, barbed wire,' he'd mumbled. 'Not so sure the job was worth it in the end, but oh well . . . You'll take this motor for me now, then?'

'Yeah. Who wants it?'

'Munce.'

'All right.'

'Good girl. I'll just leave them here.' He'd tossed the keys on to the table, looked about the flat and nodded. 'OK. I suppose I'll ring you, then.'

Before he'd reached the door, she'd said, 'I'm short, Mal. If you've got a quid to tide me over. Bus fare and all that.'

He'd fished his wallet out and handed her a ten-bob note. 'I'll get you more another time.'

She'd taken it and watched him go.

For a while, their new arrangement hadn't been much different, excepting that she didn't have to flannel herself down before she went to sleep or listen to him breathing through his mouth the long night through. A few days after she'd dropped off a car for him, she'd find an envelope pushed underneath her door. Ample cash inside to keep her in the workless state she'd grown accustomed to, but never quite enough to last the month. She'd become uneasy in the gaps between Mal's visits.

Weeks could pass without a glimpse of him or any ringing of the phone. Then, just as she'd be getting changed for bed and drawing down the kitchen blind, he'd reappear. Each time looking twice as harried, flabby at the waist. Hair all tinder dry and thin. Scratches round his collar. Once, there'd been a split in his top lip, gone plump and scabby. 'You need to eat less dripping and more greens,' she'd said. 'That shirt's not going to fit you for much longer.'

'Thanks a lot, Joy. You look rotten, too,' he'd said.

In this time, her jobs had multiplied. She'd ferried bits of gear to pawnbrokers in town and further out: new hopsack coats and suits of gabardine he'd taken from a warehouse, leather watch straps, silver napkin rings and carriage clocks. He'd got her carting boxes to the scrapyard on the bus, with sawn-off copper tubing and some pewter pipe-bends he'd ripped out of walls. They were measly, desperate jobs he must've done to ease a burden on himself. Someone had been hounding him, she'd known that much, but she'd not asked for names. By then, she hadn't cared about his troubles. Worse, she hadn't thought Mal Duggan's plight would end up being her own. She'd held the money for him in a biscuit tin below the sink. Three times, she'd woken up and found it empty on the kitchen counter. There'd been signs and plenty of them, but she hadn't heeded any.

Tonight, the Portsmouth Road was bright with freight. There was nothing but a thin white line between her and the other lane, and she was trying not to wonder what it might be like to plough straight through it, into the onrushing traffic. It was safer now to pick up speed. She even put the radio on, high volume, twisting at the dial until she landed on an unfamiliar tune. A fella with a soft, sweet voice, the sort that could bewitch you if it sang you nothing but the pools results. It soothed her for a good few minutes. He was singing about lavender and kings and queens. She waited for his name to be announced, but didn't hear it clearly. Was it Burr Lives? Pearl Ives? Shame. She would've liked to buy his record. It was decent medicine. She drove until the signal weakened, crackled out, and she lost patience tuning in for something different.

The headscarf's knot was rubbing now below her chin. She pulled it off. Her watch was stuck on ten to nine. It wasn't such a complicated route: one road going north-east until Merton, when she'd have to concentrate a little more and check the map. She didn't want to make a wrong turn and wind up in London's belly. Slim odds that she'd ever find her way back out. The city was too dense for her, unreasonable and murky. She preferred its outer edges. All the towns and suburbs. Greenery without the bleakness of the farmland. Neighbours you could call upon, who didn't know your business.

It was getting near to Christmas and, below the gutterings of ordinary houses up ahead, folk had green and red festoons hung out, with dangling clumps of mistletoe above their porches. There were holly wreaths on their front doors and stars made out of foil that twinkled with approaching lights. As pretty as it was, she couldn't raise a festive mood. At Leventree, the Mayhoods had arranged a good-sized fir. She'd watched her brother dress it up with paper chains and glassy ornaments, a dumb grin on his face; Mr Mayhood had put candles on the mantelpieces in the dining room and parlour, sprigs of leaves and berries at their bases; Florence had draped bunting up the stairs – a truly merry evening that had been. Since then, they'd all been busy with the competition work while she'd sat painting shadows at her board and asking if there wasn't something else she could be doing. 'You're being useful as things are,' Mr Mayhood had insisted. 'You're refining your technique,' Florence had said. But they were mollycoddling her and she well knew it. They were keeping her away from the important jobs, because she was a liability. All that she was good for now was *this*. Being a crook. Mal's young accomplice. The dumb pigeon he could train to carry things he didn't want to mucky his hands with. If she wanted better for herself, she'd have to find it far away from him, from here.

*

The morning it had happened was a Friday, round about the time that Charlie would've just been setting out for school. She'd been up early, heating porridge with sultanas in a pan. The phone – which hadn't stirred at all for weeks – had started chiming on the kitchen wall. And that had done it. She'd allowed the trouble in like she was lifting up a sash to get the breeze.

Mal had spoken in that callous, grumbling tone he had: 'There's something that needs doing. Sunday night.'

'I've got Charlie then. I can't.'

'You really think I care what time you're babysitting? If a job needs doing, then it bloody well needs doing. Understand me?'

'But you promised me no weekends. I don't want him catching wind of this.'

'Well, things change. Oz wants it there by Sunday night, or else we miss our chance. It's going on a boat or something, I dunno.' There'd been noises in the background then she couldn't quite make out. Voices. Clattering. 'I'll bring the keys round Sunday.'

'No,' she'd told him. 'No. You can't be here when Charlie is. He thinks we're finished.'

'I'm not asking, Joy, I'm telling. Borough Green is on the way, last time I checked.'

'Take it there yourself, then.'

'You know bloody well I can't.'

'Why not?'

243

'Certain people, that's why. Folk who've had enough of me.'

'Big club, that. I've paid my dues already.'

'All right, don't get clever. I'll be round on Sunday with the keys.'

'No, hang on.' She'd breathed in deeply. Her aunt's house was on the way to Sevenoaks. It wouldn't be impossible, but it'd have to be done properly, on terms of her own choosing. 'I'll need to get my brother out the flat first. I'm not having you around him any more. Just leave them on the table for me while we're gone. I'll keep him out till seven.'

'OK. If that's how you want it.'

'It's not, but I'll have to make it work. You said no week-ends, Mal.'

'And you said you were short of money. Make your mind up.'

Treasure Island. That's how she'd got Charlie out that day. They'd seen it once before and she'd thought Robert Newton was ridiculous and over-egged it as the pirate, but her brother had been taken with the scenery, the Technicolor; he'd even called her Billy Bones a few times after, on account of all the rum he swigged below deck. So she'd passed the local paper after breakfast and said, '*Treasure Island* must be playing still. Maybe I should give it one more try.'

'It's on at the Granada,' he'd said. 'Half past four. I thought you didn't like it, though.'

'Well, no, but I'm not always right the first time.'

'Or the second, or the third –'

'D'you want to go or not?'

'Yeah. As long as we don't have to queue for it.'

In fact, there'd been a short line at the kiosk. She'd bought him popcorn to make up for it, some humbugs for herself to suck on as a way of keeping her attention on the film. But there'd only been one picture rolling in her head that day and she was no more interested in *Treasure Island* by the time it finished. At home, she'd found her favourite tea mug had been left out on the hallway table with the keys inside. A torn-off slip of newsprint underneath it, saying:

JNE 858. 36 LWR FANT

She'd made them boiled eggs and soldiers for their supper. Round eight thirty, once the dark set in, she'd told her brother, 'All right, get your stuff together. Time we got you back.'

Charlie hadn't moved. 'Ah, can't I stay for a bit longer? I can get the nine sixteen.'

'Yeah, and who d'you think Aunt Helen's going to blame if you're not back right on the dot? No thanks.'

'OK, OK.' He'd gone and packed his bag.

It had been a mild night, but they'd had their overcoats – Charlie had his twisted up and tucked inside his bag strap; she'd worn hers unbuttoned.

'You're gonna boil in that,' he'd said.

'Yeah, probably,' she'd said.

'Thanks, Joy, for – you know – for spending time with me when you don't have to,' he'd said.

'What else would I be doing, mouse?' she'd said. 'And anyway, I should be thanking you.'

She'd thought a lot about this moment since: it had lodged inside her heart through borstal, sometimes resting happily and sometimes not. When they'd reached the lane's end, Charlie had gone left towards the bus stop, as they always did on Sundays. But she'd turned right instead.

'Oi, where you going?'

'We're not waiting for the bus tonight. I'm driving you.'

'Shut up.'

'I am.'

'Stop messing. You don't have a motor.'

'You'll see. Come on.' She'd walked them down the slope to Lower Fant Road and kept an eye out for a car parked somewhere close to number 36.

'This is daft. We'll have to wait now for the one at quarter past.'

'I told you, mouse. We're driving.'

'How, though?'

It had been there, underneath a tree, between the downy beams of street lamps. So much fancier than she'd expected. Bigger than her normal type, as well. A Jaguar. Wine red. The number plate was right, though: JNE 858.

'Here were are,' she'd said.

'Is this a joke?'

She'd simpered at him. 'I've just got to ask if I can borrow it, that's all.'

'From who?'

'My friends who live here.'

'Must be good friends, if they let you near their Jaguar.'

'Well, I can't help it if some people like me more than you do.' She'd nudged his shoulder. 'Wait there. I'll just be a tick.'

The only house with lights on had been number 45, across the road, a cottage tucked back from the rest. She'd got the shudders all right, heading up the gravel path to ring the bell, with Charlie watching from the kerbside. As the door had opened, she'd said quietly to the vexed old fella on the threshold, 'I'm sorry to disturb you, but I found these on the stones there, by your gate. I thought they must be yours.' She'd handed him two half-crowns from her coat.

'Well, I – thank you very much,' the man had said. 'The missus must've dropped 'em.'

'I shouldn't take the glory. It was really my kid brother over there who spotted them.' She'd turned and waved.

The man had gestured thanks to Charlie, too, nodding and

smiling. 'Awful good of you to bring them in. Most wouldn't. I should give one back as your reward.'

'Oh, no. What'd be the point then, eh? Enjoy your evening. Cheerio.'

'Bless you, thank you. Cheerio, then.' The man had backed away and shut the door.

She'd ambled down the path towards her brother, flashed him a thumbs up. 'All sorted.' Bringing out the keys, she'd wandered round the long red bonnet, opened up the driver's side. 'Not bad, eh?'

'It's a corker.' As soon as he'd got in, he'd started feeling up the leather, reaching out to stroke the walnut.

'Wait until you hear it go,' she'd said.

'What's it, two and a half litres?'

'Haven't got the foggiest.'

She'd not been used to driving such a grand machine. Everything had looked so different on the dashboard. The controls had been in places that she wasn't used to. The ignition on the fascia with a separate starter button. Everywhere a silver knob or dial for twisting. She'd turned the key and pushed the starter, but the engine wouldn't fire. 'That's strange,' she'd said. The petrol gauge was showing half a tank. 'It's not done this before.'

She'd given it another try. It coughed and scratched. Another try. Another.

'Joy, stop. That's not helping.'

'It can't be the batttery. What's wrong with it?'

'You've got to –' He'd trailed off quickly, with a downward glance. 'Tell you what, why don't you go and ask your friend what's wrong with it?'

'I'm not disturbing him again.'

'How come?'

'He's got an early start tomorrow.'

'Right. Works down a coal mine, does he?'

'Shut up, mouse.'

'What is he, then?'

'A doctor, if you must know.'

'How'd you meet him?'

'That's my business.'

'Is he married?'

'No.' She'd checked her watch. 'The spark plugs must need cleaning.'

He'd ignored this. 'That bloke's much too old for you. You know that, right?'

'Don't start. He's just a kind old man who likes me, that's all. He gets lonely and we keep each other company.'

'Yeah, and then he leaves a fiver on the table for you.'

'*What?*'

'Don't act surprised. I know that's how you earn a living. I mean, it's bloody obvious. You've got no job. But you can still afford the flat. And all those records you keep buying. Pretty clothes. And now some bloke just lets you take his motor for a spin? Come on.'

She'd wanted to reach out and strangle him. 'Jesus, Charlie. Are you calling me a brass?'

'Well, aren't you?'

'No I'm bloody not. Who's put that in your head? Aunt Helen?'

He'd shrugged and stared at his reflection in the window. For a good few minutes, they'd said nothing to each other. She'd sat there, seething, till the dials on the dash had blurred away. Her estimation of herself had sunk. She'd thought of prim old Helen and her godly friends, chuntering away to one another in the nave: *Of course she's got no job to speak of but she manages to keep a flat, as if by magic. Everybody knows she has no scruples, that one. Shine a penny up and she'd be yours . . .* Then her eyes had shifted to the little clock on the speedometer. She couldn't waste another moment, dwelling. 'Look, we're going to have a proper conversation, you and me – I'm not letting you go round with all that nonsense in your head. But now we're *really* late and I don't have any time to put you right. So do us both a favour, eh? Step out and have a look below the bonnet, see if you can tell what's going on with it.'

Sighing, he'd climbed out and rolled his sleeves up, leisurely about it. As he'd peered in through the windscreen at her, smirking with the pleasure of some private thought, she'd marvelled at the sight of him, how handsome he'd become. There'd been a fraction of their mother in his attitude and something of their father in the lollop of his fringe across his brow. If he'd been anybody else at all except her own blood kin, she would've clouted him right in the mouth for saying what he'd said. But it was nothing that she hadn't thought about herself. There wasn't too much difference between doing one man's bidding for the money or a hundred's, by her judgement. She might not have been a proper brass, but she was only one bad twist of fate away.

While Charlie had undone the bonnet lid and lifted it, she'd sat there having visions of her doom. Her heart had nested in her throat. Her palms had glossed. Her lips had parched. He'd stooped to tinker with the motor. When he'd come back up, his fingertips were dark with muck. 'All right. Let me have a try,' he'd said, and pushed his fringe back with his wrist. 'Budge over.'

'Nah, your feet won't reach the pedals. Have you fixed it?'

'Probably.' He'd shut the bonnet, tightened up the grips. Standing on the driver's side, he'd said again, 'Go on. Budge over and we'll see.'

'Fine.' She'd climbed across into the empty seat.

Dropping in behind the wheel, he'd said, 'How often does he let you drive this?'

'Why's it matter?'

'Tell me.' He'd wiped down his fingers on his trouser legs before he'd touched the panel.

'I dunno. A few times every month, depending.'

'Enough to know by now, then.'

'What?'

'Well. Do you see a lever for the choke? I don't.'

'Oh, *that*.'

'The starting carb's electric. If you're running it from cold like this, it's bound to give you gyp.' He'd turned the key. 'You hear that rumble? It's the fuel pump, letting fuel into the chambers. The starting carb is wired to the panel lamps, so you'll need to switch those on. And *then* you push the starter.' With one press, the engine had fired up for him and revved. 'You see? Now, when it settles down a bit, shut off the starting carb. And you can twist the throttle over here, look, so the idle speed goes up. Some days, it'll start right off the bat, no trouble whatsoever, so you must've had some luck the last few times you drove it.'

'Yeah, that must be it.' She'd gazed at the dark shapes ahead of her: rooftops laced with bowing wires, the undercarriage of the clouds. 'I'm such a clot.' He hadn't given a reply, but something had occurred to her as they'd changed seats again. 'Hang on, why'd you get your hands all dirty, then?'

'I moved the fanbelt round a bit. I thought I might as well put on a show for you.'

She'd switched the headlights on and started driving. 'Better stop your smirking,' she'd said, 'or it's going to be a bumpy ride.'

*

On Streatham Vale, the shops had CLOSED signs hung askew. Bakeries and butcher's had their awnings wound in for the night. Chemist's had their blinds pulled down. The greengrocers had taken in their sandwich boards; the hairdressers had left them folded in their doorways. There were fellas out on bicycles, scarves flapping on the breeze. Couples walking arm in arm along the pavements with their collars up, hats on, their exhalations steaming. From the junctions, rows of terraced houses branched off, decked with loose net curtains barely thick enough to blot the shadows of the folk inside. Christmas trees in every downstairs window, done up nice with garlands of red ribbon or white snowflakes cut from paper. It didn't feel like London but it was – the dull crust some would cut through just to reach the softer parts.

At the next parade of shops, she saw it – G. G. Wilson's, on the corner – and it seemed to hum with light. The paving stones outside looked buttery and warm. She drove straight past, but slowed. A little further up, she steered into a side road, parking where a street lamp wasn't working. She tied her headscarf tightly, gave herself a quiet sermon in the rear-view mirror, breathed. Stepping out, she heard the dull beat of the same announcer's voice on radios up and down the street. She didn't pass a single person on her way.

Wilson's had a side door, not a back door – that made *two* things Mal was wrong about so far. She didn't cross the road and walk right up to it. She reasoned it was better to stay on the pavement opposite, make a left, *then* cross. It was too dark now to read her watch. She looped back to the shop. If she was late, it wasn't by enough to rile anyone. She knocked and, while she waited on the street, she eyed the shop's display. So many standing lamps with frilly shades. Desk lamps, table lamps, old-fashioned, modern. Spindly craning arms and glassy hoods. Wall lights gleaming in a hundred different ways. There was an ugly fixture near the front – a gold sconce, holding two fake candles with electric bulbs. Of all the things to see. Aunt Helen had these on her landing, where the sacred photos of dead Uncle Sid were hung. She had to look away.

Footsteps neared. A lock was turned. The door swung open and a red-haired fella in a grubby topcoat stared at her. 'You're Joyce, then, are you?'

'Mr Wilson?'

The fella shook his head. 'In here.'

He led her through the hall, which stank of rising damp. The woodchip was unpainted and it curled above the skirting boards. There was a staircase, heading nowhere that she hoped to be. As the fella paced ahead of her, she noticed that he had a hammer in his hand, the lightweight kind you use to put up pictures, stubby at one end. They approached a door which said STAFF ONLY on the architrave. The red-haired fella went inside and held it open for her.

'After you. First on your left,' he said. 'You going to wear that thing all night?'

She yanked her headscarf loose and tucked it in her sleeve.

'That's better,' said the fella, head aslant. 'Now he'll see your lovely curls.'

She forged a smile and brushed right past him.

Through she went, into the brights of Wilson's shop. The countertop below the till was made of glass, as in a jeweller's, but instead of fancy rings and whatnot laid out for the customers to browse, there was a neat array of bulbs. More shapes and sizes than she would've thought possible. The carpet had gone bald where the attendants' feet had worn it down over the years. A mess of paperwork was piled up on the shelves, beyond the view of customers. In the backroom to her left, she found the man himself. Wilson was perched on his desk between two stacks of ledgers with his shoe-heels swinging in the hollow underneath. He didn't look at all as she'd imagined him, but no one ever did.

'Good evening. You're Mal Duggan's girl, then, are you?' His voice was throaty, and his Taffy accent thick. 'He told me you were tall.'

'He told me you were Welsh,' she said. 'I'm disappointed.'

There was a crack of laughter from behind her, where the ginger fella was now leaning with his hammer in the doorway.

'Very good,' said Wilson, 'very good.' He hopped down from the desk and offered her a ciggie from his silver case.

'No thanks.' For all she knew, he could've doused it in some sort of chemical.

'Have a sit down there, why don't you? Take the weight off for a bit.'

As he lit one for himself, he eyed her through the climbing smoke. The smell of the extinguished match was pleasing and it steadied her a bit. Wilson's skin had deep marks from a bad spell of the chickenpox or pimples in his youth, which must've been a long time in the past. Everything about the man was either grey or white. His bony shoulders jutted, made his blazer hang too loosely at the middle. He styled his hair so fussily, a parting at the centre deep enough to hold a pencil.

'Do you like my shop?' he asked.

She shrugged. 'It's nice if you like lamps. Must cost you, though.'

'Why's that?'

'To keep the leccy on all night.'

'You're right,' he said, and ooed some fumes out in a ring. 'It helps me shift the stock, though, and besides –' He flicked his head up as a gesture to the fella at the door, who came inside. 'We had these windows painted black all through the war. Then we had them boarded up as well. We'd get a breakage every other night. Attracted lots of bother from the wardens. Busybodies, all of them. When it was over, I decided to embrace the light, you know. And sod the cost. The punters like it. So do I now, come to think of it.' He reached to knock some ash into the plant pot on his desk, then smiled at her. The gap between his two front teeth was oddly wide. 'I believe you've brought me something, lovey. Are you going to let me have it?'

'I've been waiting,' she said, 'but you seemed to want a chat.'

Again, the laughter from behind her.

'Dear me, you're just like him,' Wilson said. 'No manners.'

'Leave it out,' she said. 'I'm not like him. I'm not like anyone.' And she unclasped her handbag on her lap. One by one, she brought out Mal's three parcels, laying them before the Welshman on the desk. For a moment, it appeared that Wilson was expecting more – he was peering at them with a wry expression – so she said, 'That's all of them.'

'Good good.'

'You need to give me what I came for now.'

'Oh, do I?' Wilson said. He drew on the last embers of his cigarette and stubbed it in his plant's dry soil. 'I think I'd better check these first, my dear, if it's OK with you.'

He went and got a knife out of his drawer and sliced the tape on all the parcels, tearing off long strips and bundling them inside his fist, until he could attack the layers of paper underneath. He ripped them back and what was left there on his desk surprised her. Three glass jars of Brylcreem, full up to the brim.

She must've taken her next breath too fast, because he looked at her and said, 'You've really got no clue what you've been carting round here, do you?'

She said nothing.

'Show her, Rick,' he said, and sat down in his chair.

The other fella tucked his hammer in his belt and came to fetch the jars. At the back end of the room, there was a small handbasin with a corded kettle on a shelf, which Rick topped up and set to boil. 'Have you got that little doo-dah, boss?' he called, and Wilson ferreted about inside his drawer again, propelling what he found across the room for Rick to catch. It seemed to be a tea strainer. Rick fetched the teapot, rinsed it out. The kettle gasped and rumbled on the shelf while he got on with twisting off the lids from all three jars. He spooned the lumpy Brylcreem out of them into the empty teapot.

'Just a minute,' Rick said. 'It works quicker if it's boiling hot.'

'Whatever's coming out of that, I won't be drinking it,' she said.

'Me neither,' Rick said. 'More than my job's worth, believe me.' When the kettle was done simmering, he poured the water in the pot and swirled it round. 'Here, grab on to this for me,' he said, and passed her the tea strainer. 'Just in case they try escaping.'

She had to hold it out over the sink while he slow-poured the milky liquid from inside, sieving out what dribbled from the spout. The steam got to her face and stung it.

'That'll do,' Rick said. 'Let's have a look what Santa's brought us.' And he put the teapot down in front of Wilson on the desk, who craned his lamp above it, lifting up the lid and blowing sharply on his fingers when it burned him.

'Ouch, I never learn,' the Welshman said. Then, looking in the pot, his eyes grew round. 'Well, goodness me. Your fella wasn't kidding, was he? I've not seen too many pure as these.'

'He's not my fella.'

'Makes no odds to me. You want to see or don't you?'

In the watery dark innards of the pot there was a diamond gleam. Fifty of them, maybe more. Each one small but dazzling. They held more colours than she knew existed, splintering the light and spinning it. As she leaned away, she felt a little dizzy. 'I'll have that ciggie now, if you don't mind,' she said, and took a seat.

Wilson let her have one from his case and lit it for her. While she sat there, relishing the smoke, Rick fished out the gems and dried them with a scrap of cloth. He laid them out upon the desk before his boss. Then, one stone at a time, the Welshman put them under his examination, a jeweller's loupe clamped in the socket of his eye, a pair of tweezers in his hand. She watched their rainbow shimmer in the lamplight as he turned them round and round. The more of them he scrutinized, the more content he seemed. 'Everything's as we were promised,' he said. 'That's good news for your fella. And for you.'

'I told you – not my fella.'

'If you say so.'

'I'm a go-between, that's all.'

He hummed. 'Let's get this done, so we can all shake hands and say ta-ra.' With this, he reached across the desktop for the telephone and lifted the receiver. As he dialled, he screened the number with his other hand. It hardly seemed to ring before the call connected. 'It's a yes,' he said. 'All's good from where I'm sitting.' Furrowing his brow at her, he hummed again. 'That's hard to tell . . . I'd say she's brought a bit of attitude with her, but that's to be expected, I suppose . . .' She could hear an outline of the voice that answered him, but couldn't understand what it was saying. 'I reckon so. Keeps telling me they're not attached . . . Enough to know what she's involved with, anyway . . . Fine. Right you are. OK.' And, suddenly, the phone was being offered to her. 'Wants to speak to you,' he said.

'Who is it?'

'It's your mother.' Wilson jiggled the receiver. 'Come on. You should never look a gift horse in the mouth, that's what *my* old mam taught me.'

She stubbed her ciggie in his plant pot, took the phone. 'Hello?'

'Hello there. I believe you're Joyce?' It was a woman's voice, or else the meekest bloke who ever spoke the language.

'Yeah, and who are you?'

'A fool for diamonds,' came the answer. 'But nobody can tell me what to spend my money on now, can they? And it seems as though we have a deal.' There was something very airs-and-graces to the voice, the t's and d's so crisp they sounded forced.

'It looks that way.'

'And yet . . . I can't help thinking I should walk away from this one. Something's pecking at me and I've not been sleeping. Would you help to put my mind at ease?'

'You're asking the wrong person,' she said. 'All I am's a go-between. That's it.' Her heart was clapping now. Her fingers had gone sweaty on the phone. The waistband on her skirt was digging at her kidneys.

The woman took a breath. 'Well, tell me this, at least. How come a girl like you winds up involved with Mr Duggan?'

'I dunno,' she answered. 'How'd *you* get involved with him?'

The woman made a throaty noise. 'With both eyes open. And I still don't like it.' There was a pause then, while some other thought was being pondered. 'I've known a few rats down the years, Joyce, I can tell you that for free. And Mr Duggan, well, he's close to being the rattiest of all. He's never been too popular and now he's made an awful lot more enemies. I wanted you to know that.'

She wasn't sure what she was meant to say. Did they expect her to defend him? 'Sorry, I don't understand this conversation.'

'I'll be clearer, then.' The woman let a moment pass. 'Those diamonds that you've brought along – they're stolen. Which is not the problem, really. No, the trouble is from *where*. From *whom*. I think it's fair to say that there are certain jewellers you don't touch in certain parts of London. There are people you don't want to pit yourself against, unless you want your tongue cut out and posted to your grandma for a lark. But that won't stop the likes of Mr Duggan. Why? It's like I told you, Mr Duggan is a rat, and rats are always desperate. They'll go anywhere for what they want, do anything eventually. And if you let them in your door just *once*, they'll keep on coming back and coming back, until you're just as desperate as they are. So, you see, I've got a problem to consider. Which is why I hoped to speak to you.'

'I don't know anything,' she said. 'I'm just a go-between.'

'Yes, so you keep insisting.'

'Well, it's true.'

'But you can understand my situation.'

'I suppose.'

'So, tell me this: are you a rat like him, Joyce?'

'No.'

'Don't rats associate with other rats? I thought they did.'

'Not me.'

'You're going to have to prove that, I'm afraid.' Next time the woman spoke, she sounded closer, louder. 'Joyce, I won't be paying you a penny for those diamonds. I've decided to dispense with Mr Duggan altogether. It'll keep the waters peaceful. Do you understand me now?'

Here they came again, the shudders.

'Speak up, dear. I need an answer.'

She couldn't get the words out. It was only when the Welshman reached to take the phone back that she managed something in a hurry. 'Yeah, OK, I think I get it. Where does that leave *me*?'

'That's going to depend on a few things,' the woman said. 'I'm giving you a chance to help me catch a rat. The easier you make that go, the sooner I'll forget that you exist.'

★

Her brother had been urging her to put her foot down. 'You've got two and a half litres underneath the bonnet,' he'd said, 'and you're driving like a sad old lady. Come on, at least push it up to forty.' She'd gone to thirty-five, no higher, but it hadn't mattered. They'd been somewhere outside Wrotham Heath on the A20. Almost back in Borough Green. She'd caught the flash of the police car's brightwork in the mirror. 'Jesus, Charlie. Now look what you've gone and done.' No sooner had he twisted round to see, the bell was ringing and the STOP POLICE sign had been lowered.

Her brother hadn't panicked – not at first. 'You'll only get a ticket, won't you?'

If he hadn't been there with her, she might well have kept on going. But she'd steered on to the shoulder of the road.

'Well, won't you?'

The coppers had drawn up close behind. There'd been two of them, but only one had trundled over in his uniform. When he'd knocked on the window, she'd obliged him, winding it right down so he could stoop and get a look at her. In one quick motion of his eyes, the copper had appraised the situation. 'Evening, miss,' he'd said. 'Is this your vehicle?'

'No,' she'd said. 'I borrowed it.'

'From whom?'

She'd peered towards the dashboard. 'I don't think you'd know him, constable.'

'I see. And here's me thinking I know everyone round here.' The copper had leaned in and spied the leather seats, the walnut trim. 'A rather fancy motor for a young girl to be driving. And expensive, too. I'll need to see your licence, please.'

'Don't have it on me. Sorry.'

'Then you'll need to bring it to the station. You've got seven days to do so.' He'd lifted out the little notebook from his pocket. 'Now then, I shall ask again, if you don't mind: who does the car belong to?'

She'd not answered. The traffic had crawled past. She'd seen three children kneeling on the back seat of a Morris, gawping at the trouble she was in. She'd waved at them. Her brother had said, 'Tell him, Joy. Go on.'

She'd cleared her throat and said, 'It's Long John Silver's.'

And the copper had exhaled. 'All right, then, miss. We're going to need you to stay put.' He'd slid his notebook back into his pocket, made a gesture to the other copper, who'd got out and stomped towards them. 'You and PC Higgs can get acquainted while I use the radio. Please don't make him have to put you in the bracelets. Either one of you. I'll need those keys out the ignition, too.' She'd passed them over. 'Long John Silver. Crikey. Your poor mother must be awful proud of you two jokers, eh? Wait there.' The copper had trudged to his car.

That's when her brother had begun to fret. 'What's going on? Why didn't you just tell him?' He'd looked confused and haunted. Mouth ajar and nostrils quivering. It was rage and disappointment on his face. Sheer disbelief, a bit of hatred. She'd expected him to cry, but hadn't been prepared for the unholy sight of it: the glut of tears, the sudden crumpling of his face, as though he were a little kid who'd tripped and scraped his elbow. Sniffing back the hurt, he'd said, 'Why can't you just be honest for a change?'

'Because I can't,' she'd said. 'I'm sorry, mouse.'

'Don't call me that. For God's sake – *Joyce*. Just tell him or you're going to ruin everything. Just tell him, Joyce. This isn't fair.'

Such a tired announcement of her name, as though he couldn't even bring himself to speak it. She'd tried to lay a hand upon his shoulder, but he'd shrugged it off. Then PC Higgs had reached her window, saying, 'Let me take your details, please. Who's going first?' There hadn't been a chance to tell her brother everything would turn out fine, the way she used to do when they were younger. They were side by side in silence on the back seat of the coppers' car before he'd even looked at her again.

*

As she waited at a set of traffic lights just south of Croydon, it occurred to her that *still* she didn't know the buyer's name. With circumstances being what they were, she hadn't thought to seek the information. Now she was in league with some posh-speaking woman with a face she couldn't tell from any other. She was being followed by two strangers in a black saloon, whose cigarettes were venting fumes out of their windows, scarcely a few yards behind her. It was doubtful she'd improved her situation – if anything, she'd only made herself more vulnerable to harm. But she felt certain of one thing: her brother would be safer with Mal Duggan gone, and she was glad of that result. No waking up in fright again because she thought she heard Mal's whisper in her ear. No more wondering what he would make her do: *take this, fetch that, drive it here, stop asking questions, shut your fucking trap, lie still*. She hoped they'd throw his body face down in a hole so he could rot there, belly first.

The route was leading her to Woldingham – or was it Oxted? She was checking her direction on the map each time she had a chance to stop. From this point, it was only B roads till she reached a crooked yellow line called Chalkpit Lane, which Mal had crossed with pencil. There was a jagged symbol on the page there, labelled WORKS, which didn't give her the most hopeful feeling. In the boot, she had an overnight bag full of sales brochures for lamps and lighting fixtures, packed for her by Rick. A layer of banknotes set on top – no more than fifty quid, as far as she could tell. A consolation prize. 'You're going to want a weapon,' he'd said, 'in case he tries to scarper – you could slow him down with it. The boss looks kindly on that sort of thing.' When she'd told him she'd come empty-handed, he'd said, 'Take the hammer,' and she'd put it in her handbag, not a word of thanks.

The lights went green. She almost stalled the motor. No beep from the black saloon behind, which made it worse. She drove on, mindful of her speed. The radio was tuned to something pretty, but she couldn't take much comfort in its noise. Her brother would be working at his draughting table now. The competition had been keeping everyone up late – there seemed to be no end of drawings to prepare and documents to write. Her only contribution had been typing. Mr Mayhood had instructed her to set up in the dining room with his Imperial and a stack of thick white paper. 'You'll need to practise first,' he'd said, 'to get your rhythm.' He'd given her the folder with the Proctor house's specification – all eighty-something pages, with their fiddly indentations and alignments. She'd known right away that it would take her weeks to get it looking right. He'd said, 'Please copy it as best you can. Every page identical to how it's been presented here. If you can master that type-writer, you're going to save the rest of us a lot of time ahead of our submission date.' Well, she'd tried – God knows she'd given it her all – but she wasn't any better as a secretary than she was at drawing elevations. Later, Mr Mayhood had come back and taken one brief glance at her attempt. He'd scratched the stub-ble on his throat. 'All right, Joyce,' he'd said. 'If typing's not your forte, we'll find something else for you to do.' But she'd only been assigned to colourwashing prints since then and reading the McGoodwin book, which, in a mindless sort of way, she'd quite enjoyed. Any scraps of competition work had gone to Charlie, and he'd given them that steady focus he applied to everything. Recently, she'd come to feel more grateful for their differences. Her brother was a special lad – she'd always known it – but she understood another aspect of him now: he grew more in her absence. Their aunty had repeated it so often – *You know he's better off without you, Joyce* – and, selfishly, she'd railed against the notion. Because she used to think it was her job to keep her brother grounded. To live in such a way that it reminded him of home – their real home, with their father, who would dangle him above the back lawn by the heels to make him squeal with laughter, and their mother, who would read him Edward Lear's daft rhymes at bedtime and make funny faces in his mashed potatoes out of peas. Except – she'd realized it lately – these weren't Charlie's memories, they were just her hand-me-downs. And when he looked at her, he didn't see their parents and their lives and what they'd been through. None of that. He saw a big dumb lump who'd landed him in borstal, a reminder of the things he'd lost, the family he'd barely known. If their mum and dad had loved them, he could only take her word for it. The painful part was to accept that Aunty Helen had been right from the beginning.

She kept driving, on and on, until it seemed as though there was no world beyond the arc of her own headlights. One place smeared into the next. The roads grew steeper, thinner, and the evergreens began to show themselves, then bare trees with their branches arching overhead, forming a tunnel. It was so much darker in the countryside. There was a frost already on the verges. She had more instructions in her head than she could hold – the buyer's, Mal's, the Mayhoods', Mr Kimball's. One day, she might get to dish the orders out herself. She was supposed to carry out Mal's plan, exactly as he'd told her, and keep him occupied until the buyer's men arrived. But what if these two hard knocks in the car behind weren't sharp enough? What if Mal had second-guessed them? What if he'd prepared for it?

Turning on to Chalkpit Lane, she braked and watched her

mirror. Seconds passed without a glimpse of the saloon. She worried that she'd made the left too quickly, but it rolled up at the junction with its indicator flashing and came after her. The tarmac was uneven now and broken at the edges. She was flanked by ghostly trunks of shrubs and saplings. Gorse and briar. Everywhere, a slop of leaves. And suddenly, her wheels were skittering downhill. She took her foot off the accelerator, let the car glide onwards. She was twisting in the dark, towards a pleasant-looking cottage with an empty driveway. Beyond that, a clutch of houses on the slope. She carried on until she caught a roadsign leaning on the bank: OXTED QUARRY. A familiar jagged symbol. Only fifty, sixty yards and she was there.

No floodlights on the outer fence. No wall. The entrance was a gravel track that led up to a gatehouse with a barrier. A dark mist loomed behind it. Two enormous chimneys puffing in the distance. She tapped the brakes twice so the men behind would see her blinking lights. As she veered towards the quarry gate, the black saloon went straight ahead. The idiots had messed it up already. She couldn't beep the horn or flash her lights at them. What now? She reached across and fetched her handbag, rooted for the hammer. It was slim enough to fit inside her coat sleeve. With her arm raised slightly, it would sit right in her elbow's bend. Not much of a defence, but it could do some damage.

She approached the gatehouse at a crawl. The lights were on inside and out. There were no other cars that she could see, although a few marked spaces were left vacant near the fence. Mal had told her that she only had to show up where he'd crossed the map and he'd be right there to meet her. So where was he? Maybe she had come to the wrong entrance. All she could do was wait.

She pulled into a parking space and shut the headlamps off. Was she supposed to let the engine run as well? She kept it idling. The hammer rested on her forearm like a splint. She held the wheel, did nothing except stare between the fence's slats, into a barren patch of land, grassed over. Then came movement in the corner of her eye. A shadow left the gatehouse, stepping out. His footseps crunched the gravel. It was Mal. He wore a uniform – white shirt, smart trousers and a chip-bag hat like fellas in the air force had – but she could spot his bulk a mile away, the slink of him. He walked up to the passenger side and climbed straight in.

'You work here now?' she said. 'Or have you joined the Boys' Brigade?' She even mustered up a little laugh, so he would see how normal she was acting.

'Filling in for someone,' he said, pulling off the hat and tossing it into the back. 'One night only.'

'I suppose the bloke who's meant to be here got a poorly feeling, did he? Out the blue.'

'You really want to know?' He grabbed her by the jaw as though it were a ripe tomato he was choosing at the greengrocer's. 'Nah, I didn't think so. Look at me,' he told her, shoving his nose close to hers. She sniffed away the shock, glared back at him. His eyeballs were a jelly of red veins. His breath was rank and yeasty. 'All right.' He released her. 'Where's my money?'

'In the boot.'

'It all went like I said it would, then?'

'More or less.'

'And how did the old Taffy treat you?'

She gripped the wheel. 'Like he was happy for the Brylcreem.'

Mal leaned back. 'He showed you, did he?'

'Yeah. He wouldn't let me go until he'd checked them.'

'All right. Good. So now you know.' He rubbed his hands together. 'Shut the engine off. I need the keys.'

'What for?'

'So I can get my money out. You'd better not have driven here with it unlocked.'

'Piss off.' She took them out of the ignition, slapped them in his hand.

Again, he gazed at her. 'You look much older, all dressed up,' he said. 'Not sure it suits you.'

'Same,' she answered.

'Well, at least you've got your figure, eh?' He snickered and got out. 'Stay there.'

A moment passed. She sat unmoving in the driver's seat, uncertain what to do or say, or how she ought to be positioned for his anger when it came. She wound the window down as far as it would go. The quarry air was dry and chalky. She could hear the faint clack of machinery somewhere. No sign of the black saloon in any of her mirrors. Those idiots had lost her. Or they'd ditched her. Either way, she was alone with him. A surge of dread burned through her guts. Her stomach was all acid. As the bootlid rose, she watched the mirror, but his face was hidden. He was rummaging inside the boot for less than half a minute. She heard him saying, 'No no no, what's this, you stupid cow, you stupid fucking cow,' and he slammed the boot shut. Then his shoes went scuffing in a hurry on the gravel. He was on the driver's side, the overnight bag in his hand. He dropped it at his feet. And she was going to ask him what was wrong, and do her best to show her innocence, but he'd already reached in through the window. Her hair was in his fist and he was hauling her up by the scalp. His mouth was right against her ear. 'Tell me now,' he said. 'They coming for me?'

'I don't know,' she said.

He heaved and twisted at her hair until her face was up against the window frame.

'I don't know,' she said again. 'What's going on?'

The door clunked, opened, and she slumped down to the gravel with her legs still in the footwell. Mal's enormous shoe was pushing on her jaw, her neck. 'Last chance,' he said. 'Who's got my money?'

But she couldn't speak with all the pressure on her throat. She croaked and gasped for air. The hard edge of his sole poked at her windpipe. He snorted inwards like a pig and spat on her. That did it – the humiliation. The warm wet shame of it upon her cheek. She worked the hammer from her sleeve and cracked it on his knee with all the strength she had.

He yelped, as mongrels do when they are beaten. Hopping, spinning, dropping. And the strain released. She sucked the air in sharply. He was wincing and he couldn't stand, but tried to nonetheless. His hobbling made her smile. 'You fucking bitch,' he said, as she got up, 'you've fucking kneecapped me!' His spit tracked down her face. He was on his backside, glaring up at her, as though she weren't a danger. As though he didn't think she would be capable of any more. She wiped her cheek against her shoulder. None of it would end unless she ended it. She saw that now. 'So are we square yet, Mal?' she said. He shook his head and spat again. Then, aiming for the thatch of hair above his brow, she brought the hammer down on him. The second time, he raised his arm to block it, but the stub end skimmed right off and struck him hard above the temple. Down he went, like meat upon the butcher's block, face up. She'd never heard a silence quite so clear.

The starry sky was dulled by all the quarry's smoke. For a moment, she just stood there, waiting for her lungs to work as normal, but she couldn't seem to fill them. Every fibre of her body shook. She couldn't think. The wreck of Mal lay but a yard from her and she was happy not to look at it. Come dawn, the crows would pick at him, make hollows of his eyes.

Next thing, a motor rumbled in the darkness. A voice behind her said, 'You done all right there. Good clean hit.' She flinched. It was a hare-lipped fella in a peacoat and a tweedy cap. He raised his hands so she could see he meant no harm. The leather of his gloves was faded at his palms.

'You took your time,' she said.

'We had our orders.'

'Well, you let him choke me half to death.'

'I would've stabbed him, but you beat me to it. Glad you did.' He scanned the yard. 'We'll sort it out from here.' The black saloon drew closer, headlamps off. Another fella climbed out and went in the gatehouse, killed the lights. She couldn't tell the near from the far. But she could feel the fella take the hammer from her fingers, saying, 'Best you let us dump this for you, eh?' The other bloke came over with a lantern, laid it at the back end of their car. He was pale and short and scarred across the eyebrow like a featherweight. She watched them lift Mal from the stones.

'God almighty. Should've hired a crane.'

'A whopper, ain't he?'

'It'll take a load of bricks to weight him down. Dear me.'

'Stop moaning.'

Top and tail, they carried him and folded him into the boot of their saloon. They fetched the bag. The hare-lipped fella took the cash and gave it to her. 'For your troubles,' he said. When she shook her head, he dropped the money through the Vanguard's window. The other fella threw the keys to him. 'You're free to go. We'll let the boss know how it happened. She'll be pleased.' He held them out until she snatched them. 'Have a pleasant evening,' he said, doffing his cap's peak and backing off into the dark. They doused the lantern, got into their black saloon and left her.

She didn't want to stay a moment longer. A swig of brandy

would've done her good. A cigarette or two. But she had neither. With the shudders in her arms, it took her a few tries to get the key in the ignition. She drove home, to Leventree, because it was the only place that she could go. It was nearly midnight and her brother would be in his bed or washing at the basin in his shorts and vest. The thought of him allowed a peace to settle in her. There were fifty pounds now on the seat beside her, give or take. She'd put it in the hidey-hole below her bed when she got back. Start saving for their future. They could go on holiday. Or she could buy a car – legitimate – and they could take it out on daytrips every weekend.

All the way to Ockham, she was driving in a state of dreaming. Imagining the happiness that lay ahead. She'd get the knack for architecture, given time. She'd put the effort in. She'd work on furniture with Mr Mayhood, till he recognized the skill she had. She'd build that greenhouse Florence wanted, labour on the farm week after week, cut back those dying trees as planned, install that irrigation system in the east field, all of it. Eventually, she'd not remember anything she'd done tonight. The judder of the hammer's handle when it struck. Mal Duggan's soft collapsing skull. The spatter of the blood. His yelp and whimper and his snuffed-out eyes. She'd done that to him. She and no one else. But she could live with it. She could. She could. She could.

*

Along the rutted track she walked, beyond the neighbour's fence where all the bracken grew. She followed the bare dirt-lines curving up to Leventree: they were as good as rails. Ahead, the squat black outline of the house revealed itself behind the elms. An ordinary place, when taken from a distance. Just a simple box of timber, bricks and slate. But home was not a building any more than music was a noise – the

Mayhoods taught her that, and now she truly understood their meaning. She felt the shudders easing, a new pain beneath her jaw. The winter rye was moving darkly in the field. A good few inches tall now. Healthy green. It seemed an age ago that she'd gone out to seed it with the old man and her brother. Lamps were shining in the parlour window and the draughting room. Another light was on upstairs. The Mayhoods were awake, and maybe Charlie too.

She'd left the Vanguard where she'd found it, with the keys inside the wheel arch, near the bend of Hungry Hill Lane. The cash, she'd stuffed into her handbag. The roadmap, she'd torn up and cast away into the hedges. On the back seat, she'd found something else and almost retched. Mal's chip-bag hat. She'd held it for a while, squeezing the fabric, thinking back to how he'd sauntered to the car in it, so full of life, and then the pale, carbuncled look of him as he lay dead. It wasn't grief for him that made her queasy; it was pity for herself, a loathing for the person she'd become. Along the Ockham Road, she'd dropped the hat into a storm drain.

Now, her heavy breaths were steaming as she walked. The track was hard and frosted. There were mocking voices in the darkness of the copse, the gossip of the tawny owls. She knew their conversation. *Hasn't any scruples, that one. Shine a penny up and she'd be yours.* As she approached the yard, she looked to Charlie's bedroom, but he wasn't there. The fast scrape of her shoes upon the gravel startled her. That crunching sound. She'd have to suffer it from this day on, no flinching when she heard it. All she needed was a cigarette to calm her nerves before she went inside. On certain mornings, in the midst of yardwork, she would pick a dog-end from the stones below her brother's window, smoke the last few knockings of it while the hens pecked in the yard. Back in borstal, one puff on a rollie was a pleasure she would beg the other girls for; it could see her through a week. She wandered over, searched the gravel till she found a dog-end, dry and decent. The hens were quietly roosting in their little hutch tonight. The tractor had been covered with a tarp to stop it seizing in the frost – lately, Mr Mayhood had been checking the barometer more often, fearing snow.

One good thing she'd done tonight was pack the matches in her bag. She leaned against the bricks with the pathetic ciggie in her lips, rehearsing what she'd say. How well her evening with her fella from the post office had gone. How sweet he'd been for taking her to watch a jazz band at a club in Guildford. How long into the night they'd danced, missing the lateness of the hour. There were certain pieces lacking in the story, but she'd make it more persuasive in the telling.

As she struck the match, the flame revealed the bloodspots on her fingers. Another dried-on spray of it across her knuckles, on her coat cuff, too. And lower down: more splashes on her skirt, her shins, her ankles. The match was scorching her; she blew it out. She thought of washing at the outside tap, but the icy water would be torture, if it wasn't frozen in the pipes by now, and blood would never shift from wool – the sleeve was speckled, wrist to elbow. Even now, Mal Duggan's mess was hounding her. He'd never be rinsed off.

What choice did she have except to hope nobody noticed? She'd do her best to hurry up to bed without being seen. The kitchen door was likely open. She could sneak in through the porch and soap her hands off at the sink. If anyone came in, she'd rush upstairs, pretend to be upset. She'd say her fella had confessed that he was married. That was reasonable. Or she could say he'd tried it on with her, got too insistent as they'd left the club. And when he'd dropped her off, he'd put his hands inside her blouse, her skirt. Nobody would pry too much for details. It was private and she didn't want to talk about it.

That'd do the job, all right. She had a plan, but now she couldn't muster up the energy to move. It had to stop. The lying. All these tales she kept on spinning to connect with all the others that had gone before, to make them hold. She was exhausted by it. Nothing in her life was ever stable. Permanence – that's what she wanted.

Everybody knows he's better off without you, Joyce. You're going to drag him under. It was too late now to fix her old mistakes. She should've listened to her aunty then. She should've stepped aside. But she'd clung on. She'd paid her visits to the graveyard every summer, laid her flowers, promising her parents she was looking after Charlie, when it was her own best interests she'd been serving. Through borstal, she'd not visited at all, and not this year. If she couldn't fix her old mistakes, at least she could prevent herself from making new ones. *Why can't you be honest for a change?* The truth was, she'd been sinking him – one bad decision at a time, one wretched piece of luck after the next – and still he hadn't cut the rope. She loved him for that loyalty, the goodness of his heart, but it was selfish to allow it. He was volunteering to be drowned. She had to let him go.

There was a sudden balance to her now that came from understanding what was right. She dropped the fag end, crept across the gravel, sticking to the darker edges of the yard. The Vanguard would still be there, on the verge, and she had money in her bag to last a while – until she found a place to settle. She could go north and taste the life up there. Or down to Portsmouth maybe, find work on the ships. The Dorset coast was nice, or so she'd heard.

Back along the track she went, towards the gate. She didn't turn to look towards the house again, in case she landed on a reason to not keep on walking. She preferred to think of him the way he'd been that evening, in the hours before they'd got called in for supper. Hair all clean and shiny, combed. The zing of coal tar soap about him. Sitting at his draughting board, absorbed in work, with no consideration for her presence or her state of mind. Forgetting that she needed supervision. That was how she wanted it to be for ever. Charlie with his back turned and his eyes down on his paper, drawing with that steadiness and skill he had. In charge of his own actions. Happy. He belonged there, in the company of better people, in the rooms where opportunities were made.

December 1952

They'd earmarked this day for ploughing but the east field had a silver skin of frost at dawn and now the prospect seemed unlikely. Mr Mayhood had assured him over breakfast, 'Oh, I wouldn't rule it out just yet until we've had a quick inspection. If it goes down any deeper than a couple of inches, we'll have to put it off. But I don't think it looks too bad.' After they washed up the dishes, they put on their woollens and walked out together, treading the compacted ground in search of where it seemed most frozen. Somewhere near the middle of the field, they stopped. Mr Mayhood pushed his fork into the soil. 'Looks all right. About an inch. It ought to take a plough, I think,' was the decision. 'We could let it thaw, but there's a danger it'd get so wet the tractor will get stuck in it – that's something Hollis warned me to look out for. Anyway, let's have that cup of tea first. Warm our cockles up before the wagon comes.'

They went back to the porch to drink the tea that Florence had left out for them, and waited for the lorry to arrive with their manure. They'd ordered it dried out and pulverized this time, less pungent than the fresher stuff.

'It's mornings like these I'm inclined to hire somebody else, you know,' said Mr Mayhood. 'Can't keep looking for a fella who refuses to be found. If he came back, we'd take him on again, but it'd be for half the wages. Florence says she'll put the word out in the village. That all right by you?'

Charlie nodded, cradling his mug and letting its steam thaw his nose. 'You've been more than fair to that old man. Too fair.'

'That may be so.'

'He wouldn't do the same for you or me.'

'That may be so, as well. But isn't that what makes it necessary?'

'I suppose.'

When the lorry came, he watched it dump the muck in one big pile in the yard, knowing it would be his job to shovel it on to the trailer later on for spreading. Once Florence had got finished with the plough, they'd have to rake the field by hand because their harrow needed welding. Even with the guarantee of Joyce's help, he'd not been looking forward to the task, and now it seemed they'd have to manage it without her. Not only had his sister been away all night with some bloke no one knew, she hadn't even had the courtesy to telephone and give her reasons – no doubt, when she offered them, they'd stink about as much as the manure.

Mr Mayhood hadn't let his disappointment with her show yet. All he'd said was, 'I don't think we ought to speculate too much about your sister. She's an adult and I'm sure she'll have an explanation when she gets back home. I think it's only right she's heard.' But Charlie recognized their method: channelling their irritation into cleaning, cooking, laundering and other preparations for the day. His aunty used to manage Joyce that way and it had got her nowhere. The only difference was the Mayhoods were a lot more persevering, more inclined to let Joyce remedy her faults before condemning her. It was a major part of why he felt so grateful to them. He could still remember those long afternoons he'd spent with Mr Mayhood in the summer, back when they'd been making renovations to his room. They'd been planing beams of ash to make his bed frame, working to the drawing he'd submitted for approval. One day, in a sweaty, resting moment, Mr Mayhood had blown out his cheeks and told him there was apple juice down in the larder, nice and cool. They'd gone to fetch the jug and stood for a while in the shady kitchen, gulping down two glassfuls each, an easy silence growing in the room, a sense of safety coming over him, until he'd got the confidence to say what he'd been meaning to for weeks.

'Mr Mayhood, could I ask you something?'

'Yes, of course. What's on your mind?'

'It's just that I've been thinking – why did you choose *me* for this? I mean, I can't help wondering if someone else deserved it more.'

But Mr Mayhood had laughed softly. 'Oh, you earned it fair and square. Your drawing was the best we saw, no question. It had real control, precision. *Vision* – most important. And a little something unexpected. That's what I was hoping we would find. And here you are, look, proving my sound judgement.'

He'd been sheepish about voicing what he'd felt, but said it anyway: 'You've changed my life. I wanted you to know that.'

Mr Mayhood hadn't answered to begin with. His eyes had narrowed as he'd put his glass down, as though thinking, *Hasn't been two months yet, lad. Bit early for that surely?* But then he'd cleared his throat and spoken: 'Not at all. *You've* changed it. I just opened up the door to let you through.' He'd leaned back on the counter, grabbing the short pincers of his false hand with the other. 'Let me tell you something I've discovered, Charlie, and I'm certain this is true. More certain than I've ever been, in fact.' He'd paused to make sure he was being listened to. 'If every person on this earth was born with just two things, they'd never have to struggle. Do you know what those things are? Belief and opportunity. Belief and opportunity. But the problem is they're gifts that other people have to give you. If you get them from your parents, then you're lucky. Otherwise you have to find them somewhere else, from people who don't know you well or owe you anything. A lot of people spend a long time searching for those things, and some find one but not the other. Some give up entirely. Me? I stumbled on them. I was fortunate. Someone cared enough to get to know me and to set his store by what he saw in me. And that's how life should be. Belief and opportunity for everyone. I'm only passing on what I was given at your age. And I don't plan to stop with you and Joyce.'

They'd gone back upstairs to plane the last few lengths of timber. As they'd worked, he'd sensed that Mr Mayhood was content to have his company, to share his purpose. And he'd thought to say, 'Who was it helped you, after you got out?'

'A fella at the Corporation up in Liverpool. His name was Mr Wheating. I didn't even think he liked me very much, but he surprised me. Aftercare had set me up in his department: city planning. On a trial basis only, mind. I knew it was a blessing, even if I earned a pittance. This is looking better now, I think . . .' Mr Mayhood had reached down to brush the shavings from the beam, and then he'd kept on planing. 'Wasn't much for me to do there to begin with. I just filed away the drawings, made the tea and organized the post. But then one of the draughtsmen went on sick leave and I asked if I could pitch in with some drawing. Wheating told me no, but I just kept on asking. I suppose he got annoyed with all my pestering and, in the end, he gave me a block plan to copy. I still remember what it was: a big municipal estate in Norris Green, and I was told to do it twice. I had those finished in a day or two and I could tell he was impressed, you know, because he had a wobble in his face – like *this* – but he just gave me something else to copy out. Another block plan, only much more complicated. Something from the Tunnel project. When I brought that back, he gave me a few more. Eventually, he calls me in to see him in his office. He says, *Look here, Mayhood, I've been speaking to some people at the architecture school. I'd like to keep you on, because I know that I could put you to good use, but I believe you'll have a brighter future over there. They'd like to meet you.* Well, next thing I know, I'm sat across a table from Charles Reilly, and he's looking over all my copied drawings. After that, I get a letter saying they have a scholarship for me. I thought it was a wind-up. All that I could think about were other lads at Feltham I'd been in with. I was just like you. I couldn't understand how I'd got all the luck while most of them were still inside or grinding out a living. But, you see, that's what I mean: belief and opportunity. They're simple things that shouldn't be so hard to find. And I'm just trying to do my part.'

It sickened Charlie that his sister had been taking this for granted. Every minute she was late, every time she muttered grievances under her breath or shook her head and scowled, it came across as an affront to the intentions of the Mayhoods. To stay out with some fella overnight and not turn up to do her chores or farmwork in the morning? Well, that shamed him just as much as it shamed her. The worst part was – and wasn't this just typical? – she'd managed to involve him in her scheming, too.

Just this morning, as he'd laid the breakfast table, Florence had stood in the doorway, fretting. 'How much do you know about this fellow Joyce is seeing, Charlie?'

'Next to nothing, really. Just a few details.' He'd rehashed the description he'd been given by his sister – brown hair, worsted blazer, specs, the post office – and recognized how terse the information sounded, how uninterested in her life it made him seem. So he'd hurried on, 'I did go down there once or twice to have a look at him myself. But there was never any sign of him, and she got moody with me when I raised it with her. That's the way she is about this kind of thing – all secretive and sensitive. She said he was some sort of manager. Goes up and down to different branches, so she told me. But you never really know with Joyce.'

Florence had blinked back at him, as though it was the first she'd heard about his sister's unreliability. 'And why's that?'

'Well, because she tends to –' He hadn't known how best to phrase it. 'Make things up. At least, she used to.'

'Are you saying you don't think this chap is real?'

'I'm saying I've not seen him.'

'Did you get his name?'

'No, miss. I'm afraid I didn't.'

'Hmm.' She'd clucked her tongue. 'Well, if she isn't back by lunchtime, I shall have to walk down to the post office myself. Agreed?'

'Sounds fair enough to me,' he'd said. 'I'm sorry that she's made you worry. But she's like an alley cat, my sister. She might vanish now and then, but you'll feel daft for getting so worked up when she comes back again.'

'I'm sure you're right.'

'I know I am.'

She'd lingered on the threshold, saying, 'Best put layers on today. Don't want you catching cold out there. We'll need you fit and ready in the draughting room.'

'I've had my thermals on all night.'

'A wise decision.'

He'd allowed her to go off without another word, which made him liable for worsening the situation. There'd been chances to report the other things he knew. For one, the Wold-ingham phone number he'd discovered on her ciggie packet that no one ever answered when he rang. For another, when he'd gone to check the nearest post offices, he'd met two clerks with neat brown hair and round-wire specs, and both of them had been in blazers, though he couldn't tell by sight if they were gabardine or worsted. When he'd asked them if they knew his sister, Joyce, they'd both returned the same bewildered look; one of them had sounded irked, the other had become uncomfortable, repeating, 'I'm a married man. Can't help you,' and then calling, 'Next!' to the old lady in the queue behind. That's when he'd tried coaxing answers out of Joyce and she'd explained about the fella being an area manager.

He should've followed her last night. He should've gone out in the cold and dark and trailed her to the Duke of Wellington until he knew for sure who she was meeting. But there'd been a lot of work to do, assisting with the competition entry, and he'd lost himself in the momentum of it all.

Her big announcement had been so abrupt it should've made him pay attention. She'd not waited for a quiet moment after lunch; she'd walked up and informed the Mayhoods while they'd been reviewing all their parti sketches at the plan chest. Progress had been fairly static for the past few weeks and Mr Mayhood had become exasperated with the project. He'd been pacing in the hallway every hour, going off to lie down in the parlour with the curtains shut, banging his claw-hand upon the tabletop when he was unconvinced by what he'd drawn and sighing heavily until his face turned ruddy. Ever since the documents had reached them from the Battersea committee – a ream of pages that the Mayhoods had been calling 'the conditions' – Charlie had been hearing nothing but the *scratch scratch scratch* of ink pens in the draughting room. Joyce had sidled up to Mr Mayhood from her station by the window and declared, 'I don't know if it's the best time to be asking, but I've been invited out this evening for a drink. I'd like to go, if it's all right with you. It's with a fella I've been getting friendly with the past few months. Would that be something I could do?' Seeing her endure the awkwardness of asking for permission had been quite a new experience for Charlie and he'd found it almost touching. Mr Mayhood had continued spreading out the parti sketches on the plan chest, circling around them with his specs clutched in his hand.

'You don't need my blessing, Joyce,' was the response, 'and you can make your own decisions what to do in your free time. Enjoy yourself.'

'All right. Thanks,' she'd said. 'I will.'

And though Charlie hadn't said a word to her, he must've looked discouraging, because she'd frowned at him as she went past. 'No one asked you, mouse,' she'd said. 'Get back to work.'

Florence, with the easy manner that she had for soothing tension, had gone over to his sister's desk and perched beside her on the stool. 'How dashing is he?'

'Average,' she'd said.

'But interesting?'

'Not sure yet.'

'I thought you said you two were getting friendly.'

'Only chatting in his place of work. It's not the same. That's why I'm going for a drink with him. To see if there's a future in it.'

'Is he going to pick you up?'

'We're meeting in the village. He's not having my address until he's earned it.'

'Good for you, Joyce. Sounds as though you've got him nicely trained already.'

'I just hope he's not too boring. I'm all right with ordinary, but boring I can't stand.'

'Yes, I know exactly what you mean.'

Mr Mayhood had begun to riffle through a sketchbook, ripping pages out and placing them into a grid with all the others. 'Everyone, please gather round a sec,' he'd called, and so they had. He'd prodded at the top left image: a more developed drawing they'd decided weeks ago had great potential. 'I still like the gist of this approach, but something's overworked about it all. We've not defined the grammar for the building yet – it's neither one thing nor the other. Mostly, it's the foyer. It's too compacted here at the south face and it's stifling the entire scheme. We've not really carried through our rowan leaf idea. The foyer really needs to have a sense of openness. It's much too sectioned off. The light should course through it as one, not like this, in slats – that isn't right.' He'd jabbed another sketch, two rows below. 'I mean, have a look at this one here. You've captured it already, Flo. You did that, when? About a week ago? I should've seen it then. The central stairwell's got that lovely tulip shape to it. I really think that's what this building needs. It has to have that sort of openness and flow. It's so much better. Don't you think that's better? I believe it's better. There's a motif there, and we can use it to define our whole approach. That tulip shape. We'll have to start again, of course, but we've got time to play with.'

Until yesterday, their competition work had been a drudge. The Mayhoods had been agonizing over whether to withdraw and claim back their deposit. But, by accident of Joyce distracting them, they'd been rewired. The impetus had carried them past midnight and he wasn't sure that Mr Mayhood even went to bed.

Now the yard was full of dry manure and they were bristling in the cold. It was the bitter kind of chill that settled in your bones. The winter sky was dismal, not a chance of sunlight breaking through.

'You might need a flask of brandy out there, Charlie,' Mr Mayhood said, eyes on the field. 'Or I could light a brazier. Take turns standing round it.'

'I'll make do with my ciggies,' he replied.

'I wish I'd never packed them in, you know.'

'You must've lost your mind.'

'Yes, probably.'

Florence came out then, with gloves on and a woolly hat, a

brown scarf hiding everything below her eyes. 'Are you sure you want to plough this morning?' she said. 'Looks more like a day for baking bread to me.'

'Last warm day for weeks, this,' Mr Mayhood said. 'We have to make the most of it.'

'You call this warm?'

'Relative to what's ahead of us, it's sweltering.'

'I'd best get knitting balaclavas, then.'

'Yes, but not for Charlie – he's got cigarettes to warm him up.' Mr Mayhood dug him in the shoulder. 'Come on, let's bring out the tractor and we'll hitch the plough. It's best if Florence makes a start out there – the ground might break the coulters yet – but you can do the last few furrows, if you like.'

Their hard work kept them warm enough. While Florence ploughed the east field, he and Mr Mayhood shovelled dry manure on to the trailer. It was mostly wordless labour, and when either of them spoke, it was an act of courtesy, a way of showing one another they were glad to share the burden. That's how it was meant to be at Leventree, he understood that now: as long as they were farming, they should never have their minds on architecture. The silence and the toil were meant to give them separation from all that, to cleanse them. And some days it did. On others, it exhausted him to the extent that he could barely hold a pencil or envision anything except the comforts of his bed. He'd never been so worn out since his first few weeks in borstal, which had been so draining that he'd fainted twice on the parade ground and been carried to the nurse, who'd given him a glass of salted water to drink. He'd toughened up quickly after that, but it had taken him a while to lose the nickname Jellylegs.

Part of him was still preoccupied with Joyce as he climbed on to the tractor for his turn at ploughing. Every time he arced around to start another furrow, his first glance was back towards the porch, in the hope that she'd be standing in her workman's trousers, ready to pitch in. But the hours passed and he and Mr Mayhood – Florence, too, before she went inside to organize their lunch – were left to haul the trailer up and down the field, edging it along the imprints of the tractor's wheels. They worked in twenty-five-yard patches, Charlie flinging the manure, spade after spade, and the Mayhoods raking it all through. Once or twice, the tractor's engine sputtered out and, when it did, a holy feeling swelled in him. The noises of the world became much sharper, more alive. The crackle of his ciggie as it burned, the straining stitches round his bootcaps as he flexed his toes, the distant lowing of their neighbour's cattle in the barn. Then Florence got the tractor going again and all he heard was engine judder, till he got that low tone in his ears like someone blowing in a bottle. And on they went again, another twenty-five or thirty yards, rehearsing the same motions with their rakes and shovels. By the time the job was done, his back was griping and he couldn't feel his nose.

After he'd washed up and changed, there was a treat for lunch – oxtail and barley stew with carrots, which he mopped up with two rounds of soda bread. Every week, he checked the rota, took note of the days when Florence was marked down for cooking. She always made hot food for them, substantial meals full of flavour; not the scrappy sandwiches with soup, or cheese on toast with pickled onions, that the rest of them would put together. Today, she even set a plate aside for Joyce and left it covered on the range, assuming that his sister would be hungry when she finally returned. She looked towards the mantel clock and said, 'It's after half past one. I think I should go down there.'

'Please don't take too long. I'd like to start on final plans and elevations by next week. We've really got to get this scheme pinned down today,' said Mr Mayhood. 'And it's your project now, your vision.'

'It's ours,' she answered. 'Last I checked, we were a team.'

'Well, either way, you're steering it from this point on. We can't be long without you.'

'Fifteen minutes, at the most. Relight the fire and I'll be back.'

'I've got a pile of useless paper we can burn, all right.'

She didn't laugh, just creased her mouth at him. 'Better yet, start writing. It'll come down to how well we can describe the scheme to them. It's salesmanship that wins you competitions and we've hardly got a word on paper that's persuasive.' Then, catching Charlie's eye, she added, 'What's the betting Joyce is coming up the drive once I get out there?'

'If she is,' he said, 'please tell her that we ate her lunch.'

'Don't either of you dare.' She went to fetch her coat, then came back through the kitchen on her way outside. He watched her from the steamy window with the hot tap filling up the sink. How was it she could look so beautiful from such a distance with her back turned and her woollens on? It was unfair to his poor heart. He scrubbed the pots and cleaned the dishes for the second time that day, and Mr Mayhood dried them. After that, they went to get a fire started in the draughting room. He twisted up some newspaper and poked it in between the kindling Mr Mayhood laid out in the hearth. They watched it all take flame and smoulder, breathing in the earthy flavour of the smoke.

'I'll put some coffee on for us,' he said, but Mr Mayhood shook his head.

'No, that can wait. We'd better take a good look at the site survey again and make sure we're not likely to encroach on any boundaries. This new idea we have is looking right, I think,

285

but if it doesn't fit the plot, we've got to work out how to alter it.'

They were still there, loosely measuring the boundaries of the site with a scale ruler, when Florence got back home. Charlie spotted her head bobbing past the window, heard the brisk thump of her footsteps on the porch. She breezed in with her overcoat on, pulling off her scarf. 'Arthur,' she said, 'could I have a word, please?'

Mr Mayhood looked at her. 'Of course.' He put the ruler down in front of Charlie. 'Hold that thought,' he said, and followed her out into the hallway.

For a moment, Charlie rested in the wing chair by the fire, lifting up his stocking feet towards the blaze. He knew they were discussing Joyce but didn't want to press his ear against the door: he'd had enough of hearing other people whisper their displeasure at his sister.

When Mr Mayhood came back in, he had an air of disaffection, striding up to gather a few papers from his bureau. 'Shall we carry on?' he asked.

Then Florence reappeared, her face a little pinked, her steps more hesistant. 'Charlie,' she said, as he stood up from the chair, landing her attention on him in the way that made his legs weak and his thoughts go drifting. There was recognition in that look she gave him – a truth they both agreed but weren't prepared to voice – and she was trailing after him, until she stopped and said, 'I'm sorry, I can't help but worry. She might well be like an alley cat. And I might well be trying to mother her. But – look – it's after two and she's not back. It seems to me that we're neglecting our responsibility towards the girl. I don't mean you, Charlie, of course. I'm trying to get through to my husband.'

Mr Mayhood was already nettled by the whole exchange. 'I'm not phoning the police, Flo. She won't thank us for it.'

'No, you mustn't,' Charlie put in then. 'That's only going to rile her up when she gets back.'

'But what if something's happened to her?' Florence said.

He couldn't stop the fast, dismissive laugh that left his throat. 'It's just the way she acts sometimes, that's all. Believe me, she's been doing this since I was little.'

'Hear that? Charlie understands what's right,' said Mr Mayhood. 'We have to let her be. This isn't school or borstal. It's a place of work and Joyce is free to come and go. We promised her as much, so we can hardly blame her now she's done it. There'll be consequences, though. She'll lag behind. She'll have more duties on the rota next week to catch up. And she'll have to stick with colourwashing prints for longer than she ought. Don't get me wrong, I won't be happy if she makes a habit of this sort of thing. But I'm not going to jeopardize her licence by involving the police. It's one late night. That's it. She'll come back when she's ready.'

Florence was subdued for a moment. Then she said, 'Like Mr Hollis did, you mean?'

'*Flo*, come on. Enough now. That's a different situation and you know it. Hollis bit off more than he could chew.'

'I just think we ought to be prepared to ring the station if she's still not home by suppertime. Perhaps we might ask Mr Kimball to advise us what –'

'Not Kimball. He's already got it in for her.' Charlie hated to be so abrupt and he could see the disillusionment in Florence as he cut her off. Her remonstrating hands dropped quickly to her sides. But he could only think of what their supervising officer might put in his report if he was told of Joyce's absence. It was just the sort of vague misconduct he'd been waiting for since they'd arrived. Not truancy, as such, but waywardness. An indication of her sliding back into her old behaviour.

Florence patted down the cushions on the sofa in a sort of protest and a storm of dust rose out of them.

He asked, 'What happened at the post office before?'

'I learned a thing or two.' She sat down, straightening her skirt. 'They said there *is* a regional manager – Mr Crottee. In his fifties. Married with four kids, and *bald*. Does that sound right to you?'

He shook his head. 'I told you, she gets secretive about this stuff. The details never quite add up. It's all because the fellas who she likes don't tend to stick with her. So she'll save a bit of face by telling you as little as she can. That's Joyce. She's hard to fathom out.' What he didn't say was that there'd been a time when he'd believed she was a prostitute. A dreadful thing to level at her and he still regretted saying it aloud. There'd been plenty of good reasons for suspecting it – he'd known enough about her circumstances, things she'd said to him, what he'd observed. But, really, he'd been nudged towards a false conclusion by a lot of gossip from his aunty and her church friends as they'd sat in their front room with fruit-loaf slices and Earl Grey. His sister had denied it – and so earnestly that he'd found himself believing her. True candour was a rare event in Joyce's life, but he could always recognize it when he saw it.

Florence crossed her arms and said, 'Till five o'clock. No longer. Supper is her duty and she knows the rota. If she isn't at that range by five, I'm phoning Mr Kimball. Understand, it's not a punishment – I want to know that she's all right.'

'Whoever she's been with, he isn't worth her time – or yours. I'm sure of that.'

Mr Mayhood was still fussing with the site plan. 'I think that's Charlie saying we should get on with our day. And, after all, he knows her best.'

And so they pressed on with their competition entry. He was glad for the diversion of the project. How much longer could he let his sister do this to him? In the throes of work, his mind would float away from her. She wasn't in the marks he put on paper. She could never stand inside the buildings he imagined, spoil their shapes, though she could break his concentration if he let his thoughts run off in her direction. Wasn't that what she was always telling him? Protect yourself. Be no one's ha'penny. And drawing was the only thing he'd ever known how to control.

On this score, he'd learned so much already from the Mayhoods. They never quarrelled when it came to architecture. They were so invested in each other's talents, sympathetic to each other's strengths and flaws, and it was always clear which one of them was leading on a project. Yesterday, while Florence had refined her concept sketches, he and Mr Mayhood had stood watching at her shoulder. In an hour, the halls of residence had found their form: a low, wide structure with a channel through its middle where the main staircase would be, a glass and steel chamber with curved walls. It had looked, from that initial sketch, as though a tulip had been darned with zigzag stitches. Today, he stood in silence behind Mr Mayhood, seeing him enhance the concept she'd begun, exploring basic elevations freehand, using charcoal, then fashioning another sequence more exactly, using pencil, with his clamp appliance on the T-square.

It still astounded him that Mr Mayhood could achieve such accuracy in his drawings. With no feeling in his right hand, he could still manoeuvre the straight edge and balance it, retaining the precision in his lines. He'd go clipping and unclipping from whichever instruments he needed, losing no momentum. When they'd first met one another, Mr Mayhood hadn't worn the arm at all – there'd been an empty space below the elbow where the sleeve had been rolled up and safety-pinned.

It had been the governor who'd organized his visit. An

officer had taken Charlie out of Sunday chapel to escort him to the office. As soon as he'd been let inside, the governor had risen from behind his desk to say, 'Good morning, Savigear. Please have a seat. You needn't look so terrified – you're not in any trouble.' Mr Mayhood had been at the window with a tea-cup. The grounds of Huntercombe were framed behind him, still and vacant, grey as pewter. 'I'd like to introduce you to the man whom you'll be working for this summer – that's assuming you keep up the good behaviour till your discharge.'

Right then, Mr Mayhood had stepped forward with a gloss of pride about his eyes. 'Hello, Charles,' he'd said, and offered his left hand. 'So glad to meet you. I must say, your drawing really took my breath away – I mean that. It's extremely nice to put a face to it, as last. My wife and I are looking forward to your being with us, very much.' They'd shaken.

'Good to meet you too, sir. Thank you.'

'I thought we'd take a little stroll outside. Just half an hour or so. And you can ask me any questions you might have. I'm sure your head is full of them.'

He'd looked towards the governor, who'd said, 'It's all right, Savigear. An officer will go out with you. You can join your working party when you're ready.'

As soon as they had got outside the sky had cracked apart. Instead of doing circuits of the garden and the playing fields, they'd had to be content with standing underneath the covered walkway as the rain fell hard on the parade ground. 'Well,' said Mr Mayhood, 'as you've got your stripes already, you can have a smoke now, I suppose.'

'I would, sir, if I had any.'

'Oh, I should've thought to bring you in a packet.'

'That's all right. I'll scrounge one from a prefect later.'

'What's your poison? Woodbines?'

'Them and rollies, mostly.'

'Some things never change. And Player's for the prefects, right?'

'That's it.' The rain had gushed down from the sloping roof and formed a kind of beaded curtain in between them and the trees. 'How d'you know so much about it all?'

'Two years in Feltham, that's how.'

'As a volunteer, you mean?'

Mr Mayhood's brow had lifted. 'No, when I was your age.'

'Oh.' His whole perception of the man had altered after that. 'You couldn't have been guilty, sir.'

'I did the crime, all right, if you can call it that.'

'What did you do?'

'I was shifting stolen goods for somebody, that's all. Wrong place, wrong time. You'll know the feeling.'

'Yeah, I do, sir.'

'Well, don't worry. It won't set you back for ever. I'm not going to let it.'

Any doubts that Charlie might've had about the Mayhoods and their contest had been washed out in the rain. What sort of barrel-scraping architects went searching for apprentices at borstal? Were they looking for cheap labour? Someone they could boss around and torment? Were they skinflints? Desperate? In dire straits? When he'd seen that missing limb, it had occurred to him that something wasn't quite as advertised. This one-armed architect was trying to recruit a dogsbody to clean his house and shine his shoes. There'd be no draughting work and no profession at the end of it. There had to be a negative he wasn't seeing. But, that grey afternoon, he'd stopped mistrusting his own happiness.

'If we had room and work enough to go around, we'd take a hundred of you,' Mr Mayhood had explained it. 'I'm not daft enough to think that every kid in borstal has the skill to be an architect, but I'm certain that they all deserve a chance to learn.

I know what a place like this can do to you. You'll have it tough sometimes, and they can work you like a mule, but they'll still treat you with respect. In Feltham, there were lads you'd never even look at in the corridor in case they beat you down, but then you'd see them working on the lathe in hobby hour and they'd have a peacefulness about them – they'd go whistling round the workshop, never bothering a soul. That's what a sense of purpose gives you. Just to know you're good at something other than the things you grow up having to be good at, out of sheer necessity, or else because somebody's breathing down your neck. I'm sure there must be lads in here who you avoid – you're probably right to. Some can't raise a smile for anything but violence. I've seen the way it goes. A lot of kids like that are just too damaged to put back together. But the point is: they weren't born that way. The world's what did it to them. Pain and suffering. Neglect. The loss of things. There's no one reason lads wind up in here. A lot of them have more of an excuse than others. But what matters is the way that you emerge from it. Believe me, with a little help, there's nothing you can't do when you get out of a place like this.'

A few weeks after that, a parcel had arrived for him at Huntercombe. He'd opened it to find a large tin of tobacco, ciggie papers and a book, *The Architect in History* by M. S. Briggs. There'd been a pencilled note: *Dear Charlie, Just some things to keep you out of trouble until June. Best wishes from the Mayhoods.* The library index card was still glued to the inside page: the Liverpool School of Architecture.

Now the first of Mr Mayhood's elevations was complete, the halls of residence were looking more coherent, but, in Charlie's view, the new design was lacking something. He went to sit at his own board to see if he could understand the problem, working from his memory of Florence's initial sketch. It didn't have that sense of openness they'd all been striving for. Perhaps if he could strip it down to its component parts, as though it were an engine, he could tune up the design. He drew it hurriedly in charcoal, trying not to think too much about his motions. What if separate structures could be formed in concrete, mirroring each another? Not triangles exactly, but right-angled shapes like this, with slopes joining their axes. Concave. Shallow. Shallower than that . . . With frames of steel rising upwards, making stairwells? See-through. They could panel them with glass. And if the buildings could be set apart, like this – perhaps a little further – the entire space would open up. A tulip shape, implied by where the two slopes merged, just like they wanted . . . He felt sure of the idea and couldn't get his vision on to paper fast enough. The more he sketched, the less he noticed how much time was passing or the twinge of hunger in his stomach. It was nearly five o'clock when he finished and the draughting room had emptied out. The embers of the fire were long dead in the hearth.

He found the Mayhoods in the kitchen. A solemnity had settled in the house, in part because the winter darkness seemed to spread so suddenly in Ockham that it prompted Florence to switch on the wall lights in the hallway by late afternoon. But more than that, the voices in the kitchen were downbeat and fitful: 'I don't know.' 'Of course you do.' 'It's odd, I'll give you that.' 'We have to, don't we?' 'Yes, but I'm still loath to do it.' As he waited on the threshold, Florence stood up from her chair. 'We're wondering what we ought to do about your sister,' she said. 'Can you pitch in making supper? She was going to bake a Woolton pie, but we've got stew left over, if you don't mind doubling up on it.'

'Sounds good to me,' he said. 'Just let me know what I can help with.'

'Maybe we could do a crumble with those Bramley apples?'

'I'll get my pinny on.' He rolled his sleeves up, fetched his apron. 'Are you going to be phoning Kimball, then?'

'We've not decided yet,' said Mr Mayhood from the table. He was reading the conditions document again.

'I'd prefer it if you waited.'

'How much longer?' Florence said. 'A day? A week?'

'At least another couple of hours. They'll get the wrong idea about her.'

'Charlie, listen. It does seem we're getting to the point where something's needed. At the very least, we should've heard from her by now. She could be hurt.' Mr Mayhood leafed another page, eyes down. He didn't seem prepared to look at anything besides the paragraph he was absorbing. 'Florence has just phoned the Duke of Wellington. No one there's seen hide nor hair of her.'

'Well, they would've had a crowd in last night, wouldn't they?'

'That's true.'

'And probably the fella would've got her drinks. She'd not have gone up to the bar herself.'

'You're right, I know, but still. First, Hollis does a midnight flit and now she's absent without leave. We can't ignore it.'

'But you *said* that she could go. You said she didn't even need to ask.' He couldn't tell who he was trying to protect, his sister or himself, though he was drained by the resistance.

'Frankly, Charlie, I don't know what's best. I really don't.'

Florence cut in then: 'I think we ought to check her room and see she hasn't taken anything. Not *stolen*,' she took care to say, 'I meant, she might've packed a change of clothes . . . But I don't want to rummage through her things.'

The silence that came after this was freighted. 'OK. I don't mind. I'll do it.'

'Would you, Charlie?'

'Yeah, it wouldn't be the first time.' This sounded much more damning than he'd hoped for and it brought a faint reaction out of Florence. 'What should I do first? The crumble or the screw's inspection?'

She threw a tea towel at him. 'Oi. You know that's not what I'm suggesting.'

'He was joking,' Mr Mayhood said. 'Right, Charlie?'

He untied his apron. 'Yeah.'

'Well, I don't care. I might be worried over nothing, but I'm worried. I can't help it.'

'Fine. I'll go up now and have a look,' he told her. 'But when she sees I've touched her stuff, I'm blaming it on you.'

'I'll live with that.'

'Just don't phone Kimball. Please. Not yet.'

'We promise we'll hold on,' said Mr Mayhood, setting down the document at last. 'And we appreciate your help with this.'

His sister's room was as she must've left it: in its customary state between abandonment and order. A wardrobe door was open and she'd hung a bath towel over it. Her bed was made with borstal corners, but she'd flung a pair of nylons on the counterpane and they were hanging from it, beige and ropey. There was still a flowered scent about the air: the fancy perfume she'd been loaned by Florence, with its bottle like two doves entwined, was resting on her desk. Her coat was gone, but that was hardly unexpected. Including her work boots, she owned two pairs of shoes and only one was missing. Tucked behind the curtains, on the windowsill, there was a ratty hardback called *The Border Legion* that she must've dropped into the bath and left to dry. Her drawers were stocked with clothes she hadn't ironed yet, or else had worn and put back in. Everything seemed right and in its place, as far as he could tell.

Except her suitcase wasn't there.

She'd kept it resting on her wardrobe since the day they'd

been assigned their rooms. It was the same make, size and colour as his own – good leather, issued to them on their discharge. That she'd moved it didn't trouble him too much, unless it was a sign she'd been preparing to pack up her things and leave. He checked the obvious spots. Behind the ottoman, beside her desk, below the bedstead – there it was. He dragged it out and laid it on the counterpane to open. There was just a cardigan inside, which looked too small for her. But as he lowered down the lid, he felt something dislodge and shift – a lump there, in the lining. He worked his fingers on the baggy fabric to make out the shape a little better. It was long and on the narrow side.

He took the case into their bathroom, got a razor blade from his shaving bag and put a clean slice in the lining, tearing it quickly. What he brought out of the cavity was shammy-wrapped and moist. A jeweller's box. There was a seal of parcel tape, already cut. He was afraid to open it, but had to know. Small pieces tumbled out at once and bounced across the tiles like pebbles. *Teeth.* Gone yellow with tobacco. Bloody at the ends of their long roots. And in the box's top there was a strip of a straw hat, torn ragged. He recognized it right away, before he'd even read the message stitched on the reverse. *For my darling Geoffrey love Maureen.*

Revulsion climbed up from his guts so fast, he didn't make it to the toilet bowl – he sicked into the bathtub. For a while, he stayed there on his knees, doing what he could to get his breath and stop from sicking up again. He rinsed his mouth out underneath the tap and washed the chunks of oxtail, carrot, barley down the plughole. All that he could think was: *Woldingham 9264.* He had to tell them now. There couldn't be another deviation or excuse. He needed to account for what she'd done.

On the way downstairs, his fingers brushed the merry bunting on the banister. He almost dropped the box. The hallway seemed a thousand miles below the ground and every step he took was noiseless, numb. Just yesterday, he'd come down these same steps and she'd been standing at the mirror with her coat on and her hair blown dry. She'd given him a look as she'd turned round: not pained, not troubled, nothing. But he should've seen it in her blankness. *Long John Silver.*

He could hardly carry his own weight by now. The duskiness inside the house bewildered him. He saw the parlour door was open and the Christmas bulbs around the tree had been switched on. And there was Florence, lighting candles on the mantelpiece. As she spotted him, she shook the flame out of the match that she'd been using. 'Charlie, what's the matter?' When he tried to speak, his voice went missing. 'Did you find something up there?' She came and took him by the shoulders, touched his forehead with her palm. 'You're so clammy. Sit down here, sit down.' She steered him to the sofa, perched beside him. 'Arthur!' she called out. 'I'll fetch him. Just sit here. I'll fetch him.' And she hurried off.

The Christmas lights went blurry in the corners of his eyes. He smelled the paraffin of molten wax. The sick cloyed hotly in this throat. He was wishing for the same thing now as he'd been wishing for two years ago: that somehow Joyce would have a better explanation for it all. But, even then, he'd known the consolation wouldn't come. The coppers hadn't taken anything she'd said as truthful either – and why should they have listened to a word she'd said? A witness had already phoned the station to report them. PC Higgs had told him so. 'He's given us a statement. Says he saw a pair of youngsters meddling with the Jaguar across the road. Revving it so loud they woke up half the street. A girl who must've been six feet, he reckons, and a shorter lad with dark hair just like yours. Coincidence or what? The girl was driving, so he reckons, but the lad was underneath the bonnet, got the engine running. There you are, see. No point acting innocent with me. You're going to be charged the same as her.' He wasn't going to take the blame for this, as well. They'd hang him for it. Hang her, too, if they could find her. He was going to retch again, but kept it down.

'Charlie?' Mr Mayhood said now from the doorway. He came to sit beside him, wrapped one arm across his back and spied the mangy box that he was turning over in his hands. 'What's that you've got? It's all right. You can tell us.'

'I –' He forced the words out. 'I just found it. In her room. Her suitcase.'

'Could I take it, please?'

He nodded and let go.

*

The caravan was pitched among the high grass on the brow of a small meadow. Mr Mayhood hadn't wanted to delay until the light of morning, so they parked the wagon by the fence and wandered up the slope with their flood lanterns. It was colder than it had been in the fields, first thing, and everyone was tired. He could see it in the pinkness of the Mayhoods' eyes when they passed through his lantern's beam and felt it in the lag of his own body. Everything was sore in him. The sharpness of the night air spiked his lungs. He couldn't smoke. It seemed insensitive and selfish. As they'd driven down the Ockham Road, he'd wondered if they should've left the house at all. 'Don't worry. If she's coming back this late, she won't be troubled on her own for half an hour,' was Mr Mayhood's view. 'I'm not leaving Florence waiting there in case she does. Nor you.' Half of him was hoping that he'd never see his sister's face again. The other half was praying no harm came to her.

They hadn't eaten supper – nobody could find their appetite – and, anyway, the sight of Mr Mayhood with that box of teeth had changed the pattern of their evening. It had made the thought of sitting down across a table with the man seem like a punishment. The tolerance he'd shown when he'd first seen them – not surprised or devastated, just cold-staring at the box, as though he'd recognized a basic failure in his sums. There wasn't any coming back from that, and Charlie knew it.

Now he followed Mr Mayhood up the slope towards the caravan, the tall grass yielding as they walked. They brought their lanterns to the door. The padlock was unbroken and the leaded windowpanes were still intact. They peered inside, but it was hard to see with the net curtains drawn and the reflections on the glass. Below the undercarriage, there was nothing but a mound of mulch and dirt.

'Charlie, shine your light around that end, please, would you?' Mr Mayhood said. 'You too, Flo.'

They did as they were asked. 'Are you all right?' she whispered to him on the way.

'Not really,' he said. 'You?'

'I don't know yet.' She sighed so heavily that he could see the breath spuming in front of her. At any other time, he might've tried to catch it in his fist. They raised their lanterns to the window at the towbar end.

'There's nothing in there,' Mr Mayhood called.

'What are we doing, Arthur?' Florence called in answer.

'Looking.'

'Yes. For what?'

'A load of nothing, hopefully.'

'So far, so good,' she said to Charlie.

There was quiet for a moment. His pulse beat thickly in his neck. Next thing, he heard the trudge of Mr Mayhood in the dark, a clanking sound. And then an urgent 'Oi! You two! Get over here!' They ran round with their lanterns shaking. Mr Mayhood was now on his haunches by the wheel. 'Do you see what's on that tyre?'

299

Florence stooped, passing her light across it. 'Mud.'

'Exactly. And it's on the wheel arch, too, look – streaks of it. The hubcap, there. But Hollis never moved this thing. I know that for a fact. I should've spotted it before.'

Charlie knelt down for a closer view. 'He's right. It's caked into the treads, all round the edge. Somebody's moved it. And not long ago.' He could make out scuffed impressions in the earth below, dried up and frosted.

'Well, if they did, they put it right back where they found it,' Mr Mayhood said.

He went towards the other end. There was a little wheel there underneath the towbar and he walked a path from it downhill, inspecting every inch of ground along the way by lantern light. Charlie followed, seeing for himself. The wheels had left a phantom trail, bending the meadowgrass in three straight lines, going ten feet down the slope, no further. Where no weeds or grass could smother them, impressions of the tyres marked the dirt.

'What do you reckon, Charlie?' Mr Mayhood said. 'You know her best.'

'I'm not sure what you're asking me,' he answered.

Mr Mayhood stared up at the caravan and started walking back. 'I think you do. But never mind for now.' As he brushed past, he gripped him by the shoulder for a second, then let go. 'Come on. You'll need to help me push it forward. I don't have your sister's strength.'

'She can't have done this on her own. She isn't capable.' There was no doubt in his mind she could've towed the caravan ten feet or more, but it was harder to accept the rest. To prise the teeth from a man's jaw and keep them in a box – that was an act of evil. She'd always been a liar, a thief, a disappointment, but she had no cruelty in her heart, and no amount of rage would bring that sort of violence from her. He was certain of that much. But Mr Mayhood tramped on through the dark without a word.

It took the three of them to shift it from its pitch. Florence heaved the towbar, guided them, while he and Mr Mayhood leaned their backs into the other end. They had to budge the wheels out of their footings first with all their weight, then it began to roll more easily and gained momentum from the incline, until Florence called, 'Stop there! That's it!' She put the handbrake on. For a moment, he and Mr Mayhood were bent double, steadying their breath. He'd felt the mud beneath his boots as they'd been edging forward, a new softness to the earth, and when he fetched his lantern, raising it above the empty space the caravan had left, the light revealed a difference in the dirt. There was a woozy oblong where the soil had been turned over and then patted down. A soil of deeper colour than the land around it – dense like clay. Their bootprints were pressed in it now, clean through its middle.

Mr Mayhood set his lantern at his feet and then sat down. 'I think we've taken this about as far as it can go,' he said. 'That's Hollis under there. I'm not exhuming him. It's time we called in the police.'

Florence only stared down at the earth. 'You're saying that's a grave?'

'I've seen enough of them to know.' He rubbed his sweating forehead and exhaled a broken noise. 'Jesus, Charlie, how could this have happened?'

'I don't know.'

'He was a gruff old bastard, Hollis, but he meant no harm. She must've lost her bloody mind.'

No answer he could give was going to be enough, but Charlie mustered one more 'I don't know.'

'Well, it's the end for us. You know that, don't you? I mean, *everything* is wasted now. It's done.' The folds of Mr Mayhood's sleeve had come unpinned and it was draping like a windless flag about his stump. There was a devastated slump about his body. 'You'd better go with Florence. Take the wagon over to the station. Don't ring 999 – they'll get the wrong idea. I can wait for them all night, if need be.'

'Do you really think that she could do this?' Florence said. 'I'm sorry, I just can't. She wouldn't have it in her heart.'

Slowly, Mr Mayhood lowered his back on to the ground. 'I never would've dreamed it a few hours ago. But that's a grave. And they're his teeth back at the house.' He lay there, gazing up, with one hand on his breast, then shut his eyes. 'Anyway, what bothers me is people thinking *we* could do this, Flo. Let's fix one problem at a time. So hurry up. Take Charlie. Tell them everything.'

'You can't stay here all night,' she said. 'You'll freeze. You haven't eaten.'

'I'll be fine. I've suffered worse.'

Charlie spoke up then. 'Or we could leave things as they are. Go home together.' It was less of an appeal than a prayer. Because the only thing he wanted was to push the caravan on to its pitch again where it belonged and never speak of what they'd found. Maybe they could drive out to the coast and hurl the box of teeth into the sea. Nobody would miss old Hollis. Nobody was looking for him. No one cared that he was gone.

But Mr Mayhood's eyes flicked open then and he sat up. 'You're right – we *could* do that. It wouldn't be too hard, at first. Just put this all back where it came from, eh? And off we go into the night.' A wreath of vapour lifted from his body as he spoke. The tolerance he'd shown before was absent now. His voice had coarsened. He was glancing to the stars, as though to curse them or commune with them. 'Forget it all. I like the sound of that. I *do*. But trust me when I say this, Charlie, you can carry on as though it never happened, but it's not the same as living. And we want a life for you.'

'You know she'll hang for it,' he said. 'They'll catch her and they'll string her up.'

'If she's a murderer, they might. But we can't let her get away with it.'

'You're asking me to be a grass and I won't do it.' He was picturing the too-bright station with the sullen sergeant at his desk, abandoning his evening paper as they walked in, flashing them a *can I help you?* face, and the eternity that he would take to write down everything they told him, only to slip off into another room to speak to his superiors and then return with tougher questions, using different names to speak of her: *Miss Savigear, this Joyce you're on about, your older sister, your apprentice, this young woman you're in charge of, your employee.* The police would take the bones of Charlie's story and discard the rest. They wouldn't care to listen when he spoke of her kind nature, how she'd screen her eyes at the romantic parts of films to hide her crying. When they asked if they could have a photograph of her, they wouldn't want the daft one of her riding on the back of a stuffed lion at Maidstone Zoo; they'd want the mugshot from her borstal file in Mr Mayhood's cabinet.

'One of us has got to do it,' Florence said, behind him. 'I can go alone, if you'd prefer. I'll tell them. Here –' She held her lantern out so he would take it. Her expression was a plea. 'You know what's right and wrong, Charlie, and this is wrong. You can't have something like this weigh you down, no matter who's responsible. And if it wasn't Joyce, then *someone* did it, after all. We can't just shut our eyes and say we didn't notice.' When he took the lantern from her, she reached out and squeezed his arm in solidarity. 'I'll see you soon.' It seemed there was no situation dire enough to stop him yearning after her. 'Try not to catch pneumonia out here. Arthur doesn't know I know it, but he's got a flask of brandy in his coat, so you can share it out between you.' Mr Mayhood gave a hum. 'You see? I told you. That should keep you going for a while.' And then she was no longer there for him to put his mind to, trampling down the slope somewhere en route towards the wagon, darkening the distance.

PART THREE

The Reasons

June 1955

First, she'd paid a visit to his aunty's place in Borough Green, where she'd assumed he was still living. It was right up on the summit of Crow Hill – one of two red-brick and shingle houses jointed at the middle by another, pebble-dashed. The close was quiet and rustic, with an island of long grass where children could've played had it been mown; some of the residents had parked their cars on it, so that's where she'd left hers. But this had caused some friction with Aunt Helen, who'd spied it from her doorway and refused to let her through the gate until she'd moved it 'off the green'. She'd followed orders and come back again. Aunt Helen had apologized in an unmeaning sort of way: 'I'm sorry to insist on that, but I've been having quite a battle with the pair at number 10 about their car and I don't want to be a hypocrite. Now tell me, Mrs Mayhood, how do you take your tea?'

Extracting information from the woman had been harder than expected. For courtesy, she'd stayed to have one cup and chatted pointlessly about her journey, her attire, her complexion, before Aunt Helen had confessed that Charlie had moved out a year ago. 'He's not the same boy I remember. These days, we can't find a single subject to agree on. And he's stubborn. Dear me, he's stubborn. He was *never* stubborn. So we both decided it was best he didn't live here any longer. For the sake of our relationship. He's got a room now in the village. Right above the hardware shop – he works there, so he gets a friendly rate from Mr Ponsonby. I haven't seen him for a good few weeks, so if you find him, tell him I request the honour of his company.' There'd been a strange tone of resentment in Aunt Helen's voice from the beginning of their conversation and this had spilled into hostility when it came time to leave. At the door, the woman had pulled back the latch, and said, 'You know, it's funny, I expected you'd be older. A lot older.'

'Oh. Why's that?'

'Well, seeing as you've got no children of your own.' They'd stared at one another and she'd seen the quiver of a smile arrive on Aunt Helen's face. 'But, looking at you, I should think it's not too late to start. They say, once you pass thirty, it gets tougher, don't they? Sid and I, we put it off too long, and then he went and died. I wouldn't recommend delaying, or you'll miss your chance.'

'I don't remember asking for advice.'

'No, but you can have it all the same. Perhaps when you get round to having your own family, you'll leave mine well alone.' Aunt Helen had held back the door a moment, nodding at the street. 'You ought to be ashamed of yourselves, you know. You've filled his head with dreams. He's not changed for the better. And I warned the boy – I told him. She was always going to ruin him eventually. It's you, though, who's responsible. Giving her free rein to do it. You're the ones I blame, not her.'

She'd let the woman have this little moment of ascendency. 'I didn't come here to upset you, so I'll say goodbye now, Helen. I appreciate the tea.'

'You just have a pleasant journey home.'

'I will indeed.' She'd bitten on these words. As soon as she'd got back into her car, she'd taken care to rev the engine loudly, giving three blasts on the horn as she drove off. The bloody harridan. The sad old witch. She wished she'd said more to defend herself, but once she'd reached the junction and the house was out of view, she felt relieved for the restraint she'd shown, because it would've made the situation worse, exchanging insults on the woman's doorstep. Still, it rankled her. The blame and accusations she'd left unreturned. And no one had a right to ask a woman why she hadn't borne a child. There could've been a thousand reasons for it, all of them as private as the next; to disregard the prospect of a tragedy along the way was tactless and unfeeling. Charlie had been right about his aunty: there was sweetness to her, but you had to suffer all the bitter layers of rind to reach it.

On the high street, she could see a hardware shop called Ponsonby's between a chemist's and a haberdasher's. The only place to park was near the Baptist church, a little walk away. Inside the shop, there were no customers, except for an old sheepdog lapping at a bowl beside the counter. A fellow with white hair came out to greet her in his apron. 'Hello, dear. What can I help you with?' he said.

'I was told that Charlie worked here – Charlie Savigear.'

'That's right. He isn't on today, though. Lucky, with it being so busy.'

She looked about the place, uncertain if he wanted her to laugh. 'Do you know if he's at home?'

'Upstairs, you mean?'

'Yes.'

'Sorry, I believe he's out.'

'Well, do you know what time he might be coming back?'

'I'm not his secretary, you know.' The old man sighed and combed his arm-hairs with his fingers. 'I expect you'll find him over at the sports ground. He's been helping out there, building the pavilion.'

'Is it far from here?'

'Just round the corner. Maidstone Road. Go left at the church and keep on going for a hundred yards or so.'

'Thank you. I appreciate it.'

'Good. Then next time, you can buy a mop or something.'

'It's a deal.' She stooped to pet the dog before she left. 'I think she's out of water.'

'Don't you worry about her – she's like a camel. Just tell Charlie I expect him in tomorrow, good and early.'

It was only a short walk and she made sure to take it slowly. The sports ground wasn't much more than an open field of turf embossed with molehills and a set of holes where goal-posts should've been. On the far side, a small team of men was gathered at the base of a half-built pavilion. Its walls were up already, but the roof's anatomy was still exposed and, to her eye, the frame looked asymmetrical. As she got nearer, she saw Charlie. He was carrying a timber joist as though it were a broom. A nubby cigarette was in his lips. It was the mildest afternoon, but he was shining with the sweat of his exertions. He didn't spot her till she made it to the edges of the site. A man called out to her, 'You'd best keep out the way, love. We've not fixed those beams in yet. I don't want any falling on you,' and that made Charlie glance in her direction. Right away, he dumped the timber, patted his hands clean. Walking over, he stubbed out his dog-end in the grass. The sweat was streaking down his forehead when he reached her.

'What d'you reckon?' he said, jabbing his thumb back at the pavilion. 'Should we call the *Architectural Review* or what?'

'It's looking well so far,' she said. '*You're* looking well.'

He didn't seem so certain, pulling at his collar, then his trousers, raking back his hair. 'You think so? I've been meaning to get down the barber's.'

'It's nice to see you on a site again. It suits you.'

'Yeah, I thought I'd do my bit, you know – for the community,' he said. 'Besides, it's something else to put down on my application letters. Shall we –' He was pointing to an empty bench across the field. As they walked, he whistled to the other

310

men and shouted, 'Back in half an hour, Mr Broad!' There was murmuring and laughter in reply, as though a bawdy joke had been returned in private. 'Don't mind them,' he said. 'The fresh air makes them giddy.'

'What's the project, anyway?'

'It's just a new pavilion for the football club. There's never been a war memorial in town and someone had the bright idea to put this up instead. It's something folk will get some use of, I suppose. The trouble is, it's taken us a while. There's only so much time these blokes can volunteer.' He dusted off the bench for her before she sat. 'How'd you know that I'd be down here?'

'Well, I had to make a few stops on the way.'

'You mean you saw my aunt. How is she?'

'Not my biggest fan. She'd like to see you soon.' She leaned back, watching the activity on site. A man was climbing to the roofline with a mallet. 'You didn't tell me you'd moved out and found a place.'

'Yeah, I'm sorry about that.' He dug his cigarettes and matches from his trousers. 'I did mean to, every time I wrote, but I just couldn't go back through it all again. She's very hard to live with. Always was, but since what happened, she's got even more opinionated. And more wrong.' The match flame wouldn't take at first – he had to strike it a few times. 'It's a funny way to love somebody, don't you think? To have a set idea of how their life should go and force them to comply with it, or else. That's Helen for you. At least she hasn't given up on me entirely. Even if she thinks she owns me.'

'You know you still have me and Mr Mayhood,' she said, meaning it, but she could only guess how circumspect it must've sounded. 'We still want to help you, any way we can.'

He stood up then and paced in front of her. 'If you've come to twist my arm on that again, you've had a wasted journey.'

'I'm not here for that, I promise.'

He went on striding back and forth, but never further than the bench's width. 'I don't care if it takes me twenty years to save it, I'll be paying my own way. You've lost too much already.'

'I know that, Charlie. Will you please sit down?'

She thought they'd come to an agreement on the issue long ago, before he'd chosen to return to Borough Green. They'd said, as soon as he was ready to apply to architecture school, they'd write endorsement letters for him, cover his tuition fees, because it was the least that they could do, to make sure of his future. In truth, they'd barely had enough left of their savings to afford more than two years of a diploma, and Charlie had inferred this, given that they hadn't paid his wages for three months by then. 'You needn't worry,' he'd said. 'I'll do something different for a while and see what happens. If there's anything I've learned, it's that there isn't any point in making plans. Things go how they want to go. That's it.'

A year had passed since then, and quietly. They'd had a regular exchange of letters, phone calls, keeping him apprised of their eventless days and putting a fresh coat of gloss on all their problems so he wouldn't notice their decline. Then he'd dropped the news into a letter, as though it were a minor detail of the view outside his window – *I've started saving up for architecture school* – and when they'd followed up with him by phone, he'd said, 'I miss it. The ambition I used to have – it was the only thing that ever got me out of bed. You know exactly what I mean. It feels as though you have a higher calling, doesn't it? The hours you put in every day are for a reason. You're doing something bigger with your life. And even if I never make it, I can't live without that feeling any more. It's just too hard to go round thinking there's no purpose to it all.' He'd refused their money outright. There were scholarships he could put in for, and if he wasn't granted any on the merits of his application, then it wasn't meant to be; he'd scrape the funds together somehow, go to any school that would accept him. 'I mean this, Florence,' he'd said. 'I appreciate your offer – everything you both have done for me – but this is something that I need to do myself.' She'd understood, of course, though it had gone against her better instincts. How could she stand back and watch him struggle when she could've helped? If not financially, then with a word to someone up in Liverpool. It had felt like a desertion. Arthur hadn't been so sure: 'We can't keep trying to atone for something that was not our fault. We have to listen to the lad, or else we *will* be doing wrong by him, and he might not forgive us for it.' As the months went by, she'd wondered more about the situation. What if Charlie had refused their help for different reasons? What if he was trying to detach his name from theirs?

He took a seat beside her on the bench now, perching on the outer edge. The fellow on the roof was malleting the beams and each strike echoed in the horsehoe bend of trees surrounding them. 'So why've you driven out here?' Charlie said. 'You didn't even tell me you were coming.' He stared hard at the lit end of his cigarette. 'You've never visited before.'

'I wanted to. We wanted to.'

'How's Mr Mayhood doing?'

'You should phone and ask him.'

'I will. How is he, though?'

'Oh, he's been better, I would say.'

'Did you decide to lease the land again?'

'No, we changed our mind on that. We're growing sunflowers in the east field now.'

'That's good. And what about commissions?'

'We've got bits and pieces coming in. It's all surveying work, but it's been keeping us afloat.'

'It'll pick up soon. It's got to.'

'Yes, I keep on saying that as well. But architecture is a reputation game and all the rumours – well, there's nothing we can do about the rumours. We just have to keep on trying to turn our luck round, but it's hard to motivate my husband these days. Getting him enthusiastic for another open competition – I'll admit, that really takes it out of me.'

'I think I get why you've come down here now.' He gazed at the pavilion, where the man was straddling the apex of the roof frame with the poise of a stilt-walker. 'I knew it was too much of a coincidence. First, I get a house call from the coppers and now you. Well, I've not heard from her, all right? I thought she might just let the phone ring twice or something on my birthday. But I haven't heard a whisper.'

'Yes, I thought as much,' she said. 'You would've told me otherwise. I would've seen it in your face.' His eyes were on her now, in that old way she used to catch them dwelling. 'The police were here?'

'Just Applegarth. He said it was a routine call, but I don't know. He gave me the impression he was after something else. You know the way he is – he's always scratching at the subject, hoping you get sore.'

She'd not seen DS Applegarth since May and she was never comfortable when he came over to the house. There was an unerring calmness to him, how he strolled about the parlour with his hands behind his back, examining her mother's trinkets and flipping through their stack of records. He was CID, which seemed to give him licence to arrive at any moment of the day or night, asking to be let inside with such effete politeness, lifting his hat and asking, every time, if he could trouble her please with a few more questions, won't take long. But his visits always lasted more than half an hour. The first occasion he'd appeared – alone – was last October, when he'd got them to review the details in their written statements to the Chief

314

Inspector, dating back about two years, as though expecting them to falter and reveal a contradiction. Arthur had grown weary of it, telling him, 'We've been through this a hundred times with, whats-his-name, Fitzsimmons. Where is *he*? Ask *him*.' But the explanation had come back: 'The Chief Inspector is a very busy fellow. He's devolved the running of this case to me. As far as I'm concerned, we haven't shut down our investigation yet – so let me ask you that again, sir, if it's not an imposition. When was the last time either of you saw Miss Savigear?' Early on in May, he'd questioned them inside the draughting room, asking to see all the work that Joyce had done while she'd been with them, and he'd even sat down in her chair a moment, searched the drawers and meddled with her instruments. He'd rummaged through the files on Arthur's bureau and disturbed the survey drawings she'd been working on. They couldn't tell if he'd been looking for some object in particular, and he wouldn't satisfy them with an answer. Still, she sensed there was a hidden method to his visits – he couldn't charge them with a crime, but he could keep them under observation and disrupt their peace occasionally, if peace was what it was. And something Arthur said had rattled her: 'If this is how he acts with us, imagine how he'll be with Joyce when they catch up with her.'

'I'm glad the shop was empty,' Charlie told her now, 'or else I might've lost my job. He parked his massive car right on the kerb outside. He asked me, *Weren't you her accomplice once before – why not again?* I said, *Accomplice? I was just her passenger, and she's my sister.* He said, *Pardon me, I must've read your file wrong. I suppose you weren't convicted in a court of law and sent to borstal, then? That wasn't you?* I told him to piss off. He didn't like that very much. But that was all the damage he could do to me, so off he went. I wouldn't trust that bloke as far as I could throw him. Joyce detested coppers – all of them. And I can't say

I've met a single one who's proved her judgement wrong.' He stamped the leavings of his cigarette into the dirt. 'I reckon I should wander back and help them with the roof. They need as many hands as they can get.'

'Don't disappear just yet. I've brought you something.' She rooted in her bag and found what she'd come forty miles to give him. 'It was in with all the post this morning.'

He took it from her, doubtingly. A picture postcard from Maidstone Zoo. On the front, there were two polar bears inside a brick enclosure. On the back, an empty space and their address, typewritten. Charlie seemed to hold his breath. He had to clear his throat to keep the melancholy from his voice, but she still heard it trembling there. 'It's her, it's – bloody hell, it's her.'

'The postmark's from a TPO in Aberdeen.'

'What's that?'

'It means she would've posted it when she was on the train. Or maybe passing through the station.'

He squinted for a tighter focus on the stamp. 'It took its time to get to you, look. *31st May*.' He sniffed it, too – she'd done the same herself, when she'd removed it from the pile of letters. It had smelled of soot. 'Who else has seen this?'

'Mr Mayhood.'

'What's his reading of it?'

'Well, he sent me here. He wanted you to see it before Applegarth showed up again.'

'I'm grateful.' He went quiet. 'She must think I'm still at Leventree . . .'

'It seems that way.'

'Then she can't know how bad a mess she's put you in.'

'Perhaps.'

'But she's alive, though – that's what matters. I mean, she must be doing all right. She's thinking of me, still.' He grabbed a handful of his hair and shook it, grinning. 'Aberdeen. It's bloody cold up there.' He rose and stood before her with his back turned. For the longest moment, he was glaring at the sky, as though in consultation with the Lord. 'Thank you, Florence,' he said. Twisting round, he put another cigarette between his lips. 'Thanks for bringing it.' He lit up, watching her.

'Of course,' she said.

'Tell Mr Mayhood that I really do appreciate it. I know it couldn't have been easy, doing her a favour.' With that, he held the bright end of his cigarette up to the corner of the postcard till it peeled away in flames. In seconds, it was just a mothy curl of black and he allowed the breeze to carry it. He shrugged at her and said, 'For everybody's sake. I got the message – that's enough.' There was a languidness about his strides as he went off, back-pedalling across the grass. The worker on the roof frame cracked his mallet. Charlie stopped, then scratched the stubble by his ear. 'Listen, can you stick around and have lunch with me?' he called. 'There's a cafe on the high street and it's not half bad. Just let me tell the fellas.'

He was gearing up to whistle at them, but she called back, 'Sorry, no, I can't – I've got to do a site inspection later.'

'Where?'

'In Sunbury.'

'Oh.' He looked subdued, until he realized what she'd meant. 'Is that still dragging on?'

'I hope this afternoon will be the end of it.'

'Don't worry, then. Another time. And I'll phone Mr Mayhood soon.'

'You'd better,' she said. It was true that he was not the same boy any more. His borstal posture had relaxed, his speaking voice was gentler but more self-assured. In her absence, he'd matured – both in his temperament and physically. She was going to tell him her good news, but knew her chance had gone. She'd tell him on the phone. 'And, by the way, you ought to walk round to your aunty's now and then. She's hurt and that does no one any good. Be kind to her.'

'Point taken,' he said, backing off into the sunshine. 'You drive home safely.'

*

It hadn't helped their chances of acquiring new commissions to be stuck in a dispute over the Proctor house. Before the defects liability period on the building work had lapsed, they'd done a maintenance inspection and amassed a list of faults that needed fixing – most of these were minor, although one or two were troubling omissions. They'd sent their list to the contractor, expecting that the flaws would be resolved within four months. At the next inspection – January last year – she'd gone with Arthur in the hope of issuing a certificate and releasing funds to the contractor, but the work had been substandard. Arthur had to steer her to a quiet corner of the site and say, 'Can you believe the brass neck of this lot? The damp-coursing's not right. And there are twice as many cracks now in those bricks upstairs.'

The situation was so fraught, it had developed into confrontation very quickly. The senior builders on the site, with whom they'd worked quite happily for eighteen months, had turned unfriendly: 'You were never bloody here to know *what* mortar we were using.' 'Busy dumping bodies, so the papers say.' 'Did I hear right – they haven't found the girl yet?' 'I suppose you didn't like her workmanship, then, either. Best watch out.' The next day, they'd been threatened twice over the phone by men who didn't give their names. The Proctors had been understanding, patient, but their confidence had worn away. They'd pursued the matter in the courts, which had delayed things even longer, and eventually they'd hired another building firm to carry out the works.

Arthur blamed himself. He said he should've been more scrupulous in tendering, on site more often, less reliant on the clerk's reports. But it was not his fault. The truth was, the contractors hadn't paid their tradesmen well enough; they'd used materials that hadn't been agreed to in the contract, cheaper and unfit for purpose. And, beyond that, Leventree had been in a suspended state for weeks, disturbed by the police and their investigation. Sacrifices had been made along the way.

From the moment they'd first spoken to him at the old man's caravan, Arthur hadn't liked the tone of their inquiries. So, that night, he'd notified a good solicitor in Guildford, Mr Fish, and hadn't cared what doubt it cast over their innocence. Mostly, he'd been worried about Charlie being cooped up in a room alone with two detectives. Mr Fish had served them well and billed them at his going rate; that is to say, their savings had depleted by the hour. He'd made sure none of them was held without a charge. Arrests had not been made. But there'd still been an invasion of their home, an interruption of their practice. All their competition work had been abandoned. 'It's something that you'll have to tolerate, I'm sorry,' Mr Fish had told them. 'Be as helpful and hospitable as you can. They'll go away after a while, once they've combed through it all.'

For days, they'd had a constable on sentry duty at their door. They hadn't been allowed to leave their drive unless a plain-clothes officer came trailing after them in a blue Minx. There'd been reporters at their gate – just local press, but stories of the HUNGRY HILL MURDER had been printed in the *Advertiser* for the next few weeks, and most of these had been regurgitated by the regional papers up and down the country. They'd got used to reading them, as time went by, although the first report had shaken them – to see their movements summarized in print so tersely:

Two men and a woman were detained at Leatherhead Police Station last night for questioning in connection with the death of Mr Geoffrey Hollis (68), found buried in a field below his caravan, near Ockham, Surrey, shortly after 10.00pm. Mr Hollis was a supervisor on a local farm. The three detained were released this morning without charge. Police are searching for another woman in relation to the incident and will soon be ready to issue a description. A post-mortem is now under way.

There'd been police in every room, disturbing their possessions, riffling through their documents, searching all five acres of the farm. They'd been questioned separately at the station and at home, with no forewarning: 'Just a few more i's to dot with you, that's all,' they'd been informed. 'You'll have to wait for Mr Fish to get here, then,' they'd said. The Chief Inspector had been thorough with his questions, not inimical; DS Applegarth was more suggestive and officious. She'd lost count of all the explanations she'd given and been glad of Mr Fish's calm assertiveness. 'We can't pay that bloke enough, believe me. He's worth every penny,' Arthur had assured her – he'd been right. Especially in those later interviews at the station, when DS Applegarth had raised the facts of the post-mortem to unsettle her. He'd been looking to dislodge some information about Joyce, but it was information that she didn't have. 'Well, our pathologist believes the old man died by strangulation with a wire. Quite likely a clothes hanger. Inflicted by a person over six feet tall. His teeth were pulled out after he'd been dead at least an hour. So, when we find Miss Savigear, she's going to be charged with murder. And you'd better do yourselves a favour now, you and your husband both, by telling us where we can find her. Or we could charge you all with aiding and abetting.' Mr Fish had answered, 'On what basis?' Applegarth had said, 'You wait and see.' There'd been mention of dismantling the root cellar, exposing what might lie in the foundations, but Mr Fish had said, 'You'll need to raise a warrant first and you don't have the grounds. In fact, you haven't any evidence at all my client knows of Joyce's whereabouts. I'd recommend we all go home.' She'd driven back to Leventree that day in tears and Arthur had been raging on the phone to Mr Fish: 'How much longer is this going to go on for? What more can we tell them?' Next day, the *Advertiser* had put out another story:

WOMAN SOUGHT IN
HUNGRY HILL MURDER

Surrey CID today issued a description of a woman they intend to question in relation to the murder of Surrey farmer Mr Geoffrey Hollis (68) from Hungry Hill Lane, near Ockham. The woman is 6ft. 1in. tall, broad-shouldered and slim, with a fresh complexion and brown hair. She was last seen wearing a fawn drape coat, a tan blouse and black wool skirt. Surrey CID declared the woman to be dangerous and they urged the public not to approach her.

When she'd collected the newspaper from the doorstep, there'd been no police in sight. Mr Fish believed the CID had changed the focus of their investigation: they'd found nothing at the house and had diverted all their resources to finding Joyce. Well, it had hardly been a cause for celebration, but Arthur had said, 'It's all right to be relieved, you know,' and kissed her forehead.

She'd felt overwhelmed with tiredness – they all had – but the matter of the Proctor house was yet to be resolved. They'd had to delegate the supervision of the build to Vernon Quinn, who'd sent them reports each week and kept in touch over the phone. But he wasn't as attuned to defects as her husband was and so important things had gone unnoticed. By the time they'd made it out to Sunbury, at last, the damage had been done. They'd been so conscious of the silence in the car and Charlie's sheer dejection. It had been a struggle to cajole him from his bedroom before noon. She'd begun to nag at him to eat his meals, to wear clean clothes, to shave. His forlornness had become a kind of bleakness. They couldn't interest him in getting back to work: he wouldn't step into the draughting room at all, refused to do a thing except for chores about the farm or smoke his cigarettes. No matter what they'd asked of him, he'd bridled at it. All the way to Sunbury, he hadn't said a word. Then, on the site, he'd traipsed round in a pall of his own thoughts. They'd never seen him so uninterested or detached, and Arthur had suggested that he go and wait for them inside the car. When they'd returned to him, he'd been asleep on the back seat, wearing his sister's cardigan.

Today, the new contractor's works were ready for inspection. She was driving back from Borough Green with visions of the Proctor house in perfect order. It had been their first commission, and their only one to date. They'd formed their practice on the basis of it. She could still remember every lunch and dinner it had taken to convince the Proctors to believe in them, two architects with no established reputation, no experience. She'd been the one who'd nurtured that relationship from the beginning, made it bloom into an opportunity.

She wanted to believe that when she got to Sunbury, it would be there gleaming on the slope: as well constructed as it was conceived. The beauty of the house, she'd always thought, was in the way her husband had positioned it within the site, so that the mitred edge of the enormous downstairs window was the first thing to be seen as you drove up the track. You could look right through the open chamber of the living room and glimpse the willows just beyond the terrace at the rear. And if it passed today's inspection, maybe something of that beauty would be salvaged. But she expected it was gone for good. The house had been a failure of their execution, not their vision. She was certain that, in twenty years from now, she'd still be taking roads that circumvented Sunbury, and telling people when they asked her, *Yes, that's one of ours, but there's a lot more to it . . .*

*

The next time she saw Charlie, she was four months in and showing. He walked into the yard as though he'd never been away, admiring the north field – the runner beans, lettuces, peas and marrows that were next in line for harvesting, as soon as they'd brought in the summer squashes. He had both his shirtsleeves rolled up, with his cigarettes distending the breast pocket. His hair was still combed back, but it was longer at the sides now, oiled to a shine. For a moment, he just stood there in a patch of August sunshine, fiddling with the straps of the cloth satchel on his shoulders. She came down the porch steps to greet him and he saw the shape of her. 'Don't look at me like that,' she said.

'Like what?' He grinned.

'Like I could pop at any minute.' They embraced, side on and fleetingly.

'Well, you look all right to me. But how d'you feel?'

'Depends what mood I'm in. It changes by the minute.'

'I hope you're not still driving that old tractor round the place in your condition.'

'I'm in *prime* condition, thank you. Like our soil. You see those crops?' She hooked her arm through his and walked him to the porch. 'How'd you think we're going to harvest that lot, with a knife and fork?'

In fact, she'd been enraging Arthur lately with her adamance about sustaining her surveying work and helping him around the farm. He didn't want her going from site to site alone these days, especially in her father's Austin with its dubious speed-ometer. Nor was he enthused about her kneeling in the fields and pulling radishes, or standing on the corn drill any more, or crawling underneath the Fordson to inspect its bodywork for fissures. She could understand his fretting, given their own doctor's apprehension on the issue: 'Thirty-nine's no age to have a baby, Mrs Mayhood, so I'd urge you to reduce your obli-gations. Rest up, do some knitting, make some jam, do paperwork – that sort of thing would be advisable from this point on. Let others do the heavy lifting for a while, eh?' Arthur hadn't once mentioned his mother, but she'd recognized the quiet spells of rumination he'd slipped into now and then, and her compass for his thoughts was never wrong. He'd said, 'I will not lose you, Flo. So if you think I'm going to let you put yourself in danger for the sake of some fool's party wall agree-ment, you're completely off your trolley. No more site visits. Allow yourself to do sod all and be looked after. That's the end of it.' In her view, sitting round all day just thinking about everything that might go wrong was more unhealthy. Still, she'd compromised to a degree. She'd agreed to let him drive her where she needed taking in exchange for certain clemen-cies regarding what she could and couldn't do around the house and farm. Because, as much as he believed that he was capable, her husband couldn't manage everything alone.

'Come in where it's nice and shady,' she told Charlie now. 'We've got a plate of beef leftover from Sunday if you're hun-gry. I assume you'll let me make a sandwich, in my vulnerable condition?'

'I'd forgotten what a stubborn streak you have,' he said. 'A sarnie would be lovely, thanks. I'd take a glass of water, too.

That bus was like a kiln.' His head was angled slightly and he seemed a little pained when his eyes landed on her next. She felt as though she were a wardrobe being sized up for a doorway.

'Charlie Savigear, you're giving me that funny look again.'

'Am I?' he said, beaming. 'It's just nice to see your face again, that's all.'

As they reached the porch, her husband's head emerged above the sunflowers in the east field, skimming through the high stalks in his hat. He was still waiting for their petals to dry out and turn a shade of brown – according to the booklet he'd been quoting on their cultivation, which he carried round as though it was a holy text, September was the time to gather and extract the seeds. This didn't quite explain why he insisted on inspecting them so often. It seemed to her that most of what he did these days was an adjournment of the work he ought to have been doing.

Since she'd told him she was pregnant, he'd been focusing his efforts on the farm, in the hope that they might turn the land to better use, if not a profit. Every morning, he'd been in the fields by five o'clock or fixing something in the yard. He'd transformed Charlie's room into a nursery and made a simple cot from offcuts of good oak and a lovely stand to hold a Moses basket. He'd built a greenhouse on his own inside a fortnight and he hadn't even let her paint its frame, claiming the strong fumes were harmful. Well, they'd grown the best tomatoes of their lives and now he'd got it in his head to make a set of cold frames for the winter, but she missed him in the draughting room. She couldn't coax the same enthusiasm out of him for competition projects or phoning round their old contacts to scout for new commissions. Month by month, she'd leafed through journals they subscribed to and discovered opportunities promoted on their pages. Twice, she'd found him at his draughting board, in the beginning phases of designs, but when she'd asked him later how his concepts were developing, he'd given her two flippant answers: 'It developed itself straight into the bin,' and, 'I don't know. Why don't you check the compost pile and see if it's improved?' The prospect of their child had bolstered him in many ways, except the most important: to their livelihood. He'd given up on architecture once before, and she was sure that he'd return to it again. But it was proving harder this time round to reassert her faith in why it mattered.

'Charlie!' he called out, and hastened to catch up with them. 'Charlie Savigear, is that a ghost or a mirage?' He removed his hat and hung it on the newel post as he trotted up the steps. 'You've actually got your arse in gear and come to see us, have you? What a privilege.'

Charlie smiled and they shook hands. 'It's overdue, I can't deny.'

'You needn't sound so shocked about it, Arthur,' she said. 'He *told* us he was coming.'

'Yes, but he's said that before and left us crying in our cottage pie.'

'In my defence,' said Charlie, looking guilty now, 'I never knew that there'd be cottage pie.'

Her husband slapped him on the shoulder, steering him towards the kitchen door. 'It's hot enough out here to bake one, that's for sure. Did Florence offer you a drink already?'

She answered for him: 'Yes, of course she did.'

'If it were up to me, she'd have her feet up and the radio on until her waters break.'

'I was about to make a sandwich for the lad,' she said.

'Oh, nonsense. I'll do that.'

She turned to Charlie. 'Do you see what I've been putting up with?'

'Yeah,' he said, 'but I'm on Mr Mayhood's side with this one.'

'That means you can have the end piece of the loaf. No water for you either.'

She wouldn't let him know it, but she couldn't quite believe that he was here again. The doubts had been there, nettling her since Friday, when he'd phoned to say that he'd be visiting. He hadn't given them his reasons, just that he'd been thinking of them and was keen to celebrate her news. They weren't soft enough to think that nothing in particular had prompted his desire to see their faces, but they hadn't pressed him.

She sliced two lemons, put them in the jug and filled it. They sat together at the kitchen table, drinking, and her husband took his shirt off to remove the straps of his prosthetic. Once he'd hung the arm upon the spindle of his chair, he looked more comfortable and said, 'So what's it going to be, d'you think? A boy or girl?'

'I don't know,' Charlie said, 'but there's a good chance it'll be an architect.'

Her husband said, 'I wouldn't count on that,' and gulped down a long mouthful. 'Not unless it takes after its mother.'

'It really is the best of news. Congratulations to you both.' Charlie raised his glass. 'Any kid of yours will be the luckiest on earth.'

'We shouldn't toast with water or it mightn't be,' she said.

'Oh. Right you are.'

'I'll fetch us something stronger in a bit,' her husband said. 'We'll have a proper toast. It's good to have you back here, Charlie. We appreciate the visit.'

'As I said – long overdue.'

She sensed that Charlie had another thought he needed to express and that too many sets of eyes were trained on him.

327

'Who wants mustard, then?' she said, and went to get the bread.

'No, thanks.'

'Lots for me, Flo.'

'Obviously, dear.'

She wiped the chopping board before she sliced the loaf. But Charlie's silence was persistent. Her husband sat there, drinking quietly and sighing with every sip. It was only once she'd come out of the larder cupboard with the foiled-up dish of beef that there was any further talk.

'Nothing else has come, you know,' her husband said. 'Just that one card.'

'I know – you told me,' Charlie answered.

'I mean, since you phoned on Friday. There's been nothing else.' Arthur cleared his throat. 'Do you think she might've settled there? In Aberdeen?'

'I doubt it. What do *you* think?'

He cleared his throat again, but harder. 'It's unlikely that she posted it herself, I'd say. She'll have asked someone to take it up there on the train. She's a lot of things, your sister, but she isn't dim. She knows how to protect herself all right.'

'You're right. I see it the same way.'

As she waited for a gap in the conversation, Arthur squared his eyes at her and drew his head back once, as if to pull her by the reins. 'Well, nothing more from Applegarth in quite a while. I don't know if that's good. I'm only glad I haven't had to look at him. He brings me out in hives, that fella.'

'I've not seen him either,' Charlie said.

'There's a chance it's all gone cold for them. They might give up on her.'

'I worry, though. She can't be on her own, my sister. Not for ever. She's already sending postcards. If she thinks it's time to pop her head up now, it won't be long before they catch her.

Anyway, I didn't want –' When she arrived beside him with his sandwich on a plate, he had to pause. 'Thank you, that looks really good.' He set it down without a bite. 'I didn't want to sit here picking at my scabs all day. I came to see you both.'

She put in, 'Wait until you see all our tomatoes in the greenhouse. You can take some home with you.'

'All right.'

'You know he built that thing from Joyce's drawing?'

Charlie faced her. 'Really?' Then he turned to Arthur.

'No point letting a good drawing go to waste,' her husband said. 'She worked on that a while. I had to make a couple of adjustments, but the bones of it were good.'

'I don't know what to say.'

'Don't have to say a thing. It's just a greenhouse, after all. Old Hollis knew what he was doing. It's all down to his advice.'

He was acting differently about it now, but in those weeks he'd been constructing it, he'd gone into that ruminative state where she could tell he was surveying his regrets. It was clear that Mr Hollis had been in his thoughts. Now and then, she'd bring him out a cup of tea while he was working at the sawhorse. Later on, she'd come out and the tea would be untouched among the cuts of timber, and she'd spot him wandering the furthest reaches of the farm, a scythe hooked on his shoulder and a bundle of pulled weeds inside a basket. 'All kinds sprouting down there by the windbreak,' he'd say, returning. 'Bindweed, by the looks of it. We've got to stay on top of that or it'll creep back in.' She'd allowed him to go on like this a while, because she knew it was his way of settling his mind. But once the greenhouse had been finished, he'd begun another project and they hadn't broached the matter with each other. It had taken her another week to notice the old man's initials in the eave on the north side, delicately carved and painted over. Some time soon, she had to tell him that she'd seen it. Not all failures were mistakes. If he wanted to rebuild this place with her, she'd do it. She'd go with him to the borstals, set the competitions up again, select the drawings, wait for their apprentices to come – and she'd make the same decisions as before. Because their reasons had been sound and they'd not changed.

'Well,' she said now, 'it's producing the best tomatoes in the whole of Surrey. We could go into the greenhouse business.'

'It might just come to that, my love.'

This seemed to prickle Charlie. He scraped his chair legs closer to the table, took a hefty bite out of his sandwich. 'Well –' he started. 'I was hoping that your offer was still standing. I've been saving up, but I can see it's going to take me till I'm fifty, working in the shop to have enough. I need to get away from Borough Green. It's going to be the end of me.' He wouldn't look at them. 'I never told you this, but there were scholarships last year that I put in for – nine of them, to be precise, and they all turned me down, so I just thought –' He trailed off, picking at the crusts. She'd forgotten his distaste for them. 'I'm sorry to be asking. I was going to raise it with you on the phone, but – I don't know – I thought it would be better, face to face, seeing as I've told you no so many times before. And I just thought that with the baby on the way, you wouldn't want the –'

Arthur raised his hand and then he landed it abruptly, softly, on the table. 'Charlie, that's enough.' He shoved his chair back, stood and went to take the jar of mustard from her hands. 'However much you need, it's yours. We made that promise to you and we meant it. I'll be honest with you: we're not in our best position, savings-wise, but that's *my* fault and I can fix it. I'll make sure you have the money when you need it. Understood?' He gripped the jar under his stump, twisted at the lid until it gave and put it on the counter. 'Where are you thinking of applying? North or south?'

'Anywhere that wants to take me. Thank you. I'm so grateful to you both.'

'We're glad to help,' she said. 'You know that.' In her mind, she was already picturing the enterprise: the letters they could write on his behalf, the calls they could put in with the instructors, all the meetings they could organize for him in town. They could help to put his work in a portfolio and run mock interviews and entrance tests in preparation.

While they ate their sandwiches, they talked it through together. Arthur said the students at the two best London schools were now the most politically engaged; in their day, the AA crowd were unconcerned with public housing schemes, but ever since the war they been more in the vanguard of the issue. Social service was their interest now, which pleased him. 'I used to work with someone on the staff at the AA. We're not exactly best of pals, but, then again, he's never been the type to hold a grudge. I'll phone him in the morning. I've a feeling you might like it there.' She didn't doubt that this was true. But she believed that Charlie was more suited to a formalist approach, a Beaux Arts training like they'd had themselves in Liverpool. No matter where he went, she knew that he could thrive. He had resilience and talent. If she could raise her son or daughter to possess the first of those, she'd never have to be concerned about the other.

'How about overseas? Would you consider that?' her husband asked.

'Of course. I read they have some decent schools in Canada. McGill – is that the place?'

'Yes, one of them. How good's your French?'

'Pathetic.'

'Mine as well. But I was thinking of the States.'

'As long as it's not Borough Green, I'm interested.'

'You leave it with me. There's a person I can write to over

there. He might not answer back, but I can try.' She hadn't seen her husband energized about the thought of architecture for the longest time and now the brightness she determined in his voice was so consoling. She took their plates to wash them in the sink and, like the old days, Charlie stood beside her with the tea towel. In the window, birds were circling the east field, ignoring the limp scarecrow that her husband had put up between the sunflowers. She'd told him that it looked too cheerful and her instincts had been right.

What had made her parents settle on this patch of land, she couldn't say precisely. They'd bought the farm soon after she was born, taking on the dentist's surgery in the village and moving from their home in Croydon. She'd always thought it came down to a simple choice to raise her in a place of safety – somewhere she could climb a tree that didn't give a view of twenty other gardens on the street. But it was more than that. It was a choice for everyone who followed after them. Her children and their children and so on, for ever. She'd inherited a way of life and she was thankful to bestow it.

Later, in the parlour, once they'd got through talking of their struggles with the Proctor house, her husband poured himself a brandy large enough to toast the population of the county. He poured one more for Charlie and the smallest nip for her, and said, 'To family, whatever form it takes.'

They drank to that. The last few moments of 'Carissima' washed into static on the gramophone.

'I was thinking,' Charlie said, 'do the police still have your film?'

'It took a few reminders, but we got it back.'

'I haven't seen it yet, that's all.'

'No one has,' she said. 'We've no projector.'

Arthur swirled his brandy. 'I was going to pick one up eventually, but I can't bear to watch the thing now anyway.' They'd

always hoped to view it from a point of distance and fulfil-
ment. To remind themselves of how much they'd achieved. To
remember all the faces that had passed through Leventree and
how their lives had changed. But it was one more project they'd
been left unable to complete, another failure of their execution. 'I've been trying not to dwell too much on how it used to
be round here. I can remember what it felt like – there's no film
on earth can give me that again. It's best to focus on the part
that's coming next.'

She'd put on Jimmy Dorsey's Orchestra, for want of better
options, and the sentiments of 'Tangerine' now seemed unrea-
sonably mournful, so she lifted up the needle. 'Do you have
one?' she asked Charlie. 'A projector?'

'No, but I could borrow one from Mr Ponsonby,' he
answered. 'And I think my aunt could get one from the church
as well.'

'Then you should take it home with you – the film.'

'Is that all right with Mr Mayhood?'

Arthur finished off his drink. 'If it'll make you happy, then
it's fine by me. Not sure what sort of state you'll find it in,
mind you.'

That afternoon, when Charlie left to catch his bus, the canister was weighting down his satchel. He'd barely crossed the
yard before he lit a cigarette, dawdling a moment at the fringes
of the field to wave at them once more. The shadows of the
elms were slanting over him. He seemed reluctant to depart.

The sky would have no rain in it for weeks, according to the
forecast she'd tuned into when she woke. They'd have to bring
the squashes in today, perhaps the lettuces and peas. As Charlie
started down the track, her husband kissed her head and said,
'All right, then. Things to do.' She watched him go along the
hall into the draughting room and, by the time she checked the
yard again, she couldn't see a hint of anyone.

The winter rye is leaning at the mercy of the breeze. His sister crouches at the bottom of the frame. She's holding out her palms to tease the awns, as though she's playing the piano. It's December – has to be. This rye will be ploughed under soon. She moves her fingers gently. Her back is to the camera, but she twists to glance over her shoulder. A look that says, 'I didn't hear you coming.' She stands up, wipes her hands clean on her hips. Her face is spectral. She strides forward with a knitted brow. As she gets closer to the lens, it's clear there's something in her hair. Half a stalk of rye she's tucked behind her ear like a flower. She blows a kiss and laughs, walks out of shot. The camera pans to follow her. Up to the porch steps she goes, and through the kitchen door, dipping her head beneath the lintel. Cut this, too.

April 1956

He was smoking in the shadow of the Plaza, no less disappointed by the building now than when he'd first approached its doors on Monday afternoon. Its sheer bland face was so imposing from this angle, thumbing him into the pavement. Eighteen storeys. Limestone at the base, but mostly terracotta cladding. A mansard roof, finished in what seemed to be a mix of slate and copper with a seaweed tinge. Across the breadth of 59th Street, where he stood, was Central Park and all its crafted wildness, captive in a frame of other roads and buildings that stretched northwards, up to Harlem, as though a better landscape had been winched in via crane from a great height. Everybody was an incidental particle upon the grid of New York City, but those who occupied a certain area at the right end of the park were satisfied their lives were meaningful, superior to the rest. It made no sense to him. In one glance down Fifth Avenue, he saw a Packard limousine, a yellow schoolbus leaking radiator steam, a horse-drawn carriage, sweaty bellhops shoving golden trolleys stacked with travel cases, scaffolding that climbed halfway to heaven, flagpoles dangling the Stars and Stripes like tasteless party decorations. How could anybody claim to practise an organic architecture looking down at all of this? There wasn't any logic to it, and it nagged him. Ever since he'd disembarked at Pier 90, he'd been bothered by the thought, and three days' trudging round the city hadn't brought him any closer to an understanding.

On Monday aftenoon, he'd been so confident about it all.

He'd strolled into the lobby at the Plaza and informed the po-faced clerk that he'd arrived.

'Whose list are you on, sir?'

'Mr Wright's. I'm meant to have an interview at two fifteen.'

The clerk had stapled a receipt to a small slip of headed paper. Then he'd leaned across the desk, lowered his voice. 'I believe that Mr Wright is out of town. Perhaps I might convey a message for you?'

How naive he'd been, expecting he could saunter in, announce himself and be escorted to Wright's suite, as though the great man had no other pressing matters in his diary that would intervene before he got there.

Everything had been arranged by correspondence. First, a letter of endorsement from the Mayhoods, urging his acceptance as a Taliesin Fellow, giving a full outline of his situation, his credentials; then, a wonderful, magnanimous reply from the great man himself, inviting him to *come out to New York for a brief interview of sorts, with myself and one or two comrades*. He couldn't quite contain his joy at seeing the red square on the envelope, the letterhead, Wright's looping signature below the second fold. *Please call the number here below to set it up. I shall look forward to our meeting*. It had seemed so wrong to smile again and punch the air as he had done, to be excited by his future prospects in the wake of what he'd lost – but, for a moment, he'd forgotten who he was. The dialling code was for Wisconsin. He'd been given a direct line to Taliesin East. It was a daunting prospect, but a thrill. He'd spoken on a bad connection to a woman by the name of Alice Kirsch. She'd told him that the Wrights were going 'back and forth from the east coast a lot right now, and nobody's too sure about his schedule for the next few months – can I telegram the details when I have them?' A fortnight or so later, he'd received the message: FLW

NYC FEB THRU MAY. CALL BACK. And once he'd checked the sailing schedule with Cunard and asked old Ponsonby for time off work, he'd organized a date in April for his interview. 'We're at the Plaza. Second floor,' he'd been informed. 'We'll put your name down on a list at the front desk. Just walk right in and somebody will take you up.'

It hadn't quite turned out as they'd described. Instead, the clerk had rung upstairs and told him to 'hang fire' until they sent somebody down. Before too long, a ping had sounded from the lifts. A lady in a long white shirt and horn-rimmed spectacles had bounded up to greet him. 'Mr Savage?' she'd said, and he hadn't bothered to correct her. 'Alice Kirsch. I'm sorry that you had to travel all this way for nothing. We did send another telegram, but I can see it didn't reach you.' She'd wiped her palm upon her skirt before they'd shaken hands. 'Mr Wright is in Long Island with a client. I'm afraid it couldn't wait. Last-minute call.'

He'd answered tamely, 'Oh, I see.'

'Problem is, he might be coming back tomorrow or next week – we aren't too clear on his plans yet. How long are you in town?'

'Only for the next few days.' His ship back to Southampton left on Friday afternoon. He had a room at a hotel in the East Village and enough cash in his pocket to last the week, if he rode the subway everywhere or walked. The truth was, he'd imagined coasting round the city until then, secure in his performance at the interview, taking in the sights.

Alice had suggested, 'Check in here again with me this evening. Call and ask to be patched through. Suite 223. You got that? *Two two three*. I'll take your number at the place you're staying, just in case. We'll keep in touch until you leave.'

He'd waited hours, busying himself in Central Park and eating pizza by the lake. A tranquillizing darkness had set in.

Small, square lights had started gleaming in the hulking shapes of buildings far away. At seven, he'd called Alice from the payphone in a grimy restaurant on Broadway. 'No luck. Sorry about this,' she'd said. And so, the next day, he'd tried three times more, and three more the day after. 'I don't know what to tell you, but it's not unusual for Mr Wright to be unreachable. Particularly when he's staying at Falaise. You see, there's always more expense on projects than you think, and fewer opportunities to beg for what you need. And it's *the Guggenheims*. I'm sure you understand.'

Despite the fact that she was such a regular purveyor of disappointing news, he'd enjoyed his chats with Alice Kirsch. Not once had she talked to him as though he was a pest or given him the feeling he was fortunate to share a line with her. He only wished that he could say New York had charmed him the same way, but all the curiosities the place had offered him on Monday had grown bothersome by Wednesday. He'd never felt so overlooked and overfed. He'd traipsed round the museums and found them enervating, bloated by too many visitors. His feet were sore. It didn't help that he'd been lugging the film canister around with him, a lumpen weight in his portfolio, because he didn't want to let it out of his sight. It was a 300-foot reel, the size of a dessert plate, and it put a fair strain on his wrist just carting it about, block after block.

This morning, he'd accepted the idea that he'd be going home without a meeting, but he was too tired and subdued to go outside again. He'd loafed in his hotel room, curtains drawn, and tried to mute the city noises with his pillow. After a few hours, the telephone had rung and it was Alice, asking, 'Can you make it here by noon? We just got word: he left Falaise this morning.'

So he'd put his clothes on and gone straight down in the lift with his portfolio. There'd been a strange electric thrum about the Village when he came on to the street, a fatty engine heat that spread from whirring units in the windows. Everywhere that slow parade of traffic, crowding him. He'd caught the 6 to Lexington and walked the rest of the way to the Plaza. There was time for one more cigarette to calm his nerves before he had to go back up those steps, beyond the smiling doormen to the lobby, with his foolish hopes revived, made lambent in his heart again.

*

When the great man came into the living room, his arms were laden with fresh flowers – bouquets of tulips, freesias, hyacinths, all bundled up in cellophane – and he was trailed by Mrs Wright, who carried two more bunches of the same. His topcoat was still on and so was his flat mushroom of a hat. He wore a long black scarf looped round his collar like a priest's stole and his cane was hooked upon his wrist. For a man in his late eighties, he moved well. There was a poise to him, a self-possession. He was muttering to his wife in a strained voice, completing a discussion they'd begun out in the hall – 'I'll write her back in a few days. I've found Miss Lee is quite adaptable' – and she hummed at him and said, 'Don't let her make you feel beholden. The publicity they get from you alone should be enough.' They both came striding in, so focused on themselves they didn't notice Charlie by the window. Somewhere, telephones were ringing – three of them at once, as far as he could tell – and none was being answered. The Wrights seemed unperturbed by this. 'If only she'd accept that as a quid pro quo,' the great man said. 'I'll talk her round. I always do.'

Charlie waited to be introduced.

There'd been a restless energy about the suite since Alice Kirsch had brought him up. For over half an hour, her colleagues had been stepping in to ask for her opinion or to cross-check certain points in documents. Tall men in suits with ties tucked in their shirt fronts; little men in waistcoats; stringy men in pullovers and well-pressed trousers; and all of them with the same harried look, the same inchoate growth of whiskers, pink below the eyes. Each time, she'd had to say, 'Excuse me for a moment, Charlie,' leaving him to marinate in apprehension. He'd sat there, getting more and more impatient, turning the film canister in circuits on his lap.

Since they'd come up in the lift, she'd been dispensing facts about the renovations Mr Wright had made to the old suite. The gold wall finishes and mouldings. The mirrored discs inlaid into the arches of the windows, backlit to create a fuller sense of space. The baby grand piano and the harp: 'necessities'. The jet-black lacquered stools and chairs that he'd designed and tasked a few of his apprentices at Taliesin with constructing (and delivering from Wisconsin in a van). The plush wool carpet, which she'd said was 'oatmeal', and those long red velvet drapes. The glinting chandelier was an original, she'd told him: 'It's a relic from the days of Dior.' But this had only rattled him, upset his conscience. To be in a gilded room that spanned the length of most school buildings while, across the park, a million other people had to go without amenities – the thought of it had soured his mood. He'd not been able to get comfortable. His sister's voice had spiked at him, repeating, *Well, it didn't take you long now, did it? Put your feet up. You'll be asking them to call you Charles next.* So he'd paced a bit, looked out of the window. From two storeys up, New York had even less appeal. All those sooted towers on 59th Street with their gravestone sadness. Flocks of bobbing heads accumulating at the crossings, waiting for permission to continue with their lives. 'I can't help thinking all of this is somehow not in keeping,' he'd begun to say to Alice, but then somebody had wandered in to interrupt by asking her advice on papers in a file. 'Sorry,' she'd said. 'Last time, Charlie. Please excuse me.' When she'd come back in, it hadn't felt appropriate to bring the matter up again. She was doing him a favour, after all. They'd sat and talked half-heartedly about his life, where he'd grown up. She'd never heard of Gillingham, or Borough Green, which pleased him. 'Are you certain that he's coming? I've been here for quite a while now.'

She hadn't even glanced towards the wall clock. 'Oh yes, Edgar spoke to him this morning. He's already set up a few meetings for this afternoon. He's definitely on his way. So just sit tight.'

'Should I go through my portfolio again?'

'Nah, trust me, he won't even look at it until he gets a feeling for your character. He's going to ask you why you want to be an architect, so get your answer ready – and it better not be stupid.'

At first, he hadn't been too sure if she'd been smiling at him with conceitedness or camaraderie. 'It's good of you to wait with me like this. But if you're busy, I'll be all right on my own.'

She'd leaned back in her chair and flattened out the creases in her skirt. 'Listen, Charlie, it's because of me your meeting wasn't scheduled right the first time. I think you ought to know that. It's my fault. I thought that everything could be reorganized and, well, I didn't think to check where you were travelling from. But I'll be damned if I can't fix this. Top of my agenda for today is making sure I get you in a room with him. And maybe, after that, you might forgive me, and it won't reflect too badly on the man himself.'

'Don't worry. I'm just grateful for your help.'

'Well, you shouldn't be. I'm hiding my incompetence, that's all this is.' She'd smiled again – it was a nice smile, he'd decided. Winsome. Not as good as Florence's, but close. Her laugh was lighter and more confident, attractive. He'd begun to wonder what it might be like to kiss her, which he took as a small indication of his progress. 'So let's hear it, then,' she'd said. 'Your answer.'

'Actually, I've got a few.'

'Oh, that won't do. You'd better pick a line and stick with it. He likes decisiveness in people. And he's looking for a spark of something, too – *originality* – so please don't tell him how it's all you've ever wanted since you were a little boy. Let's face it, that's a corny reason. And it's bullshit. No one wants to be an architect when they're a kid.'

'All right. That's my answer down the toilet.'

She'd sniggered, pushed her glasses up the short slope of her nose.

'I'm interested to know what makes *you* do the job, though, Alice.'

'Yeah, nice try. As if I'm going to let you steal my answer. Took me twenty-seven years to figure out.'

'And here's me thinking you were in my corner.'

Her eyes had moved towards the clock. Perhaps she'd started losing patience, too. 'You know, I think he's going to like you, Charlie. When he finally gets here.'

The fact was, he'd been thinking of an answer to that question for the past few years and only one had ever satisfied him. He wanted to become an architect because of Joyce.

There were other motivations. For a start, the warm, pacific feeling that came over him when he was drawing. He enjoyed the way an hour could atomize and drift away while he was occupied with a design. There was the thrill he got from solving problems in his head, inventing structures on the page, discovering the best articulation of the forms that he imagined; and, above all else, the sense of purpose he woke up with in the morning when he had a project to resume. It appealed to him, to keep those aspects of his life intact and – if he could – to be rewarded for them with a decent wage. But incentives weren't the same as reasons. He was driven to make good the sacrifices of the Mayhoods – part of everything he did now was an echo of their kindness, their example. It was vital to restore their faith in him, repay them for the opportunities they'd granted him. He was compelled by all of that. Except it wasn't *why*.

'You were right, you know, what you were saying just before,' Alice had continued, nodding at the chandelier. 'It's not in keeping. But that doesn't mean he's compromised his principles. It's more a kind of trade-off. He enjoys the culture of New York – he doesn't care much for the city.'

'Then why be here at all? I just don't get it.'

She'd gone to join him at the window, gazing up the avenue. 'Because the Guggenheim is here and they won't move it to Wisconsin. Simple. It's a huge commission.'

'I meant *here* – in the hotel.'

'Ah,' she'd replied. 'Well, that's trickier. He likes to live in the same place he works. A suite this big allows for that. And I guess it really shouldn't, but an office at the Plaza gives him sway with serious people. Money people. They love coming here. And you can't build a thing unless you've got them on your side. But I can promise you this much: if anybody wants to work with Mr Wright, that's all they've got to think about – *the work*. Here, look at this –' She went and rapped her knuckles on the lacquered backrest of a chair. 'It's plywood. Cheap as hell. It's not about how much it costs. It's all about the value, what it offers. Stick around for long enough, he might explain it to you.'

'Yeah, I'm trying.'

'Tell you what, I'm going to speak to Edgar – see if he knows how much longer the old man will be.'

'All right. Thanks.' He'd lingered by the window.

'Are you sure that you don't want a cup of coffee?' she'd said, on her way. 'I'm feeling like an awful hostess.'

'I'm sure you've better things to do than wait on me.'

'Actually, right now, I don't. I'm kind of in between instructions.' But she hadn't even reached the throughway to the office. In a blur, the Wrights had stridden through the door with their bouquets; she'd had to step aside to let them past.

She loomed nearby until they finished talking. 'Mr Wright, you didn't have to go around the block again. Your florist said she'd send them over.'

'Yes,' the great man answered, 'but I have to see them out in front of me to make the best selection.'

'Aren't they wonderful?' said Mrs Wright.

'They're gorgeous,' Alice said. 'I'll make a start on the arrangements right away.' She collected all the bunches into one big armload.

'I hoped you'd say that. We've got lunch with Haskell in a moment and they'll spoil.'

'Olgivanna has been telling everybody what you did with those hydrangeas,' Mr Wright said. 'They were splendid. Now you've got a reputation to uphold. Your secret's out.'

'I'll see if I can go one better for you this time,' Alice said. She laid all the bouquets upon the dining table. 'Welcome back. How was Falaise?'

'Productive, but a little tedious.' Mr Wright took off his coat and draped it on the armchair with his hat. 'Is no one answering the phones?'

'I'll see to those,' his wife said.

'Thank you, dear. Tell Edgar that I'd like to see him, please.'

She kissed him on the cheek and ambled off. 'I didn't find it tedious at all.'

And it was then, as Mrs Wright was heading for the office down the hall, that she caught sight of Charlie. 'Oh, I didn't see you there. Good afternoon,' she said, and nodded in a friendly sort of way as she breezed past him.

'Afternoon,' he said, though she was gone already.

Mr Wright gesticulated with his cane. 'Alice, who's your visitor?' There was a tone of resignation in his voice.

'That's Charlie Savage,' she replied.

'It's *Savigear*, actually. I should have said before.' He didn't mean for this to be embarrassing to her, but Alice flushed.

'Excuse me. Charlie *Savigear*. He's travelled all the way from England to sit down with you and – well, there was an awful mix-up with his interview. My fault entirely. So I thought we might just fit him into your schedule for this afternoon . . .'

Mr Wright no longer seemed to care. He was examining his pocket watch and winding up the movement. 'What's your publication, Charlie?'

'No, sir. I'm not here to interview you. It's the other way. I mean, the other way around.' His tongue had turned to wool. His confidence had gone. Perhaps it was the whiteness of the great man's hair under the chandelier's glow, or something in the smart arrangement of his clothes (the graduation from light shades to dark with every layer), or maybe just the pallor of his skin reflected by so many golden surfaces and mirrors – but his presence in the room was almost saintly. The air around him seemed opaque and wobbling, like the shimmer of hot tarmac in the sun. It was difficult to concentrate on anything but him.

'He's not with any paper,' Alice said. 'He wants to join us out at Taliesin. He's applied to be a Fellow.'

'Ah,' the great man said. 'A comrade in the making. Well, why didn't you just say so, Charlie?'

Hearing his name spoken was enough to put the breath back in his lungs. The phones had all stopped ringing and the quiet helped him find his words. 'I should've done.'

'Charlie Savage. Doesn't ring a bell, but I've no memory for names.'

'You asked me to set up an interview,' he said. 'You wrote to me.'

'I did?'

'Yes, sir. I've got the letter here, in case you need to –'

But the great man flapped his hand at the suggestion. 'I do enjoy how courteous you English are. Not like us Welsh.' He took a few steps closer, leaving indentations in the carpet with his cane. 'What's in the tin, there?'

'It's a film I hoped to show you.'

'I see. A film. That's good. That shows initiative.' His expression seemed amused, though, unimpressed. There was a sudden openness to his dark eyes. 'The first thing you can do is call me Mr Wright. You're sounding rather like the concierge and I don't want to have to tip you.'

'Sorry.'

'Don't apologize.' The great man was two yards away now, breathing the same air. It seemed impossible that they were standing there together, but they were: a boy from Gillingham who'd feared to go beyond the limits of his aunty's close until he turned eleven and Frank Lloyd Wright, the finest architect alive. 'The second thing that you can do is book a new appointment. I've a meeting in the Oak Room in ten minutes – and these people have beeen waiting for a good few weeks to see me. That's much longer than I've kept you waiting, I expect.' He turned to Alice. 'Could you find another time for this young man, please? Early next week would be fine.'

'I'm sorry, Mr Wright, I've really screwed this whole thing up,' she said. 'But I'm afraid it has to be today. He's sailing home tomorrow.'

'Back to England?'

'Back to England.'

The great man nodded, sighed. He stood there, twisting at his cane as though it were a cocktail parasol. 'Well – what time's he leaving for the pier?'

'Late afternoon. Is that right, Charlie?'

They were talking past him now, as certain officers would do at borstal, and he felt uninvited, out of place. His embark-ation time was two o'clock. When he confirmed this, Mr Wright said, 'All right, in that case we'll talk tomorrow morn-ing. Bright and early. You can join me in the basement while I get my shave. Alice – ask Domingo to reserve the chair beside me, would you, please?'

'Yes, of course. That solves it.'

Someone else arrived upon the threshold, leaning on the door frame. He was tall and tanned and wire-haired. 'You asked to see me, Mr Wright?'

'Hang on just a second, Edgar,' came the answer, and he turned again to Charlie with the same amused expression as before. 'We're all agreed, then. Barber's in the basement. Seven sharp.'

'I'll be there. Thank you, sir, for making time.'

'All right now. Don't blow it.' The great man sauntered past him, saying to Edgar by the doorway, 'What's all this I'm read-ing in the *Times* about the permit? I thought everything was definite.' And then he halted, glancing back at Charlie. 'Oh, and you can leave your film for me. I'll take a look at it, if I can find a moment.'

*

His sister visited his dreams again that night. He was lying on his back among the weeds. It seemed that he was hiding in the patch of grass where cars parked in his aunty's close, run through with dandelions and creeping thistles, but everything had grown so high that he could hardly see the rooftops. There was a rattling engine noise nearby and it was getting closer. All the grass was shifting like a curtain suddenly. He felt a shudder in the earth. And she appeared in front of him, pushing a lawnmower. She was a giant, stooping figure, mowing with no care for her direction. The enormous rusty blades spun round and chewed the weeds, cleaving a channel, spitting out huge lumps of green. He called her name, begged her to stop. But she was singing to herself and couldn't hear his tiny voice. Then, just in time, she cut the engine. Leaned to pick him up. For a second, he was in the bowl of her colossal hands. Her thumbs were pressing softly on his back. Next thing, she set him down and he was somewhere else – the back row of an empty cinema, alone. On the screen, there was a wooden ship and Frank Lloyd Wright was standing at the prow, his white hair flowing, pirate-like. And he was saying, *Mouse, you've no respect. You're giving me an ulcer.*

There was no more sleeping after that. He felt hot-footed, agitated. The windows in his hotel wouldn't open wide enough. He'd bought some Camels from a newsstand on his walk to the East Village; he didn't like the flavour much, but half the packet was gone before he went to bed. He knew he'd have to get more for the voyage home – the crooks from Cunard charged you twice the price for everything on board. His bags were packed already. He was running low on dollars. A pushy kid out on the street had charmed him into paying for a shoe shine and he'd done such a terrific job he'd given him a few cents extra; the kid had looked at him – 'You sure?' – as though he'd offered the last sandwich in his lunchbox. After that, he'd been through all the drawings in his portfolio several times, preparing justifications for their failings. The best work of his life was right there at the front, as Mr Mayhood had advised – his parti sketches for the halls of residence, a copy of the brief adjacent, giving context. He could talk about those drawings all day long. But if he didn't have an answer for the great man's question, *Tell me, Charlie, why d'you want to be an architect?*, then none of it would matter.

He lit a Camel, stood before the mirror to revise what he would say until it was convincing. He could speak about *belonging* – that would do it. How alive he'd felt at Leventree. How sure of his direction. How inspiring it had been to watch the Mayhoods go about their work. These things were genuine and he would mean them. Even if they weren't the truth.

He'd come to understand that it was better to pretend he didn't have a sister any longer – better to believe it. There were side-eyed looks he couldn't bear to witness any more when he was asked for information. Whatever made him leave a good apprenticeship like that? Why had those policemen visited today? What did they want to talk to him about? What landed him in borstal in the first place? He'd grown tired of the excuses, tired of having to extemporize with lies, and he was sick of having to account for where he went and what he did. He hated the suspiciousness and scrutiny. The sudden cooling off in people's interest when he told them. It was easier to act as though she wasn't in his past, because she wasn't in his present. But he couldn't just extract her from his mind the way he'd cut her from the film.

He'd borrowed Mr Ponsonby's equipment – a splicer and a viewer – and followed the instructions carefully. Frame by frame, he'd snipped her out. A wretched job. The worst. His hands had glossed with so much sweat the cellulose had slipped about and nearly spoiled. He'd gone down to the shop below for cotton painting gloves. When it was done, he'd gathered up the pieces he'd removed and put them in a jar. Eventually, he'd made another reel out of them. All Joyce. Not much footage and a scrappy edit, but it wasn't meant for anyone else to see. He must've watched it back a thousand times. In a rush, he'd put a label on the tin, *Joyce Cuts*, and now the accidental pun had stuck. She would've laughed at that. It suited her.

His sister was the reason he was doing this.

He'd known it since their first week with the Mayhoods. She'd seen the drawing on his table, showing the improvements he was planning for his bedroom. There'd been nothing special in the new arrangement he'd designed – in fact, it was a blatant copy of a boy's room he'd once noticed in a magazine at Huntercombe – but he'd been proud of how he'd used three-point perspective to describe it, all the angles measured to perfection, nice clean lines. Joyce had laid her cold hand on his neck and rocked his head from side to side – not gently – then she'd let it go. 'You're bloody good at this,' she'd said. 'I mean, I knew you would be. But you're bloody good. And I can't even get my pencil sharp. It isn't fair. I might've got the good looks in the family, but I'd rather have the talent. So unfair.' That's all it was, a fleeting moment of support, but it was honest. It had given him the sense that he could turn whatever skill he thought he had into a life that was worthwhile. He'd ridden on that confidence for weeks. And in the course of all those days beside her in the draughting room, he'd realized something: she'd become his sole responsibility. It wasn't just his future he was working for; it was his sister's, too. If he could make it as an architect, he could deliver them, at last, from their misfortune. He was trying for that now. Still trying.

*

Mr Wright was in the chair already, tilted back and covered to the Adam's apple with a sheet. He looked as peaceful as a corpse inside a casket. The shop was empty and the sign on the front door said CLOSED, but the barber had his apron on, his sleeves rolled tight, and he was thickening the shaving soap in a tin bowl. When Charlie knocked upon the glass, the great man didn't flinch. It was the barber who glanced over, waved him in. The shop door gave a tinkle as he pushed it. 'Am I late?' he said. 'I'm sorry.'

Mr Wright's pale eyelids didn't open. 'What time d'you make it now, Domingo?'

The barber checked his watch. 'I make it seven, but I wouldn't trust this cheap old thing.'

'Well, there you are,' the great man said. 'Not late at all.'

'Why don't you have a seat right over there?' Domingo made a gesture to the other padded chair. 'As soon as I get done with Mr Wright, I'll see to you. And you can leave your case there in the corner, if you want to.'

'Thanks.' He rested his portfolio against the coat stand and got straight into the chair. In the mirror, he could hardly see his whiskers, but he felt them with his palm. 'I've only had a barber shave me once before.'

'You didn't like it, huh?'

'Not much. He nicked me.'

'Well, I've never nicked no one in thirty years. Don't plan on starting now.'

The great man lay there while his cheeks and neck were coated with a lather of the soap. It seemed he was content with silence for a while – there was something almost beautiful in his repose, the trustfulness with which he let the barber go about his work, sweeping circle motions with the foamy brush, quick-sharpening the razor on a leather strop. Then he said, 'You know, it was a few months back and I've been rather busy since, so please forgive me. But I do recall it now – the letter.' He paused to let the barber come at him. Domingo had his arms bent like a crossbow, making noiseless actions of the blade beside the great man's ear, then moving in swift down-strokes at the jaw. Charlie watched it happening in the mirror. It seemed a lot of jeopardy to go through every morning – one slip of a stranger's wrist and you'd be scarred for life – but there was something quite mesmeric in the process, as spectator sport.

'I still have it with me, if you need to check.' He got the envelope out of his pocket, raised it up – the red square facing outwards, so the great man could detect the hallmark.

But then his voice came back, unbothered: 'I was speaking of the letter from your old employer. Mr Mayhood.'

'Oh.'

Domingo twisted at the great man's head until he had him peering to one side. His blade came down again and left a perfect stripe of shaven skin along the cheek.

'I get a lot of letters, as you can imagine,' Mr Wright continued. 'They arrive from every corner of the world. It's gratifying to discover people far and wide appreciate my work. It only makes me more convinced that we are doing something valuable at Taliesin. Whenever people write and say they want to join our cause, I take their applications seriously. All of them. But, naturally, not many who apply are suitable for what we do. It's hard work – very hard. It's broken more young men and women than have stuck around, but that's the process. People who can draw well are a dime a dozen. People who can draw well *and* support their fellow man, *and* break their backs out on a farm in winter, sweat their guts out in the middle of the Arizona desert – tenacity like that is hard to find. Those people will endure as architects. There's nothing you can't learn by doing. And perhaps you've some God-given talent for it, who can say? But if you can't keep going when the going's rough, you might as well do something else. You want to know –' Domingo was now standing idle. 'Excuse me, did you want to do my lip?'

'Please, you keep on talking, Mr Wright. I'll wait.'

'No, go on. Finish.'

'All right.' Domingo leaned down with the blade, shaving underneath the great man's nose, across the upper lip, and wiping off the residue. 'OK, we're done, sir. I'll just clean you up. You carry on.'

'Terrific.' Mr Wright revolved his head until he looked more comfortable again. His brown eyes were deep-set and very small, but they caught the light as readily as billiard balls. 'If you've done your preparation, Charlie, then you'll know exactly what I'm looking for in people. First of all, an honest ego and a healthy body. Next, a love of truth and nature. You'll require sincerity and courage. An aesthetic sensibility. A good imagination. Stop me if this doesn't sound like you –'

Charlie didn't know if he possessed these qualities – or all of them, at least – but kept his mouth shut. There was nothing to be gained from talking too much in the presence of a man like Wright. Listening and learning were much surer bets.

'I'll need you to appreciate not only the idea of work, but work as an idea. You understand the difference there?'

He nodded.

'What about an instinct for cooperation. Have you got it?'

Once again, he nodded.

'I'll need you to be ready to take action, not just stand there, hemming and hawing.' Reflexively, Domingo started towelling off the great man's cheeks and neck. 'And you'll have a general distaste for what most people think is elegant, but which is really just the commonplace, the inorganic. If you don't know what that means, then I can't use you.' Mr Wright began to rise now, as the barber cranked the footpump on the chair. In a flash, the sheet vanished from his shoulders and the cloth was yanked out from his collar. He sat up to approve his own reflection in the mirror. 'Thank you very much, Domingo. Like a baby's tush. Fine job.'

'My pleasure, sir, my pleasure.'

'One last thing.' The great man stood. He went to loom at Charlie's shoulder, gazing down at him. 'Rebellion – you'll need a bit of that in you. Not much. But some. It's more important than you'd think.' With that, he fetched his cane from the umbrella stand, where the portfolio was leaning – he collected this, as well, and took a seat. He had it on his lap, but didn't open it at first. 'Now, I can tell from what your old employer wrote that he believes in you. Quite frankly, I was moved – he speaks about you like a son. And I can see you've had your problems and some pretty awful luck. But here you are, still. I admire that.' The great man loosened up the clasps on the porfolio. 'I haven't watched your film yet – sad to say, I couldn't find the time. I promise you I shall, as soon as things get quieter. But all I'd like to know right now is why you want to work with us. What made you want to be an architect at all?'

Charlie had rehearsed this moment, acted out his lines until he had the whole performance so refined he couldn't even recognize how much of it was false. But now the barber was beside him, casting the white sheet upon the air until it billowed down and landed at his chest. Warm fingers probed his collar, pushed against his neck. He said, 'My sister.'

'Is that so?'

His chair went lurching back. The ceiling had an ugly stippled plaster that reminded him of home – of rooms he'd waited in before. School corridors. The nurse's office. Church. He was laid too flat to see the mirror past his feet, but he could hear the great man in the space behind him, whistling in a breath, expecting more. *Sincerity and courage* – these weren't easy to sustain. 'Honestly, I never would've come this far without my sister,' he began, and numbed himself to add the rest. 'She passed away last year, but that's just made me even more determined to succeed from this point on.' As soon as this came out, he felt no hollower, but lighter. He lay back with his throat bared while the barber whipped the soap, and didn't think about the razor. Everything that hurt had already been cut.

Acknowledgements

Thank you to my editor, Mary Mount, for vital insights on each draft and her confidence in this novel from the very beginning. Thank you to my agent, Judith Murray, for all her help and reassuring wisdom; to Karishma Jobanputra, Lesley Levene and the whole team at Penguin Viking; to Gráinne Fox, Toby Moorcroft, Kate Rizzo and everyone at Greene & Heaton. Thank you to Ruth Padel for her kindness and encouragement at a crucial time, and to Alan Read for raising my morale as I approached the final stages. Thank you to King's College London and my colleagues in the English department; to Peter Irving for his care beyond the call of duty; to Neil, Lynn and Kate Paternoster, Nicholas Wood and Katy Haldenby, and Peter and Caroline Hesz for much support along the way. Endless thanks are due to Adam Robinson for being there every Friday evening for the last two years, and to Lata Sahonta for the same. Thank you to my sons, Isaac and Oren, for every single moment. And to my wife, Steph, who lived this book with me and understands my heart completely – thank you for it all.

He just wanted a decent book to read ...

Not too much to ask, is it? It was in 1935 when Allen Lane, Managing Director of Bodley Head Publishers, stood on a platform at Exeter railway station looking for something good to read on his journey back to London. His choice was limited to popular magazines and poor-quality paperbacks – the same choice faced every day by the vast majority of readers, few of whom could afford hardbacks. Lane's disappointment and subsequent anger at the range of books generally available led him to found a company – and change the world.

'We believed in the existence in this country of a vast reading public for intelligent books at a low price, and staked everything on it'
Sir Allen Lane, 1902–1970, founder of Penguin Books

The quality paperback had arrived – and not just in bookshops. Lane was adamant that his Penguins should appear in chain stores and tobacconists, and should cost no more than a packet of cigarettes.

Reading habits (and cigarette prices) have changed since 1935, but Penguin still believes in publishing the best books for everybody to enjoy. We still believe that good design costs no more than bad design, and we still believe that quality books published passionately and responsibly make the world a better place.

So wherever you see the little bird – whether it's on a piece of prize-winning literary fiction or a celebrity autobiography, political tour de force or historical masterpiece, a serial-killer thriller, reference book, world classic or a piece of pure escapism – you can bet that it represents the very best that the genre has to offer.

Whatever you like to read – trust Penguin.

read more
www.penguin.co.uk